At the Heart of It

At the Heart of It
Ordinary People, Extraordinary Lives

Walt Harrington

University of Missouri Press
Columbia and London

Library of Congress Cataloging-in-Publication Data

Harrington, Walt, 1950-
    At the heart of it : ordinary people, extraordinary lives / Walt
Harrington.
        p. cm.
    A collection of articles which previously appeared in the
    Washington Post magazine.
    ISBN 0-8262-1078-3 (pbk. : alk. paper)
    1. Biography—20th century. 2. United States—Biography.
I. Title.
CT220.H344   1996
920.073—dc20   96-8540
                                                       CIP

Text Design: Stephanie Foley
Cover Design: Mindy Shouse
Printer and binder: Thomson-Shore, Inc.
Typefaces: Arena Black Extended, Optima, and Palatino

To my son, Matthew

CONTENTS

At the Heart of It

A Journalism of Re-remembering

> One writes in order to feel:
> that is the fundamental mover.
>
> — *Rita Dove*

Journalists are always talking about how they write to inform the public, to defend democracy, to champion the little guy against the corporate mogul, to create a better world. I began my career twenty years ago holding these high-minded rationales. But over the years, as I turned to writing about the everyday lives of people, it dawned on me that these explanations had become props: I no longer wrote stories in order to right wrongs or change the world. I wrote stories, as poet Rita Dove says, in order to feel.

At first, I told myself that I wrote stories so that others might feel. In journalism, it's always the readers who are our final justification for the great power we bear under the First Amendment. Without the defense of serving readers—the personification of "the public interest"—we in the press lose all legitimacy. So I clung to the idea that my stories were meant to make readers feel the lives of others, to take readers outside their busy, insular worlds and into the worlds of people they had neither the time nor perhaps the imagination to go meet, to take readers on a journey across the boundaries of race and class, gender, religion, occupation, age, and education—the fiefdoms that so Balkanize us today. This was a variation on the old theme: I was doing good for the commonweal, bringing empathy to the public. I still believe it's a worthy fallout of what I do. But, truth told, this too is pretense: I write stories for myself. They remind me that I am alive.

Some people jump out of planes or climb mountains. Others pray deep and hard. Others deliver meals to the elderly or take poor kids to the zoo. Others run marathons. Still others cheat on their spouses, run stoplights late at night, bellow obscenities at football games, go to horror movies. I think all their motivations share a common root: These things make people *feel*, pinch them, touch emotions wired into human beings that life today seems to dull and desensitize. I once met a man, a sociologist, who was running a huge study of women

1

who'd been beaten by their husbands. Fearful that his emotions might cloud his scientific judgment, the man said, he didn't talk to the women himself, but instead read the reports of interviewers who had talked to them. That human distance was a necessity of his job. Then, in passing, without thinking the ideas were connected, the man mentioned that he'd recently taken up fishing—what an authentic feeling it was, he said with wonder, to hold a strong, live fish in his hands as his small boat bobbed beneath a boundless blue sky.

I have a wife, children, friends who touch me daily. They are the best piece of my life. But, as is true for so many others, it's not enough. The stories in this collection are my personal answer to the hollowness, the human disconnect, of modern life. I'm not saying it's healthy or normal or good that I feel this way about my stories. I'm saying only that it's true. The words *satisfaction* and *accomplishment* don't describe the sensations I got from doing these stories. The words *awe* and *amazement* and *communion* hit closer to home.

When I stood just off stage at the Apollo Theatre in Harlem and Stephanie Burrous twisted her body into a crouch, flung her arm behind her back, and wailed out a line of gospel . . . When Shirley Rogers, after waiting months for her handicapped daughter to be placed in public day care, called the welfare office and told the woman she no longer needed her services, that her daughter was dead . . . When Bryan Stevenson's mother sat in her hospital room and told of the first time her son, thirteen years old then, was taken by the Holy Spirit and that soon afterward she, too, was reborn while standing in her kitchen watching the sun rise . . . When pro football player Jim Lachey talked of how on a perfect block of an opponent he seems not even to strike the man but instead passes through him as if he were only an apparition . . . When Rita Dove explained how she hears the "cadence of thought" in the rhythm of a phrase . . . When homicide detective V. I. Smith threw back a dead man's coat to see a cocked Uzi and for the first time in his life felt fear . . .

At all these moments, as it does for a race-car driver taking a turn at a hundred miles an hour, time slowed, bent, and elongated, voices ran at dying-battery speed, and motion flicked a single frame at a time. At all these moments, I felt what I felt once while rocking my infant son to sleep in the middle of the night, half-dozing, when suddenly I dreamed or imagined or became my father who was holding me decades before, when suddenly I dreamed or imagined or became my son who was holding his own son decades later. At all these moments, I felt what I felt as a boy after giving my confession to the priest and walking out of a dimly lit church to a sun breaking from behind dark, ominous clouds. At all these moments, I felt what I felt decades later when, no longer a believer, I sat in the tiny hospital chapel and asked any God or power in the universe to spare my father from the heart attack.

You know you are alive. You shiver, catch your breath. Your eyes tear, you blink, and inside your chest the light that is your life burns brighter, as if the electricity has surged. In that moment is everything you ever felt that was humane or even holy, a moment when you know what it is to live beyond pride, foolishness, greed, or self-pity. Naked, a moment at the heart of it, baffling and affirming. A moment of grace.

The instant passes and the space it has created inside you fills up with clutter as fast as water replaces a hand pulled from a stream. But I believe we can re-remember. Long ago, my childhood doctor, who was by then old, told me that the picture of the hand that hung on his wall had been a gift to himself, that its five fingers signified the five thousand babies he'd delivered in his more than fifty years as a physician. If he set his memory to it, he said, he could recall each delivery. He paused, closed his eyes, and said that he had just remembered my delivery, early one morning twenty-five years before. He smiled. I chose to believe him.

I've got a ritual: On a late evening after each of the stories in this collection appeared in the *Washington Post Magazine,* after the letters had arrived and readers had howled or praised, I waited until everyone in my house was asleep, left on only a single lamp in the back room, poured a glass of wine, sat down, and read my story to myself. It was time to judge. The aging Reverend James Holman stops in his tracks, glances back over his shoulder, touches the brim of his fedora, and smiles. Do the words rekindle in me what I felt the afternoon I saw him stop, glance back, touch his fedora, and smile? Do I feel the rush of it again, the connection? Do I shiver, catch my breath, blink back tears?

When grandmother Julia Shelton leans down and rubs the spot where her head hit the pantry door when she fell in her kitchen recently, and she and daughter Mary and granddaughter Karen, who are helping cook dinner, go suddenly silent, as they all realize that Julia is now old and will soon be gone, am I back in the kitchen hearing a silence that lasts forever? When Larry Jones is in the bathroom after the birth of his twins, his wife sick in bed for a month now, Larry exhausted from caring for her and the infants night and day, asking God, please, don't let me die, am I with him, feeling his swirl of love and fear and confusion? When Dan Sullivan brings his wife home the bottle of Manischewitz wine—all he can afford at $3.95—to celebrate his new job at Radio Shack, do I feel his hope as well as the claustrophobia of his life?

The answer is . . . sometimes.

It is these sometimes I've come to crave. And perhaps, if I can make myself feel these moments, readers will feel them too: Time will slow, bend, elongate, and they will sense, rub, re-remember a trace of the sensations they felt at whatever were their own particular moments when they knew they were alive. That's a worthy fallout of what I do. But, again, it's not the reason I do it. I do it because each story is for me a strong, live fish held in my hands as my small boat bobs beneath a boundless blue sky. In these moments, I comprehend what eludes me most of the time, what eludes most of us most of the time, and I am, for a redeeming instant, washed and purified in hope and in despair.

The Reverend James A. Holman today
and in 1936.

Photo by Abe Frajndlich.

The Reverend Comes Home

Georgia had never seen her father naked.

Certainly not when he was young and prideful, walking with a bantam swagger that she and her sisters called "the strut"—a walk at once jaunty and commanding, with an unforgiving posture softened by a long, friendly gait and made theatrical by arms that pumped confidently from rolling shoulders. *Make a path, folks, here comes the reverend, the Reverend James A. Holman.* Georgia's older sister, Leila, when she was a girl, would feign exhaustion just so Daddy would hoist her onto his chest and shoulder, where she'd pretend to be asleep, all the while watching with fascination over his back as his legs, like tiny rockets, launched him and her off the sidewalk with each dancing, prancing step.

That legendary strut, where was it now?

When Georgia first touched his skin in the hospital, helped turn his body in bed, or helped change his diaper, she nearly recoiled, as if meeting these intimate needs for her sick eighty-year-old father involved unnatural acts, a violation of all human hierarchy. She thought to herself: *This is not my father.*

It was not the father who had mesmerized huge revival crowds with his stunning "Take Up the Cross" sermon. It was not the father who had signed men out of jail on his word alone. It was not the father who had always arrived with pennies for her piggy bank. And, surely, it was not the father who had sat on the front porch rocking her on hot summer nights while he recited poetry.

This frail man's bones poked at his skin like sticks prodding soft leather. This man didn't recognize her, called her "Cat," the nickname for her dead sister, Catherine. This man rambled deliriously about a Reverend Johnson, asked the name of the street where his own former church stood, and insisted that one of the nurses was his dead wife, Anna Pearl. This man seemed

afraid. All hours, Georgia and Leila sat beside him, his body as light and fragile as settled dust, his skin dark against the ocean of white sheets into which
Georgia was sure he was about to disappear.

She wondered, *Where are his dreams taking him tonight?*

She wrote in her diary: "This, the man who held my hand."

But Daddy didn't die . . .

For months, Georgia Kaiser, who is now fifty, and Leila Davies, who is now
fifty-eight, took turns driving or riding the bus back and forth from their
homes in Silver Spring and Chevy Chase, Maryland, to Augusta, Georgia,
where Daddy had left the hospital and was staying with a friend. The commuting was exhausting and expensive. Georgia and Leila were schoolteach-
ers with only so many days off, and they had children and husbands who
needed their time. In theory, they had two choices: put Daddy in a nursing
home or take him into their own homes. But like many elderly people, their
father had let it be known that he'd rather die than go into a nursing home.
In a sermon Georgia remembered him preaching when she was a girl, he said,
"Some people marry their cross. Some people give birth to their cross. And
some people put their cross in a nursing home." The sisters really had only
one choice.

That was four years ago, just before Georgia cleaned out a room and
Daddy moved into her house. When he was strong enough, he began split-
ting his time between Georgia's and Leila's, only a few miles away. The
women's decision to take their father into their homes seemed to Georgia a
private choice.

But such private choices will be occurring more and more often in the
years to come. By 2025, nearly 20 percent of the population will be sixty-five
or older. In 1900, only an estimated one in ten married couples between the
ages of forty and sixty had two or more parents alive. Today, thanks to a U.S.
life expectancy that has risen by about twenty-five years in the twentieth century, more than half of America's middle-age couples are estimated to have
two or more parents living.

Despite the myth that modern children dump their parents into nursing
homes, only 5 percent of people over sixty-five are in such facilities, and nearly three-quarters of the nation's frail elderly are cared for by family members
who live in the same residence. The numbers are daunting: In 1985, there
were about 6.5 million dependent elderly in various living arrangements. By
2020, there will be an estimated 14.3 million. Hardly a family in America will
be untouched.

But Georgia Kaiser wasn't thinking about other families. First came her
duty to her father. Beyond that she worried how her own life and her own
family would be changed. Deep down, she childishly wished her father
hadn't gotten feeble. Then she felt guilty for feeling this. As Georgia packed

his things for the move to Washington, she stuffed her father's old family photos and memorabilia in a brown box and put it all away, unable even to look. She thought, *This is all that's left of him.* In her diary, she wrote: "If you should go and I remain, whatever shall I do?"

Looking back now, looking at her family as a human laboratory for what is about to touch so many lives, Georgia believes life with Daddy has turned out to be a bittersweet blessing for her, Leila, their children, their husbands— and for Daddy. Don't get Georgia wrong, it has been no picnic for any of them. But it has been no horror show either. It has made her feel good to know she has returned what was given her as a child, and it has created a time tunnel through which she, her family, even her father have looked back and ahead at their own lives. She puts it simply.

"I feel more grown up."

They are brother relics: the reverend and the curio.

He is eighty-four. The curio—a dark wooden cabinet with a curving glass front, three shelves, feet that are carved into animal paws, and a horizontal mirror that rests on a warping top—is probably that old too.

The reverend was only fifteen, working as a delivery boy at a dry goods store in his hometown of Americus, Georgia, when he heard two sisters from the family that owned the store mention that they were selling the curio to make room for a new piece of furniture. The boy spoke up, saying he'd love to buy it as a gift for his mother, and the deal was struck: fifty cents from the boy's three-dollar weekly wage for forty weeks—twenty dollars, a lot of money in 1925. The boy borrowed a truck and delivered the prize to his mother, who was elated. Sixty-four years passed. And when Georgia was packing her father's books and rolltop desk and a few other belongings, the curio was the only item he asked her to bring along.

"If you can," he said.

The curio and the boy, now antiques.

The reverend sits in a tall, flowered wing chair to the left of his curio. He is a militantly dignified man, his shoulders still erect, his head bald, his remaining hair short and snowy white against his skin. He shaves himself and does a good job, leaving only a few patches of gray beard. His face, like his body, is taut and lean, his cheeks high and hollow, his forehead remarkably unwrinkled. As always, he wears a white shirt and a tie, this day dark blue with a diagonal gray stripe and held in place with a gold tie bar. When he was young, he required two starched and ironed white shirts a day, which his wife, Anna Pearl, delivered without fail.

He crosses his thin left leg over his right leg at the knee, adjusts his wooden cane against his side, plants his elbows on the chair's armrests, and steeples his fingers. He rubs his palms together softly, barely touching, then plays with the change in his pocket. For a moment, he taps his cane with the nail of his finger, then lightly rubs his thigh with his right palm.

He does not squirm, but rather makes each move with a methodical, self-conscious elegance. He holds his hands at his chest and rubs them together slowly, as if working lotion into his skin. The hands are large, with long, expressive fingers that curl upward after their middle joints. On the bridge of each hand is a spiderweb of wrinkles that records his many years like the rings of an old tree. But his palms are as smooth and glassy as pebbles drawn from a running creek. Unlike a laboring man's, his hands were not his most precious tool.

"Let me tell you a story," he always says, his coarse, gravel voice animated by an array of rising and falling volumes and pitches and a masterful range of poetic rhythms, hesitations, and inflections. "I was sitting in the house, the telephone rang, and it was a young lady whose husband was a Pullman redcap . . ."

This is not the man who moved into Georgia's house four years ago. After what doctors called a "seizure," that man's memory was wrecked and he had to be taught to walk again. That man was so frail and confused, he spent the early days at Georgia's house in bed, not knowing where he was. He constantly apologized for being in the way. At night, he rambled about the house knocking on doors, saying, "Time to go, anybody taking me to work?" One night he got up and packed his bag for a trip he'd gone on years before. He couldn't take himself to the bathroom. He had to be reminded to eat. He had to be told, "Daddy, here's your shirt, put this on." Night after night, he asked, "Where am I?" And Georgia answered, "Daddy, you're with me." And he asked, "Now, who are you?" When Georgia returned from a brief trip, he told her that the man and the girls in the house had been very nice to him.

"Daddy, that's my husband."

"Your husband?"

"Daddy, that's Carl and those are my children."

"Those two girls? Well, they certainly were nice to me."

It was almost more than Georgia could bear. "This is my father!" She couldn't get past her perception that he was now the child, she the parent. She remembered her mother nursing her ninety-three-year-old father. "I'm taking care of Papa," her mother would say. She remembered her father's mother, who lived to be 104, sitting on the porch of the family home in Americus, where she lived with two daughters. She remembered Uncle Willie, crazy with dementia and sick with cancer, who lived with his wife until he finally died. She remembered Uncle Robert, never quite right after returning from World War II, who lived with his sisters for the rest of his life.

Georgia was a grown woman, but she couldn't accept that it was now her turn. "I was in charge of *him*," she says. "I've got to tell this man what to do . . . This is my father, who would tell *me*." She balked at the profound gap between saying, "Daddy, dinner's ready," and saying, "Daddy, come eat dinner now."

"I just hadn't grown up to that."

Her father's illness also threw Georgia into renewed mourning for her mother, who had died three years earlier. "It just made a microscopic image of the fact that she's dead, and he's alone . . . All the things that had been, never would be again." Then, in the midst of it all, her father angrily accused her of trying to steal his money. "It hurt me," she says. "I was angry. How dare he!" She sometimes thought: "I wish he were not here. I don't mean dead . . . I don't wish he were in a nursing home. But I wish it hadn't happened. That's what I wish. I wish it hadn't happened."

Georgia even found herself wondering if her enfeebled father wouldn't be better off dead. But each morning, when she went to awaken him, she worried that he might actually be dead. Then it hit her: *What if Karen or Lisa finds him dead?* From then on, she made sure waking up Grandpa wasn't one of her daughters' chores.

The oddest things irritated her. On the first evening that her father was well enough to eat at the dining room table, he happened to sit in Georgia's chair. "That night I let him," she says. But she was astounded how much his sitting in her chair annoyed her. It was silly, irrational. She knew that. But she couldn't help herself. Then she remembered something her father had told families he counseled as a minister: "People argue about what they're not angry about." Of course. It wasn't the chair: Daddy was here and her life was forever changed. She wasn't angry at *him* but at her helplessness in the face of it all. After about a week of stewing, Georgia politely said, "Daddy, you're going to sit here now." Daddy did, never knowing the little psychodrama that had unfolded, and Georgia reclaimed her place at the table.

Summer 1954, Georgia is a little girl . . . It's hot and dusty in rural north Georgia, in the towns of Gainesville and Dahlonega, before air-conditioning, a time of straw hats and cardboard fans, a time when sweaty shirts drew no disapprobation. Little Georgia, with her pretty cotton dress, is the apple of everyone's eye—the Reverend Holman's daughter, the youngest by eight years, spoiled by his undivided attention, the daughter who most takes after his outgoing manner, who, like him, loves books and poetry, a good speaker too, and polite to a fault. When the reverend comes to town on the dirt-road revival circuit, often carrying little Georgia along, the church women pretend to bicker over who'll get her for the day—for sewing or fishing or, just for fun, a stint picking cotton. She is a princess because Daddy is a king.

Every night, Georgia takes her place in the front pew. If Daddy's revival is set to start at seven, it starts at seven, not a minute or thirty minutes after. In a world of dynamic southern preachers, the Reverend James A. Holman always held his own. He'd graduated from Atlanta's Gammon Theological Seminary and in fifty-eight years of ministering rose to become a presiding elder in the Christian Methodist Episcopal Church. He ran his churches like a benevolent dictator, not only giving the sermon but picking the choir music too. And no chatter in the pews, no droning on about fund-raising picnics. No, Daddy was a choreographer of spiritual emotion. To Georgia, it was as if the whole congregation went into a magical trance, left themselves behind, and entered a realm of Daddy's making. He could "line a hymn" like nobody—prayerfully announce or echo each line, turning a hymn into a sermon in itself.

Says Georgia now, "It was a *big* life."

But three decades later, living in her home, he shuffled along the walls, his hand bracing him as he went. He stuffed bread into his pockets at the dinner table and was terrified to be alone, afraid an intruder would kill him. He picked up schoolbooks, magazines, pens, pencils and hoarded them. He hid soiled and stinking clothing in the corners of his room. When Georgia read him their favorite poem from her childhood, Rosa Hartwick Thorpe's "Curfew Must Not Ring Tonight," he did not recall it.

Again, Georgia is a girl . . . It is one in the morning and she wakes up instinctively, waiting for her father to return from his weeknight job as a waiter at the Buckhead Elks Club. She hears the door open and close and, as footsteps come down the hall, "Where's my baby?" Then, predictable as dawn, she hears her mother say, "James, don't wake her up." When the bedroom door opens, Georgia feigns sleep until her daddy says, "Here's some pennies I brought you. Put them in your bank and get back in bed."

Another time . . . Georgia comes home from junior high school three days in a row and thoughtlessly lets the screen door slam. Each day, her father tells her not to let it slam. After the third day, he stops her and says she's in trouble. Then he makes her go in and out the door five times without slamming the screen.

Sunday night, suitor night . . . Georgia's teenage boyfriend comes to the house and sits in the parlor with his beloved and they watch television. At ten o'clock, Daddy comes in to watch his favorite half-hour of TV, "The Loretta Young Show," and sees the boy give Georgia a little kiss on his way out the door. Daddy says nothing, but the next morning tells Georgia that for a boy to kiss her in her father's home is an act of disrespect. She is not to see the boy again. Every day, Georgia sneaks around the corner and calls the boy on a pay phone. After a week, her father says, "You don't have to call on the phone around there. We've got a phone, and he can come back."

But three decades later, living in Georgia's home, her father didn't always recognize her. She wrote in her diary:

"Not the man that I remember."

Sitting in the tall, flowered wing chair to the left of his curio, the reverend tells his story about the phone call from a young lady whose husband was a Pullman redcap. She asked the reverend to do an anniversary service and he agreed. He says he got down on his knees and asked God for guidance with his sermon. He thought of the Bible story about a man on his way to Jericho who fell among thieves and was left for dead. The man was passed by a priest and a Levite, before a Samaritan took pity on him, bound up his wounds, took him to an inn, and paid his way. Jesus said, "Go, and do thou likewise." In this Bible story the reverend found a good message for train porters, who, like the Samaritan, had many chances to do a traveler good. "When I preach," the reverend says, "I aim at something just like I'm shooting at a bird." He says he didn't just preach God is love. He always laid down a challenge, a tough challenge. He pauses, leans forward, cocks his head, and smiles.

"I'm sorry if I bored you."

The reverend sits on the edge of the piano bench. In movements so deliberate they seem sculpted, he shifts his cane from his right hand to his left, turns to his right, and lowers the arm of the record player onto Frankie Laine's version of "I Believe." Behind him on the chalkboard is printed, "God Is Our Refuge."

At the Holy Cross Hospital Adult Day Care Center, where he and about thirty others go every weekday, the reverend's Tuesday morning prayer meeting is about to begin. The congregants arrive slowly—two in wheelchairs, four with canes, one who is blind, one who is nearly blind, one with her chin bent violently to her chest, one with a gnarled hand, one who bobs her head repeatedly as if responding to a conversation only she can hear, one elegant old woman dressed in a bright green jacket and looking as if she's about to play golf at the country club.

The reverend, still the choreographer of spiritual emotion, intones, "We humbly ask you to give us your attention for these few minutes." His voice is tranquil, soothing, confident. He stands, leans on his cane with his right hand. With his left hand, he gestures in a half moon, his long, dexterous fingers wide and open and seeming to trail behind the sweep of his palm like the spreading tail of a comet. "Whatever else you have to discuss, social matters, jokes, let's forget them now . . . Our theme here is 'God Is Our Refuge' . . . This is a prayer meeting."

An old woman begins to read the Ninety-first Psalm from her Bible, and the reverend gently touches her shoulder and whispers, "Not now," as Frankie Laine sings: *"I believe that somewhere in the darkest night, a candle glows . . . ."* And the reverend, conjuring the magical trance Georgia remembers from childhood, lines the hymn.

"I believe above the storm the smallest prayer . . ."

"Above the storm . . ."

"Will still be heard . . ."

"Do you believe that?"

"Every time I hear a newborn baby cry . . ."

"You believe it . . ."
"Or touch a leaf . . ."
"Touch a leaf . . ."
"Or see the sky . . ."
"That's belief . . ."
"Then I know why, I believe."
"You hear those words? You *know* why you believe."

The reverend pauses for a long moment. Everyone is silent. One woman has tears in her eyes; two other women hold hands. He switches his cane from his right hand to his left, reaches out, and again touches the shoulder of the old woman with her Bible open to the Ninety-first Psalm. He nods to her and says, "Now."

It took about six months after Daddy moved into Georgia's house before she realized she had her father back. After the first few months, he'd begun spending half his time at Leila's, which gave Georgia a respite. His memory was much clearer, he bathed and dressed himself, although even today his clothes must be laid out every morning or he might put on yesterday's dirty clothes. Eventually, he agreed to wear Depends, which made his occasional accidents only a nuisance.

His sharp humor returned, and he and Georgia spent many evenings reminiscing, he telling her stories she did not recall and she telling him stories he did not recall. Georgia was once more able to think of those childhood moments with her father—when he made her go in and out the screen door five times or brought her those pennies or banished her boyfriend—without mourning that he was no longer the same man. She took out the brown box filled with her father's old pictures and memorabilia, the box she had put away, and pored over the material, laughing and crying joyful tears as she went.

Because Daddy *was* the same man, but only in flashes. When he cracked a joke about Georgia's driving: "Too bad the brakes on my side didn't work." When he asked to be taken to Metro's Kiss & Ride so he too could get a kiss. When he got sad after reading that a stray bullet had killed a child. When he put on his black fedora at that certain rakish angle, stopped, glanced back over his shoulder, touched the brim, and smiled. When Georgia took a different route to Holy Cross and he asked, "Where are we going?" and she said, "I couldn't lose you, could I?" and he beamed.

"It makes me feel that, yes, family and love and care will make a difference," Georgia says. "He's so much better." And, "I'm definitely a better person. I'm a more tolerant person . . . the change in me that I didn't think I needed to have."

Daddy had always been a hard man to live with. As a minister, he was accustomed to the spotlight, craved and demanded it. Anna Pearl also had spoiled him rotten—not only supplying his starched shirts, but getting up to fetch him a glass of water or a snack whenever he asked. Decades ago, when he smoked Camel cigarettes, no ashtray was ever so close that he wouldn't summon Anna Pearl to move it closer. Once, just after the reverend had left home for a tour of the Holy Land with a group of ministers, she hopped in the car, sped after the bus, beeped her horn, and motioned the driver to the roadside: The reverend had forgotten his favorite hat.

But Georgia soon realized that if she had changed her life to accommodate Daddy, he too had changed. For instance, he'd always been a finicky eater. A woman on the revival circuit had once packed him a lunch and later found him down the road feeding it to the hogs. But now Daddy ate everything without complaint. All his life, Daddy had refused to eat garlic, but now he did. All his life, Daddy had refused to eat chicken. Now he did. Leila even believed he'd come to like chicken. Privately, the reverend still detests it. He laughs. "I'm looking to be as easy as I can."

The changes went beyond food. Growing up in the Old South, Daddy always had a deep fear and distrust of white people, but he went to the integrated Holy Cross center and became good friends with many whites, even deferring to one white woman's insistent requests for an occasional peck on the lips. Daddy'd had a temper as a young man, but he had almost no temper now. He'd also had an opinion about everything. So when he arrived, Georgia never yelled at her daughters in front of him, sometimes took them out to the car for scolding, afraid her father would judge her a bad mother. But he never said a critical word about how she and Carl raised the girls, and he never said a bad word about the girls either, only praised them. When Georgia was embarrassed by one daughter's temper tantrum, he said calmly, "We all get angry . . . They're doing fine." Daddy also had always hated cats, but now he loved Georgia's cat, sat petting it, even let it sleep on his bed. In his own way, Georgia realized, her father was trying hard to fit into the family. At his age, over the hill, he was still growing.

Even Carl, who hadn't felt close to Georgia's father and who believed he was too domineering and self-centered, came to admire him. He loved the wise aphorisms the reverend dropped from time to time. Carl's favorite: "Just because you didn't mean to step on my toe, doesn't mean it didn't hurt." Carl had always cooked most of the family meals, and he quickly added softer fare to accommodate the reverend. He cooked the reverend's breakfast and freely pitched in to help Georgia with the new workload. That made life easier for her, but it also had an unexpected benefit: It deepened Georgia's already deep affection for her husband of twenty-one years.

Georgia's and Leila's greatest fear was what Daddy would do with his time while they and their husbands were at work. Then a neighbor told Georgia about the Holy Cross day-care center, which saved the day. Because the reverend's only income was $568 a month in Social Security, he qualified for Medicaid to pay the center's $51-a-day cost. Georgia and Leila worried that Daddy wouldn't go—he had always refused to socialize with old people and was still nervous around whites. But again, he surprised them. He said, "The people there, I could be a morale-builder for them."

Soon, the reverend was center stage at the center, eager to arrive before 8:30 so he could greet everyone in the morning, always inviting one of the women to dip a finger in his coffee to sweeten it up, always asking at the morning gathering, "What's for lunch?" And when he began his Tuesday morning prayer meetings, he was again able to do his life's work. Having people pay attention to him and listen to him, making a contribution again, being accorded special respect and status enlivened him.

The reverend's condition improved, but Georgia still struggled with her grief at her father's decline, still felt ashamed that she wished he didn't need her care, still felt guilty that his presence in the house grated on her. *He's not doing anything to bother me, she thought, but he's still getting on my nerves doing it.* She began attending the center's group counseling sessions, where she saw that her emotions were downright mundane, as she heard others caring for elderly loved ones gripe about the same kind of irritations. She thought, *Hallelujah, somebody feels the same way!*

She saw that her burden was neither unique nor the heaviest to bear. At her last session, a man explained that his wife couldn't remember where anything went in the house they'd lived in for fifty years. Another man said his elderly wife had become so incontinent that even with adult diapers, the church choir had finally asked that she retire. A woman said of her stroke-victim husband, "He's like a dummy sitting there . . . I don't know how I do it. It's getting harder and harder."

When the center's director, Bob Grossman, said that as many as half the people over age eighty-five have some form of dementia, Georgia felt suddenly blessed by the clarity of her father's memory. When he explained that people caring for the elderly often suspect that their charges are pretending frailty to get more attention, Georgia felt relief: She was not an ungrateful daughter, she was only human. Georgia learned that beyond the confines of the center was a full spectrum of elderly life—elderly people living independently, those living in group homes with special assistance, those living bedridden in relatives' homes with the help of professional aides and nurses, those living in nursing homes. The sad truth is, few elderly people die today without some period of dependency. Georgia's father could be in better health, but he also could be in worse health. For that, Georgia was grateful.

And she realized she'd been wrong: She had not become the parent, her father the child. A needful child will become *less* needful, grow in strength and self-mastery, and a parent burdened with the demands and irritations of constant care knows this, anticipates it. That anticipated future is part of the joy. In Daddy's case, the joy was strictly in the here and now, because the longer he lives the more he will decline. The more jokes he will be unable to finish, the more often he will repeatedly ask Georgia what time a favorite TV show starts, the more often he will hang his dirty clothes in the closet, the more often he will not know what day of the week it is, the more often he will apologize for boring his listeners. But there will be satisfaction later, after his death, in knowing she was a good daughter.

"When I look into his casket," Georgia says, "I want to know my mother is looking here, saying that I did a good job. And I want to be able to say, 'I did a good job.'"

Leila never attended the counseling sessions, and it amazes Georgia that her sister didn't agonize over their father moving in. Leila is a practical-minded, matter-of-fact woman. "We have little things that bother us, but so what?" she says. "This is life." Leila enjoyed hearing Daddy's stories about her childhood. She loved it that her husband, Langston, and Daddy would sit for hours talking about the Bible. She glowed with pride that he always found the strength and concentration to comport himself with dignity at her church's Sunday services, a couple of times even giving a decent sermon or prayer.

Leila took her father's presence in stride, while Georgia struggled with it. Perhaps because Georgia was the youngest by so many years, had been babied and spoiled in that role, had shared a love of books and poetry, she saw more of herself in her father. Who knows? At the counseling sessions, seeing the wide range of people's ways of dealing with their aging parents and spouses, Georgia realized there was no *right* way to respond.

She says, "It lifted a lot off my shoulders."

Back at his Tuesday morning prayer meeting, the reverend leads in reciting the Twenty-third Psalm—"The Lord is my shepherd . . ."—and then, his voice strong, his eyes closed, he prays: "Father in heaven . . . here we are now. Our heads are white with the frost of many winters, our faces are wrinkled with the furrows of age, and our bodies are bent beneath the weight of years, but in spite of all that, You have sustained us and kept us in the evening of our lives . . ." And the voice of Frankie Laine again rises: *"I believe that somewhere in the darkest night . . ."*

He is in his room at Georgia's house. It is evening. He often secludes himself here, no phone, no bother. In this room, with a blend of prayer and conversation, he talks to his wife, hears her voice when she says of their daughters, "Stand by them. They're all you have." He reads from the scores of religious books he has collected, searching for themes and passages for his Tuesday prayer meeting. For next week, he selects a stanza of poetry originally written in ancient Sanskrit: "Look to this day, for it is life, the very breath of life."

He sits on his bed, a big bed covered with a brown-and-white quilt, in a small, darkly paneled room. Around him: a picture of Jesus, a bronze relief of the Last Supper, a sepia-toned photo of his father, a handsome man with mustache, white shirt, dark jacket, and old-fashioned necktie, a photo of Anna Pearl, his rolltop desk, which is cluttered with pens and pencils, its top drawer holding the false teeth he no longer wears, his last automobile license plate—DDR 207—posted on the wall, two ties already tied hanging from a hanger on a hook near the closet. Everything washed with light turned a vague amber through a tan shade.

The reverend studies and then presses a button on the tape recorder next to him on the bed, inserts a tape, to do what he enjoys so much: listening to his old sermons, some dating back twenty years. When Georgia moved away, she asked him to tape them and send them to her so she could hear them. Now it is he who hears them. Sometimes he gets ready for bed and climbs under the covers to listen. Sometimes he paces the room, gesturing along, moving his lips to his own words. Sometimes he lines the hymns out loud. He thinks of himself as an old preacher listening to a young preacher. He is not that man anymore, but still he is.

"I'm that preacher. I'm doing that speaking now."

"That's me."

"I haven't changed."

"I still have the same philosophy."

"I was"—he hesitates—"*good.*"

"Something that I did that turned out to be magnificent."

"Be that it made some contribution."

The voice on the tape is more than the voice of the Tuesday prayer meeting, layers more. A deep, powerful, chest rumbling voice, preaching and singing at once, a voice somewhere between that of a whispering prayer-giver and that of a bellowing auctioneer: "*Anybody* can live good when there ain't nobody botherin' ya! *Anybody* can live good when they got a good job! *Anybody* can live good when there ain't nobody pickin' at your wife! *Anybody* can live good when the money is right!" In that church decades ago, amens and laughter arose.

"But if you stand with God when the chips are down!"

"Everybody! Because it's a cross."

"Jesus, keep me near the cross."

On his bed, a white handkerchief held to his face like a mask, his dark hand silhouetted against it, the reverend cries.

Living with grandpa has been a complicated ride for his three granddaughters. Leila's son, Paul, was twenty-two when he arrived, and he took the change in stride. He wasn't home much and eventually married and moved out of his folks' home. But for Leila's daughter, Ursula, then eighteen, and Georgia's daughters, Karen and Lisa, fifteen and fourteen at the time, their grandfather's arrival loomed larger. Politeness is an enforced virtue in both families, and the girls were never rude to their grandfather, but inside they often fumed as they struggled to understand his place in their lives.

"I couldn't understand why he was coming all the way here," says Ursula, now twenty-two. "I worried about having to stay home and baby-sit him. I don't mean to sound selfish, but I had my life too. I couldn't understand why they didn't put him in a nursing home nearby and we could go visit him."

It was Ursula's job to clean the downstairs bathroom, and it irked her that her grandfather didn't always hit the mark. The idea of sharing the same bathtub with an old man also annoyed her, and she always sanitized the tub before she bathed. He put half-consumed cans of soda back in the fridge. He sometimes used Ursula's drinking cup. He interrupted conversations and told the same jokes and stories repeatedly. He asked, "Ursula, you heard this one?" She answered, "Yes, Granddaddy." Then he told the joke anyway. But worst of all, Ursula was embarrassed for her friends to meet him. He was so, well, so *old*.

"It was just not cool," Ursula says. "Only in the last year have I started to pay attention to him." She has learned to put away her drinking cup so he won't use it by mistake. She has learned to say, "That's a good one, Granddaddy," when he interrupts with a joke that she has heard before, and then go back to her conversation. She has tried to imagine what it will be like to someday ask her own father, "Daddy, did you go to the bathroom?" before they walk out the door. She has listened to her grandfather tell horrible stories about life for blacks in the Old South, and she has resolved to complain less and appreciate more the opportunities open to her today. From her grandfather, she has taken this lesson: "Even though he has aches and pains and can be forgetful and had his wife die, he still seems to enjoy life."

Sometimes, Ursula will be in a hurry in the morning, running out the door, trying to get her grandfather off to the day-care center and herself off to Howard University, and he will step outside and say, "Look at the sky, not a cloud! And the grass is so green." That makes Ursula stop in her rush, look at the sky and the grass, and see that he is exactly right.

She says, "It's an inspiration."

Georgia's daughters, Karen and Lisa, nineteen and eighteen today, tell of similar journeys. In the early days, Karen couldn't help but be amused when her grandfather got up in the middle of the night and knocked on doors—it was just so weird! It bugged Lisa that he claimed a chair in the TV room as his own, when nobody had ever had assigned chairs in the TV room. When she sat in it, he shuffled around nearby, hoping she'd get up. But she didn't. Not unless he asked, which he rarely did.

Georgia didn't have as much time for the girls, and that bothered them. But once again, it was the trivial irritants that irked them the most. New, unpleasant odors filled the house. Grandpa left the toilet seat up. He tilted lamp shades to read and left them crooked. It angered Karen terribly that she and her sister had to squeeze their chairs on one side of the dinner table. He went up and down the stairs so slowly when Lisa was behind him that she became convinced he did it to annoy her. Both girls believed their grandfather acted more feeble than he was so they'd wait on him—get him a drink, a snack, a newspaper—just as Grandma had always done.

Karen harbored the deepest resentment, which she kept to herself until just last year, when she talked with Georgia about what she had come to see as her irrational anger at her grandfather. "He didn't do anything, really," Karen says. "It was me." Karen felt gypped. "I wanted grandparents like my friends' who took them shopping and on trips and to a play." She believed her grandfather's infirmity was something he'd done to himself. "I couldn't see that he was just old," she says. Karen also was angered by stories that her grandmother had waited on her grandfather "hand and foot." Unlike her mother, Karen saw nothing quaint in this. She thought, "Why should a woman have to do that?" When her grandfather seemed to expect Karen to do him small favors, she couldn't help but think he was treating her the same way, like a servant. "It disturbed me for so long," she says. "I didn't know the context."

"Looking back, I just wasn't at all compassionate . . . Now I realize he didn't like being so dependent. That's something I've thought about: What if I couldn't do anything by myself? I wouldn't feel good about it, and I'm sure he didn't either. What if I were paralyzed in a car accident? I realized that's how he must feel."

Last year, Karen began to sit in the yard and talk with her grandfather. Without being asked, she did his laundry occasionally and was surprised at how the smell of his soiled clothing no longer sickened her. She found herself listening intently as her mother and grandfather told old stories on each other and found herself imagining her own children and grandchildren someday sitting with her, an old woman, talking about the life she was living right now. And she saw herself in their stories, realized that her grandfather had seemed to act so strict when her mother was a girl but was actually quite indulgent—a carbon copy of how Georgia had raised her and her sister.

"We're all pretty much alike, as much as I'd like to think I'm different," Karen says. "But pretty much I'm not." Lisa's resentment of her grandfather was never as deep as Karen's, and she says only that she has learned patience from living with him. But Karen's silent anger was once so fierce that she still sometimes asks God to forgive her for it. She has had long talks with the man she dates about how when her parents get old, she will expect to take them into her home. Like her cousin Ursula, when her grandfather moved in, Karen couldn't understand why they didn't just put him in a nursing home. Now Karen understands. "It would hurt him to know we put him out . . . I also wouldn't want him to think I was the kind of person to put him out . . . I'm glad I grew up."

*　　　*　　　*

The reverend's room at Leila's house is larger and brighter, though it is still cluttered with his books. He sits on a stiff-backed chair, stiff-backed himself, rubs the palm of one hand lightly along his thigh, and with his other hand plays with the change in his pants pocket. A person has to understand: The *feeling* the reverend got while preaching was the most powerful emotion of his life. More powerful even than his love of his wife or his children. That's why listening to his old sermons and conducting his prayer meeting at the center mean so much to him. They touch the old emotion—the power, the joy, the intimacy with God—that he felt every Sunday and every revival for half a century. Like an aging athlete who still feels as if he should be *able* to make the mark but cannot get his body to cooperate, the reverend still feels like a young man, although his mind and body won't cooperate.

"I feel like I have something to offer . . . I'm afraid people don't want to hear it . . . It's difficult for me to come to that place, but the only way *not* to come to that place is to die . . . You adjust. You wake up on Sunday morning and say, 'Now if I was in Americus, I would have a place to preach this morning.' I don't have a place. So I put on my clothes and go to church."

The reverend, in his deliberate way, brushing his face lightly with one hand, tapping his cane with the nail of a finger, says it has been a joy to live with his daughters and their families, seeing his grandkids grow up, seeing how competent his daughters are as mothers and wives, seeing how decent are their husbands. "I had a wife who was almost a mother to me," he says. "I was known as a spoiled brat." But as an old man, living with his daughters, he has learned something about compromise, about not always getting his own way. It may have been a long time coming, but the reverend says, "I learned how to get along with people." He acknowledges that, yes, he does make little demands on his family just to get attention. He asks for juice or cookies, asks someone to recite a poem or listen to him recite a poem. "I just abhor loneliness," he says. "I do like babies, I cry." He smiles. "I need attention. I need to feel like they need me."

When the reverend was a young minister, he would go to the home of an elderly preacher he knew to help him bathe, make sure he got a haircut when he needed it. He ran errands, picked up the old man's spending money at the bank. "That man had something to offer," the reverend says, "but he needed help to do it." Once again, he tells the entire story of his sermon in honor of the Pullman redcap, which reminded the baggage handlers that they had many chances to do a traveler good. The message: "Everyone can make a contribution." At Holy Cross, the reverend knows elderly men who say little, are perhaps locked in their loneliness or debilitations. So he talks to them, compliments them, because he believes he knows what they want and need—attention. Because if a person doesn't get attention, it's as if he has disappeared.

"The ones I ask," the reverend says of Georgia and Leila, "are the ones I gave glasses of water to when they couldn't get them. Reciprocity is the order of the day . . . I feel like my daughters are obligated . . . I need it done and I feel like they ought to know I need it done." It's harder to get up and get a drink, he says, than young people realize. It's harder to take a glass down from the shelf for fear of breaking it. It's harder to pour a hot cup of coffee, and it's harder to clean up the crumbs after making a sandwich. And every day, it gets harder to remember what pants and shirt he wore yesterday. "I shouldn't have to admit that I can't do at eighty-four what I did before. You ought to know it . . . Maybe when they get to be my age, they'll say, 'I know what he means.' But I'll be molding in the grave." Maybe twenty-five years from now, he says, Georgia or Leila will think back on these last years they lived with him. "And they can be more tolerant of their children."

He tells a story: When he was a minister in Augusta, he had elderly congregants who couldn't get out of bed to eat or go to the bathroom. "If you have one on your hands," he says, "don't make them concede they have the problem. They know. Don't frown every time they call. Turnabout is fair play. Time is passing for me, but it's also passing for you . . . I'd hate to have Leila or Georgia put me in the bathtub when I was naked. I'd hate that. I still have my pride . . . I don't worry about it, but I think about it. And I believe if I come to that place, they'd do it . . . I believe this is life. You have to take it as you find it." The reverend sits forward in his chair, straightens his back, says, "There's one thing you have to know." As he speaks, his voice goes deep and clear and his arms gesture in grand designs.

> My latest sun is sinking fast,
> My race is nearly run.
> My strongest trials now are past,
> My triumph is begun.
> I know I'm nearing the holy ranks
> Of friend and kindred dear.
> I brush the dew on Jordan's banks;
> The crossing must be near.

The reverend stops, pauses for a long moment, and says, "I may be here tomorrow. I may not." He leans forward, cocks his head, and smiles. "I'm sorry if I bored you."

August 31, 1994

True Detective

A man goes twenty-two years without being afraid, without giving his own death a glance, without worrying that the map of the city's criminal ways and rhythms that he has always carried in his head might be obsolete. A man goes twenty-two years climbing the ladder from beat cop to blue-boy elite, to homicide detective. A man goes twenty-two years to earn a reputation as a "90 percenter"—a detective who puts the souls of nearly all his victims to rest by closing the book on their murders. A man goes twenty-two years, and then the waters he inhabits shift and roil with unpredictable currents, until murder isn't murder anymore, isn't a biblical sentence that friends and lovers and fathers and sons impose on each other in storms of rage and recrimination. A man goes twenty-two years and finds himself leaning casually over a corpse on Halley Terrace in Washington, D.C., about to be made aware. That man—Detective Victor "V. I." Smith—flips back the dead man's coat and sees a blue-black machine gun, an Uzi, cocked and ready to fire.

Detective V. I. Smith is fearless—at least his police buddies think he's fearless. He has waltzed into Barry Farms, one of the roughest housing projects in Washington, at four in the morning, disappeared for an hour, and returned with his suspect in tow. He has raided crack houses alone, lined up the drug heads, and sweated them for reconnaissance on the spot. V. I.'s cop friends can't imagine him being afraid of anything. But tonight, after Halley Terrace, V. I. talks and talks about his shock at seeing that Uzi. About how six of his last seven murder victims have been packing guns. He doesn't reveal it to his comrades, but V. I. realizes that for the first time in twenty-two years as a Washington cop, he was afraid. Oh, maybe he'd been afraid before and hadn't realized it, imagined his feeling was excitement or readiness or the flow of adrenaline. But there's no mistaking or denying the emotion that surged through V. I. Smith on Halley Terrace tonight: It was fear.

Detective V. I. Smith.
Photo by Silvia Otte.

Two years later . . . Everything squeaks. The heavy doors squeak. The metal swivel chairs squeak. The drawers in the metal desks squeak. The file drawers squeak. The keys of the old manual upright squeak. The room—No. 5058, dubbed Homicide North because it is isolated two floors above Washington's other homicide offices in the city's Municipal Center—is a concerto of squeaks. Its other noises—the hollering voices, the clamoring phones, the electric type-writers, *Gilligan's Island* laugh-tracking on the beat-up TV, the two coffeepots spitting mud, the handheld walkie-talkies belching static—all add layer upon layer of volume, creating finally a kind of jangled symphony.

What will stop this din and turn the entire room of nine men prayerfully silent are three words their ears are tuned to as if they were set on a private frequency: "stabbing" or "shooting" or "homicide." When the police radio dispatcher speaks any of these words, everything stops, hands reach for tiny volume knobs on radios, and everybody waits. Usually, it's a false alarm and, just as abruptly, the noise once again envelops the momentary silence like a stadium cheer after the *crack* of a long ball.

The men in Homicide North are tonight "on the bubble"—cop talk meaning that their squad of detectives is on call to investigate the city's next murder. Detective Jeff Mayberry, a short, wiry, close-cropped, jet-propelled thirty-four-year-old in a tight blue sports coat, is riding the top of the bubble in his rotation as lead investigator on whatever horror is next offered up from the bowels of the city. He has ridden the bubble aloft for four duty days now—and no murder. At least none on his three-to-eleven shift.

"You believe it?" he asks in frustration. No murder in a town that sees almost four murders every three days!

"You're bad luck," comes the rejoinder of his partner, Joe Fox, a respected and bearded forty-one-year-old bear of a detective who has a compulsive squint that constantly edges his wire-rimmed glasses up the bridge of his nose. He is called neither "Joe" nor "Fox." He is called "Joefox."

"Screw you, Joefox," Mayberry says.

Seated at the end of a row of desks in a corner under a wash of fluorescent light in front of pale curtains that hang off their track is V. I. Smith, looking out of place in this seedy domain. At age forty-six, he's quiet and self-contained, talking softly into the receiver of the old phone atop his desk, which isn't unkempt like most of the others. He's chatting with a woman who lives on W Street NW. She has been peeking out her window tonight to see if the drug boys V. I. wants to bust and shake down for tips about a recent murder are hanging on the street. They aren't.

Leaning on his elbows at his desk, talking into the phone, V. I. looks less like a tough city cop than, say, a prosecuting attorney or an FBI agent. He's six feet four. Naked on the scale, he goes a trim and powerful 230, only ten pounds over the weight he carried as a freshman basketball star at Howard University nearly three decades ago.

His face is wide and handsome, chiseled. It smiles rarely. In temperament, V. I. is terminally *cool*, never nervous or edgy. The more excited he gets, the more deliberately he speaks. And the more deliberately he speaks, the more trouble whomever he's speaking to is probably in. Even V. I.'s laugh is deliberate, with each "hah" in his slow "hah-hah-hah" being fully enunciated. In dress and style, he resembles a new-breed jazz player: His hair and mustache are short and neat, his shirt is crisp, his tie is knotted tightly and never yanked loose at his neck, and his suit, usually bought at Raleighs, is always well tailored and never cheap. Unlike some of his detective pals, V. I. would never wear brown shoes with a blue suit. He dresses to the nines because, having grown up on the streets of black Washington, he knows that a man who dresses well is ascribed a dose of respect in that world, and every small advantage counts, especially these days.

The guys in the office call V. I. "the Ghost," because they rarely know what he's doing from minute to minute. With his reputation as one of Washington's best homicide detectives, V. I. comes and goes at Room 5058 pretty much as he pleases. But if the radio calls out a murder, he's on the scene, appearing as if from nowhere, like an apparition. Of Washington's sixty-five homicide detectives, V. I. Smith figures he's the only one without a regular partner. That's because Joefox, who came with V. I. to homicide seven years ago on the same cold Tuesday in February, used to be his partner, until the green and gung-ho Mayberry arrived from uniform four years ago and was assigned to Joefox for diapering.

Joefox and V. I. eventually took the kid aside and told him how it was going to be: The three of them would be partners, meaning that any one man's case was also the case of the other two. If Mayberry listened and studied and showed respect, he would learn the art and science of unraveling the darkest of human behaviors from two of the masters. And that's how it came down, with Mayberry now a fine detective in his own right. So when Mayberry is riding the bubble, Joefox and the Ghost are riding with him.

When the bubble seems to burst tonight, it's no thriller. A man named Willis Fields, who lived in a Washington boardinghouse, died at the Washington Hospital Center burn unit today, and the death was passed on to Detective C. J. Thomas, whose job it is to investigate and certify natural deaths. But in the hospital file he discovered that the fifty-six-year-old man had told a nurse that "they" had poured alcohol on him and set him afire. Willis Fields was in the hospital ten days, but his story fell through the cracks. Nobody called the police about his allegation, which means the inquiry will start nearly two weeks cold, no leads, only an address.

"C. J., why is it every one a these things you do, you always get us?" asks Mayberry. "Remember that guy on Suitland Parkway? Been there two years? Six shots to the head?"

"And what did you tell me?" C. J. asks.

"Man, that's a natural!" says Mayberry, laughing.

"Well, here we go," says V. I., in his smooth, lyrical baritone as he palms a radio, unconsciously pats his right breast coat pocket for evidence of his ID wallet, pats his left breast coat pocket for evidence of his notebook, and heads out the door in his athlete's saunter, a stylized and liquid stroll, a modern cake-walk.

The address for Willis Fields is wrong—2119 Eleventh St. NW is a vacant lot. "They probably got it turned around," V. I. says, as the threesome mills about the grassy lot, looking lamely around, shrugging. It's just before dusk and the hot summer day has begun to cool, but except for a man staring at them intently from the sidewalk in front of the Soul Saving Center Church of God across the street, the block is empty of people, quiet.

V. I. knows this neighborhood. He spent years living nearby as a kid, attending Garnet-Patterson Junior High over at Tenth and U Streets, Bell High School at Hiatt Place and Park Road, and Cardozo High just up the hill at Thirteenth and Clifton Streets. This block of Eleventh Street isn't Beverly Hills, but it's a stable block that doesn't fit V. I.'s image of the crime at hand. An old man is more likely to be set on fire on a block where guys hang out drinking liquor, where there's a lot of street action. He nods down the road. That sounds more like the block back at Eleventh and U, with a corner market and a liquor store nearby. Sure enough, when the office checks the address the detectives were given, it's wrong. Willis Fields lived at 1929—near the corner of Eleventh and U.

Being in his old neighborhood makes V. I. nostalgic. As a boy, he seemed to live everywhere in Washington—Southeast, Northeast, here in Northwest, as his mother and father struggled and moved up from dumpy apartment to less dumpy apartment. Sometimes, he and his brothers sacked out four to a mattress. But in the fifties, V. I.'s daddy—a laborer by day, a cabby by night—bought a big old house on Adams Street in LeDroit Park, near First and W Streets NW, and the kids finally slept two to a room.

The man who grew up to be a cop was no choirboy. He didn't worry about his grades, he cut classes to play basketball, he learned to palm loaded dice, he hustled pool. By age sixteen, V. I. was frequenting the now defunct Birdland and Rio nightclubs on Fourteenth Street with his older buddies. And it was at one such club that his friend Jimmy got killed. They were hanging with a fool of a friend, who flipped his cigarette butt toward the bar and hit a dude in the neck. When the guy flicked out the narrow blade with the pearl handle, everybody scrambled, but Jimmy didn't scramble fast enough. He took the knife deep in his back, stumbled outside, and bled out his life on the sidewalk.

After that, V. I. was more judicious about the company he kept. A lot of guys he hung with eventually went bad in the ways kids went bad in those days—stealing purses, robbing people on the street. But not V. I. For some reason—

maybe because his daddy was so strict—V. I. was always afraid of the police. While other guys figured the cops would never catch them, V. I. figured the cops would *always* catch him.

One incident had frightened him good: A woman was raped in his neighborhood, and the police rounded up anybody on the street close to the rapist's description and took them to the old Tenth Precinct. V. I. sat in a holding room until 3:00 A.M., when the cops told him he could go home—they'd caught their man. That night made V. I. a believer in the "wrong place, wrong time" theory of city life. A guy had to think ahead, anticipate, cut trouble off at the pass, stay off the streets and away from guys bound for infamy. Or go down too.

After a stint in the military, after attending Howard University, after becoming a basketball celebrity on the playgrounds of Washington, and just before graduating from American University, V. I. was sworn in as one of the city's early black cops. Only a few days later, he attended the funeral of a boyhood friend, a kid nicknamed Porgy, a kid V. I. had learned to avoid. Porgy had graduated from purses to stickups, and he was killed in a gun battle with police. Almost twenty-five years later, V. I. has never stopped believing that with a few unlucky breaks, a few poor choices, he too could have gone down the toilet like Porgy. To this day, he can arrive on a street corner and find a young man who has just bled out his life on the sidewalk, and think: *But for the grace of God . . .*

At 1929 Eleventh St., nobody answers the door. So the detectives spread out and canvass the street, talking to neighbors. They have the office run the license plates of nearby parked cars, checking for the name Willis Fields. When an elderly man walks into the yard at 1929, Mayberry asks if he knows him.

"Yeah, I know 'im."

"When's the last time you talked to Willie?"

"The Sunday 'fore last."

"Who's he hang with?"

"He works at Ben's Chili Bowl."

"Where you live?"

It turns out the man lives in the room next to the one once occupied by Willis Fields. He says Fields has no girlfriend and few male friends, that nobody ever visits his room, and that he smokes cigars and hits the bottle hard. The detectives want to get inside Fields's room to check for signs of a fire, because if he was burned in his room—fell asleep smoking and drinking liquor on the bed—it would show that he could have gotten burned on his back by accident, not malicious design. But the man says Fields's room is locked and that the landlady is out.

"What happened to 'im?" the man asks.

"He didn't tell ya?" asks V. I., careful to reveal no information likely to make its way into the street gossip mill.

"Hell if I know."

At Ben's Chili Bowl, a block away on U Street, they ask their questions again. The whole time, V. I. is building scenarios, theories, in his mind. Say Fields had a buddy who often came to visit him at Ben's, but who hasn't stopped by in the last couple weeks. Good chance that guy knows something. Or say a woman always seemed to visit Fields on his payday. She's a good possibility. Or maybe Fields complained to a coworker about somebody who'd been bothering him. Or mentioned somebody who owed him money. Whatever the story, V. I. knows from experience that men like Fields usually lead very simple lives. They go from their rooms to their jobs to the liquor store and back to their rooms. So that's the bird dog's trail. Unfortunately, nobody at Ben's knows much about Fields either, except that he has been missing.

"Ooohhh, booooy!" says Mayberry.

As a murder, this case has "unsolved" written all over it. And unless V. I., Mayberry, and Joefox declare it a homicide, it will likely be forgotten. There's been no publicity, no relatives or political heavyweights demanding action. If Fields's death were declared a natural, his demise would slip into bureaucratic oblivion. It wouldn't take up their time or mess up their statistics with an unsolved murder. It would—*poof*—disappear. Except for one detail: Some dirtbag might have turned Willis Fields into a human torch, and catching the scum would bring great satisfaction. The idea is downright inspirational. Because in an era when most of the homicides V. I. gets are drug boys wasting drug boys, bandits beefing each other through the nose of a nine millimeter, or hotheads retaliating after some trivial insult, this Willis Fields case is, well, intriguing, a puzzle with most of the pieces missing. The men need to hit 1929 again, talk to the landlady, get into Fields's room. But in the meantime—since Willis Fields is still not an official homicide—Mayberry, Joefox, and the Ghost are back on the bubble.

The call comes at 9:50 P.M. . . . .

When the men arrive at Rhode Island Avenue and Brentwood Road NE, the scene, as it always does, seems not real, somehow outside time and place, like a page brought to life from a paperback novel: The shooting ground is cordoned off in a triangle of yellow plastic tape (POLICE LINE DO NOT CROSS), and squad cars and cruisers are parked every which way, as if they'd landed as randomly as dice thrown in a tornado's game of craps. The crowd of mostly women and youngsters is congregated in the vague and dreamy light of street lamps beneath huge and gnarled trees in the scrub-grass yard of the L-shaped Brookland Manor apartments. A police helicopter flutters overhead, its searchlight scorching a block nearby. The cops know this stretch of Rhode Island as a drug market, and that's the first scenario V. I.'s mind starts to build. *One shot, large caliber, left side of the head.* That's all he knows.

V. I. steps into the triangle and begins to think in the language of the scene before him. On the sidewalk begins the pool of blood, not red, but a thick, syrupy black. The blood has cascaded over the curb and run southwest with gravity for about five feet, where a pile of leaves and debris has dammed its flow. The young man who was shot was alive when the ambulance left, but this is a large pool of blood, and V. I. figures Mayberry is off the bubble. On the sidewalk is a footprint in blood. Could be that of the victim, the shooter, a witness, a passerby, an ambulance attendant. A few feet away is a lonely quarter, heads up. On a waist-high embankment, where the sidewalk meets the yard about six feet from the street, stand a Mountain Dew bottle and a can of Red Bull malt liquor.

The details seem trivial, but a homicide detective's life is a sea of details, a collage of unconnected dots gathered and collated. In the end, most will turn out to be insignificant. But at the time, a detective cannot know the revelatory from the inconsequential. He must try to see them all, then hold them in his mind in abeyance until the few details that matter rise forth from the ocean to reveal themselves. V. I. begins to link the dots in the scene before him. For instance, a man who is shot at such close range was hit either by someone he trusted or by someone who sneaked up on him. Maybe the Mountain Dew and the Red Bull belonged to the victim and to one of his friends, who were sitting on the embankment looking toward the street, talking and laughing. From the darkened yard behind them the shooter moved in. The victim fell forward, his head landing at the curb and spurting blood with each heartbeat. His buddy bolted. If the dots are connected correctly, that buddy is a witness. If not, he could be the shooter.

Suddenly, from the crowd in the dreamy light on the scrub-grass yard, comes a long, awful scream. In five seconds, it comes again. And then a woman runs wildly through the crowd, crashing into people as she goes. She disappears into a door at the elbow of the L-shaped Brookland Manor. On the chance that this might be a drug-boy shooting, V. I., Mayberry, and Joefox will not wander through the crowd or canvass the apartments looking for witnesses tonight. Until a few years ago, it was virtually unheard of for witnesses to be killed, but today they are crossed off like bad debts. Witnesses know it, cops know it, shooters know it. It's simply too dangerous for witnesses to be seen talking to the cops after a shooting, especially at night when the drug boys are out. V. I. plans to return tomorrow afternoon to do his canvass. But after hearing the woman scream, he invokes another law of experience: "You get people cryin', they gonna tell ya somethin'."

With this in mind, V. I. saunters toward the door at the building's elbow, and the crowd parts and murmurs as he passes. On the darkened stairs up to the second floor, a place filled with the smells of a dozen dinners cooking, he finds the woman's mother, who says her daughter knew the victim but doesn't want to talk to the police. V. I. doesn't push. He gets the daughter's name, her apartment number. One of the problems these days is that victims and suspects are usually known on the streets only by nicknames that the cops don't know. So V. I. asks if the victim had a nickname. The mother says, "KK."

The wanton killings of the last few years have changed everything. From 1964 to 1987, the number of Washington homicides fluctuated between 132 and 287, with 225 posted in 1987. In their first two years as detectives, the eager V. I. and Joefox drove around with their radio microphone in hand so they could lay claim to any murder as soon as it came down. Then, in 1988, homicides skyrocketed to 369—then 434, 474, and 483 in the following years, with the pace flagging only slightly so far this year. The police closure rate plummeted: By the end of 1991, only 65 percent of homicides from 1990 and 54 percent from 1991 had been closed by police, compared with 80 percent of homicides from 1986.

As homicides have gone berserk, so have the lives of V. I. and his fellow detectives. A cop used to have time to investigate his murders, interview everybody, build a case. In the old days, murder was more often a domestic affair, and a victim's killer was often found among his family. But by 1991, only 4 percent of Washington homicides were domestics, while more than three-quarters were attributed to drugs, robberies, burglaries, arguments, or non-drug-related retaliations. All of which means that for most homicides today, detectives no longer have a neat list of identifiable suspects but a barrage of friends, enemies, business partners, and competitors to investigate. Even with more detectives, the cases are constantly rolling over one another, with new murders arriving before old ones are solved. Sometimes, V. I. sits down and pores through his old files so he doesn't plain forget a case.

And the drug-boy and bandit killings are so much more complicated than the old "mom-and-pop murders." V. I. has a case in far Northeast, where a bunch of guys opened fire on a crowd one evening, killing a young man and wounding three others. On its face, it looks like a drug-boy shooting. But the chain of events is also intertwined with the lives, loves, personalities, and values of an array of individuals. The case began, according to the tips V. I. has collected from informants, a week before the shooting, when a woman friend of a suspected drug dealer was beaten by another woman. The suspected drug dealer went gunning for his friend's assailant, but shot the wrong woman. A male friend of the woman who was mistakenly shot then interceded in her behalf with the shooter, who apparently took this as a threat. With several buddies, he sought out and killed the male friend of the woman who had been mistakenly shot, before the guy could ice him. And that's a simple case.

V. I. has had cases that intertwine with as many as a dozen other murders— shootings, retaliations, shootings, retaliations. He has cases where families have been wiped out. A young man was killed, and his brother was set to testify against the shooter, and then the brother was killed. Another brother was set to testify against that brother's shooter, and he was killed. A sister was set to testify against *that* brother's shooter, and she too was shot. There's little moral outrage about many such killings because of what V. I. calls "victim participation"—meaning the victims are often as sleazy as their killers. Nowadays, half the battle is finding some reason to lock up a suspected killer on another charge to get him off the street so witnesses will cooperate and so they will be safe. This onslaught has erupted in only a few years.

But that's not the worst of it: Worse yet is what has happened inside V. I.'s heart and his head. He goes to the home of dead kids these days, knocks on the door, and tells a mother and father that their child has been killed, and they say, "Yeah, okay." Without a hint of emotion, they close the door. The homicide detective's code of honor has always been that he identifies with the dead, swears to find the killer. These days, that's harder and harder. It's hard to get worked up over the injustice of a dead man who may have killed one or two or three people himself.

But that's not the worst of it: Worse yet is that V. I. has had witnesses he promised to protect get killed. *After he promised!* So, after twenty-four years of putting his honor and duty on the line at any time, night or day, V. I. Smith stopped promising. He began saying only that he would do what he could. He has been forced to make his own moral choices outside the expectations of the law: He has let murderers stay free rather than risk the lives of more witnesses.

But even that's not the worst of it: Worse yet is that in the last few years, V. I. Smith—tough, cool, brave—has ridden home late at night and broken down in tears of private bereavement. The fabric of the city where he grew up, the city he loves, has been shredded, destroyed. People on the outside haven't grasped this yet, haven't felt the deadening weight of this sadness, this heartsickness.

From Brookland Manor, V. I. takes away only the nickname. He is famous for crashing cases at the scene, not waiting until tomorrow to investigate. He theorizes from the dots and pushes every lead to the limit. He can't interview witnesses tonight, but maybe the detectives dispatched to the hospital have a lead he can push. Maybe a brother or the mother or father of the victim named names, knew somebody who was beefing with the victim, gave the cops a line. V. I. heads back out the door, through the parting crowd, to see what Mayberry and Joefox have learned.

"He's gonna live," Mayberry says.

"That right?" V. I. asks without emotion. He glances at the pool of blood: KK is one lucky dude. Then he heads for his cruiser. He will not spend one more millisecond connecting the dots of this picture. It is an attempted murder now, another cop's glory, another cop's worry. They are still on the bubble . . .

*   *   *

At 1929 Eleventh St., the landlady is home. She seems to stop breathing when they tell her Willis Fields is dead. With her hands covering her cheeks she leads the detectives up an oddly tinted turquoise stairway to his dowdy, sweltering room. One life, one room. A round white clock on the wall reads 10:55. On the dingy carpet lie one razor blade, a bottle cap, and a few toothpicks. Half a dozen shirts hang on a rack, along with a single pair of pants, dirty. A lamp without a cover, an unmade bed, a small bottle of Listerine, nearly empty, three unopened bars of soap, a loaf of Wonder Bread. On the wall are a calendar and a newspaper photo of a woman in black hat, underwear, and stockings. Atop the television are three pens, a pencil, a nail clipper, a wristwatch, six cigars, and two packs of matches. On the nightstand is a red address book. In it are the names of people listed as owing Fields money.

"Whatever happened didn't happen here," says V. I., which means the death of Fields is probably a murder. V. I. starts theorizing, figuring maybe Fields went on a drinking binge and demanded money from one of his debtors, who went off. Lighting someone on fire isn't an efficient way to kill; it's more a murder of passion. As the detectives are about to leave, call it a day's work at 11:35 P.M., the landlady's brother arrives.

On the last Saturday before Willis Fields ended up in the hospital, the brother says, he had come out of the apartment he shares with his sister, headed to catch a plane for vacation. He found Fields passed out drunk on the outside steps going up to his room. He mentions two men—Robert and Theodore, whom Fields often hung out with on the street. He talks for a long time and the detectives are about to leave when the brother, in an aside, says, "He was layin' right there in the doorway, and this old fag was tryin' to frisk him." Mayberry, Joefox, and V. I. look at each other in wonder at what people can forget to mention.

"You know his name?" Joefox asks.

"Naw, he be down the street."

"Did Fields go in the house then?" V. I. asks.

"Stump can answer that," the brother says, explaining that he left Willis Fields in the care of one of Fields's friends, who happened along that Saturday, a man nicknamed Stump. V. I. knows that none of the people mentioned or interviewed so far tonight is a suspect, and he figures Stump isn't either, but a trail's a trail. He says of Stump, "That's where we gotta start."

For days more, Mayberry, Joefox, and the Ghost are on the bubble. *Amazing!* Still no murders on three-to-eleven. Just the luck of the draw. But when a man and his squad are on the bubble, it's hard to do much police work, because when the call comes, everything else must be dropped. V. I. has nonetheless arranged for the squad to squeeze in a quick raid one night, sweep in with some uniformed cops in marked cruisers and hit the drug boys hanging on W Street, where his source is still peeking out the window and reporting back.

Two guys argued on that street a while back and one ended up killing the other. At least that's how V. I.'s informants have explained the murder, but he has "no eyes"—no witnesses willing to testify.

His plan is to sweep in, make everybody hug the ground, scare up some guns and drugs, drag the crew downtown, and start sweatin' 'em about the murder. When a guy's looking at five-to-ten on a federal firearms rap, his memory can improve dramatically. Very little planning goes into such a raid. Eat some pizza, watch the Redskins, or *Top Cops*, or *Road Warrior*—then hop in the cars and do it. Although V. I. figures maybe a quarter of the guys on that street will be strapped with guns or have a gun hidden nearby, no detective will wear a bullet-proof vest. All in a day's work. But night after night, the drug boys don't cooperate, and the street stays empty. Word comes back to V. I. through the drug boys' girlfriends that pals of the dead man are planning a retaliatory drive-by shooting and everybody is staying scarce.

While on the bubble, V. I. works his case in far Northeast. He conspicuously cruises the neighborhood, which is a signal to his informants that he wants them to call. V. I. will collect reconnaissance as well as spread rumors—gossip that will get more people talking so his real informants will have cover, gossip that may make the shooter fear his own friends and allies are turning against him. Some guys will flag down V. I. in the street and talk to him. These are young men who have their own troubles with the law and who can tell their friends they were discussing their cases, asking V. I. to put in a good word with a judge or a prosecutor. V. I. often does. But the way the game is played, he wants payback—the names of potential witnesses, the name of a shooter, the details of the byzantine events that often lead up to a killing.

"You owe me big time," V. I. tells one young man.

"That last thing didn't work. They done me."

V. I. is unmoved. "I can't save you twice. But I did it the first time. So stay in touch. I can make it worth your while. I gotta get some eyes."

It seems that nobody helps the cops anymore just because it's the right thing to do. "You ain't got nobody helpin' ya now," V. I. says. "Nobody gives a crap. You gotta make everybody do what you want 'em to do. And you gotta be real mean to get results." The drug-boy killings have spooked everybody. V. I. can't blame folks. But that has meant more and more of his encounters with potential witnesses are hostile.

More and more, he has to threaten people to get their cooperation. He has to get them subpoenaed before the grand jury and then warn them that they can be charged with perjury if they don't tell the truth. And these are innocent people. He has even hinted that a witness's name might leak out before a suspected shooter has been jailed, unless that witness agrees to testify after the guy is locked up. He must sometimes act threatening to even the most harmless of people, which is what happens on the Saturday afternoon V. I. swings by the home of the last man known to have seen Willis Fields alive. Stump, a sixty-four-year-old man whose real name is Earl Johnson, is off his porch and headed for his front door the instant V. I.'s cruiser pulls to the curb. V. I. halts the retreat.

"Need to talk to you. Detective Smith, Homicide."

"You wanta come inside?"

"No, sir, you gonna have ta come with me." V. I. opens the creaking front-yard gate and gestures toward his cruiser.

Stump is disoriented. "I gotta tell my wife."

"You can call her from downtown."

"I don't know nothin'."

"We gonna just talk about it."

"I don't know nothin'."

Stump looks up at his wife, who is peering down from a second-story window. V. I. could have interviewed Stump at home, but he believes people are a lot like animals: They're more comfortable in their own territory. He wants them uncomfortable, so they drive off toward the station. Suddenly, the word *stabbing* squawks from the cruiser radio.

"You got a condition?" V. I. asks the dispatcher.

"I didn't do nothin'," Stump says from the backseat.

"Hey, Stump, we know you all right, man." V. I. says this in a more friendly tone, trying to calm the man down. Then he heads for the scene of the stabbing, doing eighty-five miles an hour on the Southwest Freeway. He arrives at M and Half Streets SW. The victim has been taken to the hospital, and only a dab of blood stains the sidewalk. He will live.

Still on the bubble . . .

Seated back at Homicide North, staring into the middle distance and wringing thick and worn hands, Stump is not a happy camper. He's a short man with a good belly, a mustache, and short graying hair. He wears his blue-and-white cap backward. He wears blue work pants and a white short-sleeve shirt. A ring of keys hangs off his belt.

"Never did a crime in my life," Stump says to the air.

"You know Fields?" V. I. asks.

"Right. But what happened to him, I don't know."

As these things often go, however, Stump knows more than he knows he knows. He says that before the detectives came around asking questions, a man nicknamed Bo had told him that Fields had been set on fire. V. I. knows from the hospital report that an unidentified person drove Fields to the hospital. He figures Fields must have told that person what happened. And he figures that person might have told others.

"You can't set me up for no murder," Stump says.

"I'm not tryin' ta charge you with murder," V. I. says, knowing that indeed Stump is not a suspect. "Did you ask Bo how he knew Fields got burned?"

"He said it was over on Eighteenth Street."

"Did he tell ya who Fields was with?"

"He never did tell me that."

"How'd he know about it?"

"I don't know."

"You know who lives up on Eighteenth?"

"I don't."

V. I. then takes Stump out cruising the neighborhood for Bo, but they don't find him. "I wanta go home," Stump says.

"That's where we're on the way to."

Says V. I., "Bo is the next guy to talk with."

Back at the office, V. I. finds Joefox and Mayberry yukking it up. As V. I. has been working the fringes of other cases while riding the bubble, they too have been working other cases. Joefox is telling about his informant who called and said his mother was sick in another city and that he needed three hundred dollars for airfare to visit her. He said he hated to be a snitch, but that his mother was very sick. Then he gave Joefox the address of a shooter Joefox was after. Even before patrolmen could make the arrest, Joefox's informant walked into the office looking for his finder's fee.

"They're still out tryin' ta get 'im," Joefox said.

With that, the informant picked up Joefox's phone, rang a number, and asked for the shooter by name. They chatted. "See, I told ya he's still there," the man said after hanging up.

"Man, they got caller ID?" asked an incredulous Joefox.

"Ah, I don't think so."

Anyway, the cops got a shooter, the informant got his cash, and, presumably, a sick mother got a visit from a devoted son.

It's unimaginable that Mayberry, Joefox, and the Ghost won't draw a murder tonight, Saturday night. But in the meantime, before the intrigues of darkness set in, V. I. heads out to Northeast Washington to meet Detective J. O. Johnson. They're off to look for Tony Boyce and Eldee Edwards, who are wanted for obstruction of justice for allegedly threatening a witness scheduled to testify in a grand jury investigation into a murder in which Edwards is a suspect.

The detectives cruise East Capitol near Seventeenth Street, where Tony lives. They hope to find him on the street. It's safer to make an arrest outside. Besides, if they raid the men's homes and come up empty, the men will learn the cops are on their tails and maybe take an extended vacation. V. I. interviewed Tony a couple days ago, hoping to get him to give up his buddy Eldee, but Tony hung tough. He told them to bug off, that if they were gonna arrest him, then arrest him. And call his lawyer. He wasn't tellin' 'em anything. V. I. let Tony go. But he doesn't like it when cops are treated rudely, and he's back today with a warrant. Because it's late afternoon on Saturday, there will be no judges available to process Tony's case until Monday, which means he'll cool in jail for at least the weekend. When they finally spot Tony walking up East Capitol, V. I. pulls a U-turn and hops out.

"How ya doin'?" V. I. asks in a friendly voice.

"I'm fine," says Tony, momentarily confused. He's a short, thin thirty-one-year-old man wearing a white Champion T-shirt, blue-jeans shorts, and lavender Saucony running shoes. He has a dark blue wrap on his hair. His nails are long, his body lithe and taut.

"I got a warrant for ya."

"For my arrest?"

"Yep."

V. I. is downright cheerful. He gently turns Tony toward the trunk of a car, has him lay down the leather-bound Bible he's carrying, and clamps the cuffs on him behind his back. A man walks up and gruffly asks what's happening.

"They arrestin' me!" Tony says, emotional now, with an edge of fear in his high-pitched voice. "I don't know why."

V. I.'s entire manner changes. "Sir!" he says to the man in a deep and suddenly ominous voice, stepping toward him with the full authority of his 230 pounds. "You wanta walk wherever you walkin', because you gonna be the next one that's locked up." The man opens his mouth to speak, but before the words emerge, V. I. says, *"Walk wherever you walkin'!* I don't wanta hear 'bout it." The man does not move, and V. I. goes stone calm. "Turn and go," he says in almost a whisper. "Turn and go." And the man does. Just then, a woman arrives and says she is Tony's mother. Because she is polite, because a mother has the right to worry about her son, V. I. is polite in return.

"I'll call you," he says.

After Tony is taken away in a paddy wagon, J. O. and V. I. head for the last known address for Eldee Edwards. Now that Tony has been taken, there's no hope of surprising his friend. J. O. goes to cover the back door, and V. I. climbs the steep steps to the row house's front porch. To his right is a gray cat sunning itself on a stone railing. To his left, beneath a striped awning, sits an old man in a green metal chair. V. I. asks if he has seen Eldee, and the old man nods.

"Where's he at? In the house?"

"No."

"When's the last time you saw 'im?"

"Two days ago, three days ago."

"Who's home now?"

"My daughter."

"How old's she?"

"Forty."

Walking into a strange house is a dangerous play, and V. I. has asked the old man these questions as reconnaissance. He believes the old man is telling the truth, although he has learned not to rely too heavily on his intuition in such matters because any cop who thinks he can't be successfully lied to is a fool.

V. I. has been tricked more times than he cares to remember. "Lookin' at a jail sentence," he says, "makes people great liars." He knocks hard on the door eight times. No answer. He waits, opens the door, knocks hard nine times, and hollers, "Hello!" No answer. He walks in the door. A narrow hallway leads back to a kitchen, rooms are off to the left, a stairway rises on the right. On the floor are two unopened gallons of fresh paint.

The place brings a flash of déjà vu, because it was in just this kind of house that, as a young uniformed cop, V. I. had decided to play hero when he got a report of a burglary in progress. When nobody answered the door in the darkened house, he didn't announce that he was a policeman for fear of warning the burglar, and he walked in. When he flicked on the light, he looked up the stairway to see an old woman huddled terrified on her knees and an old man standing resolutely with a shotgun aimed down the stairwell's tunnel at the intruder—Patrolman V. I. Smith.

"Hello!" he hollers again, and his voice rings like a trumpet in the cavernous hallway. No answer. He waits four seconds and hollers "Hello" again. He waits six seconds and yells, "Anybody home?" He waits five more seconds and yells "Hello," louder this time. His back pressed against the wall, his gun still in the holster, he starts slowly up the stairs. As he goes, he glances calmly back and forth between the first and second floors. Finally, a woman appears on the upstairs landing, and V. I. introduces himself as a policeman.

"I'm looking for Eldee."

"Eldee has not lived here in four or five years," she says, seeming miffed at the question.

"How frequently you see him?"

"Maybe three times a week."

"You got a phone number?"

"No. He lives in Southeast. That's all I can tell ya."

J. O. Johnson has joined them in the foyer now, and he isn't happy with what he's hearing. "I talked to you the other day myself, and I had a little confidence in what you was tellin' me, but now you make me think that you're not bein' truthful."

The woman starts to interrupt, "You know . . ."

J. O. cuts her off, "We're tryin' to be nice about it."

The woman snickers.

"We haven't been here at four o'clock in the mornin' and wake everybody up in the house and turn the house upside down lookin' for Eldee. I'm sure you don't want us to do that."

"I don't think that you supposed to be doin' that."

"You don't know what we *supposed* to be doin'. I'm askin' you to get in touch with him and have him call me. Tonight."

"Okay," she says, clearly angry.

In the car, V. I. says, "He's probably in and outta there."

"I can tell ya one thing," J. O. says, "when I break back in here 'bout four o'clock in the morning . . ."

Says V. I., "She doesn't *believe*."

When Eldee doesn't call later that night, J. O. will take his warrant and a crew of cops and hit the last known address of Eldee Edwards in the early morning hours. He will get everybody out of bed, secure them downstairs, and search for Eldee. He will not find him. But afterward, V. I. will figure the folks in that house will be more likely to lean heavily on Eldee to turn himself in. They will have been made believers.

But right now, back at Homicide North, V. I. looks straight into the eyes of Tony Boyce, who is sitting with his right elbow on his knee, his chin on his fist, and his left hand cuffed to his chair. V. I. says nothing. He gets a cup of coffee, checks the score of the Eagles-Jets game on the tube. Then he reads Tony his rights and tells him he'll be arraigned Monday morning.

"Monday morning?" Tony asks, shocked. "Does my lawyer know?"

V. I. asks Tony if he has his lawyer's phone number.

"Not here."

V. I. shrugs.

"Why didn't you arrest me yesterday?" Tony asks, finally realizing that he'll spend at least the weekend in jail.

V. I. shrugs again.

After the paperwork is done and Mayberry takes Tony, who has abandoned his cool and loosed a blast of obscenity, down to a cell, Joefox says, "He'll have a lotta company down there."

"Saturday in the big house!" says V. I. And then, out of character, he throws back his head and roars with laughter.

Incredibly, eleven o'clock comes and goes.

They are still on the bubble . . .

Over the years, V. I. has had some spectacular cases. Soon after he came to Homicide in 1986, when he was barely off the natural death detail, he solved a series of killings in which a man in a dark van was abducting women and murdering them. The seven-year-old brother of one dead woman had mentioned to V. I. that his sister kept her boyfriends' phone numbers on the backs of matchbooks and that they were spread all over the house. V. I. had the boy collect them in a bag, and the next day he began calling numbers, posing as a doctor tracking a case of venereal disease. After seventeen calls, V. I. found a man who had seen the woman the night she died. Before the day was over, V. I. had interviewed him, discovered the name of another man the dead woman had been with that night, located his dark van, and gone with his squad to arrest him.

Just last winter, V. I. and Joefox were assigned by Chief Isaac Fulwood Jr. himself to handle a high-publicity multiple murder on P Street NW, in which a man, woman, and child were found slain in a car. They were a brother and sister and her two-year-old son. When the body of the child, who had been suffocated, was taken from the backseat, it looked to V. I. as if the boy were only asleep.

He felt the righteousness rise in him, felt his revulsion for the random injustice, felt as if this could happen to his own family, his own friends. There was no "victim participation." And when V. I. and Joefox went to the home of the dead to inform their parents, who were also the boy's grandparents, the family cried, sobbed as humans should, *must*, if they are to be human. V. I., Joefox, and Mayberry, the entire squad, worked day and night for four days. As their reward, as affirmation of their own humanity, they locked up the alleged son-of-a-bitch killer, who's now awaiting trial and facing the possibility of life in prison.

That's what has changed. So many murders seem to count for nothing today. They don't embody the eternals of love and devotion and loss, recall the immeasurable value of one life, no matter how seemingly insignificant, announce through quick justice that living is safe and predictable and violence an aberration, thereby cauterizing the psychic wounds of the living. No, these murders trumpet the evil, insidious reverse: Life is cheap, easily forgotten; humanity is a fraud. At the front lines of this diminution, V. I. Smith feels his own humanity under assault, feels the fire of indignation in his belly going cold. His deep fear is that, at the front lines, he is taking only the early hit for an entire society. Because what's happening to V. I. Smith is happening to everyone who reads the paper or watches the TV news. His numbed heart is but an early warning.

"If you see the motives for why people are killing people out there now, you say to yourself, 'How can you do anything about somebody who's thinkin' like this?' It's valueless. You go into a crack house two or three months after it's got rollin' and find a family with young girls fifteen, sixteen years old who have lost everything. They've lost their dignity. They've lost their will. They've lost themselves.

"And what have you accomplished being a policeman? You're on TV: 'We got one of the biggest cocaine raids we've had and locked up two New Yorkers.' But you've left the victimized family devastated and haven't given them any alternative. But I don't have time to worry about people anymore. And it's a goddamned shame.

"I've gotten to the point where I'm not really comfortable doing what I do anymore. I've gotten to the point where I sense fear. And I've never done that before. You can't predict who's out there anymore. Everything has gone to extremes."

On the next three-to-eleven shift, with Joefox home sick, the bubble finally bursts at 5:30 P.M., probably too early for a drug-boy killing. On the way to the scene in an apartment on Twenty-ninth Street SE, just off Pennsylvania

Avenue, V. I. starts theorizing. *Female victim, inside her apartment, shot once in the head.* When a person is killed inside her home, the case is usually easier, because it's a snap to discover the last person to see the victim alive. It's also daylight, which makes any investigation easier still, and, most promising, this killing is in a normally quiet neighborhood, which hints at an old-fashioned, mom-and-pop murder, a murder of passion. When Mayberry and V. I. walk into the door of Apartment 101, they find half a dozen cops, like gawkers at a car crash, milling around. Mayberry orders everybody out.

The dead woman is lying in the middle of the room, halfway between the front door and the rear patio doors, one of which has been knocked off its track. It is an ugly scene, with brain and skull splattered on the wall and floor. The room is dark, but they don't touch the light switches for fear of smudging any prints. They wander the apartment with flashlights and find a framed photo of a woman. Mayberry flashes a light on the dead woman's face to be certain it is her.

In a matter of minutes, the dots are made whole: The woman, Crystal Johnson-Kinzer, and a male friend had walked in the door and been attacked. The male friend had escaped as shots were fired. The woman did not. Outside the patio balcony, detectives scouring the yard and garbage cans for clues find a footprint with a distinctive circle in the tread imprinted on the hood of a gray Toyota parked beneath the balcony.

When the victim's family arrives, there is—as there should be—great anguish. For months, they say, Crystal had been harassed by her husband, from whom she was separated. She'd quit a job, moved across town to this apartment, gotten a court order for him to stay away. Crystal's brother is screaming at the police: "She called y'all! And now look! Y'all come when it's too late!" He is weeping and hitting his forehead with his fist. Crystal's father, wearing the gray uniform of a working man, stands perfectly still, stunned silent. Her mother, with a rose bandanna wrapped on her head, shuffles about without expression, wiping her face again and again with a tissue. The fiancée of Crystal's brother—a woman who is a look-alike for Crystal, a woman who was often mistaken for her twin—is holding a diapered baby and sobbing.

Amid this horror, V. I. is invigorated, renewed. *This poor woman!* She could have been *his* sister, *his* daughter! A sweet twenty-two-year-old girl with a good job as a telephone operator. She loved smooth jazz, John Coltrane. She was studying cosmetology at night. She came from a nice, protective family. She'd stopped at her apartment to change clothes and head out for a picnic at her brother's. She did not deserve this. This murder is "real"—with a good guy and a bad guy. Crystal's death must be avenged. Says V. I., "You don't get many like this anymore."

Back at Homicide North, the details are gathered and collated, family and friends are interviewed, the husband's undistinguished police record is pulled. At 12:17 A.M., V. I. has finished writing the arrest warrant for Kodie Cotrell Kinzer, age twenty-one, last known address in Silver Spring. It's the home of Kinzer's grandmother, and V. I. figures it's probably where he ran to, because that's just what shooters usually do.

"They wanta go home," V. I. says.

"We gotta start the hunt!" says Mayberry, excited.

When they arrive at the Georgetown home of the judge who will sign the arrest warrant, V. I. notices for the first time that it is a lovely, perfectly clear and starry night, cool, with a light breeze. The Georgetown street is quiet, except for the soothing mantra of crickets and the conversation of what look to be two drunken college boys stumbling home. As V. I. walks through the manicured garden courtyard to the judge's town house, he sees yard after yard marked with signs that read "Electronic Security by Night Owl." It's the kind of neighborhood V. I. hasn't seen much of in his job. As the judge puts down his book and reads the warrant, V. I. studies the high, elegant ceilings in the judge's home. "You wouldn't be needin' our services too often in this neighborhood," he says, and the judge laughs.

The Montgomery County police are waiting for the three-car caravan of detectives that arrives about two in the morning. Taking down a suspected murderer is still an exotic event in suburban Montgomery, and the sergeant on duty is talking about whether he should call in the SWAT team and waiting for a captain to arrive to take responsibility for the decisions.

"They don't get to do this much," Mayberry whispers.

"It's comin'," V. I. answers ominously. "Believe me, it's comin'."

Despite the delay, the detectives will not complain. V. I. doesn't want neighboring police telling stories about how Washington's cowboy cops came out and broke protocol or acted arrogant. So they wait . . . and wait . . . and wait. Finally, it is decided that several more cars of Montgomery cops, all of whom don bullet-proof vests, will surround the apartment, and V. I. will call in on a telephone and announce the raid. This gentlemanly approach runs against every grain in Mayberry and V. I., who back home would take a couple of uniformed cops and knock on the damned door. On the phone, V. I. talks to a young man who says Kodie Kinzer isn't home and that Kinzer's grandmother is too frail to be awakened with the shock of a police raid. V. I. asks the youth to come outside, which he does. He's a nice kid, clean-cut, polite.

"Did you see Kodie last night?" V. I. asks gently.

"I came in like *late*, 'bout one or two."

"Was he in bed?"

"Yes, sir."

"Where does he usually sleep?"

"Huh?"

"Where does he usually sleep?"

"He sleeps on the couch."

"He doesn't have a room?"

"No, he's like a pass-through."

"You know of any girlfriends he might be stayin' with?"

"I couldn't tell ya."

"How old is Kodie's grandmother?"

"She's 'bout seventy."

"Is she in pretty good health?"

"Ah, not really, that's why I say I didn't wanta scare her."

"Do you expect him to come back tonight?"

"Uhm, I don't think so."

"Why not?"

"Huh?"

"Why not?"

"Ah, 'cause, ah, he was, uhm, talkin' about he was gonna go over his friend's house or somethin'."

"You ever meet his wife?"

"Nah, I never met her. I heard of her name before."

V. I. looks at Mayberry. "Think we oughta wake Grandma up?" Mayberry shrugs, but he is thinking of a line from the movie "Dirty Harry": "I gots ta know." And he knows V. I. is thinking the same thing. The kid seems honest, but V. I. has learned not to always trust his intuition. They didn't come all the way out here with seven, eight police cars to be talked away at the door. V. I. is being gentle, getting the kid used to the idea.

"Captain, whataya think?" V. I. asks, bringing the Montgomery brass into a decision that he has already made. The captain nods, and V. I. turns back to the youth. "Think it would be a problem if we talk to Kodie's grandmother?"

The young man looks suddenly shaky. "See, all those people . . ."

V. I. cuts him off. "There ain't gonna be all those people."

"I don't, I don't know . . ."

V. I. cuts him off again, this time in a voice that has once again gone stone calm: "Look, man, this is somethin' we gotta do. Prolongin' the situation isn't gonna do any good. Let's go."

Inside, buried beneath a pile of blankets, they find Kodie Kinzer. Minutes later, he's led away, his head tilted downward mournfully. He's wearing yellow shorts, a white T-shirt, white socks, and no shoes. When V. I. leaves the apartment, he's carrying a pair of black Adidas with three white stripes adorning the uppers and a distinctive circle on the sole. It will be up to Forensics to evaluate whether they could have left that footprint on the car beneath Crystal Johnson-Kinzer's balcony. But V. I. says, "I remember that tread."

It is nearly dawn by the time V. I. and Mayberry finish interviewing Kodie Kinzer, who denies that he killed Crystal. When the detectives head back to Homicide North, leaving Kinzer in a Montgomery cell awaiting extradition to Washington, the city is just waking up. The sky is brightening in the east, and people are standing at bus stops in twos and threes. A laundry truck is picking up, a Coke truck is dropping off, and the lights of sleeping cars are awakening along the roads. Outside police headquarters, a rat scurries along the sidewalk, stops, gazes about at the emerging daylight, and dives into the bushes for cover.

Life as it should be.

In the next few weeks, V. I. will keep tugging at threads in his murder case in far Northeast—the one that began when a suspected drug dealer shot the wrong woman. Before that chain of misery and foolishness concludes, five people will end up shot. He'll keep working the murder of Willis Fields, never finding Bo, the man who told Stump that Fields was attacked on Eighteenth Street. But no matter. Bo was simply repeating street rumor passed on by lots of other people. V. I. will discover that somebody who lives on Eighteenth Street owed Fields money. But it will be a long time, if ever, before that murder is avenged. In the meantime, Tony Boyce will stay in jail for weeks and be indicted for obstruction of justice. Eldee Edwards will be arrested and indicted for murder. In a few days, Kodie Kinzer will arrive at the D.C. jail, where he will await trial after his indictment for murder. Soon, Mayberry, Joefox, and the Ghost will collect half a dozen new homicides, all of which will look like drug-boy killings.

But that's all in the future. This morning, just back from the hunt, V. I. and Mayberry still have their damned paperwork to do. And in Room 5058, the coffee is cold. But that's okay. It has been a good night—an old-fashioned night, a night that affirmed the world's predictability, justice, and humanity, that healed the psychic wounds of the living, that again brought feeling to the numbed heart of Detective Victor "V. I." Smith. This horrific night has made him feel better. It has made him feel human again.

November 15, 1992

Equally Married with Children

She is upstairs in the kitchen arranging sliced summer sausage and cheese and crackers on a wicker tray. He is downstairs pulling videocassettes off the bookshelves, glancing at their handwritten legends, and sliding them back into their slots. "Honey, do you know where it is?" he asks, not loud enough for her to hear. He finally finds the cassette, inserts it in the VCR, and sits heavily at the far corner of the couch. She arrives and stands hesitantly for an instant, glancing about for a place to put the tray. Without a word spoken between them, he gets up, fetches a lamp stand, and positions it in front of the couch. He sits heavily again. She deposits the tray and sits too, but gently, like a feather floating down. She curls her left leg beneath her bottom and slides over until her back is barely touching him. Then she laughs in that way he loves and says, "This is so *corny!*"

Yet they watch this video at least once a year, for sentiment and for strength. It is the recorded memory of how Larry Jones and Donna Byers met, fell in love, and married. At the time they made the tape, their marriage was only days away. He was thirty-eight and she was thirty-one, but the camera instead captured schoolkids—giddy and goofy, laughing at each other's jokes, touching softly. In the year they'd been dating, they had never even talked about getting married. But on Christmas Eve 1987, Larry walked around all day with the ring box bulging in his right front pants pocket. Donna had been out alone for last-minute Christmas shopping and, exhausted at day's end, was surprised to find herself in a bridal shop looking at gowns. Without a word spoken between them. That evening, standing at the fridge in her apartment, as they tried to pick a restaurant, Donna said playfully, "I love you."

"How much do you love me?" Larry asked.

"Larger than a house, more than what you can contain in a box, rounder than a ball. How much do you love me?"

43

"I love you so much," Larry said, secretly relieved that he'd found a grace-ful segue into his proposal of marriage, "that I want to live with you for the rest of my life."

Larry then took the ring box from his right front pants pocket, held it out, and said, "This is just an emblem of that love and proof that it is never-end-ing." Donna started to laugh, and she kept laughing—for two, three, maybe even five minutes. Larry began to wonder if she was laughing for joy or laugh-ing at him. But she finally opened the box, put on the ring, and kissed him. It's all on the video. The whole beautiful story.

On the couch, with the summer sausage and the cheese and the crackers nearly gone from the wicker tray, the tape rewinding, Larry says, "When we were together, everything clicked."

Donna looks into his eyes, smiles what Larry calls her Mona Lisa smile, and says, "It was just comfortable."

And so they were married.

Six years later . . . With four-year-old twins, Rachel and Elijah, a new Nissan Quest, a brick house on a wooded corner lot in Silver Spring, Maryland, and more change and effort, more disagreement and tension, more tears and frus-trations than they could ever have imagined, Donna and Larry Jones have built a rare marriage—the kind so many men and women today claim to seek, but so few accomplish.

Donna and Larry are equals.

They both work, as do more than two-thirds of American couples today. But Donna and Larry also share decisions, from picking a new couch to pick-ing a new day-care center. Each has veto power over the other, no arguments. She cooks most of the dinners and usually washes the dishes, while he gives the kids baths and gets them into their pajamas. He makes the beds in the morning, gets the twins dressed. She braids Rachel's hair, makes the kids breakfast, and packs their lunches. On Saturdays, he does the vacuuming and cleans the bathroom. She cleans the kitchen and usually strips the beds. They each load and unload laundry as they clean. At night, watching TV, they fold clothes together.

During the week, he keeps the house tidy. She sorts the mail. She does the kids' art projects. He works with them on their handwriting. They both read stories to the kids. He cuts the grass and rakes the leaves. She buys the gro-ceries. They both pay the bills. When the twins were infants, they both did night feedings and diaper changes. Now they trade off days at home with sick kids. They both lug them to the doctor and dentist. He hires the workmen. She buys the kids' clothes. At night, they both put Rachel and Elijah to bed. They both listen to their prayers.

Donna and Larry make it look so natural. But for most couples, it is not. Why egalitarian marriage is so hard to achieve—and why most working wives still do the lion's share of household and child-rearing chores—is the subject of endless and contentious academic and popular debate. But the focus of sociologists and coffee klatch experts alike is often on the majority of marriages that aren't egalitarian, rather than the estimated 15 to 20 percent of marriages that University of Washington sociologist Pepper Schwartz calls "peer marriages." Husbands and wives who share duties and authority about equally, says Schwartz, author of *Peer Marriages: How Love between Equals Really Works,* also share certain traits: They have jobs that allow flexibility in their schedules, they both work outside the home, and the men almost always enjoy children. But they often share another, less quantifiable trait: These men and women seek to be friends—true, deep, soul-touching friends, *best friends.* And they organize their lives to achieve that intimacy—she changes jobs and he passes up promotions; she learns to coach soccer and he learns to read laundry labels.

Donna and Larry Jones are best friends. They came to that kind of equality for their own idiosyncratic reasons, from family background to temperament to religious faith. It hasn't been easy. Because men and women are, well, *different,* aren't they?

But Donna and Larry are better friends today than they were on the Christmas Eve that Larry proposed, and they hope to become better friends still. The evolution of their marriage and their day-to-day life together as equals is a mirror into which others can look and see their own marriages— the choices they have made, the rewards they have squandered or reaped, the equality they have given or denied, the deals they have demanded or the deals for which they have settled.

"A husband and wife are supposed to be the closest people on earth," says Larry, as he sits on Rachel's bed after having just changed the kids' bedding for the week. "We live with each other. We are the essence of each other . . . Why should I say to my wife, 'I'm a man, I shouldn't wash clothes. I'm a man, I shouldn't cook.' Especially if we're both working. She's as tired as I am." He pauses and says somberly, "I would feel less of a man." Donna, sitting next to him, touches his knee.

"And I wouldn't put up with it," she says, laughing.

Larry smiles, raises an eyebrow. "That's for sure."

"I want *Daddy* to take me home," says Elijah, whose tone manages to find that exact irritating balance between whining and demanding. It is 5:45 P.M. and he and Rachel and their mother are in the kitchen, just having arrived home from day care and work. Donna still wears her coat, but she is already opening cabinet doors, figuring out dinner. Rachel has gone straight to the refrigerator and gotten a Kool-Aid Burst and sat down at the little white table next to the big kitchen table. Elijah goes to the fish tank, seems to study the goldfish, and then starts to cry.

"What kind of snack would you like?" Donna asks.

"Peanut butter cookies," he says.

"Is there something else you'd like?"

"*Noooooo!*" Elijah whines and stomps his foot.

"Come on, come on," Donna says gently. "Settle down." She takes Elijah in her arms, hugs him, rubs his back, and as she does, he seems to wail in reverse—starts loudly but softens his cries steadily until he reaches silence in her arms. "Let's take off our jackets," Donna says. "You're a little tired tonight."

So is Donna. She's a computer graphics artist who heads a small section at Howard University's printing department. She used to be a graphics supervisor in the Washington office of the giant accounting firm of Arthur Andersen. It was nothing to work until eleven at night. But after the kids came, the job was too much. Donna earns less at Howard than she would if she'd stayed at Arthur Andersen, but she'd have been frazzled and she and her family would have suffered. This week, Donna must install the programming for three new Macintosh computers, but she hasn't yet found the time and will have to work late tomorrow night to get it done.

It was Donna's thirty-eighth birthday last Sunday, and because her mother, who usually throws Donna's annual birthday party, wasn't feeling well, Donna threw the party herself, making dinner for twelve friends and relatives. Larry, who is a federal lobbyist for the National Association of Counties, had to travel last Saturday. He got home in time to help out a little, but all the extra duty meant Donna didn't get to the supermarket or make meals to freeze for weekday dinners, as she usually does.

"What to fix for dinner?" she says absently, while peering into the fridge. She selects a smorgasbord of leftovers—greens, hot dogs, turkey and dressing, cranberry sauce, and macaroni and cheese. Larry gets home half an hour after Donna, although it seems as if hours have passed, with Elijah teetering on the edge of meltdown the whole time. Thank goodness Rachel is cheerful. Larry has brought home a red pomegranate he picked up in a restaurant at lunch. He holds it up for the kids to see.

"A pomagraner, Daddy?" Elijah asks.

"A pome*granate*," Larry says.

"I don't care!" Rachel suddenly hollers from the white table where she has been sitting quietly. "I want pancakes!" Larry and Donna look at each other—and burst out in laughter.

Oh, well, just one of those nights.

Donna and Larry are a team. Together, they earn about $100,000 a year. They tithe 10 percent of that to Mount Sinai Baptist Church in Washington and put a healthy chunk into their tax-free savings plans. After mortgage, day care, electric, phone, food, clothes, and minivan payments, not much is left for wasting. Larry figures he could double his income overnight by getting a corporate lobbying job, which would mean Donna could quit her job and stay home with the kids. They've talked about it but have rejected the idea.

Donna enjoys working, not all the time, but most of the time. After college, she worked for ten years before they were married. It's part of who she is. On the other hand, Larry will not pay the traditional father's levy of a megabuck, twelve-hour-a-day, six-day-a-week job that would buy him a full-time wife and the appearance of an old-fashioned family.

"I wouldn't see the kids," he says.

"I refuse to do that."

"I don't want to do that."

Larry, who is now forty-four, was the ninth child in a family of eleven kids. He was raised in Memphis, where his father was a janitor and yardman who worked day and night, seven days a week, just to keep food on the table. Larry doesn't remember ever being angry at his father for not spending more time with him. He admired his dad, who lived to work so his children could live decently. But there were so many events, plays, and ball games where Larry saw the other fathers with their sons, saw the fathers beam proudly and saw that pride reflected in the faces of his friends. He saw this and he missed it for himself. But, with uncommon wisdom for a child, he also saw that his father, who died two years before Larry and Donna married, was missing something too. "I think my father would have enjoyed that."

Raised only a step above poverty, Larry was an ambitious young man. He put himself through college and graduate school and came to Washington. Smart, charming, outgoing, and hardworking, he built a thriving career and became a single man about town. Always, he thought the woman he'd marry would be not only a wife and lover but also a friend. "I wanted someone I could share my deepest feelings with," he says. Deeply religious, he remembered that the fifth chapter of Ephesians in the Bible said a man should love his wife "even as Christ also loved the church." And that was a boundless love, never malicious, never selfish.

When Larry returns to the kitchen after changing out of his suit, Donna is popping dinner in the microwave. Larry empties the kids' Barney lunch boxes, which hold the remains of carrots and sandwiches, and wipes them out. He takes Rachel, who is now whimpering about an imaginary hurt on her finger, downstairs. He sits in a soft chair, lifts her onto his lap, and reads *Little Mover's Dumper*. A single tear rolls down Rachel's cheek.

"What does she have in her hand?" he asks, pointing to a character and speaking in a father's version of a child's voice. He strokes her back, brushes her hair with his hand.

"A ball." She lays her head on his chest. She is cold, so Larry covers her with a small white blanket.

"A ball, yes," he says. "Who is she playing with?"

"Kids." Rachel is calm now, that fast.

"How many kids?"

"One, two, three."

"*Very good*, Rachel!"

After dinner, which is served on red Styrofoam plates to save time on dish washing, Donna clears the table while Larry draws adjacent rectangles on paper, one for each letter in each child's name. The kids get pencils and begin printing in the boxes, chattering at a gleefully high pitch and intensity.

"Wiggle-wiggle, wiggle-wiggle," Elijah yells.

"Wiggle-wiggle, wiggle-wiggle," Rachel echoes.

Larry has gone upstairs to run water in the tub. Donna is sorting the mail into triage stacks—now, later, trash. She likes to do the dishes while Larry bathes the kids, because it gives her a few minutes to herself, something Donna has always needed. She was the oldest daughter in a Washington family of four girls and a boy. Her mother was a homemaker until she went back to work when the youngest child was about fifteen. Her father was a building facilities supervisor for the Department of Health and Human Services. He was a gentle man who never raised his voice to her mother and who gave his daughters this advice: Don't ever let a man mistreat you. If he does, he doesn't love you. He said, "Don't let a man ruin you."

Donna was a beautiful and shy young woman who thought she was in love a couple of times over the years, but changed her mind. She was married to her career. Then, at about age thirty, she began to yearn for something deeper. Simply put, she was lonely, so lonely she sometimes cried herself to sleep. She prayed: Dear God, let me meet a man who will know my thoughts, who will know how to make me happy without being told, who will always trust me, who will love me just as I am, who will never judge me. Dear God, let him be my friend.

Soon after, she noticed Larry. He was a deacon at Mount Sinai, where she'd attended church for several years, and when the congregation went to the altar to deliver their offerings one Sunday, she shook his hand and felt, oh, it's hard to describe—a little jolt of electricity maybe, a tingle of warmth. She noticed his hand's strength and softness, his smile. She noticed his voice, calm and gentle. And she noticed his head, as regal as a king's. For weeks after that, Donna and Larry played peekaboo. She'd be staring at him across the sanctuary and he'd suddenly turn and look right at her. Embarrassed, she'd turn away. One Sunday morning, Donna said this prayer: "God, if this is a person you have in mind for me, let him speak to me." Across the sanctuary that day, Larry was thinking, "Hey, the only way I'm gonna meet this young lady is to go up and introduce myself." He did. "Excuse me, I'm Larry Jones." Donna was stunned speechless. In her head she heard a voice—God's voice, she believes—"Speak, I have sent him to you." She did. "Nice to meet you."

After Donna finishes the dishes, she goes upstairs, where Larry is just patting Rachel dry and Elijah is already in his pajamas, playing with Legos and trying to figure out why the udders of his plastic cow will not give milk. This is showtime for Donna, who does not so much tuck the kids into bed as she does tickle them into bed. It is a raucous ritual that takes at least five minutes, messes up the sheets and blankets, gets the kids all wound up. Larry is a bit bemused by it all, sits quietly and marvels at how much Donna, Rachel, and Elijah enjoy these shenanigans. Finally, Donna sits on Elijah's bed, and Larry, Elijah, and Rachel sit on Rachel's bed, and he reads them a book, *The Great Amusement Park*. He begins, "The merry-go-round is my favorite ride . . ."

"Daddy," Elijah interrupts, "can we go to that park?"

"We can go to an amusement park," Larry says, and tries again to read the book. "Rides, rides, fun galore . . ."

"Daddy, can we ride on *this* ride?" Elijah asks, touching a picture of a roller coaster.

"When you get a little bigger."

"Does this one go upside down, Daddy?"

"Yes, that one goes upside down. Now . . ."

"Do you fall off the seat?"

"No, 'cause you're locked into the seat. So . . ."

"When it's off, Daddy, do you fall out?"

Larry, becoming impatient with Elijah's questions, says firmly, "If you're not wearing the safety belt."

"Daddy," Elijah says softly, "can you get in with me?"

At that instant, Larry's impatience lifts, as he suddenly realizes what his son is asking of him, realizes this is a moment for which a father should live, the kind of moment his own father may never have known with his children.

"Yes," Larry says, in a voice that commands that nothing bad will ever happen to his children. "We'll get in together."

"Okay," says Elijah, who then lays his head on his father's arm and lets him finish his story.

"I want *Mommy!*" Rachel cries.

"Well, you have to go with Daddy today," says Larry cheerfully, as he packs up the kids' Muppet backpacks and a hand puppet created out of a white sock and glued pieces of bright felt that Elijah made at day care this afternoon. "You're stuck." By the time the kids are loaded into the van, unloaded, and bundled into the house, the eyes, ears, nose, tongue, and hair of Elijah's puppet have fallen off and sit in a stack on the kitchen counter.

"Mommy will help you put everything back together."

Elijah starts to cry.

"You want a timeout?"

Elijah stops crying, turns to Rachel, who is already sucking on a Kool-Aid Burst, crosses his eyes, and yells, "I can't see!"

Rachel is unimpressed. "Why?"

"Because my eyes aren't straight."

Elijah laughs. Rachel frowns.

"Wash your hands," Larry says.

Donna isn't home. She's putting the software into those new Macintosh

computers and then running by the grocery store she didn't get to last weekend. So Larry, who spent the day explaining to a Japanese government official
how America's federal, state, and local governments intertwine, left work
early to get the kids. For dinner, he swung by KFC and picked up a roasted
chicken, potato wedges, coleslaw, and corn muffins, all for $11.99.

"Rachel, sit down. What do you want to drink?"

"I want the chicken," Rachel says.

"I want the corn bread," Elijah says.

"What do you want to *drink?*"

"Milk," Elijah says.

"I don't want anything," Rachel says.

While Larry gets Rachel a glass of Hi-C, Elijah drops his red Styrofoam
plate on the floor and feigns a stretch that falls just short of being able to reach
it. "I can't get my plate," he says. Larry ignores him, feeds the fish, goes to
change his clothes. Elijah climbs down and gets his plate. Rachel stands on her
chair, reaches up, and gives the hanging lamp over the table a slight nudge,
sits down, and begins poking holes in her Styrofoam plate with her fork. Larry
returns in a knock-around shirt and pants, but still wearing his shiny black
wingtips, untied.

"Let's say grace," he says. "Dear Lord . . ."

And then, "So, Elijah, who showed you how to make a puppet?"

Larry's vision of marriage when he proposed to Donna was this: He would
come home in the evening and she would be waiting for him, happy to see
him, feeling romantic. They would go to plays and dine out at fine restau-
rants—La Colline and Dominique's. They'd attend elegant Washington recep-
tions, she on his arm, smart and pretty, witty and well-dressed. Or they'd stay
home and cook dinner together, as they often did during their courtship,
laughing and kissing and tasting the meal. Larry, a gourmet cook, would broil
a whole fish or roast a rack of lamb, or he'd make his spaghetti sauce with
chopped red, green, and yellow peppers and fresh onions and mushrooms
and tomatoes and a touch of red wine.

They'd take long walks as the leaves were spiraling down in the fall, or
walks in the winter chill, the moist spring air, the summer sun. They'd share
their deepest fears, ambitions, and feelings—two people who lived and
thought and felt as one. Donna's vision was similar. She had prayed for a soul
mate, and God had sent her Larry. As it turned out, though, Larry couldn't see
into Donna's soul as well as God.

"There will be no treats unless you eat your food."

"Poo-poo," Elijah says.

"Daddy, do you say poo me?" Rachel asks.

"Is that a word you made up?"

The kids giggle hysterically.

"Put your foot down, Rachel."

"Elijah, eat your food."

Way back before the twins came, in the first months after the wedding, Larry felt he was moving easily into married life. He'd always cleaned his own house and thought nothing of it now that Donna had moved in, although he was newly careful to wipe the toilet and put the seat down. Little stuff bugged him—Donna's toiletries took up so much space in the bathroom, and she went through the kitchen and cleared out all his mismatched pans, dishes, and silverware, gave them all to Goodwill. She reorganized the closets, making it hard for Larry to find some of his favorite old clothes. But no big deal.

For Donna, it was another story. Almost immediately, she felt as if she were disappearing. It was funny the first few times the bank cashier pulled up her new name—Donna Jones—on the computer and twenty names popped up, and the cashier asked, "Which Donna Jones are you?" But then it wasn't funny anymore. It made sense that Donna had moved out of her apartment and into the town house Larry owned, but she still missed what had been her home for many years. And wherever they went, Larry drove—even when they went in Donna's car. To save on commuting expenses, they drove to and from work together. But Donna had often gone shopping after work and now she couldn't. If Larry was only five minutes late picking her up, she found herself inexplicably aflame with rage. One day, as they drove along, Donna broke down in tears: "I never get to drive my car anymore."

"I'll move over, drive," Larry said, clueless.

Donna had no desire to become a deaconess at church, but everyone assumed she would. "You're Mrs. Larry Jones now," a woman told her in that churchwoman voice. And when she did her hair up in wild waves on a lark, another churchwoman took her aside and said, "That's not the kind of hairstyle the wife of Larry Jones should wear." Donna thought, "All because we got married." Donna had always savored time alone. She sometimes unplugged her phone for days at a time. She enjoyed watching the sun set and could sit forever studying the petals of a flower. Every morning, she took a half-hour walk and not so much prayed as talked with God. Now her whole life was changed. In his job, Larry hit the Washington social circuit hard. At first, it was glamorous to Donna, but now it was like her job too. Overnight, she had become Larry's rib. She couldn't help it. She blamed him.

Larry sensed the distance, was hurt by Donna's rage. But every time he asked what was wrong, she broke down in tears. So he backed off, not wanting to make whatever was wrong worse. Larry was a precise, methodical, organized man who diagnosed a problem, prioritized a response, and devised a logical solution. But with Donna, he couldn't even make a diagnosis. She was immune to logic. Secretly, he wondered if they should have married at all.

Donna felt smothered, as if she couldn't breathe. She wanted to tell Larry, but she was afraid to, afraid he wouldn't love her if he knew how much time she needed for herself, if he knew how strongly she was balking at the demands of her new role as his wife. She feared that Larry wouldn't respond as a friend, with empathy and support, but would be disappointed in her, that he would judge her an unworthy wife. She wanted to tell Larry these things, but she feared that a man would never be able to understand her feelings. Her old female friends just knew: *Oh, she needs some "Donna time."* Down deep, Donna also felt she shouldn't have to *tell* Larry—that if he really was her soul mate, he should just *know* how she felt. Donna told a friend, a woman married many years, "I want to think and be like one person." The woman said, "It doesn't happen overnight. It's every day and every week." Still, like Larry, Donna wondered if they should ever have married.

At 8:30 P.M., when Donna gets home lugging four bags of groceries, Larry has cleaned up the kitchen, swept the floor under the table for crumbs, bathed the kids, gotten on his knees and washed out the tub, let them watch a Popeye video, read them a book, heard them say their prayers, and put them to bed, where they are now chattering like songbirds.

"You tired?" Donna asks Larry, who slumps his weight onto the kitchen footstool and leans his shoulder and head against the cabinets. Donna gives him a kiss and laughs at the baby powder that dusts his wingtips like light snow. The laces are still untied. She's exhausted too, but the kind of exhausted that leaves her just this side of slaphappy, silly. She kicks off her shoes.

"Mommy!" Elijah hollers, "What did you brought?"

Donna sits at the kitchen table, her coat still on, and hugs Rachel and Elijah at once. They seem to melt into her body, like young animals nursing. Larry sits quietly and marvels. In her exhaustion and joy at seeing the kids, Donna is radiant. Larry cannot help but envy her intimacy with the children. It is what so many fathers have missed. It is what he craves. Yet for all the time he spends with the children, they do not melt into him as they do with her. But then, he spends more time correcting them, regimenting their behavior, making them sit up straight, not whine or fuss. Sometimes he thinks Donna is too easy on them but not now, not looking at them across the kitchen. It's as if he is not in the room. He gets up and begins to unload the groceries and pack them away.

"Strawberry Newtons!" he says, excited.

"Always get something for hubby," Donna says, laughing.

The turning point in Donna and Larry's marriage came the first year, when she was once again crying, angry, and unable to talk about her feelings. Larry, a remarkably calm man who rarely raises his voice in anger, exploded, his face contorted, and he roared, *"We can't keep running away! We have got to talk!"* Then he stormed out the door and slammed it behind him. In minutes, he was sorry that he'd lost his temper, embarrassed. But back in the house, Donna was stunned and touched. This calm, cool man had, for just a moment, seemed vulnerable, confused, afraid. She suddenly realized that she was not lost alone in this marriage. Larry was lost with her. When he returned in a short while to apologize, they sat down and talked for the first time.

She didn't have to be a deaconess.

She could wear wild waves if she wanted.

She could drive herself to work.

She could go shopping at night.

She didn't have to do the social circuit.

She could take all the "Donna time" she needed.

It was not that Larry had *done* anything to smother Donna. He had simply acted in his confident way, revealing no weakness, no self-doubt, acting with a sense of male entitlement: Now that we are married, life will be like this. Donna had rebelled in her own passive way. When they finally reached each other, Donna learned that Larry had no desire to consume her, to dominate her, that he had no idea he was even doing it. "If your love is not freely given to me," he told Donna, "it is not love." If Larry had not been so understanding, so willing to adapt, Donna believes today, their marriage would probably have ended in divorce.

Donna started driving to work occasionally. She stayed in the city and went shopping. She went back to her morning walks, spent more time alone. She felt better, more like herself. Soon, she felt the need to do these things recede, as if knowing she could do them was all that had ever really mattered. But still, the first two years were sobering: They would not be *friends* so fast.

"Elijah, show Mommy what you made," Donna says, and Elijah fetches the pile of cloth that was his puppet. "Those are the eyes?" asks Donna, and for nearly half an hour, Donna, Elijah, and Rachel hover like surgeons over a dying patient, reattaching eyes and ears, hair and tongue, laughing and giggling, dripping white dollops of Elmer's glue all over the table, onto the kids' crackers, all over themselves, while Larry sits five feet away on the footstool so he isn't tempted to make them clean up their mess as they go, tempted to ruin the moment. He thinks, "Wow, that's really powerful." It's as if *Donna* is four years old.

"Tell me what these are," she says to Elijah.

"You put 'em on the head," Elijah says.

"Where do I put this?" Rachel asks.

"On the hat," Elijah says.

"Very good," Donna says.

"Mommy! Mommy!" Elijah hollers.

"What, honey?"

"What about this last bow?"

Finally, Larry says, "It's getting very close to nine o'clock." Donna sends the kids off to wash up, and holds out her gooey hands, palms up. In her stocking feet, she stands up flat-footed, her feet splayed, still wearing her nice checkered office dress and her blue jacket with its sleeves now scrunched up over her forearms.

"Mommies have special effects on their kids," she says, lightly.

"Daddies too," says Larry, feeling a bit left out.

Donna soothes him with a smile. "Daddies too."

They kiss and go off to tickle the twins into bed.

*　　　*　　　*

"Don't touch the stove!" Larry hollers from upstairs.

"I want some eggs," Rachel hollers back.

"Elijah, get down," Larry says as he reenters the kitchen, still wearing slippers and his red plaid nightshirt. It is 9:15 A.M. Saturday, a rare morning when the kids let Larry sleep late while Donna went off to church to help cook a meal for tomorrow. Rachel is sitting on the kitchen table, and Elijah is climbing on the cabinet next to the stove, where a pot of water is heating up to cook instant grits.

"I'm showing you where the cinnamon toast is," Elijah says.

"Thank you," Larry says, lifting him off the counter.

"Rachel, don't sit on the table."

Something is burning, but in the midst of Elijah and Rachel, eggs, grits, bacon, and cinnamon toast, Larry doesn't notice. "You know what you both need to do," Larry says. *"Sit down."* And they do.

"Can I have a piece of bacon?" Elijah asks.

"Daddy, I like grits," Rachel says.

"Elijah, you put the plates out." He does.

"Thank you. Now sit down. Sit. Sit down."

"Rachel, just sit down."

"Daddy, I want to *eeeeeeeat,*" Elijah says.

"Let's say our grace. Dear Lord . . ."

When the twins came four years ago, all of Donna and Larry's marital problems evaporated. Or rather they seemed suddenly trivial. Because nothing they had been told, nothing they had imagined, no warning they'd been given, had made them ready. Donna came home after the births and overexerted herself, collapsed unconscious, and was rushed to the hospital by ambulance for blood transfusions. She was then confined to bed for more than a month. Larry took six weeks off. He had imagined the joy of cuddling his babies, them cooing on his shoulder, warm and content. Not exactly. The twins slept and woke in two-hour shifts, but never the same two hours. He'd change, feed, rock, soothe, and put Rachel to bed, just fall asleep, and then Elijah would go off. Although weak, Donna wanted to help. But the doctor had warned Larry that she was in real danger. So he cared for Donna and cooked her meals, including mountains of liver for her anemia, and delivered the babies to her for feeding and cuddling. Then Donna couldn't nurse, and Larry began the bottles—as many as sixteen a day. Day and night for six weeks.

Late one night, Larry locked himself in the bathroom. He had never known such exhaustion. Before, he had been so tired he feared he'd sleep through the babies' crying. Now, he was so tired he feared he was dying. In the bathroom, among the new utensils of parenthood—the towels, lathers, thermometers, washbowls, soaps, and medicines—he prayed, "Dear God, don't let me die." He took a moment. Then he got up and went back at it. He told himself, "They need me. I am their dad. I have to come through."

In those weeks, Larry believes, he was made privy to the secret of life: Imprinted in his mind four years later are not the dirty chores or the exhaustion, but the moments when Rachel or Elijah was lying on his shoulder in the dark, Elijah's back no bigger than the palm of his hand, Rachel's sweet breath whispering in his ear, Elijah's heartbeat seeming to pass through into Larry's own heart, as if he and his children had become a single creature. In those moments, Larry could forget that he was blood and bone, believe that he was spirit alone. Until then, he had never realized his own ability to love. Knowing how much more he could give of himself, he believes, has made him a better father, a better husband, and a better person. What man would deny himself this gift?

But Larry also knows this: If Donna had been the kind of wife who, from the beginning, had insisted on doing all the housework and cooking and then been healthy enough to insist that she do most of the child care duties, Larry probably would have let her. "I would have fallen into that trap."

From her sickbed, Donna watched. How had she ever doubted this man? His commitment? His loyalty? His devotion? She lay in bed helpless and felt her love for Larry growing, the way the heart of Dr. Seuss's Grinch grows and grows and grows when he suddenly understands that love is not a *thing* but a feeling, that you don't give love to get it, you give love to feel it in yourself. If this was not boundless love before her, what was?

When Larry finally went back to work, it was like going on vacation: *What, only a ten-hour day? Get to drink a cup of coffee and read the paper? Go to lunch?* When Larry came home at night and Donna handed him the babies and said, "Here, I'm leaving," and raced out the door for a long walk, Larry knew *exactly* what she was feeling, didn't begrudge her a bit, knew that no matter how grueling his day at the office had been, he'd gotten the easier ride. "We felt like the only two survivors on earth," Donna says. "We had to trust and depend on each other, no matter what." Donna and Larry needed Donna's income to pay the bills, but Larry also believed that—American ideal or not—it wouldn't have been healthy for Donna to stay home full time with the kids. "He'd lived it," Donna says, and so the twins went to day care and she went back to work at Arthur Andersen several days a week before moving to the less demanding full-time job at Howard.

"What's burning?" Donna asks when she returns from church and finds Larry alone at the table and the kids off playing. She goes to the stove, opens it, and pulls out a smoldering paper napkin. "You didn't smell anything?" she asks, laughing. "Any bacon left?"

"Want me to fix you some breakfast?" Larry asks.

"No, I was wondering if there's any bacon left for seasoning my green beans." Donna begins taking dirty dishes off the table, stove, and counters and stacking them in the sink. She wrings out the dishcloth and wipes the stove and countertop. Larry gets up from the table and puts away the Hi-C.

"Will you wipe the table?" Donna asks.

"Yeah."

While she sorts the mail, Larry goes off, hauls out the vacuum cleaner, and begins vacuuming the living room. Donna pulls out a big plastic bag of fresh green beans. "Can we snap beans?" she hollers, and the kids come tumbling and squealing.

Donna and Larry can't imagine anything that would now end their marriage. From her, he has learned to relax with the kids more, not always correct, enjoy the moment, let them go. From him, she has learned to rein in the kids more, calm down, not let herself get so frazzled, leave the room for a minute, talk more slowly, say a prayer. In a world where men rarely do their fair share at home, Larry has acquired godlike status among Donna's female acquaintances, most of whom complain bitterly that their husbands don't pick up after themselves, that their sons are now taking after them, that as working wives they have *two* jobs. And at home, their husbands are like another child. Donna believes these women are seething inside and that it must infect their marriages. But when the subject comes up, she is usually silent. She believes her friends envy her marriage, and she doesn't want to seem like she's gloating. She once mentioned that Larry cooks the main dishes on holidays and makes the beds most mornings, and a friend shrieked, "Girl, you've got *nothing* to complain about!"

Donna also has had to abandon a few of her own feminine expectations. Larry doesn't only want to share the chores and the child rearing, for instance, he also wants to share in the selection of tables and curtains, couches and artwork. For a while, Donna argued that she should have greater say over home decorating. After all, wasn't she the artist? But then, after she insisted that a table Larry liked wouldn't fit in the dining room, she came home and saw that Larry had been right. She thought, "It's odd what marriages are built on."

Sometimes tradition rears up in Donna and she feels guilty that she doesn't care for her home and children pretty much alone, as her mother did. But mostly, Donna fears she takes Larry for granted. A while ago, he confessed to Donna that he sometimes wishes she'd show more appreciation for all he does. She said, "I didn't know you felt that way," and asked what she could do. "You could say, 'You go watch football games at Skip's all day, and I'll take the kids today,'" Larry said, adding that he wouldn't go without getting all his work done anyway, but that the gesture would make him feel good. In the same way that Donna, years ago, felt good just knowing she could drive her car whenever she wanted.

Donna is no longer afraid of losing herself in her marriage, and she is no longer so painfully needy of time to herself. She still worries about relying on Larry too much—he changes her flat tires, kills the earwigs, opens the pickle jars, all of which she once did herself. But mostly, she worries about relying too heavily on his emotional strength, letting him become like a father to her, because she sees his masculine strength differently now. She still admires

Larry's patience and calm, his judgment, but now she also believes he sacrifices the joy of spontaneity and that his judicious nature probably masks deeper emotions, perhaps even fears, that she hasn't yet fathomed. "I don't feel I know this part of him yet," she says. "We've only known each other seven years."

But this is their achievement so far: Donna and Larry don't live separate lives under the same roof. Each knows the joys and frustrations of work. Each knows the joys and frustrations of caring for children. Each knows the oppressive relentlessness of household chores. Each tries to know the other's thoughts and feelings. And even this: Each knows that every piece of furniture they've bought is a shared story—the haggling they went through to agree on that couch and that color, where they found it cheaper, the trip they took together to buy it, where it was to be finally placed in the room. They are friends, plain and simple.

Donna has stopped complaining that Larry leaves the lights on in every room and just turns them off. Larry has stopped complaining that Donna forgets piles of dirty clothes around the house and just picks them up. She leaves out a glass of orange juice for him in the morning and lays a blanket over him when he falls asleep at night watching CNN. He surprises her with flowers and in the winter goes out early to clean the ice and snow off her car and turn on the heater. All without a word spoken.

"Okay, kids, go get dressed," Donna says when the green beans are snapped. She pulls out a turkey breast for weekday dinners, seasons it, and puts it in the oven. She takes out ground turkey to make a meat loaf later. After doing the dishes, when she gets upstairs, she collects the kids' pajamas off the bathroom floor and goes to change their bedding. But Larry has already changed the beds, hauled off the dirty sheets, and is getting Elijah dressed for a father-son trip to the barbershop. She sits down next to him on the bed, puts her arm around his shoulder, gives him the hint of a hug, and says, "Why don't Rachel and I go along."

December 11, 1994

Amazing Grace

She's not nervous. Well, maybe a *little* nervous. One butterfly hovering, darting in her stomach, just one. At least that's the way Stephanie Burrous thinks about whatever it is she's feeling this instant, as she peers out at the fifteen hundred howling, raging, clapping, jeering, cheering people just beyond the glittering red-velvet Chinese curtain to her right. Maybe one butterfly, as she waits to take the stage at Harlem's Apollo Theatre on its famed Wednesday amateur night. From her perch among the cords and cables, pulleys and paraphernalia of the theater, she can see into the front rows to the left of the stage. The seats are filled with black people, mostly young and hip, coolsters. She wonders if this is good. It was a mostly white audience that put her over a few weeks ago on her twenty-second birthday, cheering her to a spot in tonight's quarterfinals of the Amateur of the Year competition.

But no use wondering. Gospel music isn't any Apollo crowd's favorite listening. The Apollo has been a breeding ground for just about every wave of popular music to hit America in the last half-century—blues, jazz, swing, bebop, doo-wop, rhythm and blues, rock and roll, soul, and rap. But while they all owe a bow to their spiritual and gospel roots, the Apollo has never been a bastion of gospel, and Stephanie knows it. So she's got to stay focused, remember why she's here. Find the music's power in herself and the audience will find it too. After all, folks don't have to speak Italian to love opera. Besides, this audience is not her judge, and these people will not, *cannot*, boo her, as they do so many amateur-night performers. Sure, the Apollo can be brutal, with the screaming audience often deciding in seconds whether a performer gets the hook from "the executioner," a wildly dressed character who runs on stage and chases off humiliated contestants amid a blur of horns and whistles and flashing lights.

But this *cannot* happen to Stephanie, because He would not let that happen, not now, not after that Sunday a year ago in the shaking, quaking, baking storefront Holiness church on Georgia Avenue back in Washington, just across from the Penthouse club. That morning, Stephanie was hit so hard with the Holy Ghost that she saw white light and was transported from the room, to where she doesn't know.

No, they won't boo. Still, maybe one butterfly. She smiles a tight, shy smile. She *is* only human. She crosses her arms at her chest and closes her eyes. In her meditation, Stephanie asks God to calm the wild audience so it may hear the prayer about to be sent on the wings of her voice. As she asks this, she stands slightly hunched, her left leg forward, her weight resting back on her right foot. Tense and casual at once. She wears a black leather skirt and black blouse with its shoulders done in dark suede. Not dowdy, but certainly conservative. She's short and a little stiff in her mannerisms. Her hair is curled tight and moistened to a sheen. Her right front tooth is outlined in gold in the shape of a heart. Her body carries a light scent of baby powder. Her gold-rimmed glasses sit low on the bridge of her nose and she nudges them up with an index finger. She takes them off and wipes her eyes, a little perspiration. She is not someone most people would notice passing on the street. Unless she was singing.

Onstage, beyond Stephanie, Olori Rock, a teenage rap dancer, is performing under the pink, purple, and yellow hot-lights. Before him are the old Irish burlesque hall's crystal chandeliers and its marble walls, its faux gold leaf, its killer crowd. And all around Stephanie, in the shadowy backstage light, among the cords and cables, are the others—the several dozen acts who each week mount the stage and risk humiliation in hopes of joining the Apollo's legends: Sarah Vaughan, Ella Fitzgerald, Billie Holiday, James Brown, Gladys Knight, Stevie Wonder, Patti LaBelle, Diana Ross, Michael Jackson, Little Richard, Aretha Franklin, Smokey Robinson.

Tonight, Olori Rock will not join the legends. He's gone, and Stephanie, lit by a row of yellow stage lights, has taken the short walk to right-center stage, clasped the microphone in her right hand, bent her knees, twisted her back slightly down and to her right, closed her eyes. Now, with a millisecond of dramatic hesitation, she lets it rip in a low, deep, hoarse register—the blare of a trumpet, the boom of a cannon, the blast of an alarm: "AmaAAAziiIIIng GraaAAAaaaAAAAAAce shall alwaAaAys beeEEeeEEeeEE MY-MY-MY-MY-MY-MY-MY-MY-MY soOoOong of praiAIaiAIaise . . ." Like a brass band on the Fourth of July.

That quickly, with the opening lyrics of "He Looked Beyond My Faults and Saw My Needs," Stephanie has broken a cardinal rule of gospel persuasion, a rule she learned in a lifetime of worshiping in tiny Pentecostal churches, in the Baltimore Holiness church where her grandfather and her aunt were pastors, in the churches where her father played the bass and her mother sang the hymns, where Stephanie began to sing as a nine-year-old girl, only because her folks insisted. The gospel music she was taught has been part of the Holiness Church tradition for nearly a century, growing from black field songs and spirituals such as "Go Down Moses" and "Swing Low, Sweet Chariot" at the same time that ragtime, blues, and jazz were being born. Before becoming absolutely mainstream, it was first the music of small, hole-in-the-wall urban churches filled with newly arriving migrants from the rural South. Original "hard" gospel—with its guttural-voiced quavering, straining, rasping, and growling, its low-to-high shrieks and screams, its pulsating vibrato—became a missionary tool: the Word put to music.

Black gospel has modernized, gone smooth and contemporary, but the cardinal rule Stephanie learned as a girl is unchanged: Start out slowly, let the Spirit rise, bubble. Let the emotions of joy and redemption and deliverance simmer before they boil, save something for a soaring finale. But not tonight, not at the Apollo. An Apollo talent scout, Jane Jackson-Harley, who first heard Stephanie at the Apollo's weekly auditions at Howard University's Blackburn Center in Washington, D.C., had tried to persuade Stephanie not to sing "He Looked Beyond My Faults." Too obscure, too churchy for the slick Apollo audience. Stephanie chose to sing it anyway. And now, onstage, in the old gospel tradition, she dives deep into her chest, makes a guttural instrument of her throat, and rolls and riffs and vibrates from word one. Blasted back in their seats, stunned, the Apollo crowd is silent, as if they've just taken a bucket of ice water in the face. What this silence means is still unclear, but Stephanie figured she had no choice.

Down the battered iron stairs, in the basement, is the no-longer-green Green Room, where the Apollo's victims await their turn on stage. As Stephanie sat there quietly on a straight-backed zebra-skin chair earlier tonight, her knees pressed demurely together, her hands on her lap, the top button of her blouse hooked tightly, the surrounding scene was a hip-hop version of a symphony orchestra in discordant tune-up before a concert.

Around Stephanie, amid chaos made double by the Green Room's mirrored wall, the Zulu Boys, a father/sons reggae song-and-dance act, limbered up not too limberly. Premiere, a band of five preteen rap-star wannabes, cut up in their baggy black-and-yellow outfits. The Get Busy Girls, teenagers in matching polka-dotted and curlicued black, green, red, yellow, and turquoise shirts, mugged at the makeup mirror. Everywhere, folks from five to forty-five— wearing everything from jeans and T-shirts to gaudy purple dresses, to black-and-white checkerboard jumpsuits, to shaved heads, to Rastafarian tufts, to cornrows, to hair-sprayed architectural structures—ran octaves, did splits, fussed over blouses and shirts, oiled trumpets, brushed purple sneakers, complained that the bathrooms were grodier than at any freeway gas-and-go.

Amid this blur of color and noise, Stephanie sat quietly on the zebra-skin chair, beside a dresser cluttered with curling irons and bottles of curl re-activator, and watched the stage monitor as a sixteen-year-old gospel singer from New Jersey knocked the audience dead, brought 'em to their feet. She heard the Apollo emcee announce that the girl was one of the best acts of the night. This is called priming the pump, the house picking a horse. It seemed unlikely that the audience would select two gospel singers to be among the night's top four acts who would graduate to the Amateur of the Year semifinals. Stephanie's confidence seemed to evaporate, and her determined face went flaccid, plaintive.

"She's great," Stephanie said. "She deserves to win." Then she fell silent, until someone mentioned that the girl had brought an entourage of maybe a hundred people with her, that they'd packed the center of the first floor, that they'd howled like mad dogs from the get-go. Stephanie's face suddenly lit up. "What?" she asked assertively. "A hundred people? If I brought a hundred people, I could win." She nodded her head in silent agreement with her own observation. Then she said, "When He gave her a gift, He gave me some of it too." Again she paused. "I give credit where credit is due. She's good. But I think I'm a little stronger than her, my voice, don't you?" At that moment, Stephanie resolved that there could be no simmer before the boil tonight. She'd have to reach into herself, then reach out to that audience and grab 'em like a cop making a collar.

When Stephanie sings, she feels the music as it comes out of her, and slowly that feeling starts to swell and take over, empower her. Singing is so deeply connected to her lifetime in the church, to the feelings touched in her by the emotional waterfall of spiritual conversion—her own and the hundreds of others she has witnessed—that when she sings, these feelings are rubbed and mingled and finally loosed inside her. At her music's deepest, she can forget the audience is even there and begin to sing not so much to herself, but as if there were no distinction between her mind, her body, and her emotions, as if she were not so much singing as breathing. Odd, but when she most forgets her audience is when her audience is most touched. But it can take a few bars or verses to travel to that private place—a place unexplainably similar to where she traveled when she was struck by the Holy Ghost and, for those moments, became totally devoid of vainglorious self-consciousness, totally within and without herself at once. In that place, Stephanie has a feeling so joyful she can only describe it as "free of sin." Singing at her best, Stephanie feels as if she's sitting on the back porch of heaven. From the first note tonight, it's where she must be.

So that's how she plays it. From her twisting crouch, amid the audience's shocked silence, bathed in white spotlights on the darkened stage, she flings her left arm behind her, fingers and hand extended, contorted and jerking, her face a mask of intensity. She takes a few steps to center stage, and wails: "I do noOOot knOOOOOoOoOOow just why He caAAAme to-wOo-wOo-wOo-wOo-wOo-wOo-wOo loOoOove me so . . ." With each ornamented syllable and rhythmic somersault, shivers roll down spines. The ice-water shock passes. The folks in the Apollo audience may not speak Italian, but they sure love opera. And before Stephanie is past the first stanza, they're howling, screaming, hooting, and some already are on their feet. One man hollers, "Sing it, girl!"

It is impossible for Stephanie to separate her music from her faith, although she has tried. From age sixteen until a few years ago, she sang with the Melodyaires gospel group, performing in black churches and at gospel shows up and down the East Coast. The Melodyaires once opened for the famed "singing preacher" Shirley Caesar. They even recorded an album, and a couple of Stephanie's songs got decent airplay on Baltimore's AM gospel radio station WBGR and Washington's WUST and WYCB. She sang in what's called an "anointed" style—a preaching style in the fashion of the black pulpit. She wasn't contemporary, not melodic or soothing, and her favorite songs were wrenching, old-time revival tunes—"He Looked Beyond My Faults," "Blessed Assurance," "His Eye Is on the Sparrow." She was good. She knew it. And she expected more, faster.

So Stephanie decided to sell out. Everybody from Dionne Warwick to Ray Charles to Aretha Franklin to Sam Cooke had begun their R&B careers after years of singing gospel, and Stephanie figured she'd do the same. She was tired of living with her folks in their little Rockville town house, tired of going to community college part time and working as an office clerk part time, tired of being broke. She quit the Melodyaires and began practicing Top 40 R&B songs, Anita Baker and Whitney Houston songs. She did demo tapes and sent them out to record companies. She stopped going to church regularly. She started hanging out with people who cursed and drank, smoked and danced. She didn't actually curse, drink, and smoke herself, but she did dance and wear wild clothes, pants, and jewelry. Her motives were simple: money, fame, and fun.

But nothing broke. No record companies called. Friends kept telling her to go up to the Apollo's amateur night and she agreed, but kept putting it off, drifting—afraid she would be booed. She felt more and more empty, more and more like those spacemen in photographs, floating weightless, tethered only tenuously to a mother ship. Then one Sunday morning, Stephanie, her mother, and her sister were driving out Georgia Avenue from a friend's church in Washington, when they heard singing, gospel singing. Not fancy, prettified gospel singing, but raw and undisciplined, genuine gospel singing—the tearful nasal voices, the spontaneous cries of "Praise the Lord," the jangling tambourines, the beat of the drums, the clink of the old Wurlitzer piano. Gospel music as authentic as the washboard and harmonica blues of the Mississippi Delta.

Stephanie's sister didn't want to turn around, but Stephanie and her mother did, and at 3545 Georgia Avenue they found the House of the Lord of the Apostolic Faith, Bishop J. B. Rogers presiding. Prettified the House of the Lord was not. Its front door was battered, its sanctuary was the size of a large garage, its pews were folding chairs, its flickering lights were fluorescent, its altar cross was rough wood, and its air smelled of sour diapers.

None of this fazed Stephanie, who'd spent her whole life worshiping in unadorned Pentecostal churches like the House of the Lord. They stayed for service, and when Stephanie's mother told one of the fifty or so congregants that Stephanie could sing, they begged her to sing a song. She did, the old-time "His Eye Is on the Sparrow." Everybody fussed over her and invited her back, although a month went by before the House of the Lord's preacher called and said he and his wife would pick up Stephanie at home if she'd come sing a song. She did, but in her spaceman's drift, she went back to the church only occasionally. Too lazy, too lost.

Then came November 25, 1990, a mild, sunny Sunday. Stephanie really wanted to go to the House of the Lord that day. She just had a feeling. Getting dressed that morning, she felt good, and when she got to church it was buzzing with the hum of people singing and dancing, clapping and testifying about how they were lost but now were found, praising God. In Stephanie's words, "The Spirit was high." She wasn't singing that day. She was playing the drums, just bopping along, when she began to cry. She felt sorry and happy at once—sorry she'd lost direction, run with the wrong crowd, but happy that she was now feeling sorry. Suddenly, she found herself standing before the congregation, with people crowding around her praying, singing, and proclaiming the glow on her face. But that is all Stephanie remembers, nothing else, because at that instant she was gone, touched by the lightning of the Holy Ghost in the ancient way of Saul. As her jubilant fellow congregants wept and cried "hallelujah" and anointed with virgin olive oil the forehead of the body she had left behind, Stephanie was off with God in the white light, free of sin.

From that day, no more R&B. "I can't put my all into rhythm and blues," Stephanie says. "I can put my all into gospel." Now when Stephanie sings her gospel, it's like a prayer. No, it's not the *same* feeling she felt when the lightning struck, nothing could be as intense as touching God himself. But, she believes, the feelings are somehow alike, somehow connected to the place where the mysterious human soul resides.

Before Stephanie's first Apollo appearance, on her birthday, talent scout Jane Jackson-Harley gave her the same advice and pep talk she gives to hundreds of other contestants she brings to the Apollo every year: Be yourself. Relax. If the audience boos, keep performing. Don't panic. She then warned Stephanie not to sing the nineteenth-century gospel song "Blessed Assurance," with the words "Jesus is mine / Oh, what a foretaste of glory divine . . . This is my story, this is my song / I'm praising the Savior all the day long." Too dangerous with the Apollo crowd, she said. Why not go with a more up-tempo, rhythm-and-bluesy gospel song?

But Stephanie was no longer willing to sell out. Since that Sunday morning in November, she believes, her music has changed. Oh, she could always *sing,* always wow 'em, get 'em to their feet and into the aisles. But after the lightning, her singing seemed deeper and people seemed to feel it more. And Stephanie, well, it sounds strange to say, but she sometimes felt as if she weren't in the room, as if she were pure essence singing only for the joy and wonderment of it. "I feel like I'm singing a song, but I'm not really down here singing a song," she says, still mystified by the sensation. "It's like I'm somewhere else and the Spirit just takes over." Like a mighty river, they say of faith, and that is what Stephanie believes was unleashed in her.

So on her birthday, she sang "Blessed Assurance." Onstage, even while singing, she was still telling herself, "Let go, let God do it, don't worry about being booed." True to gospel form, she started out slowly, in the middle range of her voice. By the end of her song, she found herself. Her voice swelled to a soaring, trademark gospel finish, and she tied for second place.

And tonight, politely but firmly rejecting all advice to the contrary, she insisted on singing "He Looked Beyond My Faults." Up-tempo gospel music, with the *beat-beat-beat* of popular music, distracts listeners from the music's sacred message, Stephanie believes, and the sacred message—the preaching— is why she sings. To perform a modern gospel or secular R&B song would disconnect her from what she believes is the miraculous source of her new power, and thus doom her effort anyway. No, the sophisticated, coolster Apollo audience would hear the story of Christ's death at Calvary whether they liked it or not. "I may not win," Stephanie said, "but they won't boo me. I know that."

Indeed, they are not booing. All around the theater, people in every direction are rising in waves, clapping, rejoining "hallelujah," hollering, and hooting joyously. Stephanie is saving nothing for a finale. Her eyes are still closed, the veins on her neck are swollen, her glasses have slipped down her nose. She glistens gold with sweat, on fire, holding notes and riffing the scales, for five, ten, fifteen seconds, ad-libbing her phrasing and reprising as she goes: "JesuUUUUus dieIEIEed for meEEEEeeeeEEEEeeee . . ." In the front row, Eva, a woman famous for years of dedicated attendance at Apollo's amateur night, a woman famous for never standing up for a loser, is hopping up and down, jabbing her arms in the air, screaming. Only the hundred or so people with the sixteen-year-old from New Jersey are seated quietly in the center of the main floor. They look like Episcopalians. In the balcony, in the cheaper seats, people are going nuts. Onstage, Stephanie is only vaguely aware of the bedlam. She is off on heaven's porch.

Last Sunday, at the House of the Lord, Stephanie sang and preached. It was hard to tell the difference between the two. She wore the beautiful white-and-yellow jacket and skirt and patent-leather shoes that she had worn for her birthday performance at the Apollo, and she looked very uptown for the House of the Lord, where people were neatly but not elegantly dressed. People at the House of the Lord don't lead storybook American lives. Most men work at punch-the-clock jobs and most women work as secretaries or clerks. One man—a stranger, a bum—had wandered in off the street that day after years away from any church. His brother had been shot the night before.

Another man was working the room wheedling change for a trip, he said, to Silver Spring, only a few miles away. The preacher asked how many of the thirty or so adults had *never* used drugs, and only five people stood up. A well-dressed, pretty woman said she was off the stuff now and proud of it, that she could have ended up a hooker on the street like so many of her friends.

Like the music Stephanie loves, these people's lives are rough-edged and raw, and the spirit of the music is within them. Their Sunday service was like being baptized in a river of sensation: exclamations and declarations pouring over each other so rapidly they had the sound of a foreign language; drums, bongos, piano, and tambourines; gospel hymns and dancing feet; shouted and whispered asides; faces ecstatic, scowling, or beseeching in prayer; foot-tapping and hand-clapping; everyone talking individually and everyone talking collectively in a ritualized spontaneity that has its roots still firmly planted in turn-of-the-century Pentecostalism and the riveting emotional experiences of being "born again" in the Holy Ghost, as well as the casting out of demons, faith healing, and speaking in tongues. In the House of the Lord, the congregation is a constant chorus, and the difference between who is preaching and who is listening is a very fine line.

"Hallelujah!"
"I'm not doin' the things I used ta do!"
"Pray to Jesus!"
"I know there is power in His name!"
"Oh, Lord! Oh, Lord! Oh, Lord!"
Thankyouthankyouthankyouthankyouthankyouthankyouthankyou . . ."
"Fifteen years old and tryin' ta raise a family!"
"Doitdoitdoitdoitdoitdoitdoit . . ."
"Let's give the Lord a hand!"

Nearly an hour of this had gone by last Sunday, this blending of liturgy and life into a music of its own, before the preacher stood to introduce "one of the greatest gospel singers in the world." Stephanie rose, her King James Bible in hand, and said, with the musical cadence of a song, "Thank God for lettin' us stay a little while longer." The acoustics in the House of the Lord are something like the bathroom shower, and after starting slowly to let "the Spirit descend" with the rising intensity of her voice and the congregation's emotions, Stephanie cut loose with "The Denied Stone." The place literally vibrated as she sang the lyrics and ad-libbed along the way: "You see, IIIII been doOoOoown, but I'm paAAckin' UuUp and coOoming hoOoOome, yeah, yeaAAAh, yeAaAaAah!" Stephanie went on to preach a sermon titled "Mr. Big Stuff, Who Do You Think You Are?"—about the angel of the Lord who came to Peter in prison, about how no power on Earth, no prison guards, no king named Herod could subdue or conquer Peter when he was imbued with the power of God.

She said, "Somebody ought to shout, 'Glory!'"
"Glory!"

"Glory!"
"Glory!"

She roared, "This message is for me too! Who do I think I am? Without Him, I'm nobody! I'm a nobody tryin' to tell everybody about somebody who can save anybody!" Later, she said, "It's not just singing. It's a ministry."

And so it is, win or lose, for Stephanie tonight at the Apollo. She launched her song so intensely, it's hard to imagine what can be left in the small woman to bring the song home, but she finds it: "HowOOW-Ah-Ah-Ah-Ah-Ah-Ah-Ah-Ah maAArveloUUUUUUUUUUUUUU-uh-ah-uh-ah-uh-ah-us, that graAaAaAaAace that caAAught my faAAlling soOoOoOoul." She snaps off the last note, drops her arms limply to her side, and returns her attention to the audience, which has gone berserk. Even some of the people with the sixteen-year-old from New Jersey are standing and clapping now, and as Stephanie leaves the stage, the Apollo emcee says, "Somebody pass the plate! I thought we was in church!" For her, that is the highest compliment. Stephanie is always her own worst critic, but right now—standing in the wings, her fellow Apollo aspirants congratulating her and patting her on the back—she is serene and confident. She says, "I think it was right."

It will be hours before the night is done, before all the singers, dancers, and acrobats have done their thing, for better or worse, before one man in a business suit is booed off the stage while singing "Color My World," and before a woman in a purple dress walks off the stage in tears when she can't get the words to "Harlem Blues" in sync with the music.

During the waiting, a woman from a record company introduces herself to Stephanie and asks if she's interested in singing secular music as well as sacred. With less conviction than she would hope to have, Stephanie says, no, she's not interested in singing secular music. Finally, about midnight, the audience speaks: Stephanie ties for third and earns a spot in the Amateur of the Year semifinals. At that contest two months later, Stephanie will be the fourth performer on stage, before the theater is filled, before the crowd is riled up. In a new cream-colored outfit and with a new French-roll hairdo, she will again look prim and proper for the slick Apollo crowd. But there will be little applause, as if the audience were not yet listening. Stephanie will not be among the winners, and she will grumble about going on stage too early, about the bad luck of the draw. She *is* only human.

But tonight, packing up the van to go home, outside the theater's 126th Street stage door, under the Harlem streetlights, with rap music pouring from a black Saab parked with its doors open, with hordes of vendors still hawking caps and ties just around the corner on African Square, Stephanie is a contented woman. "I gave it my all," she says. "I thought it was good. I felt close to God. I never feel that way when I sing R&B. Gospel is me." Tonight, that feeling is reward enough.

January 19, 1992

Family Matters

Norman Siegel was taking karate lessons at the synagogue when his wife called. It was a Wednesday night, a year ago last fall, and Aisha was angry, outraged, and, perhaps, feeling vaguely vindicated by what had just happened in Shauna's bedroom. For years, Aisha had been telling Norman that his daughter had emotional problems he wasn't acknowledging and that by the time she was sixteen, the girl would strike her. That night, at age fifteen, Shauna had done it, taken a good swipe at her stepmother during a struggle over the phone, shoved her against the wall, and slammed the door against her.

Aisha, a strong, assertive woman, was not in need of physical protection against a girl. She had often told Norman, with whom she had then lived for eleven years and to whom she'd been married for six, that Shauna needed a good, old-fashioned smack. The few times Aisha had smarted off to her own mother, she had been smacked. Now forty-three, Aisha was raised in North Africa, the daughter of a colonel in the Algerian army who went on to become a high city official in Algiers. To her, this "teenage rebellion" that American children pass through was simply institutionalized disrespect for the parents who clothed and fed and housed them. It was sick—bad for parents, bad for children. But that night, after Shauna hit her, Aisha raised her hand to strike Shauna and froze her arm in midair.

"No, I will not lower myself to your level."

Norman, a militantly calm, composed, judicious fifty-five-year-old man, had in the past always soothed Aisha, told her Shauna's behavior wasn't that aberrant. He secretly believed she expected too much obedience from Shauna. Aisha had once told him that when her father whistled, his children ran and stood at attention. Norman joked that if his father had whistled, he and his three brothers would have waved. This wasn't North Africa in the sixties, but

Shauna Siegel.
Photo by Larry Fink.

Rockville in the nineties. He had talked to Shauna two other times after Aisha said Shauna had tried to strike her—once during a scuffle over a coat Aisha insisted be hung up, once when Aisha tried to pinch her cheek affectionately. Shauna had said both incidents were accidents. Norman believed both Aisha and Shauna, figured each was telling the truth as she saw it. He didn't want to take sides. But driving home that night, he thought, "How can I allow my daughter to fight with my wife?"

"Where is she?" Norman asked Aisha.

"She's asleep."

Norman headed for the stairs.

"You're not going to wake her up?" asked Aisha, who now thought it was probably best to let everyone cool down overnight.

"Of course I am."

Norman remembers going upstairs, turning on the bedroom lights, and saying to Shauna, who was in bed but fully dressed: "Violence is not allowed, abusive language is not allowed. As long as you stay here, you obey the rules of this house." Aisha remembers Norman saying: "If you can't be respectful, you can't live here." Shauna remembers her father saying: "You get out of my house."

Norman, in his precise, analytic way, believed he was intervening in a specific situation, responding to a discrete act. Aisha, gifted at reading moods and tones of voice, the deeper meanings of actions and reactions, saw more. She was proud of Norman that night, believed he'd finally stood up to his insolent daughter, that they'd stood as parents always should, united. Shauna, also a reader of people, had seen that too—and more. By that night, she had come to believe that she and Aisha weren't only butting heads against each other but were locked in a war over who would wield the feminine power in the family, which woman would hold the allegiance and affection of the family's father and husband. Even as a little girl, Shauna had persistently asked her dad, "Who do you love better, Aisha or me?" That night, Shauna believed, her father gave his answer.

He didn't ask how the dispute had come about, didn't learn how, as Shauna believed, Aisha had countermanded her father's decision that she could use the phone that night, how Aisha had gotten in Shauna's face and then tried to actually take away the phone. Aisha had no right! As Shauna often said, "You're not my mother." But her dad hadn't even asked, hadn't played his usual role as mediator. He'd taken sides, chosen, laid down his trust and his love. In Shauna's eyes, she was vanquished, Aisha victorious. The war was lost. "I wasn't gonna sit by and let her take my place," she says. The next day, Shauna ran away.

The Siegels were a family lost. A family, like so many others, battered by the teen years of a child, when the flaws of mothers, fathers, and children are distorted and magnified. They were better than many families, worse than some. Better because of the love, stability, affluence. Worse because Norman, Aisha, and Shauna are all, well, hardheads. Nobody likes to be wrong, nobody likes to give in.

Many of their tensions were ordinary, except that the Siegels took them to extremes: Shauna ran away and Norman and Aisha refused to take her back. Then, in an effort to save their family, the three of them launched an exploration into their shared lives, asking painful questions, facing painful answers, struggling to decipher what it means to be a family. They haven't figured it out. Does anyone, ever? Or is the exploration itself enough?

As they searched they kept circling back, looking for the beginning of their story. But when would that be? After Norman's divorce from his first wife or after his marriage to his second wife, Shauna's mother? Or when his father decided he'd have nothing to do with Norman's new wife because she wasn't Jewish? Or just after the joyful birth of Shauna? Or just after Norman's terrible arguments with Shauna's mother that Shauna, a few years old at the time, still dreams about? Or after Norman's father died, when Norman told his stepdaughter his only regret was that his father never said he loved him?

Or would the beginning come during the years when Norman and Shauna were best friends, when he ran a contracting business and Shauna proudly bore the title "Daddy's Number One Helper," when Shauna begged her father to come into her classroom so the other kids could see what a wonderful daddy she had?

Or would the beginning come with young Aisha, in the refugee camps of Tunisia in the fifties, while her father was off fighting for Algeria's independence from France? Or later, when Aisha saw her father hit her mother? Or after they'd become a prominent family and her parents divorced and her father married a woman Aisha despised? Or when Aisha, at twenty-one, confronted her father in his regal office, told him his children hated him, said defiantly, "I smoke!"?

Or would the beginning come after Aisha immigrated, became a U.S. citizen, met Norman while taking Israeli folk dancing lessons, and converted to Judaism? Or during the years after, when Shauna still lived with her mother, when she'd visit, slouch over the table, and shovel food onto her fork with her fingers, when Aisha would ride her mercilessly to learn manners? Or when Aisha got down on the floor with Shauna to play for hours with the first Barbie she gave her, the first of fifty-two? Or after Shauna told Aisha she wanted *her* to be her mommy?

Or would the beginning come after Shauna's mother, arguing that Norman wasn't fit to be a father, denied him visitation, when Norman, despairing in his efforts to see his daughter, told Aisha, "What's the point?" and Aisha made him drive to Shauna's house at the usual visitation hours so Shauna would know he wanted to see her?

Or would the beginning come when Shauna would peek around the corner of the window and see him sitting in his car with so sad a look on his face that thinking about it still brings tears to her eyes? Or after one of the times Shauna remembers her mother telling her that she was ugly? Or after one of the times Shauna remembers her mother drinking so much wine that Shauna had to tuck her in bed, turn off the lights, turn off the TV? Or after Shauna moved into the basement of her mother's house at about age eight and began coming and going as she pleased, day or night? Or when Shauna sneaked into the rooms of the people who rented from her mother and stole money to buy Christmas and Hanukkah gifts for her friends and family? Or the many, many times she'd lie to her mother about breaking a dish or staining a shirt to avoid her temper?

Or would the story's beginning come at the saddest of moments, after Shauna, at age eleven, went to her room after an argument and prayed that God would kill her mother? Or later that same night when Shauna found her mother in bed, stiff, mumbling, shaking, her eyes vacant, skin cold, and she ran from neighboring house to house until she found a phone to call for help? Or soon after, when her mother went into the nursing home, and Shauna, still believing her mother's debilitating seizure was somehow her fault, had moved in with Aisha and Norman and their newborn son, David?

Aisha believes she saw the trouble coming. "Norman had poop in his eyes," she says, meaning he didn't see it coming, that all the years he'd struggled as a divorced father to earn Shauna's affection had blinded him to her problems, which the two of them interpreted differently. Aisha is an orderly person, perhaps obsessively so. She styles hair at a Washington salon and spends her leisure hours painting intricate gouache illuminations in incandescent colors. She believes shoes should always be taken off at the door and replaced with slippers to save wear and tear on the Oriental rugs. She believes coats should be hung immediately in the living room closet, never draped over a couch or chair. She believes mail should be read and disposed of promptly.

Norman believes none of these things, does none of them, perhaps obsessively so. He skirts the slippers rule by wearing soft-soled shoes outside and in. He hangs up his coat only if he's not going out again that day. He accumulates mountains of mail—in the living room sits a stack dating back three years. In his basement office, from which he runs his real estate business, Norman's desk and floor are a blizzard of paper. Upstairs, Aisha's side of the bedroom is neat. Norman's is a disaster.

So Aisha nags. Norman ignores.

It's a kind of detente.

From the time Shauna was little, she was more like Norman. But early on, Aisha became convinced that Shauna wasn't just lovably disorganized like her dad, but that she literally didn't know how to live in a civilized fashion. After Shauna's mother was stricken, it was Aisha who went into Shauna's basement room and discovered how she lived—dirty and clean clothes strewn every-where, empty cereal boxes, cookie crumbs, dust, and dirt. Healthy people, she believed, didn't live this way. The mess symbolized deeper troubles. To Aisha, it was as if Shauna had been raised by wolves, raised with no rules. While Norman saw in Shauna an outgoing, cheerful girl, a survivor, Aisha saw "dys-function." It became her mission: She would teach Shauna to live like decent people.

Even Shauna says it was Aisha who taught her not only how to sit up at the table and use a knife and fork but also how to carry on a conversation during dinner rather than watch TV. Shauna says Aisha taught her to bathe and brush her teeth properly, to comb her hair thoroughly. For these lessons, Shauna thought she hated her stepmother. Aisha is not a soft-spoken woman. Her directions sounded like commands to Shauna, who wasn't used to following anyone's commands. Shauna says Aisha wouldn't say, "Can you please pick up that piece of paper?" She'd say, "Pick up that paper!" And so Shauna would snap, "No, you do it!" Aisha, raised in a family where "kids were pret-ty images," where if Aisha even thought the word *no* her mother would hear it, was faced with a child who not only thought the word *no* but said it—will-fully, defiantly, disrespectfully. At age ten, Shauna told Aisha, "Shut up!"

Aisha warned Norman that trouble was brewing. He didn't see it, not in Daddy's little girl. Aisha was developing another image: Shauna as charming manipulator, con artist. One day, Aisha found detergent swept under the bath-room rug. She asked Shauna if she'd spilled the detergent, and Shauna said no, absolutely not, not her, no way. Aisha told her it was okay if she had, just clean it up. But Shauna, who had spilled it, denied it to the death.

Aisha's favorite earrings, the first gift Norman had given her, turned up missing from her bedroom. Shauna denied that she'd touched them, although she'd actually worn them to school, lost one, and tossed out the other, think-ing Aisha wouldn't notice. Even after Aisha found the remaining earring in Shauna's trash, Shauna continued to deny that she'd worn them. Aisha noticed that clothes in her closet were turning up stained. Shauna, who'd worn and stained them, denied all knowledge. Dishes turned up missing. Shauna, who'd broken them, feigned ignorance.

Looking back, Shauna believes she was just acting as she always had at her mother's. Her mom might get terribly angry if Shauna accidentally broke a plate or stained a shirt, so she learned to deny all offenses. Her mother would never persist, the subject would be dropped, Shauna would be off the hook. "I'd just get away with everything," she says. But not with Aisha, who told herself Shauna might despise her strictness now, but she'd thank her later. Aisha could live with that. It was Norman who irritated her. He wouldn't stand behind her, didn't see Shauna's habits as hints of deeper troubles. He saw Aisha as a neat freak. He was comfortable with some disorder around him, and so was Shauna. Norman was more likely to see their disputes as those of two stubborn females clawing for space. He'd ask Aisha, "Are you having your period?" As if talking to children, he'd say, "You two have to learn to get along."

Norman was playing his usual role as mediator, but to Aisha, he was making the say-so of a child equal to the say-so of his wife, undermining her authority. Secretly, she began to question Norman's strength—was he so weak that he'd let a child bully his wife? Was this the man she wanted to be the father of her son? Was their marriage a mistake?

Then came Gettysburg—Shauna's bedroom. Aisha couldn't stand the mess. Yes, she believed Shauna had learned lousy habits that needed to be corrected for her own good. But, fancy justifications aside, it drove Aisha crazy to see clothes thrown in piles, bread tossed under the bed, a banana peel on the floor, dirty spoons everywhere. Aisha was on her constantly. To Aisha, this was *her* house, as her mother's house had been *her* house. Mother ruled; children obeyed. To Aisha, Shauna's room was a brazen act of disrespect, a slap in the face.

Norman, as usual, didn't think it was that big a deal, and Shauna played her parents' differences deftly: Look at Dad's office, look at Dad's side of their bedroom. To Shauna, it was all a struggle for control—Aisha wanted to dominate her and she would not be dominated.

By Shauna's junior year at Wootton High School, the ultimate escalation had begun. Shauna was cursing Aisha, calling her a bitch to her face. When Aisha talked to her, Shauna would stare into her eyes and mutter the obscene lyrics from rapper Dr. Dre's "Dre Day," something Shauna knew drove Aisha wild. The family went to a counselor, a woman named Connie, who, after talking with Shauna privately, told Aisha in front of Shauna and Norman that her North African upbringing had been more strict than that common in modern-day America. If she couldn't tolerate Shauna's room, she should close the door. Shauna beamed. Aisha, her confidence shaken, reluctantly agreed.

Aisha then talked to her own mother. "Maybe you have to be a real bull," her mother said. "Stand your ground even if you have to be called a bitch." So Aisha decided: No, she wasn't wrong; America was wrong. It was a sick society—the violence, crime, disrespect for parents. Shauna's room came to symbolize it all. Aisha would not have her young son, David, living in a house terrorized by a child. She told Shauna to clean up her room.

"We talked with Connie . . ."

"Connie is out!"

Aisha decided Shauna would understand only one language, her own. She went close to Shauna's face: "Now, listen to me good, you little bitch. You want to mess with me? I'm gonna be breathing down your neck. You're gonna see a true bitch in action." Did this help? "I felt great!" Aisha says. But no, Shauna's behavior toward Aisha and Aisha's behavior toward Shauna got worse and worse, right up to that Wednesday night.

*   *   *

On Thursday, a counselor called from Shauna's school and said, "I understand there was a problem last night." He said Shauna wanted to stay at a friend's house to cool down, and he asked Norman if that was okay. Norman said yes, as long as he knew where she was. When Shauna called later, she used a pay phone because she knew her dad would check his caller ID and then look up the number in his computerized cross listing of numbers and addresses to locate her. She refused to say where she was staying. "You don't love me, so I found people who will take care of me." Shauna was playing her own game of brinkmanship, trying to make her dad realize how much he'd miss her.

For almost a week, Norman and Aisha didn't know where Shauna was. They called the police, who said they could pick her up at school and bring her home but she'd probably just run again. Norman and Aisha weren't really worried. They believed Shauna wasn't tough enough to run away and hit the streets. And she was still attending school. No, they figured, she must be with a friend. When they thought back to the Wednesday night scene, they remembered she was fully dressed in bed and figured she was planning to bolt even then. Norman finally learned from the mother of a friend of Shauna's that she was staying with a girlfriend. Shauna had falsely told the girl's mother that her father knew where she was. Norman called the woman, who said, "Shauna's a wonderful girl. She's welcome to stay here as long as she wants."

"You wait!" Norman thought.

Actually, Shauna hadn't plotted her escape. She was dressed in bed that Wednesday night because she anticipated a blowup when her dad got home and planned to "book" out the door for a while if she had to. She took no extra clothes or even a toothbrush with her the next day to school. She figured she'd go home that night and face the lecture and the grounding that were sure to come. Then her new friend Crystal Steele, a good student who neither drank nor did drugs, got an idea. She was about to have a birthday party Shauna knew she wouldn't be allowed to attend, and Crystal suggested that Shauna stay at her house at least until the party. Shauna, eager to avoid the hassle at home, eager to attend Crystal's party, enlisted a friendly guidance counselor as a go-between. "It was a long six months of a night," Shauna says.

Shauna was the guest who came and stayed. It was a standoff. In a snit, she'd set out to prove how much her dad would miss her when she was gone. Norman and Aisha decided they'd do the same. Aisha told Norman, "She wants her freedom, give it to her." Life at home had become intolerable. Shauna was like a wild mare that had to be broken. She was going to follow the rules—talk to Aisha respectfully, keep her room clean, do her chores, go to school, get decent grades, tell Norman and Aisha where she was going, and come home at the designated hour. Or she couldn't live with them.

Shauna was to be ostracized, shunned. She wanted to live on her own, so let her—no clothes, no financial help, no visits with her little brother, no visits with her father, no Thanksgiving dinner with the family. Shauna thought they'd miss her; well, she'd learn that she'd miss them, too. When Shauna called and told Aisha she wanted a favorite pair of shoes, that she'd paid half their cost, Aisha said, "Okay, you want the right foot or the left foot?" In a move calculated to shock, Aisha told Shauna over the phone that since she no longer wanted to be a member of the family, Aisha was dismantling her bedroom, boxing up her belongings, and giving David the bigger room. Shauna was devastated by this symbolic act, but she stuck with her demand that Aisha be out of her life, that she have no authority over her. She would obey her dad. Norman rejected the demand. Shauna asked, "You're willing to lose your daughter over this?" Norman answered, "You'll always be my daughter, except you won't live here anymore."

It was a harsh conversation. But when Aisha overheard it, she was elated, believed she had her husband back. "I understood he was on a mission," she says. "He showed me he was a man." At that instant, Aisha knew no child was going to rule their family, destroy their marriage. As ever, Norman remained cool and rational. Shauna called and said she missed the times they'd go out for bagels or pizza together. Didn't he miss them, too? "I still do that stuff with David and Aisha," he told her calmly. Looking back, Shauna insists she wasn't trying to manipulate her dad's emotions. She says she only wanted him to say he missed her, he loved her. "My dad doesn't tell me that he loves me."

Aisha is reluctant to admit it, but the months when Shauna was gone were great. In recent years, she had felt her love for Shauna seeping away. "I had gotten such a cold heart toward that kid," she says. After all Aisha had done for her—more than Shauna's own mother had done, Aisha believed—this was how she was repaid. Aisha reminded herself of Shauna's tough childhood, that she was just a kid, but still she became embittered. When she found nasty notes Shauna had written about a girlfriend, she let that bitterness get the best of her and gave them to the girl. "I'm human," she says.

With Shauna gone, Aisha and Norman didn't argue once. He picked up Shauna's chores, spent more time with David because Shauna wasn't there to help out. Without having to worry about whether Shauna would come home on time, they went out more. Truth is, life was better without her. The other truth is, they wanted her back. Shauna suggested she be allowed to move to Atlanta to live with her half sister. Norman and Aisha refused. "We were not going to ship her problems off to someone else," says Aisha. "Her place was at home. The whole idea was to get her back home."

Shauna loved Aisha and she hated her. Looking back now, she knows this. Aisha once told Shauna that she looked at Aisha—at her beauty, confidence, success, ability to run a household—and saw what she wanted her own mother to be and despised Aisha for it. Aisha believed this because she had despised her own stepmother for living in the house that should have been her mother's house, Aisha's house. Shauna says Aisha was wrong. She envied Aisha, but she didn't wish Aisha's traits for her mother—she wished them for herself. Shauna hated Aisha's self-mastery, because Shauna felt she had none. "She was so strong," says Shauna. "Next to her I was low."

As her father did, Shauna saw herself as a survivor. She'd learned to look confident, never show weakness. She could charm birds from the trees. She was a relentless flirt, and she came to believe she could win over any guy if she tried. But she didn't feel good inside. She'd sit naked in front of the mirror in her room and cry at the sight of her body. She was beautiful but thought she was fat. And those guys who liked her, truth was, they were usually bad guys, guys who wanted one thing, and when she wouldn't give it, they'd dump her.

Worst of all, she felt she couldn't live up to her adored Daddy's expectations. She was a good competitive swimmer, but he wanted her to improve her time every week. "When I didn't," she says, "he looked down on me." Norman says that isn't true, that he simply believed it was good to set a high standard, to set personal goals and strive to achieve them. But sometimes the perfect can be the enemy of the good. Shauna quit swimming. Her grades then were average to above average, but Shauna felt they weren't good enough for her father, who had a college engineering degree and an MBA. If she got a B, it was, "Why isn't it an A?" If she got a 99 percent, it was, "Why isn't it a hundred?"

Aisha, who was a terrible student and who had felt stupid as a girl until she discovered her gift for art, believed Norman expected too much, that C's and B's were fine. Norman believed Aisha underestimated Shauna, that she only needed motivating. His parents had motivated him by setting a high standard in school, and he'd achieved it. "We find ourselves being our parents," he says. Her sophomore year, Norman made Shauna draw up a study plan for how she'd earn a 3.5 average. Yeah, right, Shauna thought, what a joke! She told herself she had no interest in being such a goody-goody. Actually, she believed she was too dumb to get high grades. "I gave up," she says.

Norman wanted Shauna to hang out with bright, successful kids like those in the Jewish youth group at their temple, felt it would rub off on her. Shauna went but hated it. To her, they were snobs, A students who made her feel stupid. If she asked about a math problem, it was always, "Gosh, all you have to do is . . ." She preferred to hang with kids who weren't as good in school as she was. It made her feel smart. At youth group, she'd sneak outside and smoke cigarettes. She portrayed herself as a rebel—cool and screw-you confident. Inside, she felt weak and afraid. She recognized this contradiction, which made her even more afraid.

Shauna began smoking cigarettes in seventh grade and took her first puff of marijuana in eighth. She and a girlfriend would sneak out at night, meet guys, and roam the neighborhood. By high school, she'd affected the baggy-shirted grunge look and begun listening to rap music. Freshman year, she downed a bottle of ibuprofen to commit suicide, became afraid, and told her father, who got her to vomit. Shauna says she was just mad at life, wanted to show everyone that they would miss her when she was gone. Her father remembers that it was over a boy. Either way, he didn't think it was a serious attempt. Sophomore year, Shauna began skipping classes. By the beginning of her junior year, when all hell broke loose, Shauna was hanging out with kids like herself—kids lost, angry, and afraid, in pain, kids who cursed at their parents, kids who were hit by their parents, kids who hit back.

"Losers," Aisha called them.

Norman attributed many of Shauna's problems to the bad influence of these kids, which still makes Shauna laugh. The bad kids hadn't sought her out, she'd sought them out. She was looking for them, looking for kids even more messed up than she was, kids who made her feel not only smart, but masterful. Driven to feel better about herself, Shauna stooped to conquer.

Meanwhile, as she and Aisha were degenerating into their cycle of rudeness and recrimination, Shauna and her father remained close. "I can't even tell you how much I love my father," she says. "I have just always loved him so much. He was always there for me. He was more than my father. He was my best friend." Before Shauna ran away, they'd sit in the kitchen almost every afternoon and talk about her day, or go out for a snack. There was a lot Shauna wasn't telling her dad, but she always believed that if she needed him, he'd be there.

Her sophomore year, Shauna had told her dad she had something to say, and, please, don't tell her he was disappointed. She could never stand that. When she was little, she'd ask him to spank her, but don't say he was disappointed. Then she said she'd been smoking cigarettes and marijuana. She'd quit both. She wanted him to say he was proud of her for quitting. Norman, who believed it was always important to maintain a high standard, said he couldn't tell her he was proud of her. And, yes, he was disappointed. "I thought more of you," he said. This time, Shauna wasn't crushed by her father's comments. This time, she was angry. When she lit up her first cigarette after that, she said, "This is for you, Dad!"

"What's left," Aisha told Norman after Shauna ran away, "is tough love." Problem was, Shauna saw the tough, but not the love. To her, everything Norman and Aisha did seemed to confirm that she was unwanted. She'd get off the phone after talking with her father and burst into tears. She'd complain bitterly about Aisha to Joan Steele, her friend Crystal's mother, but she'd never say a bad word about her dad. She'd only repeat what he had said—and Joan would be appalled. She couldn't believe a father could treat a child so coldly. She told him, "You have to remember that Shauna is the child and you are the adult."

Shauna seemed like a pretty normal sixteen-year-old to Joan. It irritated her that she'd talk on the phone forever. It upset her when she learned Shauna was skipping classes and her grades were falling to C's and D's. But Shauna was going through a rough patch, and Joan believes there's little one person can do to make another person change. It must come from within. "I think she liked it here because we accepted her the way she was," says Joan, who never saw the totally irresponsible child Norman expected her to see. Shauna was careful not to skip any class more than five times, because after that came an automatic failure. She was never more than a few minutes late for her curfew. She washed her dishes and kept her clothes picked up without being asked. She was always pleasant.

Shauna was touched by the Steeles. They weren't well-off, lived in a crowded little house. Joan was a housekeeper, her husband a painter and wallpaper hanger. But on Shauna's sixteenth birthday, they threw her a party with presents and balloons. At Christmas, Joan split the four hundred dollars or so she'd saved for Crystal's presents and bought gifts for Shauna, too. The Steeles are Pentecostal Christians, and Shauna, who had formally embraced Judaism at the age of thirteen, began attending their church. She was overwhelmed by what she saw as the congregation's warmth—compared with what she saw as the stiff, intellectual traditions of Judaism. Everybody hugged; near strangers said, "I love you." Joan noticed that Shauna seemed to crave these expressions of affection.

The Steeles weren't made perfect by their faith, and they imposed their own kind of family expectations—they'd once ordered Crystal to stop dating a black boy. "We're from the South," Joan says, and it would have torn her family apart. But Shauna chose not to judge the Steeles as she might have judged her parents. To her, the Steeles were the storybook family she had craved since she was a girl. Of her father and Aisha, she said, "They're too much into money and not enough into love." Shauna decided that the warmth she saw in the Steeles and their church emanated from their love of Christ. She began wearing a cross.

No other act, no words, no weapon could have cut Norman more deeply. Shauna swears her conversion was real, that she had no thought of getting back at her father by rejecting his faith. Her mother was a nonpracticing Catholic who celebrated Christmas heartily. Her half sister and half brother are Christians. She was never comfortable with Judaism—the kosher rules, the Hebrew prayers she couldn't understand, the intellectualism. Shauna loved praying to Jesus in plain English, talking person to person. It calmed her, strengthened her, diminished her anger. "This is what I needed," she says.

The standoff continued. Meanwhile, tension grew between Shauna and Crystal, who was having her own problems as a teenager and who came to believe Shauna was stealing her place in the family and the church. Shauna, outgoing to Crystal's withdrawn, was always the center of attention. Although the girls are still good friends, sometimes they didn't talk for weeks during Shauna's stay. Then Shauna pulled a dumb stunt. She spent the weekend with a boyfriend. She just disappeared, didn't tell Joan, and Joan got scared. If something happened to Shauna, she was afraid Norman would sue her.

When Shauna turned up, Joan laid down the law as Norman had done: "I love you, but if you do this again you can't live here." Although Joan never asked Shauna to leave, Shauna knew it was time. But she also knew she couldn't just move back home, that she and Aisha would pick up where they'd left off. If their "tough love" plan was supposed to have made Shauna appreciate the family, she says, it backfired. She felt more unloved than ever. She told her father she wanted all of them to go to family counseling. "We don't need counseling," he said. "You do."

Through a friend, Shauna heard about Open Door, a home for runaways. Kids move in and go through individual and family counseling before moving back home. Every night for weeks Shauna called hoping for an opening. When it came, she moved in and saw Norman and Aisha for the first time in six months. They sat on the couch and held hands.

"All kissy-face," Shauna says.

Emotions are mysterious to Norman. He will quickly cry at a sad movie, and Aisha and Shauna believe that, although he'd never say so, his feelings are easily hurt by rude remarks from them or even from six-year-old David. But Norman doesn't allow himself to think with his emotions, is proud that he doesn't. And if Aisha likes shoes, coats, and mail in their place, Norman likes emotions in their place, safely under control.

It's a family joke that Norman was once wrong. But he says, also joking, that he can't remember when it was. When he looks back at his choices he doesn't remember any he'd call mistakes. Norman believes that everything happens for a reason and that every painful experience carries a kernel of redemption. He had a terrible marriage with Shauna's mother, but Shauna came from it. And if he hadn't gotten a divorce, he wouldn't have met Aisha. In his life, Norman was confronted with realities and opportunities. He analyzed them, decided what to do, and did it. Sure, things didn't always work out the way he planned, but he can't say his choices were wrong. Some had consequences he hadn't anticipated, but that's not the same as being wrong. His judgment was solid, based on the knowledge at hand.

Norman grew up the oldest son of a well-to-do Boston entrepreneur. After college, he tried working in the family business, but when he told his father he wanted more money, his father said, "You want more money, so find somebody else to pay it." Norman did. They were never close, really, and when Norman divorced his first wife, a Jew, and married Shauna's mother, a Christian, his father would have nothing to do with her. Looking back, Norman wonders if his second marriage, at age thirty-three, wasn't his own rebellion against his father. Norman, too, was judged by high standards. He told his stepdaughter, Shauna's half sister, that he never was able to live up to his father's expectations. And his elderly mother recently told Norman that he hasn't been the success she expected him to be in life, that his father was smarter.

Norman is a traditionalist—he honors duty, responsibility, and trust. Asked to describe his hopes for Shauna as a woman, he says, "Responsibility, honesty, integrity. A responsible member of society." He doesn't mention happiness or love, as Aisha does when asked the same question. When boys visit Shauna, Norman expects them to sit and talk with him. He asked one boy, "What are your intentions toward my daughter?" Over the years, Norman's Jewish faith has become more important to him—from Friday night Shabbat dinner to Sabbath services to Passover seders to keeping kosher to reciting kaddish, the mourner's prayer, at the temple on the anniversary of his father's death.

But perhaps above all, Norman honors trust. And as Shauna moved into her teen years, she lost his trust. Despite Aisha's warnings, Norman believed she was doing fine until her junior year began. Her grades were okay. She'd passed her lifeguard exam and had worked as a lifeguard that summer. He trusted her and let her come and go without too many questions. Later, when he discovered she'd been running wild, he felt betrayed. "I felt Shauna would listen to me and I didn't think she would lie. Aisha felt that she didn't listen and she did lie." Aisha, he says, was closer to correct. "Sometimes it's easier to be unaware."

Norman found cigarettes in Shauna's room—this after she'd told him she quit. He tore them up and left the mess on Shauna's bed for her to clean up. Norman listened to Shauna's rap recordings and was appalled at their violence and obscenity. He confiscated them. Shauna's time on the phone was limited to a certain amount each night. When the phone kept being busy when he called home, Norman monitored it and discovered Shauna was exceeding her limit. He suspected she wasn't keeping kosher dietary restrictions, eating pork or eating beef and cheese together, when she was away from home, and he was right about that, too.

Then the Friday night before Shauna ran away, she came home and said she was skipping Shabbat dinner for a high school football game. Norman said no. Shabbat was nearly a sacred tradition in his home. Missing Shabbat had to be approved in advance. But when two scraggly, slouching, shuffling guys came to the door, Shauna—as angry and defiant as she routinely was with Aisha— said, "I'm going and you can't stop me." She got her coat and left. Good Lord, what had happened to Daddy's Number One Helper? Overnight, everything had gone to hell. Overnight, emotions were no longer in their place.

After two weeks at Open Door, Shauna finally came home. Norman and Aisha believe she was a wild mare broken, her back against the wall, with no place else to go. Shauna scoffs at that notion. She went to Open Door, she says, because she knew the center would require her father and Aisha to go into family counseling with her as part of the program. Shauna genuinely wanted to go home. She'd learned a lot—or maybe just grown up a lot—while she was gone. She decided that 95 percent of all the conflict with her dad and Aisha was her own fault—she'd been lost. During the months she was gone, she mostly dropped the friends Norman and Aisha hated. She decided they were bad for her. She began noticing when other kids talked rudely to their parents, and decided she didn't like it. They sounded like brats, babies. She began to feel good about her body and her looks, to believe she was pretty. She began to think about college and about buckling down at school. She began to think about getting a good job someday and having a family of her own.

Although the Steeles had paid her way and Norman called her time with them "a six-month pajama party," Shauna believed she'd done all right without her family. True or not, believing she could get along without them somehow freed her from the need to prove she could get along without them. Whether it was a matter of getting away or growing up, she no longer saw her right to live in a messy bedroom as a powerful symbol of her autonomy.

Her view of the future changed: Putting up with her dad and Aisha through high school no longer looked like forever, as it did when she was thirteen, fourteen, fifteen. Shauna now looked ahead and saw that she didn't want to someday have children with no grandfather. She'd seen Joan light up her grandkids' lives, and she wanted her father to do that for her children someday. But, finally, Shauna simply loved her dad more than she could ever say, couldn't bear losing him. Although he may not say it, she knew he loved her, too.

It was the lifeline between them.

Six months after Shauna moved home, she and Aisha have become friends, and Shauna often wonders why it is so hard for her to tell Aisha she loves her, why it is so hard for Aisha, too, to say those words. Shauna now keeps her room tidier, not tidy enough to suit Aisha, really, but at least she doesn't leave dirty spoons and half-eaten snacks lying around anymore. Aisha lives with it. Like Shauna, she reminds herself that Shauna will be gone soon. Aisha doesn't get home from work until late, and Shauna often cooks dinner, does the dishes, helps David with his homework, gets him ready for bed. Shauna has realized that some of her anger toward Aisha grew from listening to her yell at her father for not always doing these chores as Aisha would like. Shauna couldn't stand hearing her talk to her dad as if he were a child. So she has picked up the slack herself.

The family has continued to meet with an Open Door counselor, who doesn't see all the family's troubles as Shauna's fault. Instead, she probes the family dynamic that helped create their mutual troubles. She has even called Shauna a "stabilizing force" in the family: By focusing on her problems, Aisha and Norman have been able to avoid their own. Behind these closed doors, Shauna has learned more than she wants to about Aisha and her father's lives and relationship, even about their sex life. She has learned adult secrets—that as the real estate boom has gone bust, her dad's confidence has suffered. She now believes Aisha is dominant in the marriage, and that she and Aisha are driven to take care of her dad, who is emotionally numb yet loving in his own distanced way. The counseling has moved on to Aisha and Norman, and Shauna now believes Aisha's love is more important to her father's happiness than Shauna's love. They'll be together long after she is gone.

The counseling has changed the way Shauna and Aisha talk to each other. The accusatory tone, the bitterness, is gone. Shauna has noticed that Aisha thanks her far more often for her help around the house. Aisha sometimes thinks this is silly—that people shouldn't be thanked for doing what they should do anyway—but she has realized that Shauna appreciates it, seems to need it. She has noticed that Shauna has been thanking her more, too.

Aisha is still angry at Shauna. She still doesn't believe Shauna's version of why she came home, figures she's gilding the lily, that she wore out her welcome and needed a place to land. But Shauna *is* different, and that has made Aisha different. Not long ago, Shauna called Aisha at work, said her dad and David weren't home, and asked what time she'd be home. Aisha, distrustful, beeped Norman and said, "She's up to something." Norman went home and found Shauna up to nothing. For her cynicism, Aisha felt ashamed.

Shauna is still angry at Aisha, too. She gave her friend those nasty notes, but most of all, she stole Shauna's bedroom and gave it to David. Shauna doesn't sound grown up when she talks about this, but childish and whiny. It means something deep to her that her bedroom disappeared, makes her feel unwelcome, like a guest, as if she too could be made to disappear. It hurts her in a way that's hard for Aisha to understand. After all, it's only a bedroom. But Shauna has reined in her temper. She prays a lot to Jesus and says this calms her. When she came home a little late after school the other day and her father said she should've called, she said, "You're right, Dad, I should've called. I'm sorry." Soon after, Aisha gave Shauna a house key, which she'd withheld, believing it symbolized responsible family membership. "I think she feels I've grown up a lot," Shauna says. "I hope."

Aisha, the former Evil Empress, has even become Shauna's ally. Norman, still feeling that Shauna violated his trust too many times, that she's too irresponsible, insists that she call home when she arrives at, say, the movie theater with a date, and then call home again when she's leaving the theater. "I just feel more comfortable knowing where she is," he says. Aisha believes that at seventeen Shauna should have a curfew, let them know where she's going, call if she must be late or if there's a change in plans. Right now, for every minute Shauna is home past her curfew, her father demands that she arrive home half an hour early the next time she goes out.

Shauna: "He just wants to protect me."

Aisha: "It's just plain control, stupid control."

Aisha has told Shauna that she doesn't want her to smoke cigarettes, that it's a filthy, deadly habit, but that she can't really stop her. If Shauna does smoke, she should smoke weak cigarettes. Aisha has told Shauna that it's best to defer sexual intercourse, but if she's going to have sex, she should use birth control and latex condoms for AIDS and venereal disease prevention. Norman tells Shauna she should absolutely wait until college to have sex and never smoke cigarettes. His reasoning, naturally, is logical: Too many sexual diseases are abroad, and if she smokes cigarettes she violates the terms of their low-rate nonsmokers' insurance plan.

But Shauna has begun to wonder if her father's vaunted rationality may sometimes mask emotions that are really ruling his decisions. Maybe he just doesn't want his little girl to have sex yet? Maybe he just doesn't want her to smoke? For more than a year now, he has told Shauna that she's not responsible enough to get her driver's license. He told her she needed to have a B average, be acting respectfully at home, and have a part-time job to pay her car insurance. Shauna did all those things.

Then she came home late one afternoon before she got her house key and found that her father had left home and locked the door. He later said he just wasn't thinking, but at the time Shauna figured he was mad because she'd gotten home a little late. It was bitterly cold, and Shauna, in frustration, kicked in the screen door. Her father told her she couldn't get her license until she paid for the door. Shauna wonders what new, rational requirement will come next.

At Wootton, where Shauna is a senior, her counselor and several of her teachers are surprised to hear that her father believes she's immature and irresponsible. Says a teacher who has known Shauna for years, "He doesn't see a thousand children a day." At Slade's American Grill, where Shauna works as a part-time hostess, the manager says she's an exceptionally responsible worker. And at Open Door, they'd like Shauna to return as a "peer counselor" to help other runaways.

Norman: "In a year, I'll have very little control." Maybe being strict to the end will keep her from making a few last bad mistakes—maybe, in that year, she'll get good sense.

Aisha: "He's having difficulty letting go."

Shauna has for years said that when she turns eighteen, she'll stop using the name Shauna in favor of her middle name, Mellyssa. The name Shauna, she says, belongs to the fat, ugly, frightened little girl she used to be. Norman has told her he won't help pay for college if she drops the name Shauna, which he chose because of the Hebrew name, Shoshana, meaning lily or rose. Shauna is so far considering only Christian colleges, and Norman hasn't objected. "My dad has been really good lately," she says. "I think his devotion to me is winning out." But Norman has fussed about her wanting to attend a Christian school to Aisha, who told him Shauna must find her own way, he cannot find it for her.

"I really have a lot of trouble with Shauna and her Christianity," Norman says candidly. When he talks about this, his eyes water. He tells himself Shauna isn't really a Christian. He once told Aisha, "The day she stops being a Jew, she stops being my daughter." When Shauna moved back, she agreed to practice Judaism in the house. On the other hand, Norman agreed that she could also go to Christian services if she could get a ride. Norman wouldn't take her. She couldn't have Christian images in the house, and she could only wear a cross around her neck inside her shirt. Norman can barely tolerate seeing Shauna wear a cross. "Every time it comes out of my shirt," she says, "my dad almost rips it off my chest."

It doesn't help Norman to remember that he married a Christian woman perhaps to rebel against his father. His Jewish faith has been handed down. It's who he is. He'd be friendly with Shauna and her future family if they were Christian, but he couldn't celebrate Easter and Christmas with them. And his grandchildren wouldn't know the Hebrew prayers. After he dies, Shauna wouldn't recite kaddish in the temple on the anniversary of his death. "My family gave me a religion," he says, "and I have to give it to my children."

Shauna insists her conversion isn't a repudiation of her father. "I love my dad so much," she says. But her response to his anguish is uncharacteristically cool: "He's not going to give up his religion for me. Why should I give up mine?"

Shauna can't wait until her little brother, David, is a teenager. Aisha and Norman think *she* was weird, wild, dysfunctional. They'll find out! She was just a typical kid! Aisha thinks David's perfect, just wait! Shauna's going to laugh and laugh! She teases Aisha about this all the time. And Aisha teases back, says she can't wait until Shauna has teenagers. The girl wants four kids, good God! She'll learn that Aisha and Norman weren't so crazy. Wait till she knows what it is to worry over a child. Then she'll thank Aisha, who plans to live long enough to gloat. Back and forth they banter, with a new affection and respect.

Aisha: "She's a fabulous kid."

Shauna: "She's a good woman."

And Norman, always so sensible, so confident he'll find a kernel of redemption in each painful experience, well, he's not able to be so flip as Shauna and Aisha, not yet able to make light of what has transpired, to fashion from their story a triumphant ending. He wants to get there. He doesn't know if he will. He's angry and hurt, in pain, afraid that he'll lose Shauna to her new faith, that he's facing something he truly can't control. What does it mean to be a family? Norman hasn't figured it out. Does anyone, ever? Or is the exploration itself enough?

How will it all come out?

"I have no idea," Norman says. "It's still going on."

February 11, 1996

To Have and Have Not

In her dream, Sara's apartment in Florida is much like her apartment in Gaithersburg, Maryland: a fair-size living room, a dining room niche, a cramped kitchen with old appliances, and two bedrooms, one for her and Dan and the other for the boys, Patrick and Connor. Patrick, at age four, sleeps in a bed that was her uncle's boyhood bed back in the thirties. Connor, a year old, sleeps in a crib that was not only her uncle's, but later her mother's, her older sister's, and then her own. Sara doesn't think of the bed and the crib as heirlooms but as hand-me-downs. In her dream, which she has every couple of weeks, the apartment in Florida is always more cheerful than her Gaithersburg apartment, filled with light and laughter. She is always relaxed, never frantic. In her dream, she drives a Ford Taurus station wagon. She and Dan don't argue about whether to pay the electric bill or the phone bill first. Dan, who just turned twenty-eight, isn't worried about getting more hours at Radio Shack, and Sara isn't worried about how she'll afford a birthday gift for Dan or about losing her job as a phone operator on the three-to-eleven shift at the Holiday Inn. No, Patrick is running in the surf and Connor is playing in the sand, or, sometimes, they're all at Disney World, where she went with her own father twenty years ago, when she was six years old, before her feet began to splay outward and the rheumatoid arthritis was diagnosed. Over the last few difficult years, with marriage and children and barely getting by, Sara has had this dream so often that she now looks forward to its coming and enters into it comfortably, knowing even in her sleep that it is a dream, and dreaming it anyway.

In Dan Sullivan's pocket this morning, a Tuesday, are three dollar bills and 71 cents in odd change. In Sara Sullivan's purse are nine dollar bills and $1.50 in change, which is a lot of spare money for her. It's left over from a particularly frugal weekly trip to the supermarket. In their savings account this morning, they have $12.53. That's a total cash reserve of $26.74. On Friday, Sara will get a paycheck for two weeks of work, seventy-seven hours at $7.02 an hour—$540.54 gross, less $58.09 in taxes and Social Security, 78 cents for $40,000 in life insurance, $11.08 for dental insurance, and, the killer and the godsend, $69.23 for medical insurance. That's $401.36 take-home for two weeks. Dan's last two-week take-home paycheck, after all his deductions, was $219.53, about what his next paycheck is also expected to be—down about $100 each from his checks before Christmas, when sales were good and before the new Radio Shack opened nearby and siphoned off customers from his store.

Together, Dan and Sara will have about $1,240 to live on for four weeks. In 1994, they grossed $20,478—about a third more than the $15,142 poverty level for a family of four. Dan and Sara receive no state or federal assistance, although this year they do expect to get $843 from the federal Earned Income Tax Credit for poor and lower-income workers. They also get $816 a month in day-care subsidy from Montgomery County's Working Parents Assistance Program. Sara's mother and Dan's parents have been paying the $597 remaining on their monthly day-care bill. Even with the help, if either one of them lost their job, they'd be destitute in a month.

Dan and Sara Sullivan live in the American netherworld between poverty and the middle class. It is a world in which more and more young families have found themselves in the last fifteen years, as their median income has dropped dramatically, well-paying jobs have become harder to find, and the value of a college degree has risen steeply. Many of the forces driving these changes are global, but their consequences on families like the Sullivans are deeply personal.

Dan and Sara were raised in middle-class families in the suburban Maryland towns of Olney and Bethesda. Dan's father and Sara's mother finished college, as did Dan's brother and Sara's sister. But Dan and Sara didn't get through college or trade school, made other choices, and now find that they have reversed the classic American climb up the generational ladder of mobility. Dan and Sara weren't the best and the brightest or the most mature of kids. They drifted while others made tracks. They had children early, which limited their chances to make up for lost time and bad choices. So maybe they alone are responsible for their predicament. But maybe the narrow options society now offers them, the slimness of their hold on security, and the impact this has on their parents and their own children should be a wake-up call for all Americans. Because, responsibility aside, Dan and Sara are among a rising population of struggling, disoriented young people learning to live without the comforts and advantages they took for granted as children.

"Reality hits you like a brick," says Sara.

"I'm older and wiser," says Dan.

The Sullivans' estimated montly expenses:

Rent and heat . . .$705	Phone $50
Food $160	Cable $25
Car gas $60	Laundry $24
Electricity $30	Car Payment $287

Total. $1,341

Monthly shortfall $101

This does not include any money for medical bills before reaching their $200 family insurance deductible each year, day care, upkeep on the car, Christmas and birthday gifts for each other and the kids, clothing, vacations, an occasional romance novel for Sara or a classical CD for Dan, taking Patrick and Connor to *The Lion King* or a meal at Roy Rogers, not to mention any savings for college, retirement, or emergencies. Yet right now, Dan and Sara are in better financial shape than they have been in years. A few weeks ago, they sat down with Dan's parents, who still live in suburban Olney, and Sara's mother, who now lives in Frederick, Maryland, and figured up their total debt— more than $5,000. Dan could only shake his head in disbelief. He'd been putting out of his mind what he couldn't pay anyway—the credit card bills from years ago to cover diapers and car repairs when Sara was unemployed for eight months, an $800 extended warranty on a Ford Festiva Dan sold three years ago, long-past extravagances such as a $40 meal at Bennigan's and a $75 trip to the Renaissance Festival, as well as $2,000 in medical bills from Connor's prenatal care and delivery and an operation Sara had to have after the birth, plus her tubal ligation.

Dan's and Sara's folks, who aren't wealthy, agreed to pay off the bills. In return, Mary Ellen and Jerry Sullivan, who at fifty-five and sixty-one are nearing retirement, insisted on taking over the couple's finances—actually taking their paychecks in hand—for the next few months and setting up an accounting system and a budget so Dan and Sara know exactly what is coming in and going out. Otherwise, Dan's parents and Sara's mom, Margaret Magruder, feared that the financial woes of the new generation might eventually destroy the financial security of the old. Because as long as they have a dollar, they will never let their grandkids live in poverty. But they are afraid. As Dan's folks say, even in their toughest days, when they were starting out, they never struggled like Dan and Sara, never saw so little light.

If Sara's dream is pleasant and down-to-earth, Dan's is strange and esoteric. In his dream, he is reading, say, philosophical passages from the mystical Jewish cabala, and he notices an intriguing, previously unconsidered, passage that he shares with a famous archaeologist. Later, in a faraway land, they uncover a great discovery that will earn Dan neither money nor fame but will transform mankind's conception of itself into something better, more decent, more enlightened. It is a grand and noble dream. It makes Sara squirm.

"Let's stick to the present," she tells Dan, who has taken a deeper interest in religion in the last year, not only in his traditional Catholicism, but also in the teachings of the Jewish Torah and the Islamic Koran. When Dan bought those books, along with several by the Catholic theologian Thomas Merton, Sara was annoyed. As if they could afford it! When Dan told Sara recently that he'd like to someday become a deacon in their parish church, she was annoyed again. As if he didn't have enough to do with his time! Dan tells Sara that all the great books of religion teach the same message: Be good to one another. In the last year, since Dan has, as he puts it, made God his silent partner, a calm has descended upon him. He believes he is more tolerant of difficult customers in the store, hence a better salesman, and more patient with the boys and Sara, hence a better father and husband. He now believes that if he puts his future in the hands of God, his life, his family's life, will work out for the best. He paraphrases a promise in Matthew, chapter 6: "If He cares for the birds of the air and the lilies of the field, how much more will He care for you?"

Sara sighs and looks away.

Dan is a tall man with narrow hips and wide, angular shoulders. He speaks slowly, without inflection, and he moves with deliberate grace, this morning combing his thick brown hair back off his forehead with his right hand again and again. Dan and Sara have run out of the Aqua Net hair spray Dan usually uses to keep it in place, and Sara hasn't budgeted the $1.99 to replace it yet. So as fast as Dan combs his hair, it flops back over his forehead. Sara laughs warmly. She will get the Aqua Net next time she goes shopping.

Sara is a short woman with a rounding figure. She has gained fifteen pounds since she met Dan seven years ago. She's more animated than Dan, laughs often, talks faster, has a nervous energy to balance his laconic calm. Her hair is short and dark and bushy, and for her 20/1600 vision she wears thick glasses that magnify her eyes to prominence on her face. Perhaps as a consequence of her arthritis, she is more cynical than Dan, less trusting of people, even a touch bitter. Face it, she says with certainty, not many men as handsome as Dan would have married a woman who looks like her. Over the years, the arthritis has curved Sara's shoulders, knotted her knuckles, eaten holes in her bones, destroyed joints in her toes, made her walk stiffly, and left her in pain.

Tonight, they sit eating dinner among the items of their lives: A dining room table Sara's sister gave them two weeks ago when she got a new one. Dishes and silverware that once belonged to Sara's mom. Two small framed pictures on the dining room wall that depict Parisian street scenes and that also came from the home of Sara's mother. A silk flower arrangement from her sister's wedding two years ago. Two matching table lamps Sara's mother bought with Green Stamps three decades ago. A grandfather clock that runs on one AA battery that Dan and Sara got as a prize for touring a new trailer park resort near Fredericksburg, Virginia.

A set of shelves that was a gift to Sara on her fourteenth birthday and now holds their thirteen-inch TV. A tall bookcase that once belonged to Sara's mother and now holds a large collection of movies, most of which were bought years ago or were gifts from their parents. A short bookshelf Dan got in the fifth grade. A cabinet stereo that once belonged to Dan's grandmother. A CD player Dan's parents gave him for Christmas in 1986. A lot of brightly colored children's toys, mostly gifts from Dan's folks and Sara's mom. A rectangular coffee table and an octagonal side table Dan traded for an old stereo soon after they were married. A Beta player Sara bought for $15 at a yard sale. A VHS player Dan's parents gave him in 1992. A long, worn, green couch that came from friends of Sara's stepfather's. A microwave Sara's sister gave them when she got a new one. In their bedroom is a bed they bought used at Cort Furniture for $99. Two master bedroom dressers from Sara's girlhood room. Two bedroom end tables that were her mother's. In the boys' room are the bed and the crib handed down in Sara's family for three generations and two dressers, which were donated by Patrick's old babysitter, a friend of Sara's mother's.

"I don't wish to be rich," says Sara.

"Being a millionaire is not my main objective," says Dan.

"I would like to be comfortable," says Sara.

Sara would like to take a vacation, go to Ocean City for a few days, and play on the beach with the boys. Or take a boat ride from Annapolis to St. Michaels and back. She'd love taking her dream trip to Disney World, but that's pie in the sky. They went to Kings Dominion once, and Sara couldn't enjoy herself knowing they were spending the electric bill. She'd like to painlessly plop down five dollars on an Iris Johansen romance novel, pick up a half-gallon of ice cream at the supermarket whenever she wants, and buy Chef Boy-ar-dee ravioli even when it's not on sale.

She'd like to take Patrick to a movie, a matinee for four dollars a ticket. She can't now, because she'd spend the whole time thinking about how four dollars is two loaves of bread and a gallon of milk. Someday, she'd love that Ford Taurus station wagon from her dream so she could drive the boys and their friends around in "mom's taxi" in that idealized suburban way. Someday, she'd like to spend two hundred dollars and throw Patrick a big birthday party at the Discovery Zone. She'd like to have been able to buy Connor nice gifts for his first Christmas and first birthday. But, believing he wouldn't yet know the difference, she got him diapers and baby food.

Sara has bought herself only two pairs of jeans, a top, and an inexpensive dress in the last year. Dan hasn't had a new shirt or tie or jacket in years, unless his folks gave it to him for Christmas or his birthday. So Sara would love to buy a nice dress just once a year and wear it out to dinner with Dan, who could get dressed up, too. They'd go to—why not dream big—Maison Blanche. She went there once in high school with a date, when her mother loaned them her credit card—and the bill was sixty-five dollars!

If they ever get flush, if Dan gets the Radio Shack manager's job he's working toward and is earning $25,000 or $30,000 a year, she'd like to buy one of those diamond tennis bracelets she sees in the Evans discount jewelry ads, $249. And a set of the gold earrings, $59.99. She'd like to go to the Kennedy Center's "Shear Madness," and just once she'd like to go hear the National Symphony Orchestra live. With tickets from $10 to $43, that's fantasy.

But more than anything right now, Sara would like to buy clothes for Patrick and Connor, which she never does, because Dan's folks are generous enough to buy them. It's embarrassing to admit, but Sara doesn't even know what size her own sons wear. Wouldn't it be special to go to Penney's and just *buy* the boys each an outfit, pay from her own purse? She'd never say this to Dan's folks, of course, afraid she'd sound ungrateful.

Dan would like a new couch. Theirs is coming apart at the seams, and little pieces of plastic innards are beginning to poke through and prick their skin. He'd like a *new* couch, one nobody else has sat, snacked, or snored upon. He'd like a twenty-seven-inch TV because TV is about all they can afford for entertainment. He'd like a used ten-dollar video once in a while, too. They've watched their favorite videos—*The Last of the Mohicans; A History of the World, Part I; The Terminator; Jurassic Park*—so many times they've memorized the faces in the crowd scenes. Dan would like updated Trivial Pursuit questions for when their friends Paul and Hale come over for their regular Saturday night get-together. They've got all the answers memorized. He'd like to buy a new CD maybe once a month—starting with Mussorgsky's "A Night on Bald Mountain" or Rafael Fruhbeck de Burgos's version of Carl Orff's "Carmina Burana." And just once a year, he'd like to take the family to the Outback Steakhouse and never even look at the prices.

Dan has never mentioned it to Sara before, but he has seen her eyeing those Evans ads, heard her say, "Oh, that's beautiful." He thought, "Maybe next year around Christmas time I can grab some of that stuff and put it under the tree." Then on Valentine's Day, he'd like to have flowers sent to Sara at work so everybody can ooh and aah over how much her husband loves her. This year, he couldn't even afford the $1.99 roses at the 7-Eleven. He laughed darkly to himself: "I could get flowers but wouldn't have gas in the car to get them to her."

Dan would like to own a house, wants his boys, as he did, to grow up in one. A town house instead of a split-foyer would be fine, as long as it is a place with their own rooms, a place they know is *their* home, with that feeling you get. And someday, way down the road, if either Patrick or Connor calls for financial help in the way that Dan and Sara have needed help from their folks, he'd like to say, "Just come by. I'll help you out." But more than anything right now, Dan would like to take Patrick to Lakeforest Mall, let him wander the stores, and then, without even thinking, buy him a gift, maybe a Power Ranger doll for ten dollars. Dan can't do that. He doesn't even like to go to the store with his son because it makes Patrick learn to yearn for things Dan can't provide. Fearing his son's judgment of him someday, Dan wants to land that manager's job before Patrick is old enough to realize how much his father can't give him. Before Patrick is old enough to compare his own father with those of other boys.

Get out of Sara's way, because she is on a mission: rush in and out of Weis Market as fast as she can, spend as little as possible, and save a bundle. Her mother-in-law has budgeted $40 a week from their paychecks for groceries, and Sara has an additional $30 left over from money her mom gave her. "Dan doesn't know how to shop the way I do."

Esskay pork-and-turkey hot dogs are on sale for $1.39, compared with $2.79, $2.39, and $1.99 for other brands. Sara's got plenty of hot dogs, but the price is too right and she snatches two packs for the freezer. Weis Quality grape jelly, thirty-two ounces, is $1.49, compared with Smucker's grape at $1.75. A package of Weis Noodles and Sauce Alfredo is $2.80 a pound— Lipton's is $4.32. Weis ravioli is 71.4 cents a pound—Chef Boy-ar-dee ravioli, full price today, is $1.31 a pound. Unlike most other Weis items, the store-brand ravioli tastes awful to Sara. So she'll wait for Chef Boy-ar-dee to go on sale. Usually, Weis butter spread is the best buy at 49.5 cents a pound—compared with Fleischmann's at 96.5 cents. But today, Sara notices, Touch of Butter is on sale for an amazing 33 cents a pound. She gets three pounds. "You gotta check your bottom line."

Weis toasted oats are $1.80 a pound—Cheerios are *on sale* at $2.78 a pound. Weis pot pies, which Dan takes to work for lunch every day, are 50 cents each—Banquet pot pies are 59 cents and Swanson's are 87 cents. And soda? It's almost a crime to Sara. She used to buy it from the machine at work for 50 cents a can, or $6 a dozen. Then she switched to buying twelve-packs of Weis soda for about $2.50 and bringing them to work with her—a $3.50 savings. For home, Weis cola is 31.2 cents a quart in the biggest bottle—Pepsi is 60.8 cents a quart. And bread? It *is* a crime to Sara. *Two* twenty-ounce loaves of Weis Big One bread cost $1.18—*one* twenty-two-ounce loaf of Wonder Bread costs $1.85. Sara is satisfied with her shopping trip. "That's how my mother taught me to shop."

Although Sara grew up in affluent Bethesda, she was no rich kid. Her mom divorced when Sara was a year old, and they moved in with Sara's grandmother. Her mother, a nurse with a degree from Georgetown University, went to work for Montgomery County and eventually earned her master's degree.

But there were rough years. Sara sometimes wore secondhand clothes, and her mother always shopped with an eagle eye.

In high school, Sara missed many months because of her arthritis—therapy, operations, casts, walkers. She graduated on time with average grades but was afraid she couldn't make it at a four-year college and went to Montgomery College, where she earned more than a year's credit, until she failed a required algebra class. Discouraged, she went to Katharine Gibbs business school and landed a job as an office clerk earning $6.25 an hour, although her arthritis has always made typing hard. She and Dan met at church. Dan was dating a friend of hers and they palled around as a threesome, until Dan and the friend split and he and Sara started dating. Dan sent her flowers at work. They spent a weekend at Ocean City. After only a few months, he asked Sara to marry him. They got engaged in 1990 and married in 1991. Her pregnancy with Patrick was unplanned, and they had him with little thought or worry about how he would change their lives. After all, Sara was working full time earning $250 a week as an office clerk, and Dan was working fifty hours a week at Hi-Gear Discount Auto Parts, earning $6.50 an hour, $325 a week.

"Those times were nice," says Sara of the days before Patrick. "But then you get into the reality of it, moving away from home and having to pay for everything yourself. That's when reality kicks in . . . If we didn't have our families, we might have had to put the kids up for adoption. That's just the way it is."

Soon after Patrick's birth, Sara lost her job and spent eight months searching for work, three and four interviews a week. The whole time, she was never offered a job. "I applied for all these jobs and nobody accepted me," she says. "I started to wonder why." She believes her arthritis scares off employers. But the employers have also scared off Sara. A couple of years later, when Dan's mother told Sara about a phone operator's job open with the federal government, Sara baffled her mother-in-law when she didn't even apply. But by then Sara, badly bruised by so many rejections, had her job at the Holiday Inn, and she feared having still another employer tell her she wasn't good enough.

While Sara was out of work, she and Dan were living rent-free in the Bethesda house of Sara's mother, who had remarried and moved into her new husband's house. Still, they spent Sara's $2,000 in savings and ran up credit card debt just paying their basic bills. Once, during her months out of work, Sara applied to Montgomery County for heating fuel assistance—they had accumulated a $432 winter heating bill. She was denied aid because Dan earned too much money, and Sara bitterly recalls a humiliating exchange with a woman who spoke imperfect English:

"Why don't you walk?"

"Why don't I walk?"

"No, why don't you *work?*"

"I'm unemployed."

"Well, what do you spend your money on?"

Sara was unaccustomed to being talked to that way. Of this and other trips to social agencies where she was also told Dan earned too much money for them to receive government help, she told her mother, "They treat you like scum." Finally, three years ago, acting on a tip from the mother of a friend of Dan's, Sara landed her phone operator's job at the Holiday Inn Crowne Plaza in Rockville, Maryland. Believing they were financially set, Dan and Sara moved into an apartment of their own, and Sara's mother rented her Bethesda house.

At Weis Market, Sara is in and out in half an hour—six bags of groceries for $60.26. She's always nervous that she won't have enough money to cover her purchases and that she'll have to turn back a bottle of cola or a bucket of butter. But it's an embarrassment she's gotten used to, and she has plenty of cash today. Compared with others in the checkout lines, this is what Sara *did not* spend money on: potato chips or corn curls, cookies, ice cream, roast beef, or Bounce sheets for the dryer.

"If Dan wants a snack, he drinks milk."

"My son doesn't like sweets."

"We've still got a little ice cream."

"I get pot roast three or four times a year."

"So my socks stick together, big deal."

Dan wants to impress his new Radio Shack regional manager, who has asked for a video recording of the inside of the Viers Mill store. So before Dan shoots the video, he studies the most recent shelf-display Plan-o-Gram sent out by national headquarters and then rearranges the shelves to match. He separates the cheap phones from the expensive phones, moves the $50 ones within easy customer reach and the $150 ones up high to deter shoplifters. He puts the answering machines all in one location and moves the boom boxes behind the counter. He hopes his manager will see the video, notice the perfect shelves, and say, *"Man, looks good!"*

Dan was not always so determined to please. While his younger brother breezed through school, got a scholarship to Rutgers, and entered law school, Dan struggled in school. The calls from teachers began in kindergarten—Dan didn't pay attention in class. Later, there were schoolyard fights with other boys. Once, after he had lost his pencil repeatedly, a teacher tied it to a string and hung it around his neck, an incident he still remembers with pain and anger. While other kids in the neighborhood were outside playing ball and roughhousing, Dan preferred to stay in the house and draw or play alone.

"He hears his own drummer," says his dad.

"Danny fits into his own category," says his mom.

"He's a thinker," says his dad.

"Danny is an artist," says his mom.

"Danny was a challenge," says his dad.

Dan was bright. When he was in elementary school, his folks were even told that he was gifted in the arts. But Dan was a dreamer, with a laser focus on whatever obsessed him at the time. When he got into dinosaurs at age five, he was like a little paleontologist. While other kids were doing math in school, Dan was drawing Corvettes, Camaros, Mustangs, and Firebirds to precise wheelbase scales he had constructed for each model on the back of his school notebook. He became a master of the role-playing adventure game Dungeons & Dragons. For a while, he immersed himself in Greek and Roman mythology. At age thirteen, he noticed a neighbor throwing out a hundred car magazines. He took them home, read them cover to cover, and memorized stats about engine cubic displacement, torque, and zero-to-sixty acceleration times. "Oh, wow, check it out," he'd tell friends. "You can buy a Nissan Maxima with an overhead cam straight six, which is almost as advanced as what you get in a Jaguar, and a Jaguar costs $30,000 and this Maxima is only $12,000."

Dan graduated from high school with average grades, could have gone off to college or art school. His parents would have paid. But he couldn't stomach any more school—round peg, square hole. He believed kids who excelled in school were simply best at sucking up to the teachers. He recalled stories about college graduates delivering pizzas for a living. A Ph.D. he knew once asked him to program his VCR. Although his mother, who took third place in a nationwide spelling bee as a girl, and his father, who worked his way through college and became an elementary school principal in Montgomery County, constantly lectured him about the role a college degree plays in getting a good job, Dan never took school seriously. He took classes at Montgomery College in art and auto mechanics but never worked toward a degree. He tells a story that captures his attitude: He had saved enough money from a boyhood paper route to buy himself a 1969 Camaro Z-28. When he saw a high school teacher he despised driving a little Datsun, he thought to himself, "He drives a Datsun and I've got a Z-28. What the hell is he doing telling *me* what to do?"

Was it arrogance, naïveté, defensiveness? Perhaps it was all of these. But once Dan, who still lived at home rent-free, began selling cars at Glenmont Chrysler-Plymouth after high school, knocking down $18,000 a year, he figured he was on his way—*his way*. Looking back today, Dan knows he mistakenly believed that if he just kept doing what he wanted, as he got older, the comforts of his parents' middle-class life would naturally come to him, as if they were a birthright. "I didn't need school then," he says with self-mockery. "I was a big-time car salesman." But Dan was working sixty to ninety hours a week to make his $18,000 a year. And he was blowing it as fast as he earned it, on nights out in Georgetown and a parade of souped-up cars—a '68 Cadillac Coupe de Ville convertible, a '72 Cadillac hardtop, a '78 Chevy Malibu.

When Dan got burned out working such exhausting hours, he took a job at Radio Shack, where he'd worked before selling cars. Then he moved to Hi-Gear. Then the parts department at Paul Brothers Oldsmobile. Then Paul Brothers, plus Radio Shack part time. Then Radio Shack full time. Then Radio

Shack part time and back to Hi-Gear full time. Then just Hi-Gear. Then back to Radio Shack full time. Dan made each move for slightly more money, better hours, or what he thought was greater opportunity. Then, last September, he cut back to part time at Radio Shack again and went off to sell vacuum cleaners. When the supposedly lucrative job turned out to be a sham, he went back full time at Radio Shack. He told himself: "It's crazy! I'm twenty-eight years old, I got a family, and I'm jumping around jobs like a high school kid. That has got to stop." It hit him: "Oh my God, I have to have food on the table."

"I always worked hard but not smart."

"I'm trying to play ball now. I *am* playing ball."

The other day, Dan got a ninety-three on his first test in his beginning electrician's class, and he was one of only a handful of the fifty or so people to turn in the homework in his Radio Shack management class. Today, Dan talks about the arcane world of Radio Shack with the same excitement and obsession he once reserved for dinosaurs and automobiles. He ticks off the steps of selling—greeting, defining need, meeting need, selling add-ons, closing the sale, leaving the customer with a good feeling. His motto: efficiency up, costs down. He knows that one out of three people will buy a five-dollar calculator if asked. He knows that two out of three will buy batteries if asked. So he sweats the small stuff—cable-TV splitters, cable wire, speaker wire, antenna wire, and antenna splitters. They add up to big money, usually an average $35 sale. Forty sales at $35 each is a $1,400 day—with his 6.25 percent commission, that's $87.50 in Dan's pocket. He knows that tape decks come with connecting wires, but stereo equalizers don't. So on a $119.99 equalizer sale he remembers to ask a customer if he needs the wires, probably a $10 sale, and he remembers to ask if the customer's amplifier at home has an equalizer jack. If it doesn't, Dan will likely lose a sale, but he'd lose it anyway when the customer brought back the equalizer for a refund. That would cost Dan time and also anger a customer who might feel bamboozled.

Dan used to take ten minutes every couple of days and run over to the Coffee Beanery in Wheaton Plaza for a 65-cent cup of coffee. No more. Not only was it wasted money—ten cups is $6.50, or three loaves of Weis bread and two gallons of milk—but in the few minutes he was gone, someone might have walked in and bought a $1,000 stereo, costing him $62.50. It has never happened, but it could, and Dan will no longer chance it. Each morning, he brings a twenty-four-ounce jug of coffee—made at home from Hills Bros. blend, $2.99 a can on sale—and during the day he heats up cups in the microwave.

On Wednesday and Thursday nights now, Dan takes his electrician's class. If he doesn't get a Radio Shack manager's job, maybe he could go on to become an electrician. But in the meantime, the class has already helped him explain to several customers how to install Radio Shack's home security systems, making him a better salesman. Last year, he took a management class that has helped him in dealing with coworkers.

Dan is no longer cynical about school. He would give this advice to a teenage boy: "Get a Chevette. Keep it stock. Stay in school." Sometimes, he wonders what he'd be doing if he'd worked harder in high school, gone to college. Or if he'd gotten serious about his classes in auto mechanics. Instead of five to seven dollars an hour, maybe he'd be making twenty dollars an hour working on cars. "Or maybe I'd be doing something I can't even imagine." Recently, he told his mother that reading the Bible and the Torah has made him think that he'd like to go back to college and teach religion someday. His mother, reminded of Dan's youthful fascination with mythology, was nearly moved to tears. "We're past that," she said. "Maybe someday, but now is too late. You've too many responsibilities."

Back in the store, a man asks Dan if he has an electric harness hookup for a Kenwood car radio. Dan doesn't, and the man is upset because he has been everywhere searching for one. So Dan does something he hates to do: He sends the man—his $13 purchase and Dan's 81-cent commission—somewhere else.

"Did you try Marty's Electronics?"

Yes.

"The Road Shop at Circuit City?"

Yes.

"Greg Auto Sound in Rockville?"

The man shakes his head no.

"Out Viers Mill. Turn left on 28. Turn left on Rockville Pike. Near Belby's Beer and Wine."

When Patrick was born, Dan and Sara decided they needed a bigger car, a four-door. Dan's little Ford Festiva was almost paid off, it had only 35,000 miles on it, it got fifty miles to the gallon, he still owed on its five-year warranty, and the car was in great shape. But Sara's arthritis made it hard for her to lift Patrick in and out of the backseat and hard for her to drive its stick shift. But Dan also had another concern, one drawn from an expectation rooted in the world his parents had created for him—a world of vacations to Yellowstone, summer camp, new jeans from Sears, a world Dan has been unable to re-create for his own family: The Festiva didn't have air-conditioning. All his parents' cars, even the Ford Torino they'd bought new way back in 1973, had air-conditioning. For an infant, wasn't air-conditioning a necessity? So they traded the Festiva for a new '92 Ford Escort LX—and $287 a month in payments. In July, the balloon financing on the Escort comes due, and they must get a loan to square the final $4,000 payment or sell their car and buy a used one.

"Reality creeps up on you," says Sara.

"It would have been smart to keep it," Dan says of the Festiva.

"I'd like to get a Taurus," says Sara, who drives one every couple of weeks in her Florida dream.

"I don't know about a Taurus."

"Well, something along those lines."

"I was thinking more of an Escort wagon."

"Well, some kind of wagon."

"We can't get anything much bigger with our money."

"Well," says Sara, subtly clinging to her own expectation of life's necessities, "it depends on how much it costs."

This is Dan's plan: He and Sara cut their expenses to the bone, and get used to it. No more $1.59 bacon-cheeseburgers at Little Tavern for him. No more books by Thomas Merton. He has applied for a job at the Radio Shack on Rockville Pike. That store is busier, so he'd get more hours and sales, which he figures would up his income at least $200 a month and cover their shortfall in basic bills. Dan's going to work his butt off in his Radio Shack and electrician's classes. His mother told him that whenever he feels too tired to study any more, he should let the faces of Sara, Patrick, and Connor flash across his mind. Dan believes he doesn't need to play that motivational trick on himself. He knows now. This is life. His life. Sara's arthritis limits her chances to ever get a high-paying job. So nothing good will happen unless Dan makes it happen. Pretty soon, Patrick will be in Head Start and out of costly day care. Connor will be out of costly diapers and baby food. But, really, the future all rides on Dan getting that Radio Shack manager's job.

"It's not a matter of, if I work really hard I *might* get it," he says. "It's more a matter of, if I work really hard I believe I *will* get it." Dan *must* believe. He can't be negative, or he fears it will eat him up. Down deep, he knows disaster could strike—Sara's arthritis could flare up and she could need medical care. Or Sara could lose her job. The Holiday Inn where she works is being sold, and no one's sure if the new management will rehire everybody. If Sara lost her job, they'd lose not only her income but her HMO health insurance that pays everything except $10 toward each doctor's visit. Or he could be killed in an accident. No life insurance. What would Sara do? Or they could wreck the car, which has no collision insurance because it costs too much. "Let's face it," he says with bitterness, "I'm not going to be sending my kid to Harvard."

But Dan can't let himself think that way very often, just like he can't worry about what *might* have happened. "What if I went to college?" he asks with irritation. "Well, what if my parents had hit the lottery?" He can't think about what if. He's got to think about *what is*. For at least a year, until he knows if he'll get that manager's job, he and Sara will need the help of their families and the county's day-care assistance. Dan hates taking any of it. "You're raised to grow up and depend on yourself," he says. "I would rather be able to say,

'Patrick, I bring money in here, your mother brings money in, and we have the family supported.'" Frankly, it irks Dan to be dependent on his parents. Yet four out of five of his best friends—none of them with college degrees—are either living at home or getting help from their parents. The only friend who isn't getting help inherited money after his dad's death and got a big insurance settlement after a car accident.

"You're going to come to a point in the next ten, fifteen years where you're going to have the haves and the have-nots," says Sara. "The people who have the college education and the people who don't . . . But there has to be an alternative for people who either don't finish college or can't afford college."

"My parents should be relieved of duty and get their own vacations," says Dan. But last year, Sara's mom spent more than $5,000 on day care for Patrick and Connor. In the last fourteen months, Dan's folks have spent about $7,000 on day care, clothing, and other help to the family. Altogether, that's more than half of what Dan and Sara earned themselves last year. Dan's father is retired from Montgomery County schools but works full time as a film librarian in an X-ray lab. He'd like to retire, but can't—not only does Dan need help, but his ninety-one-year-old mother is in a home that costs him $300 a month more than her retirement income.

Dan's mother, who works as a secretary for the federal government, has 10 percent of her income deducted and put into retirement savings and $200 a paycheck deducted and put into savings bonds for the grandkids. Recently she's been spending virtually all her remaining take-home pay, which is $774 every two weeks, helping Dan's family. On top of that, with Sara working the weekday night shift, Dan's folks baby-sit the several nights a week Dan attends classes or works until 9:00 P.M. His parents are terrified about what would happen to their grandchildren if they and Sara's mom were no longer able to pitch in. Sara's mom never in her life imagined that one of her children could end up living so close to the edge. "They'd be on welfare," says Dan's mother. "They can't make it." She and her husband consider Dan and his family their obligation, believe it's not fair for society to support them as long as their parents are able. After all, says Dan's mother, Danny had opportunities he didn't take. "I have two sons," she says. "And one listened and one didn't."

Again and again, Dan's mother has asked herself, "Where did you go wrong? Where did you fail?" Are Dan's troubles her fault? She asked her son this just recently and believes that it was a sign of his new maturity when he said that his bad choices had been all his own. He told her, "I couldn't have had a better mother."

Working with their parents on a budget has been a relief to Dan and Sara. They were embarrassed to do it at first, to admit they needed the help. But getting those past bills paid, getting rid of the bill collectors who'd scream into the answering machine, "I know you're in there! Pick up the phone," knowing where every one of their pennies is going has taken the constant panic out of their home. In the past, Dan and Sara argued over amounts of money that would barely be noticed in middle-class homes—Dan buying those religious books for $25, Sara those $5 romance novels, Dan those 65-cent cups of coffee. Harsh, bitter arguments. Dan's mom scolded them: "Stop blaming each other. You've got to be a team." More than anything right now, the team of Dan and Sara wants a house, wants the life they lived as children for their own children. They can't let themselves even think about how impossible it will be to save, say, a $15,000 down payment.

"This situation, if we work hard enough, *will* not last forever," says Sara.

"You gotta work towards something," says Dan. "Or you're always gonna just stay in the same pit."

"We're struggling," says Sara, "but a lot of people are worse off."

"We're struggling," says Dan, "but on the verge of getting the upper hand . . . I am very hopeful."

This, too, is Dan's plan, the Dan who still hears a different drummer, Dan the dreamer: For the last few years, he has been creating a role-playing adventure game with Sara and two friends. Dan believes it's better than Dungeons & Dragons. He has devised far more elaborate charts to determine the strength, charisma, constitution, dexterity, willpower, wisdom, swordsmanship, appearance, and intelligence of his game's characters. Dan has set his game in fifth-century North America. He has studied the geography of the land and populated his fantasy world with Native Americans and fictitious European explorers. All his charts, maps, and instructions will be run off on a friend's Macintosh computer and put into three-ring binders. "One book, thirty-five bucks," says Dan, which is dirt cheap compared with some fantasy games. Dan plans to have his game finished and copyrighted by the end of the summer and then take it to Wheaton's Barbarian Book Shop, whose owner has agreed to sell it on consignment.

"Gas money," says Dan, smiling.

Saturday night, and Dan has a surprise for Sara: a $3.95 bottle of Manischewitz Concord Grape wine. On Monday morning, he starts at the Rockville Pike Radio Shack. Besides the promise of an extra $200 a month, the store offers a bonus—it's five miles closer to home, which means Dan will save about $2.50 on gas each week. Dan takes the candles down from the tall bookcase that once belonged to Sara's mother, puts them on the dining room table that Sara's sister gave them, lights the candles, and pours Sara a glass of wine. Then he cooks dinner—grilled hot-dog-and-cheese sandwiches, with macaroni and cheese and a tossed green salad. Dan says grace, which he's doing more often lately. He has told Sara that perhaps God will help them if they become more faithful to him: "The Lord restored the prosperity of Job."

The kids are in bed. It is a quiet and comfortable evening. "Once all this is over," Dan has told Sara, "I think we'll be so much closer." They eat dinner and clear the table. Dan pours Sara another glass of wine. Then they sit before the thirteen-inch TV on the long, worn, green couch, with its plastic innards beginning to poke through and prick their skin, and they watch *Jurassic Park*, a movie they have watched more than a dozen times before.

April 23, 1995

Mothers and Daughters

A woman *is* her mother. That's the main thing.

—*Anne Sexton*

Like detectives at a crime scene, the women are bent over the place where Grandma Julia Shelton fell last week, leaving blood smeared ominously on her kitchen pantry door and a deep diagonal gash in the back of her head. After she'd spent a week in the hospital and had every test imaginable, the doctors said it wasn't a stroke that had made her lose her balance, but a middle ear infection. So Grandma Shelton is feeling better, even though she's still a little woozy and homebound for a while. Just now, she and her daughter Mary and her granddaughter Karen have interrupted their making of stuffed zucchini for dinner and are trying to reconstruct the trajectory of her fall, examining her pantry door, wondering exactly how she cut her head. On the doorknob? No. Not sharp enough. On the edge of the countertop? No. The blood was on the door. Grandma leans down and softly rubs the spot, which has been wiped clean. A sudden silence breaks the patter. Oh, well, Mary says cheerfully, just thank God that Grandma's fine.

"Mom, you want me to cut the mushrooms?" Karen asks.

"I would love to have you mince the mushrooms."

"How do you mince a mushroom?"

"You slice it and then you chop it."

Karen rolls her eyes, smiles, and reaches for a knife.

Three generations of Shelton women, three generations of mothers and daughters: grandmother Julia Shelton, seventy-eight, who was born before American women even had the right to vote, who gave up her job to raise a family, then went back to graduate school in middle age, graduated number one in her class, and rose through twenty-seven years as a social worker to run her own staff at Norfolk's Tidewater Rehabilitation Institute; daughter Mary

101

Clockwise from top: Mary Pence,
Karen Pence, and Julia Shelton.

Photo by Tom Wolff.

Pence, forty-nine, who came of age with the women's movement of the sixties and seventies and went from activist housewife to partner in the prominent Washington, D.C., domestic relations law firm of Feldsman, Tucker, Leifer, Fidell & Bank; and granddaughter Karen Pence, twenty-three, who never imagined that she wouldn't have a career, who studied economics at Swarthmore, and who, fresh out of college, landed a job as a research assistant and computer programmer in the Washington office of Mathematica Policy Research, the prestigious Princeton, New Jersey, consulting firm.

Three generations of women who are at once ordinary and extraordinary, women who, like so many others, have struggled to blend men, children, educations and careers, personal ambitions and family responsibilities into a life that is also their own. Mothers and daughters, linked in grand design by family intimacy, by the qualities they like in each other and the qualities they don't, by their public confidence and their hidden doubts, by the world of women that changed around them and the world around them that they helped to change. Three generations of women bound as well by smaller connections—hair that fades from girlish blond to womanly brown, fair complexions, hands with long and lean fingers, smiles that match, and thoughtful pauses that linger between sentences.

The Shelton women: history within history.

"I'm quite hungry," Karen says in her gentle, almost faint voice, her words seeming to float momentarily in the air.

"I'm sorry," says Mary, who, like her daughter, speaks ever so softly, leaves space between her words, and often lets her sentences trail away tentatively, as if they all ended with question marks. Mary, as usual, is in charge of the cooking, and dinner is an hour away. "You want some cheese and crackers?"

Julia, who has been rhythmically mincing the scooped innards from the halved zucchinis that now resemble tiny boats, says to her granddaughter, "You do have some better shoes, I'm glad to see." She looks down at Karen's plain white tennis shoes, which are tonight worn with a casual sweater and blue jeans, office wear at Mathematica, where Karen runs state food stamp data through her computer to constantly reassess the program's costs and benefits. Karen recognizes her grandmother's deadpan dig but doesn't take the bait, keeps chopping, or rather *mincing*, the mushrooms. "They don't have holes in them," Julia says, still prodding. "Okay, Mary," she says, scraping the zucchini into a neat pile, "I don't know if these are minced enough."

Mary, wearing a blue-and-white-striped apron over her expensive lawyer's suit, cocks a spoon in her right hand, leans toward the table, and eyes the pile over gold-rimmed granny glasses riding low on her nose. Looking and acting like the professor of the kitchen, Mary nods her approval, then says: "You want to put it in that bowl?" Julia knows this is not a question. She puts the zucchini in the bowl.

"This calls for six cloves of garlic," Mary says, as she stands over her cookbook. "Why don't we do two?"

"Two?" Karen asks, raising her voice. "I put *four* cloves of garlic in a cup of spaghetti sauce." Everyone pauses.

"You want to vote for three?" Mary asks, and they do.

The line of Shelton foremothers hails originally from Indiana. Karen's Great-Great-Grandmother Lizzie Mehaffie was born in a log cabin and never finished grade school. She married a railroad mechanic who worked long hours six days a week, meaning that Lizzie, who volunteered with the Women's Christian Temperance Union and baked bread and angel food cakes for household spending money, ran the show at home. Her kind, soft-spoken husband once said he wanted to marry a strong woman who'd fight his battles for him, and he did, although he also paid a price. Sometimes, family legend has it, he pretended to be deafer than he was to keep from hearing Lizzie's strong opinions on just about everything.

It was the Mehaffies' daughter Mary who later became Great-Grandma Gemmill, the Shelton women's matriarch. After high school, Mary worked as a teacher, one of the few professions open to women then, but she wanted to go on to Indiana University. So by teaching part time, she worked her way through and earned a bachelor's degree in math in 1910 at age twenty-six. For the next five years, she taught public high school. Then she married Robert Gemmill and quit teaching, as was the tradition in those days. The couple set up housekeeping in Toledo, Ohio, where Robert worked as a railroad postal clerk who made weekly three-day runs to St. Louis and back. He loved the job and refused promotions to office work, which angered his wife, who wanted him to have not a job but a career. In 1929, when Julia was only thirteen, he injured his knee on the job and died of blood poisoning.

After her father's death, Julia lowered an emotional veil in her life. As she explains this, she passes her open hand before her face like a stage curtain closing. She mentions his funeral. "I was bound and determined that I was not going to cry," she says. "The effort not to cry was just horrible." But she didn't cry. And she's certain her mother didn't either.

After the funeral, the family simply stopped talking about Father. They didn't tell stories about him or share fond memories. Julia believes his death was just too painful for everyone. She can remember little about her father. But not long ago, when she asked her brother, Henry, about him, he told animated stories—how their earnest mother would laugh red-faced and breathless at his jokes, how he was a big, muscular man who exercised every morning and often roughhoused with Henry, how he drew pictures and composed and recited rhymes. Henry's memories of his father were "pure joy." Julia, looking at old black-and-white photos of him today, draws a blank. "I think his death was so traumatic to me that I tried to block a lot out," she says. "He was gone and I didn't think about him anymore."

This would be only one deep sadness in one woman's life, except that Mary struggled all her childhood with what she saw as her mother's emotional distance. Mary admired her mother's strength, but she craved greater closeness with her. After listening to her mother talk for the first time recently about her own father's death, listening as she spoke without passion or intonation, Mary believes she now understands why her mother could not sense her girlhood anguish. "I wanted her to listen to my pain, and she couldn't," Mary says. "And the reason she couldn't is because she couldn't listen to her own pain."

"Let's see," Mary says. "You guys are gonna hate me for this: 'one-half cup of finely minced almonds.' I bought *chopped* almonds, but they're going to still need to be minced." Mary, who is tall and angular to her mother's shorter and rounder, delivers the bag of almonds to the table and stops to look over her spectacles at Karen's handiwork. She shakes her head and says reluctantly, "I don't think that garlic is finely minced enough." Karen, taller and leaner, more fragile looking than her mother, has a slow, graceful way of throwing back her head and combing her long, still slightly blondish hair out of her face with open fingers. She combs back her hair, smiles, and rolls her eyes again, reaches for a knife.

"Be careful of your fingers," Julia says.

Then, out of the blue, Mary mentions that her husband and Karen's father, Danny, has lost twenty pounds in the twenty-six years they've been married. She wonders if it is her fault.

"It's a compliment to his good habits," Julia says.

"Mom," Karen says with feigned nonchalance, as her knife dances *click, click, click* on the white plastic cutting board, "isn't that an outdated view of a relationship?"

"Very outdated," Mary says, smiling at her daughter's gentle gibe. "I'm just an outdated kind of a woman." There is a long pause, which is the conversational way of all the Shelton women. "You think he should take responsibility for himself?"

"I do," Karen says.

Mary is at the stove mixing the rice and the minced zucchini, almonds, and mushrooms in the bowl. She glances at Karen's cutting board again. "Awesome garlic. You did a great job."

The saga of the Shelton women is a vintage American tale. The widowed Mary Gemmill, with children ages fourteen and thirteen, takes a job as an actuary at Washington's Union Labor Life Insurance Co. in 1930, rents a cramped Georgetown apartment near Western High School, by reputation then the city's best. Her son and daughter have their teeth straightened. Julia learns to play piano on the Steinway upright her parents had bought in Indiana. Mary Gemmill takes her children to see President Hoover in person. She takes them to art galleries and museums. Her daughter graduates number two in her Western class and wins a scholarship to Barnard College, sister school to the Ivy League Columbia University. After graduation in 1937, she marries a Harvard Law School graduate and becomes a social worker. Mary Gemmill's son, Henry, graduates as the "top boy" in his class at Western, wins a scholarship to Yale, and goes on to become managing editor of the *Wall Street Journal*. "She did things for us in just a very quiet way," Julia says, "without letting her own needs get in the way."

But there is a subtext. While her daughter was at Barnard and her son at Yale, Mary Gemmill had a breakdown. Little is known about it, except that Union Labor Life had transferred her to New York, where she was miserable working under a harsh new boss who often made sexual advances to the younger women in the office. At this, Mary Gemmill fumed with indignation. But Henry believed it was probably the gap between his mother's demanding expectations for herself and the limited horizons she faced that was at the heart of her depression. Mary's ambition, dating back to when she wanted her husband to take promotions into the front office, had for years been channeled through her children. To Henry as a boy, the names Harvard, Princeton, and Yale were just names. It was his mother who knew their significance, edited his letters of application, handed him the envelope from Yale, and beamed when he opened it and read of his scholarship. But all those years, the college-educated, self-made Mary Gemmill worked at a "little job," as Henry said, with no chance of promotion.

"I remember that she had some psychiatric treatment at that point," Julia says of her mother's depression, which caused her to quit her job and move in with her sister-in-law in Philadelphia for two years. "I think her sense of self-worth was very badly eroded. She never really discussed it with me. This is just what I've picked up." Said Henry, "She managed everything beautifully, but her desires were much beyond that, so she thought she'd never done too much. So she projected them on us. We were to become *somebody*. She unreasonably worshiped people who were *somebody*."

Yet as the mother's life unraveled, the daughter's life got exciting. Julia was something of a wallflower in high school, and she hated it, wanted badly to date and have fun. She remembers rejecting the idea of becoming a librarian when she realized she would meet few men in that profession. In college, she began dating not only Jim Shelton, the man she would marry, but many others, having a great time. She knew the unwritten code of the era and, although smarter than many of her dates, she consciously dummied up around them. This, at a time when women in America's elite colleges saw themselves as a new breed—as Margaret Mead, the famed anthropologist who graduated from Barnard in 1923, or as Frances Perkins, President Roosevelt's secretary of labor, or as the many women who ran the nation's vast network of private social welfare agencies in the tradition of Jane Addams and Hull House.

The women at Barnard were rethinking everything from careers to sexuality. "We felt we were pretty smart, pretty clever, pretty important," Julia says. And while at Barnard, she did something she believes would have shocked her mother, who never spoke to her about sex. She went to a doctor, said she was getting married, and got a diaphragm. Then she and the man who would be her husband for fifty-five years rendezvoused at, as she remembers it, the Shelton Hotel in New York City. Other women she knew at Barnard were having sexual relations. It was a modern thing to do. But Julia also had *un-modern* goals. She didn't want to become one of those Barnard career women who ended up living alone the rest of their lives. She wanted a career, but she wanted a family too.

Social work was her choice. Yes, it was a woman's profession, but Julia now saw this as an advantage—at least all the good jobs wouldn't automatically go to men. But when she told Jim she planned to work for a few years after their marriage and before children, they had a "blowup," as Julia calls it. Jim was six years older and wanted children right away. But Julia would not relent. "I had a role model of education and working and being self-sufficient," she says of her mother. "A paid job always meant something to me." So for three years, she was a social worker near Philadelphia and then Washington, years she loved. She was good at it, and she knew it. Still, when she quit to have her first child in 1941, it would be eighteen years before Julia would work for money again.

"All right," Mary says, still studying her cookbook, "stir in lemon juice. How much lemon juice? Three tablespoons."

"What else, honey?" Julia asks.

"Start stuffing."

As they fill the six halved zucchinis, Karen uses her fingers to taste her mother's concoction, licks her lips, flashes the Shelton women's smile. "If these almonds were just a little less finely chopped, they'd be crunchy in an unpleasant kind of way."

"Are you criticizing, young lady?" Mary asks.

Karen laughs. "Appreciating."

As a girl, Mary always thought her mother was different from the other kids' mothers. Her mother never sat around the kitchen table drinking coffee and gossiping in the mornings. She hated to cook and wasn't very good at it. She didn't enjoy browsing through department stores, always shopped with a *purpose*. Mary's mother and father sat down and paid all the bills together, and, because of her father's congenitally poor vision, her mother also drove everybody everywhere and did most of the minor fix-it chores around the house.

She volunteered at the League of Women Voters. Mary didn't know what the league did, but it seemed important.

"She was a doer," Mary says.

Her mother remembers things a little differently. For the first twelve years of her marriage, Julia had to move her family and household seven times, as Jim's job as an attorney for the Labor Department and then the Internal Revenue Service took him from Washington to Atlanta to New York to Atlanta to Birmingham to Detroit to San Francisco and, finally, back to Washington. The ritual was always the same: Jim would fly ahead to his new job. For the long road trips, Great-Grandma Mary Gemmill, who'd gone to work in Washington for the Post Office Department and then Commerce doing the routine math calculations that computers do today, would arrive at Julia's house and together they'd pack up for the movers. Then Mary Gemmill would fill a box with chocolate chip cookies and another box with grapes, and the whole family would head out in the car. Julia's four children had come like stepping stones, one every two years, and she was harried not only by these incessant migrations but also by diapers, scratches, schoolwork, music lessons, doctors, dentists, dishes, sick kids, bedtime stories . . .

Looking back, Julia wouldn't trade any of it. But she does know what Betty Friedan meant in her 1963 book, *The Feminine Mystique*, when she labeled the frustration many women felt in their homemaker roles as "the problem that has no name." As a young woman, Julia never questioned her nomadic life in pursuit of Jim's career. He was the breadwinner. He worked hard. It was the way of the world. Only lately, after being asked about it by Mary, has she acknowledged that deep inside she craved more, yearned for achievements and satisfactions that were hers alone. In 1957, when Mary was twelve, Julia went back to graduate school in social work at Howard University. She and Jim said it was because the family needed more money for the upcoming college tuition bills.

For a long time, Mary suspected it was something more. And when she recently asked her mother if the money was a cover, an acceptable excuse for getting out of the house and back to her career, her mother broke out in a huge grin. "It was wonderful that we needed the money for college," she said. She talked about how hard it always was for her to put her own needs first, ahead of Jim's and the children's, and how good it felt to be back in school and then back at work. "To do something that somebody felt was worthwhile enough to pay me for felt good," she says. Then, this woman the world has always seen as strong and capable makes a remarkable admission: "I have a very poor opinion of myself mostly." Echoes of her own strong and capable, yet doubt-ridden, mother.

Somehow, as a girl, Mary knew this about her mother. She doesn't know how she knew it, only that she did. Perhaps it was because Mary herself knew the feeling. Her brothers and sister were all top students. Mary was not, got average grades in elementary school. Her father had a steel-trap memory, loved playing games of mental recall: Recite the state capitals from East Coast to West Coast or list the Bible's minor prophets. He was an avid bridge player, and all the kids became expert players. But Mary hated the memory games, hated bridge. She was smart, and by the time she got to high school, she had begun to excel. In college she was Phi Beta Kappa. But as a girl she lived in a world of imagination, spent hours playing make-believe alone under the second-floor eaves, read storybooks hidden in her schoolbooks. She was desperate for approval. She felt stupid. And it was this pain—and her loneliness and self-doubt—that she wanted to share with her mother, but never could.

On a rainy day in 1959, Julia graduated at the top of her Howard class. For Mary, it was a revelation: "I always knew my father was smart, but I never knew my mother was smart. I knew she was competent, but competent and smart are two different things. I remember being surprised and pleased and proud. I was glad for her." And, "She was doing something significant with her life and I was going to do something with mine."

"Let's eat," Mary says.

The women sit down at the dinner table, and when they extend their arms to clasp hands while saying grace their generations are revealed and recorded in their hands—from Julia's that are blemished to Mary's that are blemishing to Karen's that are as soft and smooth as a child's cheek. For this casual dinner, the women have treated themselves nicely. The place mats are colorfully flowered beneath white plates. A single red rosebud floats in water in a clear brandy snifter that once belonged to Great-Grandma Gemmill. Each woman has a small salad of beets, corn, and grated carrots. Karen has a glass of white wine.

"This is a zucchini canoe," Mary announces. Glancing at Karen, she adds, "It has wonderfully minced garlic."

When Karen was born in 1970, Mary was determined she would always hear and share her daughter's pain in a way her mother never had. But in other ways, she followed her mother's path—finished college, married, trailed her husband around the country as the Navy shipped him from post to post, taught school for a few years, got a master's degree in remedial reading, had Karen and son Brian, and became a housewife. The family settled in Ann Arbor, Michigan, where Danny was sent to teach ROTC at the University of Michigan and where he capped his earlier engineering degree with an MBA and took a job in the emerging computer industry.

"I had hitched my wagon to his star," Mary says.

Then came the changes.

Women's Liberation was everywhere in the air in the seventies, and Mary became a convert. Modern feminism spoke to her. Like her mother, she had great difficulty convincing herself that her own needs should ever come before those of her husband or her children. "I wondered if the experience of being the piece of baggage dragged around the country had had an impact on me," she says. "It's harder to value yourself and to see yourself as having equal worth." As Danny moved up at the office, Mary moved up to become the president of Ann Arbor's chapter of the National Organization for Women. She was elected to the school board, where she championed contraceptive education and more equitable funding for boys' and girls' sports. She worked on a study that revealed rampant sex stereotyping in Michigan's public school textbooks. She was a prime mover behind the opening of the city's first shelter for battered women.

With Karen in tow, Mary marched for equal access to credit for women, for legalized abortion, for the Equal Rights Amendment. Danny came home excited one day because the two of them had been invited to a management retreat in Florida. Sorry, Mary said, she couldn't go because she was boycotting the state for its failure to pass the ERA. Danny argued. Danny beseeched. Mary refused. She wrote a letter to Danny's boss explaining why she couldn't go. So intrigued was the boss that he invited himself and his wife to the Pences' for dinner. He told Mary that if she would go with Danny to Florida, he would write an endorsement of the ERA on company letterhead to every Florida legislator. Mary went, although the whole time she was there—reading Marilyn French's *The Women's Room* at poolside by day and dolling up by night—she was annoyed at having to play the good corporate wife. "I played the role," she says, "because I care about Danny."

Karen was to be raised in the new order. She had trucks and blocks galore. Mary wouldn't let her have a Barbie doll until Julia finally bought her one. Mary read *Ms.* magazine's "Stories for Free Children" to Karen. Mary fumed when Karen came home from first grade and said the boys chased the girls around the playground while the girls screamed. Mary's mother, like her mother before her, had told Mary nothing about sex. By the time Karen was four, she could converse about the intricacies of the uterus.

Still, at home Mary was a housewife. For the era, she and Danny had a modern marriage: He cooked and took the kids when she had a school board meeting, a rally, or whatever. He marched for equal rights. He built a desk for her NOW phone line, which rang incessantly. He was no mossback. But home was still Mary's bailiwick. Danny was still the breadwinner. Then, in 1978, he was transferred to Washington. "I didn't want to come, but I did," Mary says. "I did it with a smile on my face." But she was angry—angry at herself. After all the other moves, she'd gone and made a life for herself. That was a real skill. Her mother had that skill, and she admired it. But this time, she'd given up so much. She wondered why she'd done it so willingly. In her mind, it raised an old question: What am I worth?

Neither Danny nor Mary mentioned divorce, though Danny believes it may have crossed Mary's mind. With Danny's blessing, Mary took a policy analysis job at Commerce, where she saw lawyers no smarter than herself making a lot more money. She decided to go to law school. But like her mother, Mary had discovered that she loved earning a paycheck for the first time in years. She could feel her confidence rising. So she kept her job *and* went to law school. And the family entered the *new* new order: mom as superwoman.

"I was a lunatic," Mary says, shaking her head.

"You want another canoe?" Mary asks, getting up from the table.

"Half a canoe," Julia says.

"I'd like a third of a canoe," Karen says.

"They're *good*," says Julia, who marvels that her daughter is always willing to try out a brand-new dish on friends or family. Julia would never do that, would always stick to the tried and true until she'd tested the recipe on herself. She admires that in Mary.

This evening, the Shelton women eat at an Indiana walnut table owned by Great-Great-Grandma Lizzie Mehaffie more than a hundred years ago. Behind them on the wall is a clock, refinished and in working order, owned by Lizzie's parents as far back as 1837. Beneath the clock are Julia's photo albums—photos of Great-Great-Grandma Mehaffie, whom Julia remembers clearly; photos of Great-Grandma Gemmill, whom Mary remembers clearly; photos of Julia, whom Karen obviously will remember clearly. After two generations, the memory is lost. But the imprint lives on.

Mixed among the photos are Great-Grandma Gemmill's pocket-size account ledgers—green, black, brown, maroon. Meticulous, handwritten records: the inventory of her estate after her husband's death in 1929, which included five parcels of land worth $7,400, cash in the amount of $67.59, the Steinway worth $50, and household goods worth $150. Great-Grandma Gemmill recorded everything, from her net worth of $25,043.41 in June 1949 to the 70 cents she expended for rat poison in May 1950. She reports a trip back home to Logansport, Indiana, in July 1954. She left on Tuesday morning, July 6, and arrived at the Ben Hur Motel on July 8. Her room cost $6.00 a night. She left with $100.30, spent $76.80, and arrived home in Arlington on July 14 with $23.50 remaining.

"Mother," Mary asks after she returns with second helpings, "have you shown Karen Grandma Gemmill's account books?"

"No."

"You should."

Karen knows little about Great-Grandma Gemmill.

"She was very much in charge of her own life," Julia says.

Karen was nine years old, and Karen was miserable. During Mary's first year in law school at George Washington University, she didn't once eat dinner with Karen and the family on a weeknight. She didn't get home until nine or ten o'clock. Dad cooked spaghetti a lot. But worst of all, the house had become a tense, frazzled, confusing place. Tempers rarely flared, but beneath the propriety, Karen sensed something different, something she hadn't sensed in Ann Arbor, where her mother brought birthday cupcakes to her class and was waiting with a meal on the table when Karen walked home from school at lunchtime. Karen recalls Ann Arbor as idyllic—"very Norman Rockwell." This new life was different—an "unsafe atmosphere." Mary felt guilty for leaving her children at home but couldn't help herself. For the only time in her marriage, she had tunnel vision: She was going to be a lawyer.

For all her complaints, Karen also admired what her mother was doing. And when Mary finally went to be sworn in as a member of the Maryland bar, Karen went with her, feeling the same kind of pride Mary had felt at her mother's Howard graduation.

Mary has a photo of herself and Karen from about that time, and it is one of Mary's favorites: mother and daughter sitting and smiling brilliantly in the garden at a Pennsylvania summer home the Pences then owned with others in their family. They are wearing identical blue T-shirts emblazoned with the letters *ERA*. At the supermarket, a man once asked Karen if that stood for earned run average, which she found hilarious. But even then, Karen was silently questioning what she saw as the gap between her mother's feminist outlook and the way she lived her life.

"I didn't think of her as a strong woman," Karen says. "I had a perception she was too needy on my dad . . . I thought she should have more strength in herself and less need of my father . . . Wanting my dad to have all the answers. Or wanting him to take care of her . . . I thought she was too passive . . . She didn't seem to have the sense that she herself was competent." In her mother, Karen sensed what Mary had sensed in Julia and what Julia had sensed in Great-Grandma Gemmill: "It's what I perceive as her ambivalence about her own self-worth."

Looking back, Karen is glad she had all those trucks and blocks to play with, that her mother disdained Barbie dolls, that she preached feminism. "My mother's explicit actions were very good," she says. "They were just undermined by her implicit actions." Karen remembers that whenever her mother, who is weak in math, would want help adding or multiplying, she would always ask Danny. If he wasn't around, she'd ask Karen's brother, Brian, who was three years the younger. At first, Karen would say, "Mom, you can ask me too." Still, she didn't. So Karen got mad. But even then, after Mary realized she was doing her own kind of sex stereotyping, it was hard for her to stop. "She wasn't as able to cast it off," Karen says. Karen decoded other messages. She vividly recalls a time the family came home from church on Sunday morning and found a dead mouse on the porch floor. Mom said to Dad, "*You* take care of that. *I'll* fix lunch." Her father was a gentle man who showed little emotion. He seemed to Karen to handle stress calmly. Her mother would sometimes cry when she became emotional, and Karen noticed that once she became a lawyer she had a hard time sleeping on nights before big trials. Her father always seemed confident. Her mother seemed unsure of herself, doubtful.

"It bothered me a lot," Karen says.

But Mary lived up to her resolution from years before: "I wanted to be a shoulder Karen could cry on, which my mother wasn't able to do for me. I felt it was a gift I could give her." Being open with Karen was hard for Mary sometimes. She remembers when Karen once asked if she and Danny had made love before they were married. They had, but Mary told Karen she wouldn't answer because she didn't want Karen to make a choice based on what her mother had done. Mary meant it when she said it, but for all her efforts at openness she also knew she felt very uncomfortable talking about this intimacy with her daughter. And Karen, although she didn't mention it, also knew her mother felt uncomfortable.

Karen could be remarkably candid with her mother. The young Mary would never have criticized her mother to her face, but Karen had no such qualms. She freely criticized her mother's driving, her taste in clothes, her slipups in grammar. Until a few years ago, however, Karen did not speak of deeper matters. Then, during a family vacation in France, as she and her mother were walking back to the hotel, Karen said she thought her mom was too dependent on Danny. Karen brought this up because she was dating a man at Swarthmore and she'd come to feel "needy" of him, feared she couldn't be strong without his help. "That was a very scary feeling," she says. And she blamed her mother. She believed she'd seen Mary behave this way with Danny and now she was following suit. Mary got angry that night in France. "I've made the choices in my life that I want," she snapped, "and you're free to make your own choices with your life." Then she stormed off. It was among the worst arguments they ever had. But a couple of years later, when Karen mentioned it, her mother couldn't remember the incident. Mary decided she must have buried it because Karen had cut too close.

By then, Mary had begun to wrestle with the matters that had bothered Karen even as a young girl. Mary didn't believe Danny dominated her. That was the view through a child's uncomplicated eyes. Danny was an engineer, an efficient, organized man. He did the carpentry, kept the cars running, planned the best route between here and there. Mary spent most of the household money, kept the kitchen cabinets stocked. Danny did dead mice. Mary did curtains. It was a traditional division of labor, but it was also a sharing of expertise, a partnership. No, something else haunted Mary: Like her own mother, she still didn't feel right putting her needs first. But her seemingly selfless behavior for her family was rooted not only in altruism but also in an abiding sense that she didn't *deserve* to come first.

It was the smallest of events that brought this to the fore. When Danny and Mary remodeled their bedroom three years ago, Mary told Danny exactly how she wanted the shelves in her closet built. Danny, the engineer, told Mary he feared her desired shelf design would compromise the closet's strength. Oh, okay, Mary said. But the next day, it hit her: It was her closet! Nobody else's needs were at stake. If ever there was a time she should speak up for herself, wasn't it now? So she did. And Danny said fine, he'd figure out a stable way to do what she wanted. It was that easy. Since then, there have been many times Mary has simply spoken up, explained, pressed for her way. "I wasn't sure I was worth having the closet the way I wanted it," she says. "It sounds so silly now."

But at sharing her daughter's pain, Mary succeeded—perhaps too well. "She takes it harder than she needs to," says Karen, who has been forced to censor what she tells her mother. When Karen was living for a college semester in Cameroon, for instance, she was mugged, living with a family that frightened her, and sick with malaria. But she wrote home about all the nice produce available in the marketplace. The truth, she believed, would have hurt her mother too much. "I hate it when she cries," Karen says. "It's scary to see your mom cry. You want to think of your parents as invulnerable." She pauses. "Maybe that's a childhood fantasy I should outgrow."

"Coffee, anyone?" Mary asks. "Dessert?"

Into the evening the Shelton women sit at Great-Great-Grandma Mehaffie's dinner table and talk about their lives. The conversation takes place each with all, each with another, and each with herself alone. When each woman speaks, she can hear her own voice, as well as the voice of her mother. But if each Shelton woman *is* her mother, as poet Anne Sexton writes, then each Shelton woman is also *not* her mother. Each also has lived in conscious reaction to, if not rebellion against, her own mother. Each comes from a family in which worldly accomplishment is enshrined and tied to sense of worth. But each also lives in a world that makes accomplishment far harder for women, while demanding that they raise a family too.

"Mixed messages," Karen calls it.

Mary remembers a picture that Great-Grandma Mary Gemmill always displayed prominently. It was of Henry, Julia's brother, with President Richard Nixon. Mary Gemmill showed everyone that photo, as proof that her son—and perhaps that *she*—had arrived. "My mother didn't have a picture of herself with Richard Nixon," Mary says. While Henry was building a career at the *Wall Street Journal*, a career his mother could prize, Julia was raising children and trekking across the country. She became a hospital social worker who coordinated patient care with doctors, nurses, and social workers. She was a woman to be reckoned with. But it wasn't the same. "The men got the executive jobs," Julia says. "I didn't waste any time on it. It was just a fact of life."

"Did it matter that my mother wasn't editor of the *Wall Street Journal*?" Mary asks. "I can only tell you that later in my grandmother's life, I sensed on the part of my mother a concern that she wasn't valued as much."

"It's true Henry had more status," Julia says, "but I think my mother respected me." And then, "She expected a lot."

This year, Mary is the lay leader of Christ Congregational Church in Silver Spring, Maryland, where her mother was the lay leader exactly thirty years ago. Mary noticed recently that although her mother wasn't the first female lay leader, she was the first to list her own name instead of her husband's in church records—Julia Shelton instead of Mrs. James H. Shelton. Mary believes this was significant, evidence of her mother's nascent desire to stand alone in her accomplishments.

Mary herself is still caught in the psychological double bind of career and family. She still worries that going to law school hurt Karen deeply, especially since Karen recently told Mary she sometimes fears she might do something to make her parents stop loving her. Karen can't imagine what that might be, but she sometimes has feelings of impending doom for no good reason. Mary fears her daughter's dread is rooted in those miserable law school years of Karen's childhood, years when she perhaps felt abandoned by her mother, creating fears that echo in her today. Mary has done well as a lawyer. The satisfactions are great. But so is the guilt. "Boy, this is such a conflict," Mary says to Karen. "Going to law school was the best thing I ever did for me. And maybe it was the worst thing I ever did for you. Was it?"

"At the time, it was bad," Karen says, "but later I was proud." Karen believes she better understands the balance in her parents' marriage today. She wonders if she mistook her father's emotional reticence for strength and her mother's emotional openness for weakness. Karen hadn't known that her mother had placed the ERA campaign ahead of Danny's Florida retreat. Today, Karen believes her mother's confidence has grown manyfold since she became a lawyer a decade ago. Mary has become confident enough to let preening, macho male attorneys believe they are controlling negotiations with her, to not engage in their games, and still get her way. She once faced down a male lawyer who would tell her the filthiest jokes imaginable, in what she figured was some weird exercise of male dominance. She walked into the man's office and told him the raunchiest joke she'd ever heard—and the man never told her another dirty joke. Nowadays, when Karen hears her mother on the phone, confidently talking to clients, it's as if Karen is hearing a stranger—not "the mother in my house."

Julia says that the guilt she felt when she went back to school has receded, because she has had time to see just how well Mary has done and because she believes she did the best that she could. Hers is a different regret. Over the years, she has silently watched Mary act out a relationship with Karen that Julia knew was consciously different from her own relationship with Mary. She was envious of this, just as she was envious that Mary had good female friends with whom she could discuss the common women's experiences Julia's generation often faced alone. If Julia had known how badly Mary wanted to be closer as a girl, she would have tried her best. She doesn't know how well she would have done, but she would have tried. She regrets this but doesn't feel guilty about it. "I think I was coping with as much as I could cope with."

Before she went into the hospital last week, Julia had never told Mary these things. But from her sickbed she said she was sorry she hadn't spent more time with Mary as a girl, sorry she hadn't listened more carefully, and that, if it was all right with Mary, she would like to try to do better now. Tonight, she turns to Karen and looks intently into her face: "I'd also like to get to know you better. It would mean a lot to me." It is a turnabout: Karen, so free at sharing her feelings, is caught off guard.

"I'd like that, Grandma," she says.

What's striking to Julia is a similarity she sees in all their lives. "One of the main things that bothered me," she says of her own marriage and her own husband, "was that all these moves we made were because of his decisions." Mary did the same for her husband, and now Karen is thinking about leaving her job in Washington and moving to Cambridge, where her boyfriend is studying at Harvard. Julia says, "It seems to me the men get the preference."

Karen isn't sure what she'll do. At Swarthmore, most women believed it was terrible for a woman to change her career for the sake of a man. But Karen believes she's simply not as driven as many men, who seem to plan out their lives degree by degree and job by job, as if they were on a forced march toward some known point in the future. She doesn't want to be like men who can't work together easily and cooperatively—in the way her Great-Grandma Gemmill and Grandma Julia used to pack up the house and car and in the way she, Mary, and Julia prepared dinner tonight. Men seem to have a single-minded sense of career entitlement that many women don't share. Men seem to lead one life, while women lead many.

Karen has always been competitive. Her brother, Brian, remembers that she was determined to throw a ball as well as any boy. Unlike her grandmother, who steered away from male professions, Karen was attracted to economics because it seemed to her that women weren't supposed to enter the field. She also got "tremendous satisfaction" when she outscored her boyfriend on the Graduate Record Exams. But Karen also has seen the toll careerism took in the frenzied lives of her parents, and she's not sure she wants that. Right now, following her grandmother, she's thinking of going to graduate school in social work. But like the Shelton women before her, she also wants a husband, family, and, yes, a daughter.

Karen believes she's more confident and assertive than her mother was at her age. She doesn't believe she has nearly the problem speaking up for herself. But Karen still shares a trait with the Shelton women before her. "I don't have as much faith in myself as I would like." And when it comes to men, she sees another similarity between herself and her grandmother: Julia believed men would find her more attractive if she didn't outshine or challenge them, and Karen believes it too. She believes "ninety-seven-and-a-half percent" of men like it when women act less competent, as if they need to be taken care of by men. What irritates Karen is that she sometimes finds herself willing to play the part, just as Julia did. But Julia never questioned the protocol, while Karen resists it, feels guilty if she does it, gets angry at herself. Still, she's drawn to that comfortable place of dependency, the role she believes she saw her mother play.

"I've been consciously trying over the past year to learn to live independently and have confidence in myself and in my own ability to solve things," Karen says, "as opposed to thinking I have to have this man to solve things for me."

Mary knows the implications of Karen's words. In the way that her own relationship with Karen reflected back on Julia, Karen's desire for autonomy reflects back on Mary. Growing beyond your mother, Mary believes, is the hardest thing. "If I perceived my mother a certain way, can I be different from her?" she asks. "Or does she have to change before I can change? It has to do with self-esteem. I thought it unfair of me to want to feel better about myself than my mother felt about herself. I felt it was a kind of disloyalty."

So Mary is at once proud and envious of her daughter. Karen was tempted to marry right after college as Mary did. But she didn't, decided she was attracted to marriage for the wrong reasons—fear of being alone, the desire to be protected. She believed living independently would build her confidence, and it has. It's the one thing Mary would do differently—she'd marry later, give herself time to learn that she could rely on herself. Truth is, she knows Karen wasn't wrong in her girlhood perception that Mary once needed Danny's approval to feel good about herself.

"You didn't want me to want his approval?" Mary asks.

"Not for things like your closet. You should be able to say, 'It's *my* closet!'"

"You wanted me to be able to say it when I was twenty-five?"

Karen nods.

"Like I didn't practice what I preached?"

"'Stories for Free Children' meet real life," Karen says.

Mary smiles. "But look at it this way, sweetheart. You're gonna do it better than I did. Isn't that wonderful?" Then Mary hollers, *"Great! Fabulous! Wonderful!"*

And the three generations of Shelton women all laugh, especially Karen, the forebear yet to bear, the daughter who hopes to be the mother who hopes to be the grandmother, the daughter who will someday clasp the unblemished hand of a girl yet unborn, a girl who will herself reach back and unknowingly brush the hands of Lizzie Mehaffie and Mary Gemmill and Julia Shelton, women whose memories will be lost in the dimness beyond two generations, a girl who will love and judge her mother as Karen has loved and judged Mary, a girl who, if strong and confident, will be disloyal enough to grow beyond them all.

She will have blond hair. It will turn to brown.

April 17, 1994

Rita Dove.
Photo by Fred Viebahn.

The Shape of Her Dreaming

Bed, where are you flying to?

—A line jotted in a notebook in 1980 by
Rita Dove, United States poet laureate

February 5, 1995, 5:35 P.M.

Twilight is not the time Rita Dove prefers to work. Much better are the crystal hours between midnight and 5:00 A.M., her writing hours when she lived in Ireland the summer of 1978, before her daughter was born, and Rita was young, with only a handful of poems published, before the Pulitzer Prize, before she became poet laureate of the United States. In Ireland, she and her husband, Fred Viebahn, a German novelist, would spend the late afternoons selecting dinner at the fish market, filling their sherry bottle from the merchant's oak cask, strolling Dublin's streets. They would cook dinner, write letters, read, talk, make love, watch TV into the late night, and then Rita would write, or do what people *call* writing, until the milkman arrived at sunrise and it was time to go off to sleep.

No more, not with her twelve-year-old daughter, Aviva, the trips to Washington, the phone and fax, the letters, speeches, interviews, the traveling—oh, the traveling. It's the worst. It doesn't respect a poet's frame of mind. Rita can't go off chasing a shard of thought about the three-legged telescope her father once bought, or why it is that hosts in southern Germany fill up a guest's wineglass before it is empty, or whether a forest's leaves can be both mute *and* riotous at once (they can, of course). While traveling, Rita must catch a plane, look both ways, always muster the dedicated, logical mind of a banker or a plumber.

But this afternoon, for the first time in a while, she sits at her desk in her new writing cabin, which stands down a sharp slope from the back door of her house in the countrified suburbs of Charlottesville, where she teaches at the University of Virginia. The cabin is small—twelve by twenty, a storage shed with insulation and drywall, a skylight so tiny it's more like the thought of a

119

skylight, a wall of windows whose mullions create miniature portraits of the woods, pond, mountains, and sunset to the west. No phone, fax, TV, no bathroom or running water, hardly any books by others and certainly no copies of her own nine books: "They're done. They have nothing to do with the moment of writing a poem." On a small stereo, she plays music without words—lately, Bach's Brandenburg concerti and Keith Jarrett's jazz piano.

The last few days, Rita has been thinking about three poems she'd like to write—"Meditation," "Parlor," and "Sweet Dreams." She began to ponder the last poem after she reread a few lines she'd scribbled in a notebook in 1980. For fifteen years, she had looked at those lines every couple of months and thought, "No, I can't do it yet." She wrote three hundred other poems instead. But just seven weeks from today, Rita Dove will consider "Sweet Dreams" done—with a new title, new lines, new images, and a new meaning the poet herself will not recognize until the poem is nearly finished.

It will be a curious, enlightening journey: one poem, one act of creation, evoked from a thousand private choices, embedded in breath and heartbeat, music, meter, and rhyme, in the logic of thought and the intuition of emotion, in the confluence of the two, in the mystery of art and the labor of craft, which will transform random journal notations, bodiless images, unanchored thoughts, orphan lines of poetry, and meticulously kept records of times and dates into something more. Words with dictionary meanings will become words that mean only what the experiences of others will make of them, words no longer spoken in Rita's voice but in whispering voices heard only inside the heads of those who pause to read her poem.

In 1980, living in a fifty-dollar-a-month, one-room walk-up in West Berlin, Rita was sick in bed one day. For light reading, she picked up *Das Bett,* a German book about the place of the bed in history. She was leafing page to page, when she came upon this sentence: "Vergleiche man die Wände der Wohnung mit einer Nußchale, so wäre das Bett jene feine Haut um den Nußkern, den Menschen."

She stopped. She loved the sentence, its meaning—if the walls of an apartment are like a nutshell, then the apartment's bed is like the fine, delicate skin around the kernel, which is the human being. But she also loved the sentence's sound. In the way that the sensuous glissando of a harp, the haunting blue note of a trumpet, or the hypnotic percussion of a drum can touch a person's mood, Rita's mood was touched by the *sound* of the German words said together in their sentence. As a composer might hear a bird twittering and a woodpecker pecking and suddenly hear instead a melody, Rita suddenly felt "the cadence of thought."

The sentence said something beautiful and it sounded beautiful: "And that is the essence of poetry." It is language as idea and sensation at once: "the clay that makes the pot." Rita copied the German sentence into her notebook and wrote, "Bed, where are you flying to?" She imagined the bed as a home, the bed as a magic carpet, the bed as a world: "That's the inspiration. I have no idea what the leap is."

Soon after, she wrote:

> sic itur ad astra
> (such is the way to the stars, or to immortality)

> Bed, where are you flying to?
> I went to sleep
> an hour ago, now
> I'm on a porch
> open to the world.

> I don't remember a thing,
> not even dreaming.

> and Chagall shall play
> his piebald violin.

> we'll throw away
> the books and play
> sea-diver in the sheets—
> for aren't we all children
> in our over-size shirts (clothes),
> white priests of the night!

Rita enjoyed the lines, especially the first stanza. Like the sentence in *Das Bett*, it seemed to have a music all its own and to carry the exuberance and spontaneity of a child's dream, although the stanza also baffled Rita: "I wasn't quite sure what it meant."

Rita has, after a fashion, a filing system—plastic folders in yellow, blue, red, purple, green, pink, peach, or clear. She doesn't file her nascent poems by subject or title, as a scientist or historian might file documents. She files poems by the way they *feel* to her. Red attracts poems about war and violence. Purple, Rita's favorite color, accumulates introspective poems. Yellow likes sunshine. Blue likes the sky. Green likes nature. Pink—after a line she wrote about her daughter: "We're in the pink / and the pink's in us"—is a magnet for poems about mothers and daughters. But the categories aren't fixed: Blue is the color of sky, but blue is also the color of the Virgin Mary's robe.

Rita's flying bed poem went in the clear folder, which holds very little: "The clear folder wants to be pure thought." A clean, fresh, pure lyrical poem: "It was a daunting folder. Very few things ever made it out of that folder."

But when Rita sits down at her desk this fifth of February, as she goes through her ritual of laying out her folders, looking at each, and waiting for the door to her intuition to swing open and reveal to her which she should pick up and thumb through, she reaches for the clear folder, reads the old poem, and thinks: "Maybe I can do it now." Maybe in this cabin, clean and fresh and pure as a lyrical poem, she can finally finish it: "It was now or never."

At 5:35, she writes:

SWEET DREAMS
— *Sic itur ad astra. (Such is the way to the stars.)*

Bed, where are you flying to?
I went to sleep nearly
an hour ago—now I'm on a porch
open to the stars!

I don't remember a thing,
not the crease in the sheet,
the neighbor's washing machine.
I'm a child again, barefoot, catching
my death of cold,

in my oversized nightshirt
and stocking cap . . .
but so are all the others,
eyes wide, arms outstretched in greeting—
white priests of the night!

Rita is fiddling, playing, just seeing where her mind takes her words. She has changed the poem's title to "Sweet Dreams." She has lost Chagall and his piebald violin, the sea-diver in the sheets. She has gained the neighbor's washing machine, the crease in the sheet, and the barefoot child catching her death of cold. She has altered punctuation. But as she rereads the poem, it is the stanza she wrote fifteen years ago that grabs her—the porch open to the *world* has become the porch open to the *stars:* "It changed without me even thinking about it."

What did that mean?

She jots these notes on her poem: "The original impulse of the poem—it was meant to be magic, pure impossible magic. The speaker goes to sleep & wakes into a journey—is it a dream or the lost feeling when you wake & don't know where you are? . . . How to capture the ecstasy, the spontaneity?"

Rita now enters a strange and magical place in the creation of her poetry, as she begins to carry on a kind of conversation with her poem, as she tries to actually *listen* to what the poem she has written is trying to tell her, the poet.

And the poem begins to create itself.

Rita uses this analogy: One of her favorite books as a girl was *Harold and the Purple Crayon*. With his crayon, Harold drew before him on the blank page the places he wanted to go—a street, a hill, a house. He created the world into which he then entered. But once inside that world, it was real, not an illusion. For Rita, writing a poem is like Harold drawing his way through life: Once a line is written she can step out onto it. The line is like a train and she a passenger curious to learn its destination. Each line is an idea that carries her to the next idea. Yes, she is taking the poem somewhere, but the poem is also taking her.

Some people's minds run from point A to point B with the linear determination of an express bus roaring from stop to distant stop. Theirs are minds trained to avoid detours, to cut a path past the alleys and side streets of distraction. Rita's mind is more like the water of a stream swirling randomly, chaotically, and unpredictably over the stones below as it still flows resolutely downstream: "It's hard to describe your own mind, but I am really interested in the process of thought. Sometimes I catch myself observing my own thoughts and think, 'Boy, that's kinda strange how that works.'" Rita is not like those who see tangential thoughts as distracting digressions: "I'm interested in the sidetracking."

When her poem's first stanza was written, for instance, its character was in a dream, flying on a bed, feeling a child's excitement—"open to the world." Perhaps, Rita asks herself, she unthinkingly changed "world" to "stars" in a later version not as a simple slip of the pen, but because the world is really what her dreamer *wants* to leave behind? Perhaps the stars—or immortality, the word Rita wrote beneath the poem's title fifteen years ago—are her character's real destination? And, she tells herself, that isn't just exciting but also frightening, meaning that "Sweet Dreams" was never meant to be only a joyful, childlike poem.

"That's what had stopped me all these years."

February 10, 4:30 P.M.

In her cabin, Rita stands at the *Schreibpult,* the stand-up writing desk that her father, an amateur woodworker, built as a surprise for her two years ago when she turned forty. While visiting her folks, Rita saw the desk in their basement. She came upstairs and said to her father, "That's a pretty nice desk down there." And he said, "Well, when your birthday comes you can take it home." It had been a decade since Rita had mentioned to her father that she'd like such a desk: "It was astonishing."

Rita is sick today, coughing and feverish, but the jobs of wife, mother, professor, and poet laureate go on, with the job of poet taking a backseat. It has been a satisfying and grueling time that will ease this summer when her two-year tenure as laureate expires, but the fame that it has brought will forever change her life. She can no longer write in her university office, because someone will stop by to visit. She can no longer sit in an outdoor café in town and read, because someone will recognize her. Some days she hasn't the time to make a single entry in her notebook—not a fragment of conversation, a recipe, a fresh word. She has a new book of poetry just out, *Mother Love,* but still feels a creative emptiness in the face of so many demands, is afraid of losing the human *connection* to the clay that makes the pot: "It's harder and harder. Fame is very seductive. I'm tired of hearing the sound of my own voice. I want to be silent." Often, she has asked herself, "Was I writing for prizes? No. I wrote because of those moments when something happens in a poem." She once wrote these lines: "He used to sleep like a glass of water / held up in the hand of a very young girl."

"That was a great moment."

Rita loves the image, although she doesn't know exactly what it means or even feel the need to know. She remembers a line written by poet Stanley Kunitz: "The night nailed like an orange to my brow." Kunitz once said that for years he lived in fear that someone would ask him to *explain* that line. He didn't understand the image, Rita says, but he wasn't going to touch it. "Sometimes you have those moments. Those are the moments you live for. There are some that change your life. When I write, I feel like I am learning something new every second. But I'm also *feeling* something more deeply. You don't know where you've been. That's the mystery of it. And then to be able to put it down so that someone else can feel it! I feel incredibly alive."

Outside Rita's cabin windows, two Canada geese are nesting at the pond beneath the little pier Fred built last year. Never before has she had so comforting a view from the windows of a study. The years she and Fred spent in Europe, they lived in dark apartments that looked out onto concrete. In Arizona, she gazed out at a decaying swimming pool in the backyard.

This cabin is doing something *to* Rita. When she was a ten-year-old girl, a few months before her first period, she daydreamed a house for herself: "It was small, one room . . . This dream house would stand in the backyard, away from the house with its clinging odors but close enough to run back—just in case." Her cabin is eerily reminiscent of the fantasy. And like Harold's purple crayon, like a poem that begins to create itself, the cabin is casting its own role in Rita's life. When she comes here, even for an hour, she writes at least a line or two. In this cabin, even in the middle of the day, it seems like the crystal hours from midnight to 5:00 A.M.: "It's a harkening back."

On her desk, Rita has put the tiniest clock she could find, and she has decorated her bulletin board with pictures. A photo of a Colorado sand dune that resembles the torso of a woman: "I just love this. I don't know why I love it." A postcard depicting a solarium (her grandmother's house had a solarium) in which sits a violoncello, an instrument Rita played as a girl: "It's a room I'd like to be in." A snapshot of Rita and her daughter, who is almost totally obscured by shadows, standing in a dry riverbed in Arizona: "You can barely see her, but I know she's there." What do the pictures mean? Rita has no idea. "These are things that make me start to dream. They open my mind."

She writes in her journal:

"What I love about my cabin—what I always forget that I love until I open the door and step into it—is the absolute quiet. Oh, not the dead silence of a studio, a silence so physical that you begin to gasp for air; and it's not the allegorical silence of an empty apartment, with its creaks and sniffles and traffic a dull roar below, and the neighbors' muffled treading overhead. No, this is the silence of the world: birds shifting weight on branches, the branches squeaking against other twigs, the deer *hooosching* through the woods. It's a silence where you can hear your blood in your chest, if you choose to listen."

February 20, 5:45 P.M.
Rita has identified her problem: She's like an opera singer who must—without exercising her voice, humming a bar, hearing a note struck on a keyboard—hit a perfect B-flat. She has been away from the first stanza of "Sweet Dreams" so long, she likes it so much, that it's like one of her published books—it's *done*. She can't read the lines and rekindle the emotions that created the lines in the first place—and so she can't hitch a ride on those emotions into the rest of the poem. In the language of the poetry craft, she can't "make the turn" from the first stanza to the next. So she ignores the first stanza, begins without it.
    In her cabin, she writes:

> I'm a child again, barefoot,
> catching my death of cold
> in a nightshirt I've never seen before
> fluttering white as a sail . . .
>
> moonlight cool as peaches above me,
> below,—but I won't look below.
>
> Bed, come back (here), I need you!
> I don't know my way back.
> Bed, at least leave me my pillow

Rita is writing lines and stepping out onto them. She decides to break away from "the tyranny of the typewritten page." In the margins, at odd angles, she writes: "purple crayon," "blow," "languid," "fluid," "landings," "whispering, happy landings." She is searching for the feeling of flying. Suddenly, she's frustrated: "Can I fly? If I could only remember! How does one remember?" She continues to scribble: "I've lost my feet," "with its garden of smells," "aromas," "crushed smells," "its petals whispering happy landings." She picks up a book of poetry by Wallace Stevens, thumbs through the pages, and jots down words that strike her: "confusion," "hermit," "fetched." She scrawls: "purple hermit of dream."
    At 6:02, she writes:

I'm a child again, barefoot,
catching my death of cold
in a nightshirt I've never seen before
fluttering white as a sail.

Above me, moonlight cool as peaches.
Below . . . but I won't look below . . .

Come here bed, I need you!
I don't know my way back.
At least leave me my pillow
with its crushed aromas, its
garden of dreams, its purple petals
whispering *Happy landings*

"*I'm a child again.*" Too explanatory. The poem should have the *feeling* of childhood without needing to announce it.

"*Catching my death of cold.*" It goes on too long. This poem must be a collage of fleeting images, as in a dream. But Rita likes the line and would like to find a way to keep it.

"*Moonlight cool as peaches.*" She likes that line, too, may use it someday in another poem, but to mention food while in flight is too corporeal, too earthly. Still, she'll leave it in for now.

"*In a nightshirt I've never seen before.*" The image is too surreal, gives the sensation that the poem is a real dream rather than the sensation that it is *like* a dream.

"*I won't look below.*" Not believable. Her poem's character wouldn't need to remind herself not to look below at the world. She's yearning to leave it behind—for a ride to the stars.

"*Come here bed, I need you!*" Wait, the poem is talking to Rita again: Its traveler is ambivalent about her journey. She craves the stars but, like a child, also the comfort of her bed.

"*I don't know my way back.*" The word *back* is too narrow, too referential to the world. This traveler isn't worried about the way "back," but the way to the stars, the future, immortality.

"*Garden of dreams,*" "*purple petals,*" "*Happy landings.*" "Yech!" "Awful!" "Disgusting!" But Rita doesn't stop to change them. They are placeholders for the poem's cadence. New words will come.

On and on it goes—each line, each word examined. At 6:10, 6:15, 7:33, and 7:44, Rita begins new versions. She now believes that the complicated emotions in her poem can no longer be described as "Sweet Dreams." She hates it that people always accuse poets of being "hermetic"—hard to understand, obscure—but she goes back to the original Latin title from 1980 anyway.

Unlike an essayist, who must keep in mind readers' tastes, interests, biases, and education the better to convince them, Rita never thinks of her readers: "That sounds awful, I know. But to me a poem can't possibly be honest if I'm thinking about my readers."

It is a paradox: Rita has a better chance of reaching the emotions of her readers if she doesn't consciously try to reach them, if she doesn't worry about how people will respond to a certain poem. Pondering that would put a kind of emotional membrane between herself and her material, making it less authentic and more distant from the unmediated emotion she is trying to feel and then evoke, reinvent, in her readers: "If I start thinking about 'the world' and about the reception of this poem in the world, then I'm lost. I'm lost. It's not gonna be a poem."

Rita deletes "crushed aromas" because the word *aroma* is too "thick," not simple enough. That allows her to replace "garden of dreams," a cliché, with "garden of smells." She likes that change, because a smell, unlike an aroma, can be either pleasant or sickening. "Purple petals," which probably referred back to Harold's purple crayon, is excised. It's, well, too purple. Now, without "crushed aromas" and "purple petals," she adds "crushed petals." She plays with the poem's enjambment—the way sentences run on or break from line to line—looking for meanings that she didn't see at first: "Catching my death / of cold in a fluttering nightshirt," for instance, can mean something far different from "catching my death of cold / in a fluttering nightshirt."

At 7:44, with Keith Jarrett playing, she writes:

SIC ITUR AD ASTRA
—*Thus is the way to the stars.*

Bed, where are you flying to?
I went to sleep nearly
an hour ago, and now
I'm on a porch open
to the stars—barefoot,

catching my death of cold,
in a fluttering nightshirt
white as a sail. Above me,
moonlight cool as peaches.
Bed, come back here,

I need you! I don't know
my way. At least leave me
my pillow, with its garden of smells,
its crushed petals whispering
Lay back. Relax. Gentle landings.

On the poem she jots "dreams" and "worries of the day," reminding herself not to lose the poem's dreamlike feeling and to add the idea that traveling to the stars is also a way to leave the trivial bothers of daily life behind.

February 24, 5:35 P.M.

In her journal, Rita writes: "I want more intriguing, surprising metaphors . . . I want the language to imitate the clarity of children's literature . . . I'm looking for an image as wild and apt, as wonderfully penetrating yet impenetrable, as Gabriel García Márquez': '. . . and death began to flow through his bones like a river of ashes.' If I could catch a fish like that, I'd be ready to die. No, not really. But the contentment would be immense and would last my entire life."

But not so others can *read* the line and admire her as she admires Márquez, but so she can *feel* the line's creation. It's an addictive joy, a feeling of exhilaration, yes, but not of pride. It's beyond pride, or maybe before it: "I feel very humble: 'Thank you, line. I don't know where you came from, but you're greater than I am.' You have those moments. They're the ones that keep you writing. You're always after the next fish."

It is 6:20 now, sundown out the cabin window. Rita takes up a new pen and writes: "Now we'll see how this pen works. Sungown. Dundown. The light quenched. Oh, fennel bloom. Another ladybug—perennially cute, ladybug, body and name. Too many make a plague of luck. Ah shame on you, duckie: You've lost your quack. For an ounce of your prattle I'd hang up my traveling shoes."

What does it mean? Who knows.

Gone fishing.

March 13, 4:23 P.M.

Rita was going through old notebooks earlier today, trying to unclog her mind, searching for inspiration hidden in a line or even a word: "A word that will knock this damn poem back on line." It was a beautiful seventy-three-degree day outside, but Rita was at her desk imagining the sensations of flying on a bed at night: "The absence of incidental 'white noise,' the smells and the cool feelings that night floats up in us, almost like the earth is emitting a faint subterranean sigh."

She wants to write this poem, but the world is relentless: *USA Weekend* has asked the U.S.A. poet laureate for an original poem to publish; she must plan her laureate's farewell poetry reading at the Library of Congress, organize the panels for an upcoming literature conference, write the opening remarks for the Nobel Laureates in Literature convocation, finish writing her lecture for the university faculty colloquium, and write the foreword to an anthology of stories written by children. That's for starters.

But then, going through a tiny black-and-red notebook, Rita comes across a snatch of forgotten poetry she jotted down while at a conference in Morelia, Mexico, in January 1994.

READING BEFORE SLEEP

Bed, where are you flying to?
One minute ago I climbed
      into the cool
waters of night & now
        (end of day)
I'm on a porch
open to the sky
      world!
If I close my eyes
I'll sink back
into the day, made
    strange—
but no, my eyes are open
and I am falling it
    seems
forward

Rita is amazed. Just the other day, she made a note to remind herself to add to her poem the idea that traveling to the stars was also a way to escape daily life—"the worries of the day." Now she finds, in the forgotten Mexico notations, these lines: "If I close my eyes / I'll sink back / into the day." She thinks, "This thing has been haunting me for all these years." She writes in her journal: "Somewhere there's a few lines about melancholy. Where is that sheet of paper?" Then, dutifully, she spends the afternoon and the evening working on a poem for *USA Weekend*.

March 17, 5:47 P.M.

Fred has asked Rita to go with him and Aviva to the stable where Aviva keeps her horse. Rita, who hasn't been out to the stable in months, hears Fred's plea and agrees, although she plans to sit in the car, watch Aviva and her horse trot around the track, and work on "Sic Itur." But once she gets to the stable, she can't capture the poem's mood. The grounds are too much of the earth, not the stars. So Rita works on "Parlor," one of the three unfinished poems she considered working on way back on February 5. She works for an hour, scribbling additions and deletions and notations on her copy. Then Fred climbs into the car, out of the cold, and turns on the radio news.

"Does that disturb you?" he asks.

"No," Rita says, lying. "I think I'll just stretch my legs."

Walking out along the fence line in the descending darkness, Rita asks herself, "I've had all this time to write. Why can't I give up this few minutes?" She wants to be in her cabin writing, but she wants to be with Fred and Aviva. She wants to be with Fred and Aviva, but she wants to be poet laureate of the United States: "I want to fly as a poet." She takes out her notebook and writes, "Sic Itur Ad Astra: You don't want to come down. Immortality—it's loneliness. You long for the pillow's smells, the earth you are leaving but that's all you can take—the recycled breath, the memory—into the rarefied air. The dear worries, the sweet troubles of dailiness."

And it has happened.

Rita's poem is creating itself—it is a train, she its passenger: "For the first time since I wrote that stupid title down I realized I wrote it down because it had that line about the way to immortality. I realized I was talking about fame."

Naturally, people reading Rita's poem will know none of this. They'll see the poem's themes through the lens of their own ambivalent feelings about whatever are the conflicting demands in their lives. But the tension Rita feels between the satisfactions of fame and accomplishment and the joys of everyday life is *her* particular lens—and the emotional juice of her poem. Because a new meaning has emerged for that first line written in Rita's sickbed in Germany in 1980, before her life had become a dream ride from earth to the stars: "I want 'em both."

"It's just that I've felt lonely."

"Where's my life? I want a life."

March 19, 4:30 P.M.

It comes quickly. Yesterday, the Brandenburg concerti playing for two hours, Rita ripped through four versions of "Sic Itur." Today, the Brandenburg concerti still playing, she whips through five versions. She has found her old musings on melancholy, cribbed an image—"tiny dismissals"—and combined it with the lines on life's trivial irritations from her Mexico notations: "If I close / my eyes, I'll sink back into / the day's tiny dismissals."

Rita has turned a corner. Forced to work on her poem for *USA Weekend*, impelled to work on "Parlor" at the stable, her mind was somehow freed, her attention distracted momentarily from "Sic Itur," which, inexplicably, allowed Rita to finally see her poem clearly. These so-called distractions cleared a path so that her poem could happen *to* her, as if she is not the creator of insight, but its recipient. Rita keeps a single quote, in German, tacked to her cabin's bulletin board, the wisdom of Austrian poet Rainer Maria Rilke: *It is not enough for a poet to have memories. You must have very great patience and be able to wait until the memories come again.* Memories remain, but the poet changes: "You have to wait until it all comes back in a different form to find the meaning."

Rita is loose now, playing—with words, images, punctuation, enjambment, and stanza size. She writes a line, walks out onto it, looks ahead, continues or steps back, tries another. For the first time, she can hear the rhythm of her poem before its words are written, as in a song that doesn't yet have lyrics. "It's very weird."

She writes:

> Bed, where are you flying to?
> I went to sleep nearly
> an hour ago, and now
> I'm on a porch open
> to the stars! If I close
> my eyes, I'll sink back into
>
> the day's tiny dismissals—
> bagged lunch, the tiny dismissal of a glance—
> but no, I'm wide-eyed and barefoot,
> catching my death of cold,
> nightshirt fluttering white as a sail.
>
> Bed, come back here, I need you!
> I don't know my way.
> At least leave me my pillow
> to remind me what I've rested my dreams on—
> my dear/crushed pillow, with its garden of smells.

Rita is suddenly hit with an image that grows from the lines she wrote way back on February 5: "I don't remember a thing, / not the crease in the sheets."
She writes:

> What will they do when they come in
> and find me missing, just the shape
> of my dreaming creased in the sheets?

The lines make Rita shiver in the way she once shivered when she wrote, "He used to sleep like a glass of water / held up in the hand of a very young girl." That *feeling*. So much of writing a poem is less like saying a prayer than it is like putting together the weekly shopping list. Then comes a sacred moment . . . For Rita, these lines are a fish to keep—a rare poet's epiphany in the muck of craft: "I don't know where it came from. It just came."
Then:

> Bed, where are you flying to?
> I went to sleep nearly
> an hour ago, and now

I'm on a porch
open to the stars—barefoot,
catching my death of a cold
in a nightshirt fluttering white

as a sail. Come here, bed,
I need you! I don't know my way.
If I close my eyes, I sink back
into the day's bagged smiles,
the tiny dismissal of a stranger's glance . . .

Oh, what will they do
when they find me missing,
just the shape of my dreaming
creased in the sheets?
Who will tell them what it's like here?
No one else knows but my pillow—

my poor, crushed pillow with its garden of smells!

Then:

Bed, where are you flying to?
I went to sleep
nearly an hour ago,
and now I'm on a porch
open to the stars!

Close my eyes
and I sink back into the day's
tiny dismissals; eyes wide
and I'm barefoot, in a nightshirt
fluttering white as a sail.

Come here, bed,
I need you!
I don't know my way.
What will they say
when they find me missing,
just the shape of my dreaming

creasing the sheets?
At least leave me
my pillow to remind me
what misery I've fled—
my poor, crushed pillow

with its garden of smells!

Out Rita's window, the sun is lingering three inches above the mountains. The days are longer now, but she has been too busy even to notice that it is spring: "Why is spring a she? What gender are the other seasons? Summer is female, surely. And winter, too. Fall? Actually, they're all female." Rita's mind, again, is swirling like water over stones in a stream.

"I had given up on this poem."

"It's a great feeling."

"I'm rolling!"

Rita has deleted the sappy line, *"Lay back. Relax. Gentle landings."* She has again included "catching my death of cold" but then excised it as too "cutesy-wootsy." "Bagged lunch" has gone in, become "bagged smiles," and gone out: "I don't know what a 'bagged smile' is." She has finally taken out "moonlight cool as peaches," and the cliché "wide-eyed" has become "eyes wide" and will later become simply "open wide." She has added "the tiny dismissal of a glance," which has become "the tiny dismissal of a stranger's glance," a cliché she hates, and which has now become simply "the day's tiny dismissals." She loves the sneering sound of the *hiss* in the word *dismissals.* The line "Bed, come back here" has become the more direct "Come here, bed."

Remembering her notation to emphasize that this poem should have the feeling of a dream, Rita has added, "I've rested on my dreams," which she hates as a cliché. But she thinks, "Oh, hell, I'm just gonna put the dreams in and see what happens." Working from her epiphanic flash, the lines have become "just the shape / of my dreaming creased in the sheets," which have now become "just the shape of my dreaming / creasing the sheets." Rita also has added a stanza space between "just the shape of my dreaming" and "creasing the sheets." That space will force a reader to pause after the word "dreaming," float in the space, and ponder the image before moving on to the next line. The newly added gerundive i-n-g ending on the word *dream* also carries action—and the sense that the act of dreaming, not the dream itself, is leaving its impression on the bed of real life. As with her poetry, the product is inseparable from the process. In the words of Yeats: "How can we know the dancer from the dance?"

Rita has added "my dear / crushed pillow," although she knows it's too corny. She has quickly changed it to "my poor, crushed pillow." Despite the truism that a poet should never use two adjectives when one will do, she wants two adjectives to precede the word pillow. Less for the words than for the double *beat* of emphasis, which is meant to mimic the intense affection of a child for a blanket, toy, or pillow: "It's not always the words themselves that bring you the nostalgia but the sound and the rhythm of the words."

This is Rita's ideal: She wants to take a reader to the place she would go as a girl when she read a poem and suddenly felt her breathing begin to synchronize with the poem's cadence: "Before you know it, your body's rhythm is the rhythm of the poem. That's one of the things poems do. You don't even notice that it's happening. But what convinces you is the way the poem influences your breathing, your heartbeat. It becomes a physical thing. You want people to get there."

Rita has realized that the final sentiment of her poem is mundane. After visiting the stars, her traveler discovers the wonder of what she has left behind: "my poor, crushed pillow / with its garden of smells!"—meaning her ordinary life with Fred and Aviva, the days Rita cooks those quick meals of frozen fish fillets, sliced fried potatoes, and salad with Caesar dressing, the evenings they all plop down at the TV and watch Aviva's favorite show, *Star Trek: Voyager*, and then Rita quizzes Aviva for her test on earthquakes and volcanoes, and Aviva is curled up on the chair, and in the silence between Rita's questions and Aviva's answers Rita can hear the sound of the leather creaking as her daughter adjusts her body, which makes Rita think to herself, "There's no sound in the poem. Is there sound in dreams? Sound does funny things in dreams—it's like telepathy."

Of her yearning to travel to the stars and her irritation with daily life, Rita asks herself, "Where you gonna go? Is there anything really better than this?" And how else to be a poet? Aren't the trivial, even irritating distractions of life the wellspring, the clay that makes the pot? A poet free from "the day's tiny dismissals," living only among the stars, will not be a poet for long: "It sounds like the old, corny notion, 'Love will bring you back,' but you know that's what it is. How many different plots do we have in this world? Not many."

For the first time, Rita stops to analyze the poem's rhyme and discovers a surprising array of rhymes, half rhymes, and "cousins" of rhymes: barefoot/nightshirt, my way/they say, creasing/sheets, fled/bed, smells/dismissals, sail/smell. Although a reader wouldn't consciously notice the rhymes, they still weave the poem together, like the reprising melodies of a minuet: "Okay, I'm ready!"

Rita has been writing versions of "Sic Itur" with different stanza configurations—experimenting, seeing if stanza breaks at different lines carry meanings she hasn't recognized, in the same way that playing with a poem's enjambment can reveal a new insight. But now she realizes how she wants the stanzas constructed: "It's really, really picky." But if "Sic Itur" is a journey *up* to the stars and back *down* to earth, it demands a narrow, vertical silhouette on the page: "To lift you up in the sky." And if it is to evoke the simplicity of childhood, it also must *look* clean and pure on the page. The idea is to reach people not only through words, ideas, images, sounds, rhythms, and rhymes but also through the pattern of ink their eyes see on the page.

She goes through tightening lines to narrow the poem's width and extend its height. Then she adjusts the number of lines in each stanza. From top to bottom: one-and-a-half-line title, five-line stanza, six-line stanza, six-line stanza, five-line stanza, one-line stanza: "It's like a mirror image," which makes the tug of the stars and the pull of the world equal in visual weight on the page.

At 5:24, she writes:

SIC ITUR AD ASTRA
Thus is the way to the stars.

Bed, where are you flying to?
I went to sleep
nearly an hour ago—
and now I'm on a porch
open to the stars!

Close my eyes
and sink back to
day's tiny dismissals;
open wide and I'm
barefoot, in a nightshirt
fluttering white as a sail.

Come here, bed,
I need you!
I don't know my way.
What will they say
when they find me missing,
just the shape of my dreaming

creasing the sheets?
At least leave me
my pillow to remind me
what misery I've fled . . .
my poor, crushed pillow

with its garden of smells!

Rita has a few nits . . .

"I'm dotting the i's."

She worries about the word *fluttering* in the line "fluttering white as a sail."
Is it necessary? Does it add enough for the space it takes? Unlike prose, which
Rita compares to walking through the woods and describing everything you
see, poetry is like walking through the woods, coming upon an old, deep well,
and describing only what you see as you stare down its casing. Poetry is a narrow world made wide. So every word, every line in a poem must stand on its
own. But without the word *fluttering*, the line is lame: "white as a sail." Pick
any line: "just the shape of my dreaming" or "and sink back to." Each adds
something—action, an image, lyricism, intrigue, an idea. But wait . . . that one
line: "At least leave me." What does it add? Nothing: "It just sits there."

"This line and I are going to battle."

Rita's not sure about those three i-n-gs in a row—missing, dreaming, creasing. And she's not sure about the line "Close my eyes"—she might add a

comma at its end. Today, she's not even sure about the title—maybe she should go back to "Sweet Dreams," which now carries a touch of irony. But adding "Sweet Dreams" would put too much type at the top of the poem and muck up her mirror-image construction of the stanzas. And for the poem to make sense she still needs the Latin and its translation—"Thus is the way to the stars." Come to think of it, maybe she should go back to translating "thus" as "such"—"Such is the way to the stars." Less pedantic. And she'd better look up the quotation. Turns out to be from Virgil's "Aeneid," which she didn't know: "Oh, shame!" She must attribute it. No room for "Sweet Dreams" now.

Maybe she should move down "Come here, bed, I need you" and move up "just the shape of my dreaming creasing the sheets," so the poem's character flies from sky to earth, earth to sky, sky to earth—a trip that ends back home, where Rita has realized she wants to be. But then she'd lose the spatial pause between "just the shape of my dreaming" and "creasing the sheets." And that word *misery!* Rita wants it to be self-mocking. "What misery I've fled . . ." is supposed to mean that her daily life wasn't misery at all. But the word is too strong. "I think there's a different word that won't ring as many bells. One word. And it should be three syllables, but it might end up having to be two."

March 26, 1:43 A.M.
After allowing herself a week of distractions, a week for her poem to simmer, Rita writes:

> SIC ITUR AD ASTRA
> *Thus is the way to the stars.*
> *—Virgil*
>
> Bed, where are you flying to?
> I went to sleep
> nearly an hour ago,
> and now I'm on a porch
> open to the stars!
>
> Close my eyes
> and sink back to
> day's tiny dismissals;
> open wide and I'm
> barefoot, nightshirt
> fluttering white as a sail.
>
> What will they say
> when they find me
> missing—just
> the shape of my dreaming

creasing the sheets?
Come here, bed,

I need you! I don't know my way.
At least leave my pillow
behind to remind me
what affliction I've fled—
my poor, crushed pillow

with its garden of smells!

"A poem is never done. You just let it go."

In her cabin, Rita hears the distant woof of a dog. Outside the open window is a faint wind: "The sound of air moving—not quite a breeze, but a sighing— all that the word *zephyr* implies." She remembers a time as a girl when her father said that word. At a gas station, as the attendant filled his tank, her father stood and stretched, faced off into the horizon, and said as naturally as if he were asking for the time, "What a lovely zephyr today." Young Rita never forgot the baffled look on the attendant's face. Where are those few words she jotted?

Ah, here they are:

> Meek, this fallen leaf
> reminds me of a word
> my father used to say—
> zephyr, tilting back to
> gaze up under his brimmed fedora
> as if to coax the air along
> his brow: "What a lovely zephyr
> today." And the gas station
> attendant scratched himself,
> instantly ashamed

And once again, Rita steps out onto the lines . . .

May 7, 1995

Bryan Stevenson.

Photo by Paul Robertson, ABA JOURNAL.

The Mystery of Goodness

> On the threshing-floor, in the center of the
> crying, singing saints, John lay astonished
> beneath the power of the Lord.
>
> —*James Baldwin,* GO TELL IT ON THE MOUNTAIN

I am not an expert on religion, far from it. But somewhere along
the way, I learned that in ancient Jewish legend there is told the story of the
lamedvovniks, the thirty-six Righteous Men who were sent by God to live and
work among us, always poor, unnoticed and without glory, unaware of their
own perfection. If a Righteous Man were ever discovered, various versions of
the legend went, he would deny his identity, disappear, and reappear,
unknown and unknowing, in a distant place. I do not believe in *lamedvovniks.*
I do not even believe in God. But over the years, I've sometimes puzzled at the
idea of these Righteous Men living secretly among us, been reminded that
what it means to be truly good was as mysterious to those who lived a thousand years ago as it is to us, with all our modern sophistication.

Lately, after meeting Bryan Stevenson, I've found myself puzzling over
these questions once again. But then, that often happens to people after they
meet Bryan Stevenson.

This morning, Bryan—thirty-one, a lawyer, and a black man—is on the road
out of Montgomery, Alabama, where he lives, headed for Phenix City, a tiny
Alabama town where Bryan's black client George Daniel has been locked in
the Russell County jail awaiting his execution for murdering a white policeman. Just yesterday, a federal court overturned his conviction and ordered that
he be given a new trial.

That is what Bryan Stevenson does. He files appeals. He is one of those
much-maligned lawyers who supposedly clog the courts with frivolous peti-
tions meant only to postpone deserving men's dates with the electric chair, gas
chamber, or needle.

At the Russell County jail, Bryan is ushered into a small room where George
Daniel is waiting. As Bryan tells him that he'll have a new trial—which might
literally save George's life—the thin, thirty-four-year-old man smiles blankly,

139

squeezes his nose tightly, rocks his body gently, and bounces his legs to some rapid, internal rhythm. He wears a white jail uniform that is filthy at the crotch. The last time Bryan visited George, his cell was dirty with his own urine. Court records show that at least once during his incarceration George Daniel ate his own feces and that he is mildly retarded. "I need cigarettes," he says finally. Bryan promises to get cigarettes, and George is led away. As Bryan leaves, a guard stops him at the jailhouse gate and says of George Daniel, "I think he's crazy. I really do. That's just my opinion. We have to make him take a shower and change clothes. I think he's crazy. Some people are playin'. I don't think he is."

Outside, past the electric door and the tall wire fence, Bryan says, "George is one of the men America believes is so evil he must be strapped into an electric chair and killed." He doesn't say this harshly or self-righteously. He says it gently, with eerie understatement. "You know, people always ask me how I can defend these 'animals.' I never understand how they can ask that. The criminal justice system is so corrupt, so racist. I wouldn't want George Daniel out fending for himself. He can't. He's ill. But a civilized society does not execute people like him. Chief Justice William Rehnquist can restrict legal options for the convicted, because he can't imagine himself or anyone he loves ever being in George Daniel's situation. But how would Rehnquist feel if his son were in George's place? In the end, we are too frail to make these decisions."

I met Bryan Stevenson by chance while traveling through the South, which boasts more than half of America's death-row inmates and about 85 percent of its executions since 1977. Right off, Bryan fascinated me. A graduate of Harvard's law school and John F. Kennedy School of Government, he's the director of the Alabama Capital Representation Resource Center, which is involved in some way with most of the 119 death-row inmates in Alabama. He was offered $50,000 to $60,000 a year to take the director's job, one of the center's board members told me, but Bryan said it was too much money. He settled on $18,000—now up to $24,000. In corporate law, he could make five to ten times that.

Bryan worked seven days a week, still does, often from 8:30 in the morning to 11:30 at night. On Saturdays and Sundays, he knocks off early to do his laundry and maybe catch a movie. These days, he has little time to play his electric piano, compose music, play basketball, or attend church, all of which he once did regularly. He hasn't had a vacation in years. Once a voracious reader, Bryan has read three books for pleasure in the last year. He sometimes worries that he doesn't laugh enough anymore. Simply put, the man was hard to figure. A person didn't need to believe Bryan's cause was noble, or even correct, to be touched and fascinated by his passion. All through the eighties, while most of his Harvard classmates got rich, he defended penniless murderers. His parents—working people from rural Milton, Delaware—certainly didn't understand what their son was doing. "Take the money," Bryan's father said, more than once. With all his degrees, Bryan still drove a beat-up Honda Civic. His mother drove a jet-black BMW 325i. She couldn't figure her son either. What had made him so different—from his folks, his classmates, from America, really?

"I've asked him how he does this day in, day out," said William Newman, a Massachusetts lawyer in Alabama to work with Bryan on a death-row appeal. "It's Bryan. It's who Bryan is. I'm telling you, Bryan is a prince. I bet you won't find one person who *doesn't* say that. I'm telling you, he's a saint. You can't say that, I know, but he is. That's exactly what he is." Another Massachusetts lawyer, Stewart Eisenberg, also in Alabama working on an appeal, said, "I am extraordinarily impressed with Bryan, but I'm curious about why a black Harvard Law School graduate who could write his own ticket spends his time earning next to nothing in Klan country on the back roads of the South."

His curiosity was my curiosity. Bryan Stevenson had rejected America's reigning view of success and money, even justice. Perhaps understanding him—America's reverse image—would tell us something about ourselves. So, not yet having the legend of the *lamedvovniks* in mind, I set about trying to discover what had made Bryan Stevenson so unlike the rest of us.

The road is home to Bryan. He spends more time driving than he does in his apartment, which is furnished with a single folding director's chair, a stool, two end tables, two small ceramic lamps, a television, and a mattress and box spring on the floor. At the office, the phone rings incessantly. Bryan advises about sixty private lawyers who work on Alabama death-row cases pro bono. He handles an additional twenty-four death-row cases himself. He supervises a staff of five young lawyers who deal with about thirty cases. At the same time, he must raise about $200,000 a year in private or foundation grants to go with the $300,000 the federal government gives to the center. So it is only in his car, now a gray Toyota Corolla, on the back roads of the South, that Bryan has time to himself. He thinks, meditates, sometimes prays.

He is a thin, athletic man, just shy of six feet, a soccer star in high school and college. He wears short, natural hair and a short beard. He wears unstylish clothes and clunky sunglasses. He talks so softly that I must sometimes strain to hear him. He has no discernible accent, strictly Middle American. In phone conversations, prosecutors and defense attorneys who don't know him usually assume he's white. Once, when Bryan suggested that a defense lawyer try to plead his client down from a death sentence charge to life without parole, the lawyer said, "Didn't I tell you? He's a nigger. Can't get a life plea for a nigger in this county."

"I have always felt," Bryan says, as he drives toward Atlanta to visit another death-row client, "that I could just as easily have ended up as one of the men I am defending. I've had friends, cousins who fell into trouble. It could have been me." Bryan says this quietly and deliberately, with little emotion. When he talks about the death penalty, he talks mostly facts and fairness. He talks like a lawyer. Unless asked again and again, he rarely speaks about himself, not even in the little asides through which most people reveal so much. When I later read his words, I will see that he was, more or less, on a soapbox, plunging point by point through his list of horrors about the death penalty. But as I sit next to him, listening, a gentle intimacy in his manner masks his single-minded agenda.

"I could go through the South's prisons and put together five death rows of men not condemned whose crimes were far more vicious," Bryan says. "The people who end up on death row are always poor, often black. And almost always they had bad lawyers—real estate lawyers who never handled a capital case and who had to be dragged screaming into the courtroom. In one case, the judge actually sent the defense lawyer out to sleep off a drunk. Appointed lawyers, paid a maximum of $1,000 in Alabama and several other southern states, often do almost no work on their cases. It takes eight hundred hours to do a capital case. The Supreme Court declared it unconstitutional, but prosecutors in the South still keep blacks off capital juries by giving bogus reasons to strike them. In one rural Alabama county we found potential jurors labeled by the prosecutor as 'strong,' 'medium,' 'weak' and 'black.'

"Maybe it would help the congressmen who are so hot for the death penalty if they thought of it this way: Imagine a senator is accused of stealing campaign funds and he is told that he gets a lawyer who's a drunk, who's being paid $1,000. Then the senator is told, if he's a Democrat, that only Republicans will sit on his jury—just as blacks are still tried by all-white juries. That's our system of justice today. Why do I do what I do? How can anyone do anything else?"

Bryan Stevenson was always different. In rural southern Delaware, he was the only black child in his first-grade class in 1965. His mother, who migrated from Philadelphia through marriage to Bryan's father, had volunteered to put Bryan and his older brother in the white school even before formal integration was in place. She had only to look at the ramshackle schoolhouse black children attended to know where her kids were going. Years later, when Bryan was put in a slow-learner class with the black children who had arrived with integration, it was Bryan's mother who went to the school and raised hell until he was bumped to the top class.

Alice Stevenson was a firebrand by the yardstick of southern Delaware. "Don't be a fool, don't be silly and grin," she'd tell her two sons and daughter. "You are here to make a mark. Otherwise you will be the mark." Appalled at the docility she perceived in southern Delaware's blacks, she admonished her children never to show false deference to whites. She insisted on perfect grammar, diction, and pronunciation. And there was one absolute rule: "I never want to hear that you can't do something because you're black. You can do anything you want."

Bryan's father, Howard, a native of southern Delaware, gave less assertive advice. The child of a prominent black mechanic in nearby Georgetown, he had grown up playing with the children of the town's prominent whites. He recalls few incidents in which he was mistreated by whites. In fact, because he dressed nattily—refusing to wear the jeans and overalls then worn by most of the blacks he knew—it was more often blacks who insulted him with the charge that he was highfalutin. Howard's advice to his children—born of his own unusual experience—was that most white people will treat you well if you treat them well. Between the two of them, Howard and Alice Stevenson sent a singular message: Whites were not to be feared.

Both had good jobs. She was an accounting clerk at the Air Force base in Dover, and he was a lab technician at the General Foods plant. They bought three acres on County Route 319 and built a little ranch house that was elegant by local black standards of the day. Up the road, their neighbors lived with dirt floors and no running water. In a sense, the Stevensons were local black gentry. Alice worried about her children being in school all day with whites, worried they'd be picked on, worried they'd forget they were black. In high school, where Bryan was popular, she worried about the white girls who kept calling the house. "Please don't marry a white girl just to do it," Bryan's mother pleaded. Today, she says, "I didn't order him, but I did beg." On the other hand, Alice worried too about her children hanging around with too many black kids who said "mens" for "men" or who said "I be fixin' to go home now."

But most important, she worried about a more profound influence. Howard was a deeply religious man with a Pentecostal bent to his faith. Alice had realized this near the time of their wedding while they were attending a service at her white-gloved black Baptist church in Philadelphia. Out of the blue, Howard was struck by the power of the Holy Spirit. In the words of the Pentecostals, he "got happy"—and he stood and danced wildly in unconscious, joyful exultation. The ushers came to restrain him. The fiercely proud, urbane, and proper Alice was mortified. And back in Delaware at Howard's Prospect AME Church, it was more of the same. To Alice, the congregation's emotionalism was ignorant and hickish. It did not fit with her plans for her children.

The Stevenson kids all did well, went to college and graduate school. But Bryan was always the family's darling. Howard Jr., the oldest, came to resent his father's strict discipline. Christy, the youngest, used to sneak off to listen to rock music. But Bryan—as far as anyone knows—did none of these things. Not to say he was perfect: He picked on his sister sometimes, fought with his brother, bent a few of his father's strict rules. But all in all he was about as good as kids come. A self-taught musician, he played organ and piano at the Prospect AME Church and learned to shift his tempo to the spontaneous outbursts of congregants as they, like his father, "got happy." He showed no interest in being a minister, but he could preach up a storm.

In his overwhelmingly white high school, Bryan was president of the student council. He was a star athlete. He was a straight-A student who would eventually graduate number one in his class. He would be pursued by Ivy League schools but take a soccer scholarship to Eastern College, a small Baptist school in Pennsylvania, where he would lead the gospel choir and a Christian fellowship. In high school, he was a champion public speaker, and he played the lead in *A Raisin in the Sun*. After thirty years of teaching drama, Harriett Jeglum still remembers it as the play of which she is the proudest. At Cape Henlopen High, Bryan held an odd status. He was one of only a handful of blacks in the advanced classes, and it was common for black kids in that situation to be teased, even harassed by other black kids—accused of "trying to be white." Bryan's sister, Christy, got some of that grief, but she and her brother and other old acquaintances of Bryan's say he never did.

"He was just so kind and decent," says Kevin Hopkins, a childhood neighbor of Bryan's. "Nobody would ever have thought of saying anything like that about Bryan, black or white."

Bryan's mother tells this story: When the kids were young, she always told them they could make requests for their favorite meals and she'd do what she could to fix them. Christy and Howard made requests, but Bryan never did. "He just ate whatever I cooked and said it was the best food he'd ever eaten," she says, still sounding a bit puzzled. "That's just the way he was about everything. If I was in a bad mood, he was always the first to notice it. He'd say, 'You all right, Mom?'"

Back on the road to Georgia's death row: "I had the happiest childhood," says Bryan, finally loosened up and talking about himself for a change. "I was at church two, three nights a week, all day on Sundays," he says. "At school, I knew everybody—the white kids from class, the black kids from sports. But we lived in the country, and I didn't hang with any clique. My parents cared about me and I wanted to do things to make them care about me more. Years later, at Harvard, so many kids I met felt that if they hadn't gone to Andover and Harvard, their lives would be over." He smiles. "But I always figured that people with even zillions of dollars couldn't be happier than me.

"I had fights with the white kids on the bus. They'd call me 'nigger.' In first grade, I remember holding my hand up and never being called on. In second grade, a teacher's aide made me get off the monkey bars while the white kids were on them. When they did integrate the schools, all the black kids were in 3-C. I was the only black kid in section A until junior high. Year after year, the counselors tried to get me to take vo-tech: 'Everybody needs to know how to make bricks,' they said." Finally, as Bryan talks, it becomes clear that the racism he has experienced, mild by the standards of the generation before him, is still tightly woven into his work against the death penalty.

"The reason I always say I've never met a client whose life isn't worth saving," he says, "is because they are like me—except they didn't get in 3-A. They were in 3-C. A few breaks the other way, and I could be on the other side of the table. You know, as a kid, I spent my summers at my aunt's in Philly. You couldn't get police to come to her neighborhood. You had to call and say a police officer had been shot. My grandfather was murdered, stabbed dozens of times, in his own home. The killers pleaded to a low charge. I had a black friend raped on campus, but the case was never pursued. She was leaving town, had no family there to pressure the prosecutor. That's our justice: We over-prosecute crimes against whites and under-prosecute crimes against blacks, because whites have political power and blacks don't. I saw it in my own life long before I studied the death penalty. But when I did, and discovered that a man who murders a white has a 4.3 times greater chance of getting the death penalty in Georgia, I saw it as a symbol of all the race and poverty bias in our society. We're not yet capable of valuing the life of a black mother of four in the projects the same way we value the life of, say, the ex-president of Chevron. We're just not capable.

"Do you know that in Montgomery, Alabama, there's a paper called the *Bulletin Board* that still runs ads seeking white renters? I spent weeks looking for an apartment. On the phone, a man said, 'You don't sound black, but I ask everyone.' I lost all humility. I told one woman I was a lawyer with a Harvard degree. She said the apartment was $250. I put on a suit, but when she saw me her whole body sagged. She said the rent was $450. It's very demoralizing and debilitating. None of my Harvard degrees, my suits, meant anything next to my little black face.

"All these things are of the same cloth."

At the Georgia Diagnostic and Classification Center, which houses that state's death row, Bryan's client, Roger Collins, is waiting in the visitors' room, a deep narrow place with a wall of screened bars and a long row of empty stools. After four years of handling his case, Bryan has come to think of Roger as a friend. Roger stands to greet him, takes away his sunglasses and puts them on, hams it up. He is a black man and Bryan's age exactly, thirty-one, handsome, with short hair and a close-cut beard. He is on death row for brutally murdering a black woman thirteen years ago. Roger was eighteen. His accomplice was twenty-five. They had separate trials. Roger got death. His accomplice got life. Roger could get an execution date any day.

Bryan tells him about his appeal and about how Congress might pass a law that would help his case. (As it turned out, Congress did not.) "I understood right from wrong," Roger says. "I did, yeah. It just started out one thing and ended up another. I've done some hellful things in my past." When he was thirteen, Roger says, he and his father and brother would go to Florida from Georgia and rob places every weekend. In ninth grade, he still couldn't read. He thinks, but isn't sure, that his mother and brother are in prison. His father, who eventually went to prison for murder, is out now, and he visited a few weeks ago. "He said they went for the death sentence," Roger says, "and missed."

"It looks real good," Bryan says. "Don't get down."

Roger says, almost to himself, "Ain't set no date."

Outside, on the road again, Bryan says, "I meet people like Roger every day. Their lives are a mess. Half of my clients have had somebody in their families murdered. They are always getting their electric turned off, or their telephone. Or they mention that their daughter has been in jail for six months, and, by the way, what should they do about it? They live at the margins of society, with no sense of control over their lives. We've given up trying to help them. To mention it is to be ridiculed as naive and weak. You know, as a boy George Daniel was hung in a sheet from a tree when he wet the bed, and beaten with a bat." Bryan is quiet for a long time. Then he says, "I'm afraid they're going to kill Roger."

Something happens to idealistic young people at Harvard Law School. On the first day, Bryan recalls, his entering class was asked how many planned to practice public interest law after graduation, and probably 70 percent of the hands went up. But very few entered the field. Last year, only about 3 percent of Harvard Law's graduates went directly into legal or public service organizations. In Bryan's class, the overwhelming majority of graduates took prestigious clerkships or cut to the chase and took $70,000-plus jobs with big law firms. "Everybody came into law school wanting to help the poor," Bryan says. "But when the big law firms offered $1,500 a week, they all went."

It was a seduction. On that first day, students were told to look around at their five hundred classmates. "They tell you that you're sitting with future congressmen, leading partners of important law firms. You are pushed to compete, get to 'the top.' Only nobody ever stops to define 'the top.' There's no value orientation about finding meaning in what you do." Students are encouraged to feel special, he says, as if they are better than everyone else and therefore deserving of wealth, power, and privilege. It can be a very appealing pitch, especially to youngsters from the bottom, who yearn to be accepted by the elite and who are willing to pay the price of distancing themselves from their roots. Bryan didn't bite. It sounds hokey, but Bryan seems instead to have cut a swath of goodness through his years at Harvard. In the remarks of his former classmates, there is an unmistakable tone of testimony.

"He is just this incredibly exceptional person," says Jeffrey Nussbaum, a lawyer in San Francisco and a former Harvard Law classmate. "Bryan radiated a sense of goodness and kindness, which sounds so mushy. But he definitely radiated it. He has some kind of inner peace." Nussbaum says Bryan was once harassed by a gang of whites in Cambridge. "He wasn't angry. That was the thing. How can I put it? He felt sorry for the people who had attacked him."

Another Harvard classmate, Jerry Salama, now an assistant to one of New York's deputy mayors, even remembers Bryan once talking about his opposition to the death penalty. "What about the guy who cuts people in fifty pieces?" Salama asked pointedly. First, Bryan mentioned that his grandfather had been savagely murdered. Then he said something Salama has never forgotten: "It's not right to kill them back." Says Salama, "He just couldn't fathom the idea of wanting to 'kill them back.'"

Again and again, old Harvard classmates mention that Bryan, who clearly didn't share the law school's dominant values, never criticized anyone for wanting to get rich and powerful by serving the already rich and powerful. "A lot of us were talkin', talkin' all the time about helping the poor, but very few of us did anything about it," says Kimberle Crenshaw, a former Harvard Law classmate and now a UCLA law professor. "Bryan never talked about it. He just did it. He didn't do it to win other people's approval. He did it for himself. He was one of the few people not tainted by Harvard. He's got something else that gives him energy. I don't know what it is. I don't know anybody like him. I think Bryan is religious. I don't know how religious."

Bryan's old classmates mention repeatedly that they "think" Bryan is religious, but they say he never talked about that either. They knew he went to church, but nobody knew where. In fact, Bryan went to church in a poor black Cambridge neighborhood, where as a volunteer he helped people fight their way through the city's housing and welfare bureaucracies and gave kids free piano lessons.

"Bryan is the kind of person who, even though I don't see him much anymore, I will always consider a close friend," says Frederick Smith, a lawyer in New Jersey and a former Harvard Law classmate. "The word for Bryan is *seminal*. It's hard to be close to him and not be profoundly influenced and deeply changed. I very quickly fell under his wing. Bryan was from a little country town, and I had gone to prep school, Harvard College, and spent two years at Oxford, but I had to run to keep up with Bryan, literally." He laughs. "It sounds like I'm talking about someone who is older, but I'm five years older than he is.

"I always assumed that what happened to me would happen to Bryan. 'Well, now's the time to grow up. We have bills to pay.' Everybody else in the class, like lemmings, hopped off the cliff and went to large law firms. But not Bryan. I have another friend from Harvard, and he and I still talk about the phenomenon of Bryan Stevenson. What makes him what he is? We talk about how much we hate what we're doing. Why did we fall so short and Bryan is out there as a beacon? I hate to admit to character flaws, but maybe Bryan is the clearest example of what true character is all about."

Bryan Stevenson doesn't like to hear this kind of talk about himself. It is, he believes, another kind of trap, not unlike the one Harvard lays for its "special" young students. "I know they are trying to be nice," he says, as he drives off to yet another rural Alabama town, this time Monroeville, to talk to the family of his death-row client Walter McMillian. "I hear it when I go to a reunion or I run into an old classmate who's doing something he hates. These people act like I'm a priest, making such sacrifices. I'm not. It's easy for me to do what I do. What people don't understand when they say I could be making all this money is that I *couldn't* be making all this money. I could *not* do it. I could not get up in the morning and go to work. If the death penalty were abolished tomorrow, I wouldn't be a corporate lawyer. I'd probably be a musician. When people say I'm great, what I'm doing is great, they aren't talking about me. They're talking about themselves, about what's missing in their lives."

Bryan has struggled with the idea that he is special, denied it, all his life. "Whites have always treated Bryan like he walked on water," says his brother, Howard Jr., a psychologist and visiting professor at the University of Pennsylvania. "But the label of specialness is impossible to swallow, because to be black and special to whites means you aren't really black, which puts a distance between you and your people, who are to whites very unspecial. To accept the label of special is to absolve people of their responsibility to be good. It's a different kind of control. It's the desire to take what you have and make it their own."

As Bryan cruises toward Monroeville, past cotton and cane and giant pecan trees, past Alabama's Holman Prison and its death row, I recall for the first time the legend of the *lamedvovniks,* the Righteous Men, who forever deny their own virtue. Bryan would understand why ancient legend required good men to deny their goodness: To believe you are good, special, better than the rest, is to be neither good nor special.

Finally, I ask, "How important is your faith?"

"It's very important," Bryan says. He explains that in the 1970s he was involved in the charismatic Christian movement. It was a modern version of the backwoods Pentecostalism—with its emotional and sublime encounters with the Holy Spirit—that Bryan's father had practiced all his life. In the 1960s, the faith burst forth and profoundly changed America's stodgy and ritualized mainline denominations. Yet, traditionally, Pentecostalism was a faith of the dispossessed—the poor and the uprooted, from white Appalachia to black Los Angeles. And Bryan knows this.

"Church is not so important to me today," he says, "but I still glory in the charisma and spontaneity of the black church, still love to play the piano for a person who stands and dances to the Spirit. It is restorative. A grandmother who stands up and says, 'I've lost my son and daughter in the fire, all my belongings, but I'm here with my grandson and we're gonna make it'—it is more restorative than praying with people who are thankful for their wealth. I must return to that well. If there's an afterlife, that's who it's for—those whose lives have been hellish and who've struggled to be better. That's who Christianity is for—the rejected, despised, and broken. And those are my clients."

It's dark when Bryan arrives in Monroeville and meets Walter McMillian's sister, niece, and nephew in the cold wind outside the IGA food market at Ollie's Corner. He tells them an appeals court has ordered the local court to consider whether the county prosecutor had secret deals with the two main witnesses against McMillian, a forty-nine-year-old black man who was convicted of killing an eighteen-year-old white woman in cold blood during a robbery. One witness against McMillian was his alleged accomplice, who pleaded guilty to the murder and got a life sentence. In many of Bryan's cases, it's clear that his clients actually did murder someone. But the evidence against McMillian is strictly circumstantial. Eventually, Bryan will prove McMillian's innocence beyond a doubt and he will be set free. His release will make the front page of the *New York Times*.

"Is everything else going all right?" Bryan asks.

"Did my daughter call you?" McMillian's sister asks.

"From Mobile, yes. I haven't had a chance to call back."

"They got her son for capital murder."

"Is that right?" Bryan says, masking his shock with studied calmness. "Have her call me. Make sure she tells him not to say anything to the police. Does he have an attorney?"

"No."

"Make sure she calls tonight."

"How late?"

"Anytime, anytime."

Back on the road, Bryan says, "It's probably too late."

As always, Bryan worries first about the man accused, but right now I can't help thinking about the victim, for whom it is already too late. And I ask the question that is unavoidable, the one so many people believe challenges Bryan's entire work: "But what about the victims, the people your men kill? What about their husbands and wives, their kids? Don't these murderers deserve to die?"

Bryan is silent for a moment. He has, of course, heard the question many times before. "I feel worse for the families than I do my clients. It's the hardest thing." He is silent again. "But I tell them, 'I don't care what you did, how awful it was. I'm here to get you off. I don't believe you should be killed.'"

"It's not right to kill them back?" I ask.

"It's not right to kill them back," he answers.

By now it's late, nearly eleven, and on the drive back to Montgomery, I close my eyes, very tired. But Bryan is wide awake, ready to go back to the office tonight to work on several briefs and to meet with Amnesty International representatives who are in town visiting his center. The schedule is grueling, and Bryan does sometimes yearn for regular hours, a wife, kids. But he finds working with his clients so absorbing that he doesn't think much about what he's missing. Besides, he figures he's still young, with plenty of time for a family later. After a while, when we are nearly back to Montgomery, I ask, "Your parents have never understood why you do this, have they? They think you could be earning gobs of money."

Bryan laughs. "They've come to understand me recently."

The next week, on a beautiful autumn day, I leave Washington and drive to Milton, Delaware, where Bryan grew up. I find his home, the little white ranch house on County Route 319, and his father, Howard Sr., a short, trim man with dark gray hair and black plastic glasses. He takes me to the Prospect AME Church on Railroad Avenue, past the road signs riddled with bullet holes, past Vern's Used Furniture. It's a small, not so sturdy, white clapboard church about the size of some living rooms I've seen. The sanctuary is adorned with bright flowers, a cloth rendering of the Last Supper, and a piano and an organ, much like the ones Bryan once played here on two, three nights a week and all day on Sundays. The church, with its vaguely musty aroma, is the very image of the tiny churches that dot rural America, particularly in the South, the very image of the backwoods church that embarrassed Bryan's mother when she first moved to Milton decades ago.

It's a long way from Prospect AME to Harvard Law School, but somehow Bryan made the distance look short and easy. I am marveling at this when I notice that Bryan's father is standing before the little altar, framed by the bright flowers and the cloth rendering of the Last Supper, lost in thought. He shakes his head, looks around at the empty sanctuary, and says wistfully, "Bryan used to set me on fire when he prayed out loud." And once again I am reminded of how often Bryan's behavior—in childhood, in law school, still today—evokes inspiration in those around him, even his own father.

Back at the house, I see that Bryan's old room is filled with storage boxes now, but that the walls are still papered with dozens of his awards from childhood: the Golden Scroll for the Promise of Greatness, the Thespian Society Award, awards for music, sports, student council—you name it, the guy won it.

"Bryan said you only recently came to understand him," I say. "What did he mean by that?"

Without hesitation, Howard jumps up from the couch and dashes to the television. He roots around in a cabinet full of videotapes and pops one in the VCR. "This was last April," he says. "Bryan spoke to the national youth conference of the AME Church." In a few moments Bryan, all grainy, comes on the screen. And for half an hour, he speaks, starting slowly and then, moved by the power of his own emotions, quickly, like rapids. He says we execute the retarded, the young, and the mentally ill. He says we execute men for killing whites far more often than we do for killing blacks. He talks of the defense lawyer who was drunk and of the blacks who are so often struck from murder juries. He talks of the judge who said of a convicted man's parents, "Since the niggers are here, maybe we can go ahead with the sentencing phase."

Then Bryan says, "It's not enough to see and deal with these things from a humanistic perspective. You've got to have a spiritual commitment. So many talk that talk, but they don't walk that walk. We've got to be prepared to pay the cost of what it means to save our souls." Then he quotes the Bible—Matthew 25:34-45: "Then the King will say to those at his right hand, 'Come, O blessed of my Father, inherit the kingdom prepared for you from the foundation of the world, for I was hungry and you gave me food; I was thirsty and you gave me drink; I was a stranger and you welcomed me; I was naked and you clothed me; I was sick and you visited me; I was in prison and you came to me. . . . Truly, I say to you, as you did it to one of the least of these my brethren, you did it to me.'" The place is bedlam. "I wouldn't exchange what I'm doing for anything," Bryan says, voice rising. "I feel the pleasure of God."

Bryan's father gets up quietly, rewinds the tape. Tears are in his eyes. "I didn't understand his faith until this talk," he says. "He never talked about himself, ever."

Sadly, Bryan's mother, Alice, is in the hospital being treated for a life-threatening illness, and his father and I go to visit. Her lean, elegant body and handsome face are the image of her son's, as are her slow, deliberate mannerisms, perfect diction, and clear, accentless voice. She sits in a robe in a chair next to her bed, illuminated by a single lamp. Seeming tired, she closes her eyes as she speaks. "I told him he was not going to live in the sticks all his life. Please do not be satisfied." She opens her eyes and laughs. "Sometimes I think he listened too well. He is so far away. I miss him so. Did Howard tell you we didn't understand him until April of this year when we heard him speak? He never talked about himself. Me, I've been a money-grubber all my life. But now that I've been sick, I see that Bryan is right. Really, what are we here for? We're here to help one another. That's it." After a pause, she says, "You know, a college friend of Bryan's once asked me, quite seriously, 'Could Bryan be an angel?'"

Alice and Howard Stevenson talk into the evening, and just as I'm about to leave, Howard says, "The Lord touched him." And Alice tells this story: When Bryan was thirteen, in a hot little Pentecostal church in Camden, Delaware, where she'd taken the Prospect youth choir to sing, "Bryan went off in the Spirit. He got happy. He danced." I ask what that means, and Alice and Howard chuckle at my naïveté. "It is to be in a realm of complete and absolute joy," Alice says, although that day she did not feel joy. "I cried because I never wanted that to happen to Bryan. I didn't want him to be a backwoods cultist Christian. He broke out in a sweat, completely physically immersed, and the Spirit took him over. I held him, hugged him, and cried." Because for all the years Alice—proud, urbane Alice from her white-gloved Philadelphia Baptist church—had gone to Prospect AME, she'd never been a true Pentecostal believer.

"But this was my child, my darling, my flesh. I knew there was no falseness in him. So I knew this was a real gift from God. I stopped turning my nose up at it as something only ignorant people did." And looking out the window one morning soon afterward, watching the rising sun, Alice was suddenly overwhelmed with the presence of God. Simply put, Bryan had saved his mother. "That feeling," she says, "can't be put into words."

Perhaps not, but I remember that James Baldwin seems to have come very close in the final pages of *Go Tell It on the Mountain*. And rereading his words at my home late that night, I try to imagine Bryan as Baldwin's character John, try to imagine how transforming must have been Bryan's experience—whether spiritual or psychological. Baldwin wrote: "And something moved in John's body which was not John. He was invaded, set at naught, possessed. This power had struck John, in the head or in the heart. . . . The center of the whole earth shifted, making of space a sheer void and a mockery of order, and balance, and time. Nothing remained: all was swallowed up in chaos. . . . His Aunt Florence came and took him in her arms. . . .

"'You fight the good fight,' she said, 'you hear? Don't you get weary, and don't you get scared. Because I *know* the Lord's done laid His hands on you.'

"'Yes,' he said, weeping, 'yes. I'm going to serve the Lord.'"

I put down the book, and I think again of the thirty-six Righteous Men: The ancient legend, I now realize, isn't the answer to what it means to be truly good; it is only one more way of asking the question. With or without religion, maybe that's all good people can ever really do: live their lives as a question posed to others. I think of a priest I once knew. He told me that Christians would have no need to evangelize if only they lived their lives as mirrors of goodness in which others could glimpse the goodness of Christ—and thus the goodness in themselves. And I think of Bryan: His deepest mission, I now see, is not to save the lives of convicted men, but to live in such a way that his own life is a question posed to others. "I want to be a witness for hope and decency and commitment," Bryan had said, before I understood what he meant. "I want to show in myself the qualities I want to see in others." Bryan's own motive is to "feel the pleasure of God." Yet whether graced with the power of God, the power of a strong, decent family, or the power of some buried psychological zeal, Bryan's life is like the priest's mirror: Looking into him, people see their failings and possibilities. Like the *lamedvovniks*, Bryan must deny this power—not because he will disappear in a flash of God's will, but because if others can call him "special," they can excuse their failings and avoid struggling to find the goodness in themselves.

January 6, 1991

Tough Games, Tough Girls

The girls get this *feeling* . . .

The soccer ball sails in a giant arc toward Missy Somadelis and the attackers rush to overtake it just beyond the center line, greedy for a goal. In a blur of red uniform, Missy—short and strong and fast as thought, the Chantilly Storm's sweeper, its last defender before the goalkeeper—splits the attackers, cocks back her right leg, halts its motion, locks her eyes on the descending sphere, swivels her hips for power, sees her knee cross her body and her foot fly forward and collide with the ball a blink before it hits ground. In a one-touch maneuver, Missy rockets it back upfield, the ball's black-and-white markings rotating slowly on its axis, making it seem to float serenely on a river of air, while back on earth the Storm's offensive swarm is already sprinting, faking, cutting, and bullying its way toward the point of touch down and the crowd is erupting in shouts, screams, and cheers.

Then comes the *feeling* . . .

Exhilaration, accomplishment, acclaim: Missy can't easily find words to describe the sensations firing through her. She hears the Storm's fans and moms and dads, sometimes even her own mom and dad, hollering wildly on the sidelines, hollering louder than they ever holler for the Washington Redskins or Baltimore Orioles. A jolt of energy surges through Missy's muscles and mind. Her body feels instantly stronger and her confidence spikes.

"I know I can do it again!" she thinks.

When a shot rockets toward Mary-Pride Kirven, the Storm's goalkeeper, she dives, blocks it, bounces hard in the dirt, scrapes her knees to bleeding, but feels no pain, just this: "Everybody is looking and watching me." Jessie Martello, the center halfback, shoulders the ball from a girl and feels a tingling so good, so addictive, that she wants to feel it again and again. Striker Christie Schied does a roll-over fake with her right foot, cuts the ball with the outside

Christie Schied and the Chantilly
Storm at practice.

Photo by Charles Emmett Freeman.

of her left foot, pivots, fires, scores, and it's—how else to say it?—the best feeling she has ever known. Stopper Diane Rutkowski volleys the ball upfield with a thunderous *boom* and feels like Superwoman. Left halfback Erin Bullock steals the ball with an expert slide: "You don't think about anything. You're just so happy. Like nothing bad will happen, like nothing can make you feel bad.

"Nothing can ruin it."

No, the girls can't imagine any emotion as good as the *feeling*. And, no, they can't imagine that dim, dark, ancient time of their mothers' childhoods when girls grew up without knowing it.

The sweat begins: On the hot days of summer and early fall, after stretching every muscle, a half-mile jog around the practice field at Virginia's Fox Mill Elementary School, speed dribbling, change-of-speed fakes, ball cuts, leg-lifts, and tuck-ups—an excruciating exercise in which the girls jump in place and lift up their legs at the knees—the well-tanned, affluent girls of the Storm, most of them thirteen years old and in eighth grade, sweat like roadside ditchdiggers, their T-shirt sleeves rolled up over their shoulders, shirts soaked from their necks to their stomachs, shirts wet across shoulder blades and down the middle of backs. Sweat cascading over eyebrows. Sweat smeared across foreheads. Sweat matting the flyaway hairs of their ponytails to their necks. Sweat that stinks.

"Christie, twenty-five tuck-ups!" screams Sheri D'Amato, the Storm's coach. She's thirty-one years old, an all-state soccer player in high school, a member of the 1985 George Mason University NCAA championship team, once named the nation's high school female coach of the year during her eight-year stint as West Springfield High's girls coach. Sheri's command, in a voice that manages to be both deep and shrill, echoes among the trees that surround the field like mute, towering spectators—and Christie starts tucking up.

"Who knocked that cone over? Twenty-five tuck-ups! . . . Catch 'em! Catch 'em! Catch 'em! . . . That's it! . . . You've gotta keep your concentration! . . . Starting next practice, every time your shoe comes untied, you owe me fifty tuck-ups . . . You guys slowed down. Tuck-ups! Tuck-ups! Come on, get those knees up. *You gotta want it!*"

Sheri D'Amato is short, with an athletic build and a jock's spring in her walk. She wears old Pumas and baggy black shorts. She stores lip balm in her right sock. She yells orders as she stands with her arms plaited across her chest, her feet planted at the width of her shoulders, bouncing up and down on the balls of her feet. In a quick, jerky motion, she flicks back her head and swipes her bangs back off her forehead. She sucks her lower lip. Her right elbow is scabbed yellow, her left calf is scabbed red, her right knee is scabbed rose, and the skin around it is bright red in a ring of soreness. She plays softball, third base, in shorts. Her T-shirt reads: "There Is *No* Off Season."

Jessie's T-shirt: "Don't Dream It, Be It." Alaina Brown's T-shirt: "Aggressive By Nature, Soccer By Choice." Kristin Claussen's T-shirt: "Practice Doesn't Make You Perfect . . . Just Better Than Them." Ashley Wallace's T-shirt: "In Your Face."

"Okay, take a break," Sheri says, her voice going smooth and resonant. The girls pant, wipe brows, turn and amble to their water bottles, wash and spit out the first mouthful, knock down the second swallow, pour water over their heads, rub water into their faces, spray it off in a dog's shake, exhale, wipe hair from their eyes, gather round their coach.

"I like your nail color," somebody tells Sheri.

"Thank you," she answers.

"My nails are, like, ugly."

Laughter.

"I don't have any nails."

Giggling.

"I bite mine."

Chattering.

"I bite mine, too."

"Blueberry fingernails," says Sheri, smiling toward Kari Sartorius, who has painted every other nail a deep blue.

"They look neat," somebody says.

"I have fluorescent pink on my toes."

More giggling, more chatter.

"All right," Sheri finally says. "You've gotta block out all the other stuff, focus." Then she asks the girls what they are supposed to see while they're shooting the ball.

"Knee over the ball," the girls yell in chorus.

"Knee over the ball," Sheri repeats.

"Follow through," they all yell.

"Follow through," Sheri repeats.

"Rotate your hips," the chorus cries.

Sheri flicks back her head, swipes at her bangs, nods, and repeats, "Rotate your hips." Then: "Follow through, direct it, run towards goal . . . When you see the ball coming across the field this weekend, relax, just relax. See the ball coming, see it strike your foot . . . Block out 'Oh, my God! Oh, my God! I'm gonna mess up!' Forget the negative stuff. Plant the foot, see your foot strike the ball, and follow it . . . See it, plant, strike, follow through."

Think to yourselves: *"I'm in control!"*

Their mothers knew a different childhood. No competitive sports for girls, not really. No soccer. Basketball in which girls could dribble only three times and in which "snatching and batting at the ball" were illegal. A little field hockey, maybe. Cheerleading, with those tiny skirts that flipped up over their bottoms with each bounce. Nice smiles, perky rah-rahs, and, always, great enthusiasm for the boys' team. *Two bits . . . four bits . . . six bits . . . a dollar. . . . All for McNamara . . . stand up and holler!* That's a cheer Christie's mom, Cathy Schied, remembers she and the other cheerleaders used to do in high school for the boys. Today, she loves to hear people cheering for her daughter, believes Christie's dedication to competitive soccer has given her a confidence her mother didn't get until much later in life. "I think, God, why couldn't I have been more like that?'" says Cathy. "Soccer has made her think she is equal to any male. I believe her career will be in a male field."

"She decided this week," says Christie's dad, Biff, "to be the field goal kicker on varsity football in high school."

"She's dead serious," says Cathy.

"She knows she can kick a soccer ball," says Biff.

"Why not a football?" asks Cathy.

This should be the Storm's year. The conference season starts Saturday against the Braddock Road Magic, probably the Storm's toughest competition in the league. It's the test. When Sheri D'Amato took over last fall, the Storm was in trouble. For a total of $9,600 a year, which pays for the fall and spring seasons, Sheri and her former West Springfield High assistant Pam Cox began rebuilding. Practices twice a week in the drop-dead heat of July and August, running on a third day, individual workouts twice a week, food diaries so the girls can see all the junk they scarf. Sheri and the girls worked on basics—trapping the ball, dribbling, throw-ins, shooting. They worked on tactics—passing the ball to the feet of nearby midfielders but high in the air and across field to downfield attackers. They worked on defensive positioning—keeping a visual triangle from themselves to the girl they're guarding to the ball. They worked on "field composure"—seeing the whole game at once, slowing down the rapid-fire action to slow-mo by staying calm, cool under fire. But most of all, they worked on attitude—concentration, commitment, toughness.

Stereotype or not, Sheri believes girls, particularly young girls, don't play with the abandon of boys, with a disregard for injury to themselves or others. Girls, even athletic girls, flinch, hold back. They are tentative. So many boys don't care what their teammates think of them—they want the ball, want to score, to be the star. A coach's challenge is to teach boys to be less selfish, less self-aggrandizing, to play as a team. For girls, it's the opposite. They fear the spotlight, hate the idea that teammates might call them ball-hogs. They shrink from glory.

Stereotype or not, Sheri believes boys don't care if their opponents think they're mean and nasty. To be feared, to intimidate is a badge of honor. But girls want to be liked, not feared, even by their enemies. And that attitude saps their edge. Yeah, yeah, you can debate the chicken-or-the-egg question all night—are boys and girls born different or socialized differently? And not all kids fit Sheri's model: Some boys are meek; some girls are aggressive. Yeah, yeah, but leave that stuff to the sociologists and the shrinks. No matter the reasons, if the Storm was ever going to play kick-butt soccer, Sheri had to breed confidence into them and softness out.

"Walk away with this for Saturday," she tells her team. On an indirect penalty kick, how many girls front the ball on defense?

"Two."

"And where will my forward be?"

"Up top."

"If they're in shooting range?"

"Three or four in the wall."

"What are the critical points?"

"Stay together. Don't use your hands. Don't duck."

They try it: Everybody scatters, everybody ducks.

They try it again: Everybody holds.

"Better! Better! Better!"

Last weekend, the Storm swept to a five-game tournament victory. The girls scored twelve goals—their opponents scored zip. That was a big switch from last season, when they lost as many games as they won and parents were up in arms. They'd hired Sheri to turn the Storm around, prepare the girls to make their high school soccer teams. The coaches, fees, equipment, travel, and accommodations for out-of-town tournaments were costing each of the team's seventeen families about $1,200 a year. Sheri told the parents to calm down, the girls were learning how to think about the game and how to play it. Pretty soon, they'd learn how to win.

Phil Martello, Jessie's father, never thought he'd see the day when the girls on the Storm would "take out" an opponent—retaliate for a dirty play against a teammate. But he has seen it. Likewise, he never thought he'd see his wife, June, stand on the sidelines and scream, "Knock her down!" But he has seen that, too. It bothers June that boys play soccer much more aggressively than girls, so she's always admonishing Jessie to play tougher: "I want you to be physical, take some shots, don't back off." During the games, she hollers, "Get her, Jessie, get her!"

"She really gets into it," says Phil.

"I have learned that I can be loud," says June.

June is the controller for a realty firm, with sixty people, most of them women, working under her. Too many women, June believes, don't know how to work as a team, can't raise up their heads and see the big picture—the team strategy, so to speak. And too many women don't know how to fail—they fall apart under criticism, believe it's a personal attack, cry. June used to be timid like that. Even when she became the boss, she hated to reprimand people, resolve thorny personnel problems. And to terminate an employee? "They'll hate me if I fire them," she'd think.

"As a girl and young woman, I never was in a situation to learn these skills," says June, who didn't have the chance to play competitive sports in her rural hometown. "Girl Scouts was baking cookies and sewing." June is talking about what she calls leadership skills—taking responsibility for balancing people's needs with the needs of the group, the organization, the team. "It's hard to stand out from the crowd in a large organization," she says, "and I hope Jessie learns from soccer to speak up and lead and not just be a sheep who follows along."

June wants Jessie to learn this: how to separate her personal feelings from her organizational decisions. She believes soccer has helped. The year before Sheri took over the Storm, the coach cut one of Jessie's good friends. "I think it was good for Jessie," June says, although it almost cost the girls their friendship. Jessie told her mom, "Maybe it will hurt her feelings if I stay on the team." But she stayed, the friendship endured, and Jessie learned that people can look out for themselves and still be friends. June believes boys and men have always known that. Look at Gus Frerotte and Heath Shuler, competing Redskins quarterbacks who are still friends.

"This is real life," says Phil. "There are people who want your position, and they may be your friends. Life is ruthless." A few years ago, he says, June had to fire an employee the day before a big holiday. But by then, it didn't bother her.

June shrugs. "The person deserved it."

Most of the Storm girls have been playing soccer since they were six or seven. They began on one of the Washington area's hundreds of community "house" teams where everybody plays and fun is the goal. The teams are coached by dads and moms. But by about age nine, most of the girls had moved up to "select" teams that are divided into higher to lower divisions based on the girls' skills and commitment. More and more, like the Storm, these teams have paid coaches. The Storm was in Division I but slid to Division II, where the team plays today. Sheri's plan is to be back in Division I next season.

What is she teaching her girls?

Cooperation.

Commitment.

Concentration.

Time management.

It's okay to be competitive.

How to accept criticism.

Tolerance for pain.

Accepting victory.

Handling defeat.

To play for themselves, not their parents.

Sheri was a jock from the crib. Her father played semipro football; her mom was athletic. Sheri was the oldest, with a sister and four brothers. The neighborhood kids hung out at her New Jersey home and played sports year-round. She was the best quarterback among them. She remembers her father's football truism: "If the back of your jersey is dirty, it's a bad game. If the front of your jersey is dirty, it's a good game." She discovered soccer and became a star. Soccer put her through college and taught her the value of hard work and attention to detail, lessons that have helped in her career as an elementary school teacher and now as an assistant principal at North Springfield Elementary. But soccer also taught limits: She broke her toes her freshman year in college, but was afraid to tell her coach. So she played for weeks with broken bones. By the time she saw a doctor, the bones had fused improperly and had to be rebroken and reset. Over the years, she had surgery on both knees and an ankle. "I fell apart," she says. "I don't have any knees or ankles left." By the time Sheri's senior year came, she was no longer a star, no longer a starter. By then, she was thinking about getting married, getting a job. "My priorities had changed."

Sheri never had a female coach, and neither had most of the girls on the Storm before she arrived. Sheri believes it matters to them, because she knows what they're going through—from their personal troubles, to their fear of pain and injury, to their worry that boys will not like athletic girls, to their desire to be seen as nice instead of tough, to their inexperience with aggressiveness. In high school, Sheri would hold back in gym class, afraid of being seen as brutish and unfeminine. In coaching at West Springfield, she saw her girls gear back their aggressiveness at home games when their boyfriends were in the stands. Because she is a woman, Sheri is more empathetic. But because she is a woman she can sometimes be tougher. She once noticed a dad leading a girl off the practice field, his arm around her shoulder.

"What's wrong?" Sheri asked.

"I'm having my period," the girl said.

"That's it?" Sheri hollered. "Get back on that field!"

"I know what it is to be a girl," Sheri says. "And I know what it takes to compete. They have to make up their minds."

It is mother-daughter role reversal. When Beth Belle, the mother of Mary-Pride Kirven, sees her daughter's dedication to soccer, her determination to play well, her certainty that the game means so much to her, it's as if the daughter is taking the mother to school. Beth feels not only proud of Pride but inspired by her: "She has a lot more guts than I ever thought she did. She's got what I haven't got."

Pride sometimes used to come off the field in tears, and the assistant coach's brother, Mike Cox, would say, "No crying. It's not acceptable." Beth has seen Pride get so much tougher since she's been playing soccer, not only on the field but also with her brother and at school. Pride's new confidence has even forced Beth to reflect upon her own life. "I've always been a people-pleaser kind of person," she says. "That's one of the things I still have to deal with. She's learning that not everybody's going to be your friend . . . It's brought up with me how we *never* competed with boys, never wanted to outshine them." Beth drifted through college, into teaching, got married, had kids, all without much thought. She believed a career was what a woman did until she got married. Now, seeing Pride's confidence and determination, Beth has told herself: "I can do something." She has decided to go back to nursing school.

"She already knows she wants to do well in school," Beth, still a bit incredulous, says of Pride. "Church is important to her, soccer. She seems so much more sure of herself. I like the changes. I think it's great."

Corner kicks. They shouldn't need to practice them, but in last weekend's tournament, the Storm blew their corner kicks—when the ball comes to them after an opponent kicks it out of bounds past her own goal line and a Storm player gets to kick the ball from the corner of the field to a horde of teammates waiting in front of their opponent's goal. It's an optimum moment for a score, but the girls muffed it.

So line up: two giant steps in front of the eighteen-yard line, in line with the center of the goal, tight, facing the goal, one behind the other—Linny Kulp, Carin Miller, Erin, Jessie, Christie, Ashley. Linny, raise your hand to tell the corner kicker, Diane, that you're ready. Diane, raise your arm and drop it just before you take your step to kick the ball. On Diane's dropped hand, Linny, angle fast directly toward the goalpost farthest from the corner kicker. At the six-yard line, break hard—cut, zig, like a football player—to the near post of the goal. Carin, race straight, set up one step in front of the goalie, block her view. Erin, follow Linny's path, but zig sooner, land in front of the goal behind Carin on the six. Jessie, count to three, fake left or right, cut straight up the middle, halt just behind Erin. Christie, race toward the back edge of the goal, stop at the six. Ashley, duplicate the pattern, a bit wider, stop two steps behind Christie.

"Questions?" Sheri asks.

No questions.

"Just drop your little butts over there."

They run it—again, again, again, again.

Then, in a burning red sunset, beneath a three-quarter moon, the crickets chirping in waves of call and response from the woods, ripped up clumps of dirt casting a thousand tiny shadows across the huge empty soccer field, the girls whooshing and slapping at mosquitoes, Sheri asks, "Can you beat Braddock?"

The whooshing and slapping stop. "Yeah!"

"First and foremost?"

"Intensity!"

Sheri's voice goes slow and deep. "It doesn't matter what I think. It doesn't matter what your parents think. It matters what you think. And you guys gotta want it. I want you guys ready. That means I want you thinking through your runs tonight before you go to bed. Every night your homework assignment is five minutes of quiet time in your bed staring up at the ceiling with the lights out, thinking about the runs. *Think*: 'If Sheri put me at right wing and the ball was on the left side, what would I do? Now, if the ball was on the right side, what would I do?' Work it through in your heads." She laughs and needles them lightly: No flailing around Saturday, screaming, "Where am I supposed to go?"

"Come ready."

Boys and girls are different. Sheri believes that—and so do the six Storm girls who sat for long conversations about themselves and soccer. They sometimes look at the opposite end of the Fox Mill practice field and see teenage boys drilling one-on-one, battling as if their lives depended on it. The Storm can't reproduce that gamelike intensity at practice—the girls won't play that hard against their own teammates, afraid they might hurt each other. Says Jessie, "You're just used to being nice to people." Diane: "I always thought that if you pushed somebody, then they would think you're mean or they wouldn't like you." Missy: "Sometimes boys can be tougher and push more, aggressive." Erin: "Girls aren't more wimpy. Girls can be more sensitive."

It's why most of them love having a female coach. "I think the whole team feels much closer to her," says Pride. The girls can talk to Sheri more easily than a man coach—from questions about menstruation, to school, to boys, to being afraid on the field. "She understands us and can teach us more," says Jessie, "because we listen to her because she's a female coach and we think that if she could do it, then we could do it . . . She works us but she makes it fun."

Sheri has nicknames for them—Mighty Mouse Missy, Jessie Marshmallow, Alaina Mosquito, Christie Christmas. Men coaches, the girls agree, don't seem to joke around much. They holler a lot, seem to discipline by belittling: "How many times have we been over that?" they roar. The girls marvel that boys don't seem bothered by this kind of treatment, seem to thrive on it. "If they're yelling at us nonstop, then we can't really learn," says Jessie. "Girls take it harder." They get self-conscious and flustered when screamed at, Missy says, can't think straight, might even break down in tears. Then, says Erin, they'll just flub up again, be afraid to try anything new. "It's the way girls are."

"Sheri doesn't yell," says Diane.

Well, that's not exactly true—Sheri yells. But the girls seem to take it better from her. They hear constructive criticism, not derision. On the sidelines during games, Sheri always compliments for a second or two before she criticizes for a minute or two. It's just good coaching. Men can do it, too. But these girls attribute it to a special feminine sensitivity. Biff Schied, Christie's dad, believes a lot is in the eye of the beholder: If a man were as tough on the girls as Sheri is, their parents would be raving that he was brutalizing them. Because Sheri is a woman and an athlete, the parents give her more leeway than they would a man. And because she is a woman and an athlete, she expects far more of the girls than either their parents or the girls themselves do. It seems to have worked.

"I like the competition," says Jessie. "I like it when I come out to a game and I play against really good players. My heart starts beating and I get nervous and I really like it." Jessie, who used to feel afraid on the soccer field, has now realized that if she feels intimidated when some player knocks her around, then other players will likely feel intimidated when she knocks them around. Jessie has had this epiphany: When she is feeling most afraid is when she must be most aggressive.

"I was afraid," says Christie. "But I've taken a couple of hits, and it would hurt for a second and then it goes away . . . I've gotten over it."

"When you cry, you act like you're a wimp," says Diane. "When you're playing soccer, you have to act tough so people will be afraid of you." And, she has learned, when you act tough, you begin to feel tough. And when you think you've reached your limit, you usually haven't. Go harder—play through the exhaustion, the fear, the pain. Diane used to cry when she'd get hurt on the field. Now, she says, "I usually go to the ball and if it hurts I just deal with the pain." Diane says—and Jessie, Pride, Missy, Erin, and Christie agree—that their growing sense of physical power on the soccer field has washed over into the rest of their lives.

"All sorts of confidence," Diane says. "My mental confidence: I know I can play soccer. And it's physical confidence: I know I can run, I know I can kick the ball." At school, Diane has found herself less willing to put up with shoving bullies. She's far more likely to speak up or even shove back. "You're playing soccer and you have to try and be in control and push somebody and get the ball. In school you don't want to be like that, push everybody, but you still want to be in control. You want to know that somebody respects you. In soccer, you want to be feared. But then in school, you want everybody to like you. You have to get used to doing both."

The girls relish that sense of physical power and prowess. Christie remembers a time she went one-on-one in gym class against a boy and beat him bad. He turned beet red, got enraged, couldn't believe a girl had zapped him. Christie loved it. "They're always like, 'Oh, I'm awesome!' But I know I can challenge them to soccer, and beat 'em . . . So they don't get too cocky about everything."

This is what Sheri meant when she said the girls of the Storm needed to learn how to win—they needed not only skill but also mental and emotional grit. At practice the other day, Missy and Erin were having trouble getting their long kicks on target. They kept saying to each other: "We can do this. We know we can do this. Sheri knows we can do this." After that, they did it, sent their kicks arcing perfectly down the field. They looked at each other, amazed.

"Wow, it worked," Missy said.

"She's learning to be tough, independent, and to hold her own," says Kathy Somadelis, Missy's mother, who is a social worker. "It's more difficult for a woman to say, 'No, I want it this way.' You're a woman and you're not supposed to be assertive. It looks like you're mean. You're supposed to be soft and kind and empathetic. But you have a job to do . . . I see that life is tough and you have to be tough . . . It's a lesson for life: Hurt a little, you keep going. Crying is not acceptable if you want to be treated as equal. In a business setting, you lose all credibility."

Kathy remembers once watching a bunch of kids play football, and one team had a girl on it. The boys on the other side kept hollering, "Get the girl!"—rabidly, as in the days when whites would scream out racial epithets at a rare black ballplayer on an opposing team. But like those early black athletes, that little girl was one of the toughest players on the field, and Kathy saw that the boys on her own team treated her as an equal, as a comrade in arms.

"I *loved* it," Kathy says. "She had their respect."

It is a philosophy of life that Sheri teaches. She doesn't look down on the girls who used to play on the Storm, those who decided they didn't want to dedicate their lives to soccer, who moved down a division or two or three to play for fun and exercise. Some of them were upset about leaving the team; some of their parents were even more upset. But Sheri believes she knows what it takes to compete at the highest levels in high school and college sports. And it's delusional to imagine you'll ever make that cut if you don't give up to get. If you don't give up junk food and parties on the nights before games. If you don't give up lazy spring breaks and languid summer vacations. If you don't jog and practice ballhandling on your own. If you don't think often about the game away from the field. If you don't put everything else out of your mind at practice. If you don't give all that you've got. Because other girls will.

So it's simple: Get with the program or go. It's often not a girl's physical ability that falls short. It's her commitment, or desire, or dedication, or priorities. Sheri's priorities changed her senior year in college. She lost the raging dedication. For other girls, priorities change when they discover boys, painting pictures or writing poems, surfing the Internet, getting straight A's, basketball or baseball, partying.

Under Sheri, the Storm's parents have recognized and begun to ponder these choices, too. All the girls have missed weekend sleep-overs for years to be fresh for the next day's games. Jessie's father knows Jessie likes to draw but hasn't drawn a picture since soccer began last July. Erin's mom knows Erin could have taken an accelerated algebra class but decided it would be too much with soccer. Missy's mom knows Missy would like to be in the drama club but doesn't have the time. Pride's mom talked Pride into giving up a planned three-week trip to Rome last summer so she could stay home and go to soccer practice. After she did, she began to wonder if she'd done the right thing, if something wasn't out of whack.

Truly competitive sports can boil down to choices—pianos not played, science camps not attended, books not read, math teams not joined. After all, how many great athletes go on to win a Nobel Prize or to write a great novel or to found Microsoft? No, to walk away from competitive sports, Sheri knows, isn't a moral flaw. But without the raging dedication, the love of competition, the compulsion to win, it won't happen for you. It's a delusion. You will be found out. Sheri knows, for instance, that Pride has been skimping on her running at home, because she used to finish in the front of the pack on laps but now finishes way back. She knows Kristin has been working diligently on her footwork, because at practice her balls are under control from the first touch. She knows that for some reason Erin hasn't been playing her best so far this season. She knows that Missy gets distracted under the burden of schoolwork, and she knows that Diane loses a notch when her mom can't make a game. You can't fake excellence.

Sheri is crazy about Pride, believes Pride has a sixth sense as goalkeeper, that she can anticipate shots instinctively, that she has a quickness and foot speed that are rare, and that she's aggressive and fearless. If Pride grows to be as tall as her mother, she could play in high school, even college. But Pride has always been a natural athlete who wowed her coaches and fans and who never had to face serious competition for her goalie's job. This year, Sheri took on another goalie, Sarah Slocum, as a backup in case Pride got hurt. Sarah could barely run a lap when she started, and Sheri told her she wouldn't play. But Sarah worked her butt off, got in shape. When Sheri talked, Sarah's eyes were locked to hers. Sheri saw a fire in Sarah.

"Pride is a lovey," says Sheri, but Sheri can't let her personal feelings interfere with her organizational decisions. Pride seemed to shrink from the very idea of competition. When Sarah announced one day that she planned to become the Storm's number-one goalie, the air seemed to go out of Pride. Then, when Pride jammed her right thumb in warm-ups before the first tournament game and decided she couldn't play, Sarah played and did well. Because Sarah did well, she became more inspired. The better Sarah did, the more it seemed to sap Pride, who continued to complain about her sore thumb. Then Pride wanted to sit out the first half of the second tournament game.

Sheri was unsympathetic. "There's some point where you just suck it up and play," she says. Sheri knows Pride gets jittery before games and that sitting out the first half would calm her, let her see the competition, get up her confidence. But in the long run, not facing her fear would hurt her. Sheri wanted to push Pride, but not break her.

"It's all swollen," Pride told Sheri.

"Can you move it?"

"Yeah, but it still hurts."

"Either you go the first half or you don't go at all."

Pride forgot her sore thumb, played, played well.

"I just think I know Pridy," Sheri says. "She doesn't believe how good she really is." She's got competition for the first time and she's looking for reasons to retreat. "The whole bit with her thumb opened the door for Sarah. If I hadn't pushed her, she'd have sat out the second game." Pride didn't realize, Sheri says, that she herself was helping turn Sarah into a better goalie by letting her play, getting her psyched, letting her prove herself. "Some kids respond to head-to-head competition and other kids back away and say, 'Hey, I'm not good enough.' And they let 'em take it." Sheri believes it's her responsibility to make Pride confront her crisis of confidence, because coddling her would do Pride no good. Pride must experience Jessie's epiphany: When she is feeling most afraid is when she must be most aggressive. If Pride wants to play competitive soccer she's got to rise, not fall, in the face of competition. As a freshman or sophomore on the high school varsity, Pride will have to give 100 percent at practices even if she never plays in a game. As a junior or senior, she'll have to fend off underclasswomen hungry for her job. It doesn't end. It only gets tougher, more fierce.

Sheri recently has had the same talk with other girls, including Erin. "You have to decide to step up and play or step back," Sheri told her. Kristin and Ashley are new to the Storm this season, and they're bucking for Erin's starting job. "The last two games she played better, but I still think she's sitting on the fence. Does she want to be a true athlete or just play the game? She has the ability but this year she has to decide."

Step up. Or step back.

It's not a moral flaw.

But it is a fact of life.

Karen Rutkowski, Diane's mother, began coaching her oldest daughter's pee-wee soccer team a decade ago. Although she'd played no organized sports as a girl, Karen coached because nobody else would. So Diane went to her big sister's soccer practices from the time she was three years old. But when she joined the Storm last year, she was still a little round and a little fearful. Under Sheri, she trimmed down and toughened up. Now she's one of the Storm's fiercest competitors.

"She's been so happy this year," Karen says. "The harder they work her, push her, the more she finds she can do." Most important to Karen, her daughter has gotten comfortable hollering directions to teammates on the field and, likewise, taking direction. "At age twenty-one, I didn't know how to do this—

afraid to hurt people's feelings and very sensitive about what people said to me. I interpreted constructive criticism as belittling . . . How could I play a competitive game? My mother was always there in my head—'Be nice, be kind, don't hurt anybody.' . . . I was passive and meek, let people walk on me. Typical stuff. I wanted people to like me and I wouldn't say anything to anybody . . . I think our society has for a long time pushed girls to the back burner. I don't think it's fair."

As she advanced in nursing, went through a divorce, Karen got more assertive, more confident. She figures that was learning the hard way. Seven years ago she joined a women's over-thirty soccer league. "It's a natural high, a great feeling," she says of competing at a sport for the first time in her life. "All these old women running around in jog bras. We love it!" She only wishes she'd started when she was young. "I think it would have been the answer to gaining the maturity and self-confidence we all struggled with."

The girls of the Storm are standing with soccer balls hugged to their chests or with balls hanging like holstered six-guns between their hips and wrists. A couple of girls have a foot resting on balls sitting on the ground. They toe them gently. They've warmed up, listening to Coolio's "Gangsta's Paradise," singing along to its tough-guy lyrics: *"I ain't never crossed a man that didn't deserve it / Me be treated like a punk, you know that's unheard of."* They wear intense, pensive faces. They stand without fidgeting, strong, healthy girls with erect postures, lean and fit, smart and pretty, girls from comfortable families. Someday, they'll be coaching their own daughters—and sons. But today, it's their confidence that Sheri, as usual, is bolstering. No matter what, Sheri has learned, girls at this age need that constantly. Sheri's telling them that they can beat this Braddock team, that they have the skills to win their season opener, that only a failure of will, intensity, commitment could lose it.

"You guys are good. Do you believe it?"

"Yes!"

"Go out there and prove it."

It is a philosophy of life. Every game, every day you continue to play, the demands get greater and the gradations of criticism get finer. You can't fake excellence. It's the lesson beyond the soccer field that the girls are supposed to be learning, the lesson that's supposed to have been so great an advantage in the lives of men, the lesson that is supposed to prepare them for the new world of women and the marketplace: Life is a competition. So get with the program.

In the tournament last weekend, the tournament the Storm swept in five games, the tournament in which the girls played their best ever, Carin had some great passes, but whenever her opponent beat her to the ball she would back off and concede it. In soccer, in life, you concede nothing. Jenny Conlin, too, lofted some beautiful crossfield passes last weekend, but she also has to toughen up. Erin laid off some nice balls, but there was a split-second hesitation before she did, an instant when she waited, an instant of self-doubt, that gave her opponent a chance to recoup. When you have the advantage, you take it, always. Christie was trying some new moves, which was great, but because she's been so good for so long she sometimes touches the ball too many times before passing. As the competition gets tougher, she's got to get ever quicker on the trigger. Missy always tries her hardest, but she kept trapping the ball on the ground instead of taking it on the inside of her foot and sending it upfield. She's got to one-touch it today.

Last weekend, Linny sometimes backed off after her opponent collided with her. Got to dish it out, girl. Ashley, a solid, consistent player, suddenly began twisting her in-bounds throw-ins instead of catapulting them straight in. Can't have that. Kristin, one of the toughest girls on the team, found herself distracted and put off her game by an opponent who kept sprinting at her full speed as if she were going to ram her. Don't back down today. Kari was playing more aggressively, just as Sheri wanted, but when she got a penalty and had to play with the risk that another serious infraction would get her tossed and leave her team a girl short, Kari lost her edge. No good—it's 100 percent or nothing. Last year, the Storm was happy just to play well, lacked the killer instinct. Today's the test. Step up. Or step back. Sheri: "Today, it's who wants it more."

Pride's thumb is still sore, but better. While she was standing on the sidelines after being forced to play the first half of that second game last weekend, she was laughing and relaxed, seemed to have realized that the pain had receded with her fear. Kristin has a huge raspberry on her hip today. Missy, Ashley, and Lindsay Chamberlain have blisters on their heels. Linny has a slightly swollen left eye where a ball socked her. Her leg, which required surgery after she broke it in a game last year, is feeling strong. Christie's kneecap was mal-aligned, but the physical therapy and the elaborate taping seem to have corrected it. Jessie broke a bone in her ankle a while back, but the doctor says she can play unless the pain is too great to tolerate. She will play. Carin has Osgood-Schlatter disease, a painful adolescent inflammation of the shinbone just below the knee, but the doctor says she too can play if the pain allows. Carin is also recovering from ligament strain in her knee from last season, and it sometimes aches. The lip that bled profusely after she got slugged by a ball last practice is nearly healed. Caroline Valentino's shin is too sore for her to play. The doctor couldn't tell from the X-ray whether she's got a stress fracture or shinsplints. It makes her limp badly. In hopes of playing soon, she puts ice on and off her leg every twenty minutes whenever she can and has been treading water in the pool for exercise.

Beneath a satin blue sky, hazy and hot, the game begins. It's been so hot so long that the field's grass is parched and brown and the ground is dry and hard. The ball bounces like crazy. When a gang of girls rushes to a free ball, the cloud of dust is so thick you can't see anything below their knees. It looks like they're stamping out a fire. The ref is letting the girls pound each other, calling few fouls. It's rough out there. Carin gets knocked to the ground and comes out afraid she's hurt her knee again, but in a few minutes she's forgotten about it and is back in the game. Tori George twists her ankle, comes out, gets it taped, and goes back in. But the Storm is playing flat, uninspired. The girls are passing one-dimensionally—not passing the ball diagonally downfield to break down the defense. Today, Sheri is so excited, so lost in the game, that she races up and down the sidelines like a dog chasing a car, barking orders. Today, the yellow scab on her elbow has turned dark and is ready to fall off, the red scab on her calf has gone rose, and the rose scab on her knee has gone yellow, its ring of redness having disappeared. Today, Sheri has only one volume, maximum.

"Alaina, I better not see you lagging behind!"

"Hey, Missy, you're gettin' too frazzled!"

"Talk, help each other!"

"Guys, we need to shoot!"

"Diane, you've got to nail that ball!"

"On that like a fly on poop!"

"You're playin' halfheartedly!"

"You guys gotta want it!"

Then, something happens. To the surprise of the girls of the Storm, they realize that they are better than the Braddock Road Magic, that they are beating them to the ball, that although the score is zero-zero, they are dominating them. Nobody says this. It is collectively acknowledged without a word. It's as if Sheri can suddenly hear the whole team think to themselves: *"God, these guys aren't really better than us. We can beat them."* Sheri can see the change, see their belief in themselves alter their play—alter their aggressiveness, quickness, decisiveness. Then, in a red blur of uniform, Lindsay passes Jessie the ball as she splits two defenders. Jessie touches it across the middle in front of the goal, just as Kari steps through a pack of defenders, just as the goalie abandons the goal to risk grabbing the ball, just as Kari touches it off the inside of her foot—and into the net: One-zip. Game and victory.

Then comes the *feeling* . . .

The girls' muscles grow stronger, their energy surges, their confidence spikes. They hear the fans and their moms and dads shouting, screaming, cheering in honor and praise. Nothing can ruin the moment, the best in their lives so far—exhilaration, accomplishment, acclaim. A feeling so euphoric, so empowering, so addictive that the girls of the Storm know they will want to feel it again and again and again, maybe for a lifetime.

November 26, 1995

Mrs. Flossie Reed.
Photo by Sylvia Plachy.

An Older, Wiser Woman

The backyard is a mess, but it's not a mess that Flossie Reed sees just now. Instead, in her memory's eye, the tree stump hunched along the property line is still a giant maple, maybe ninety years old—older even than Flossie Reed's eighty-six years. She can still see it shading her treasured flower and vegetable gardens, which have been gone for more than a decade. Years ago, today's unkempt grape arbor was manicured and much larger, and the old gray concrete bench that's now stored in the carport was set perfectly, poetically, beneath the arbor's arch. Today, the crape myrtle bush is huge, ten feet tall. But when Mrs. Reed, as she prefers to be called, bought it with the money that her son—in his first year in the Army during World War II—sent on Mother's Day, only a few shovels of earth needed to be turned for its planting. That day, a lady who lived next door said, "It looks like you could have bought something more than a plant." Mrs. Reed replied, "No, I don't think so." The woman is dead now.

The red and pink roses are growing wild and tangled today; only a couple of the white peonies are still alive; and the mulberry tree that guards the yard's rear corner has gone shabby, having been cut back only once since Mrs. Reed's husband, Gibby, got sick, suffered, and died in the living room of the house, which he and she built in North Brentwood, Maryland, with their own hands in 1939. Half a century later, the yard's lush grass is gone to crab, clover, thistle, lamb's-quarters, dandelions, and buttercups, and it's hard even to see where the rows of carrots and spring onions once grew. Gone too are the two pecan trees from the farm of Grandma Patsy, who is long dead. Of her yard, Mrs. Reed says, "It was a showpiece."

The other day, when Mrs. Reed told a friend, a woman who is old like herself, about her once beautiful yard and garden, the woman said, "So the flowers withered, so we withered." Without a trace of her usual humor, Mrs. Reed said, "I don't wanta wither." Standing in her backyard, amid the ruins of her showpiece garden, speaking without nostalgia or despair, Mrs. Reed says, "When you can't keep things, you gotta let 'em go."

Flossie Reed is a philosopher of old age. For twenty years she has shared her knowledge and insight—gently or bluntly, whatever it takes—with scores of elderly people she has visited week in, week out as part of Prince George's County's Home Visitation Program for the elderly. She's the county's oldest and longest-running visitor and something of a legend in North Brentwood. There the sight of Mrs. Reed driving deliberately behind the wheel of her '82 Ford Fairmont—baby blue and showing only 20,350 miles—brings waves and hellos from old people and kids alike. With America's population aging faster than ever, with one in four people expected to be over sixty-five by the year 2050, public policy makers, sociologists, and psychologists are rushing to fig-ure out the secrets of what's called "successful aging." In short, what makes a person good at getting old? Why does one old person stay active, sharp, and happy, while another withdraws in bitterness and frustration?

"Age is something you know is coming," she says. "If you live long enough, it's gonna get ya." It was about fifteen years ago, for instance, that Mrs. Reed developed the allergies that made her beloved gardening a struggle. So she quit gardening—that quickly, without complaining or agonizing or whining. Over the years, she has done more or less the same with coffee, ice cream, pork, beef, the annual treks to the World Series, the weekend house in New Jersey, long walks, praying on her knees, bridge games, cleaning house, and Lord knows what else. "I'll tell you, you miss things, but you learn to say, 'I can't have them.' Why worry about it?" A lot of old people can't do that, not only can't let go of small habits, but also can't accept the more profound loss-es of old age—energy, sight, memory, hearing, mobility, friends, spouses, and, most of all, independence. "I'm determined I'm not gonna be like that," Mrs. Reed says. "If I can't have it, I can't have it." Flossie Reed has got to move on.

At moving on, keeping on, she is the master. She's up each morning at five, reading her Bible, taking her bath, dressing, eating toast. After one of her two heart attacks, Medicare paid for a woman to come to her house in the morn-ing to help out. But by the time the woman arrived, Mrs. Reed was always up and done, the dishes washed. By then, she might even have been dancing to her daily exercise tape—rotating her neck, swimming her arms, prancing her feet. So she fired the woman.

At ten in the morning, heading out the front door, Mrs. Reed is a vision of vitality in slow motion. She wears a simple blue-flowered dress and a white sports jacket, opaque stockings, white flats (she wore short heels the other day and the vanity cost her a strained muscle that hurt so bad she could bare-ly walk until she doctored herself with Ben-Gay), and a pretty turquoise beret, beneath which she tucks her short dark-gray hair. Dangling her brown leather purse, which is more like a small suitcase, over her cocked left fore-arm, Mrs. Reed slowly, slowly *reeeaches* for the door's lock with her right arm, *tuuurns* the lock, *puuulls* the door slightly ajar, *steeeps* back to swing it open, *baaacks* through the door, *puuulls* it shut behind her, *steeeps* away from the door, *cloooses* the screen, *tuuurns* to face the descending steps, *reeeaches* for the black iron railing . . .

Nothing and nobody hurries Mrs. Reed. None of her motions is fluid, one linked seamlessly to another. Instead, she moves with a kind of mechanical efficiency, like a person reading one word of a sentence at a time, but reading the sentence still. She knows her bounds; she knows her possibilities. She knows that walking down the steps is harder, more dangerous, and more painful to the arthritis in her knees than is walking up the steps. She knows she can no longer make up for lost time on the way to an appointment by hus-tling just a little bit more. She has turned scheduling the hours of her day into a science. She knows, for instance, that it will take a good two minutes to get out of her blue Fairmont—to *slooowly* open the heavy door, *slooowly* swing her left leg from behind the wheel to the ground, *slooowly* swing her right leg to the ground, then rise, rise, rise to her feet, where she will pause for a second, stretch her body that has been cramped into the car seat, take another breath, check that she has her purse, check that she has her keys, depress the lock, glance left up the street, glance right down the street, step away from the car, turn, and close the door gently, not wasting any precious energy.

She is five feet two inches tall. Naturally, she used to be a bit taller. She weighs 140 pounds. Naturally, she used to be a bit heavier. Her face is thin, and the bones that made her a knockdown beauty when she was young are still high and elegant. Her skin is still supple, and its most prominent wrinkles aren't those of old age but rather the laugh lines that radiate like ripples in a pond from the corners of her mouth. What dominates Mrs. Reed's face these days are the thick glasses that magnify her eyes. But even magnified, the eyes aren't tired or baggy. Closing in on ninety, as these things go, Flossie Reed is still a beauty.

"I was supposed to be a pretty girl," she says, as she tools along at thirty miles an hour in a thirty-five-miles-per-hour zone on Queens Chapel Road. "I believe I was when I was young." She laughs—*hee-hee*—cackles, really, with disarming charm. She's great fun, great company. She believes her failed des-tiny was to be a comedian. "If I don't toot my own horn and say I was pretty, nobody else is gonna." She cackles again, goes silent. There's not a lot of con-versation when Mrs. Reed drives, because she concentrates deeply, takes it very seriously, with her hands locked at ten and two on the wheel. She used to be able to drive and chatter, read a map, jot a note, but no more. Now, it's one thing at a time—tune out the distractions, focus. Mrs. Reed wants no tickets, no accidents, no bad driving record, because when old people lose their licens-es, they close the book on the first ten chapters of their lives. "I know it's coming," she says. "I'll adjust." But in the meantime, she'll fight like hell to keep the privilege. That's part of the secret, of course: Fight like hell, deny that age is closing in, resist, sabotage the twilight. Then let it go—get a bus schedule.

This morning the cars zoom past "Betsy," as Mrs. Reed calls her car. (The nickname was far more fashionable when Mrs. Reed was born in 1905.) People fly out in front of Betsy at intersections. In traffic, they tailgate impatiently. In Betsy's rearview mirror, Mrs. Reed can see an occasional driver hollering angrily as he leans into his steering wheel and glances in his mirror, waiting for the chance to hit the pedal. As these types jet past, some of the worst even honk their horns in bombastic indignation. Mrs. Reed is in the right, but the world is so fast and so rude that it makes *her* seem to be in the wrong. "I don't pay any attention," she says calmly. "They're young and they've got things to do." She pauses, cackles—*hee-hee.* "Young people, they don't get it."

Mrs. Reed was already well into grade school when Evangeline Jennings was born in 1914. But that difference means little today, especially with the seventy-seven-year-old Mrs. Jennings homebound in her wheelchair, the left side of her body limp from a stroke she suffered twelve years ago. She was stricken when her husband and brother died and her son committed suicide within a few days of one another. Overnight, Mrs. Jennings went from feeling young to feeling old. With only one arm and one leg to propel herself, Mrs. Jennings is even slower than Mrs. Reed, and it takes her a good five minutes to answer the knock on her door. Mrs. Reed waits patiently until Mrs. Jennings opens the front door. Then Mrs. Reed shakes the screen door violently and hollers in mock anger, "Open that door!"

"You're a good *old* soul," says Mrs. Jennings.

"I'm a good *young* soul," says Mrs. Reed.

The two women have known each other to say hello for half a century, but they only became good friends in the last year, after Mrs. Reed began visiting Mrs. Jennings once a week as part of her county visitation duties, for which she is paid a nominal $5.50 an hour, plus gasoline money and health benefits. Mrs. Jennings shares a house with an adult son, and three other children and several dozen grandchildren, nieces, and nephews live nearby. They visit her regularly, take her to church, out to dinner occasionally. But visiting with someone of her own age, of her own era, is special in ways hard to explain. It's comforting in the way that fairy tales told again and again are comforting to children, the way that fish stories are comforting to old friends, the way that watching grainy footage of Babe Ruth motioning to center field is comforting to all Americans. Something shared.

It can be trivial. Take Mrs. Jennings's first name, Evangeline. As with the name Betsy for a car, almost nobody is named Evangeline anymore. But then, almost nobody is named Flossie either. Or take their slang. Not many people the age of the women's grandchildren would say they were going to the kitchen to make a "Dagwood"—after the multitiered sandwich creations of Dagwood Bumstead in the cartoon strip *Blondie*. Imagine baby boomers in forty years remarking that someone has the ambition of "Zonker," only to be met by the blank stares of forty-year-old youngsters loyal to comics still twenty years from invention today. And take the poems the women recite to each other from memory, poems recalled from childhoods seven decades past.

First, Mrs. Jennings:

> There was no crown for Him of silver nor of gold.
> There was no diadem for Him to hold . . .
> He wrote His love in crimson red,
> He wore the thorns upon His head . . .
> A rugged cross became His throne.
> His kingdom was in hearts alone.

Then, Mrs. Reed:

> No flowers, please, when I must die.
> To those who always passed me by,
> You need not on that occasion try
> To force a teardrop from your eye . . .
> No flowers, please,
> This is my plea.
> But if you have some love to show,
> Please show it now before I go.

And they share understandings unspoken. They've buried their mothers, fathers, grandparents, friends, and they've buried their husbands. Mrs. Reed was married to Gibby for sixty-two years, Mrs. Jennings was married to Pete for thirty-six years. "The worst thing that ever happened to me was when my little grandson collapsed," Mrs. Reed says. "It still hurts to think about it. I'd never seen my husband cry as long as we had been married, but he sobbed like a baby when my grandson died. We loved that child so." Mrs. Jennings nods, doesn't speak.

The women even understand each other's dreams. "I'm in bed and I was awake," says Mrs. Reed. "Not really, but I thought I was awake." And Gibby came to her. "He came on the side of the bed where the telephone is, and he got in that bed just as nice and just as real as somebody climbing in bed beside you. And I looked to see him stretched out, but nothing was there. I sat up and started crying and said, 'Gibby.' But he was gone. It was just so real." And Mrs. Reed dreamed she was walking on the sidewalk in the bright sunlight, across the street from her house, hand in hand with Gibby, as if they were youngsters courting again. But in her dream they weren't youngsters. They were an old man and an old woman, still in love. When she awoke, the dream seemed so real that Mrs. Reed got up and looked out the curtains to see if maybe it really was daylight. It was dark.

Says Mrs. Jennings, "Premonitions."

Mrs. Reed cackles. "They say the dead watch over the living, so, Gibby, I guess you've been looking out for me."

Mrs. Reed was born on a farm in South Carolina and delivered by her Great-Grandma Hester, with her Grandma Patsy assisting. In the view of Mrs. Reed's mother, nobody knew more about delivering babies than Great-Grandma Hester. Mrs. Reed's mother had left the farm for New Jersey, where she'd married her husband, a farmer and train station attendant, and made a home. But for each of her nine babies, she'd packed up and taken the train back to Great-Grandma Hester. In Mrs. Reed's family, there were no sorry old people. Hester lived to be nearly 100 and Patsy lived to be 97. She was out in the barnyard feeding the chickens when she had the fatal stroke. Not long after she died, a cow knocked down Mrs. Reed's grandpa, and he died soon after. He was 103. So dignified were the old people in Mrs. Reed's family that as a girl she thought, "I wish I was old."

Mama Ford, as they called Mrs. Reed's mother, was cut from the same cloth. She was bossy as a young woman and bossy as an old woman, but she never dawdled a moment in her life, and she never lost her memory or got senile. On the day she died, Mama Ford went to church three times. She heard her daughter Flossie sing "I Must Tell Jesus All of My Trials," and she heard her brother Claude preach. Then when the congregation stood and raised hands to the hymn "Leaning on the Everlasting Arms," Mama Ford collapsed. She was eighty-seven. She was buried on July 4, 1957. Says Mrs. Reed, "The Fourth of July hasn't ever been the same for me."

After her mother died, a fog descended on Mrs. Reed. A grayness literally engulfed her for months. Then she had a dream: Her mother came to her dressed all in white. She cried, "Give me up!" and smacked the Bible—*bam!*—with her hand so hard the sound shook Mrs. Reed out of her sleep. Out loud she sobbed, "Oh, but Mama, it's so hard. We miss you so." A few days later, as she was riding with Gibby in the car, Mrs. Reed suddenly exclaimed, "Gibby, honey, the sun is shining!" She says, "I don't know what had happened to me. I don't know whether I had had a stroke. I don't know. But the sun didn't shine for me from Mama's funeral on the Fourth of July until September, when we were coming down the highway. I don't understand, but this is the way things happened. It was like a dream. And that's what they say: Death is only a dream. You lay down and go to sleep, just like a dream."

The old woman is asleep when Mrs. Reed arrives in her room at the nursing home, and she calls the woman's name to awaken her. The woman sits up and shouts, "You'll have to come close! I'm hard a hearing and half blind!"

"Well, thank God you're not fully blind," says Mrs. Reed. "You should know this voice. Who is this?"

"I don't know," the woman says with irritation.

"I'm Mrs. Reed."

"Oh, my God! Let me hug you! My Lord!" The frail eighty-four-year-old woman has a surprisingly strong, staccato voice. Mrs. Reed knows the woman well, has been visiting her for more than five years, first at her house, now in the nursing home. "She complains, she complains, she complains," Mrs. Reed will say, laughing. "She's a chronic complainer." Over the years, Mrs. Reed has learned that it's a myth that people's personalities change as they get old: As a rule, sweeties are still sweeties and grumps are still grumps. The woman in the nursing home is proof of that. Before Mrs. Reed, the county had sent several other visitors to the woman's house, and all had eventually begged off the assignment. But Mrs. Reed toughed it out and has even come to like the curmudgeonly old woman, who is elated at Mrs. Reed's visit today.

But almost instantly, the woman's tone goes sour. "You don't know but I'm dying here. I lost another pound today, down to 113. See my face?" She touches a pale face with pale palms. "I can feel it." She's lost so much weight, she says, that her dentures don't fit anymore. "I can't eat the food. It makes me sick." It tastes awful. It's got no seasoning. They won't serve pork, sausage, or bacon. No this, no that. "I've got gas something ungodly." She says she fell three times recently. Her roommate died, but she doesn't want a new one. Too much trouble. "I don't like it here. My son put me here. I didn't even know it. I get these spells of falling down. He put me here and I do not approve of it, because half the people are nuts. That's the truth. If you were here, you couldn't stand the food."

"I was in the hospital a long time," Mrs. Reed says cheerfully. "I didn't like it either, but I kept eating."

"I lost my apartment, my money, everything. I have nothing. Sometimes I figure I'll just have to kill myself to get out. Mrs. Reed, you know I was an independent person. I'm not gonna say I was a sweet person. I was a spoiled brat. I've never really been happy. Life has been awful hard for me."

"And that made you mad and made you bitter."

"I'm hard to please. Always was."

"Your head's harder than mine."

"That's the truth!"

"It's what we talked about so many times," Mrs. Reed says. "You have to adjust."

"If they put garbage in front of you, would you eat it?"

After an hour of this, Mrs. Reed says, "I'll see you when I come back." There isn't a hint of exasperation in her voice.

The woman says, "I sure appreciate you coming to see me."

＊　　＊　　＊

On the road, back in Betsy, Mrs. Reed says, "You gotta be strong to deal with life. Life is so complicated. I'd fight city hall and everybody else if you told me you were gonna pull me outta my little shack. Nobody is taking me outta there." Of a nursing home, she says, "It's not for me. Let somebody tell me what to do? No way! Long as I can creep or crawl, I'm stayin' right in my own little two-by-four." But when Mrs. Reed hears old people say they'd rather die than go into a nursing home, she doesn't agree. "I believe I could make the best of it," she says. "You have to be flexible." Rather than complain about the food, she'd get a friend to slip her some seasoning. She laughs. "My mother used to say, 'Cunning is more important than strength.'" Now that Mrs. Reed is old, the insight is even more important. Rather than complain about being blind, she'd listen to the radio or books on tape. She'd help people worse off than herself, talk to them, cheer them up. She says, "I believe I could adjust."

To Mrs. Reed, life isn't about adding up accomplishments until a person gets old and begins to subtract losses. From the beginning, life is about loss—loss of childhood, adolescence, innocence, ambitions, dreams. Marriage often isn't all it's cracked up to be, parents die, children and grandchildren grow up and move away, don't always become the people you'd hoped. Jobs become routine and promotions stop. But a long time ago, Mrs. Reed began to learn that wrapped within each loss is a gift. While in her late twenties, Mrs. Reed was working as a clerk-typist for the federal government. She was a member of the fraternal order of the Eastern Star, an officer in her church's missionary society, a member of the church choir, and active in the PTA at her son's school. Then without warning, she was stricken with a rare muscle condition that left her unable to walk, almost completely helpless. She landed in the hospital in Baltimore for six months.

Her marriage wasn't perfect in those days, and if it hadn't been for their child, Mrs. Reed might already have left Gibby, who was a truck dispatcher for the Bureau of Engraving and Printing. But when she was sick, he got off work and drove to visit her every day. *Every day!* Once when he arrived, she was under the covers sobbing, because she'd been given her hospital bill and knew they couldn't afford her illness. Gibby asked what was wrong, took the bill, and left the room. He returned and told her to never worry about it again. Says Mrs. Reed, "I never saw another bill as long as I was in that hospital." When Mrs. Reed came home, she was still hobbled, able only to go up the stairs on her hands and knees and come down on her backside. It was years before she was back to normal. Gibby could be a hard, cynical, jealous, undemonstrative man, but during her illness she saw his utter devotion. And she saw herself: "I was wrong. I was attractive. I knew it. Everything—my shoes, my pocketbook, my hat had to match. I got sick and went to the hospital, and I didn't care whether they matched or not. I learned clothes don't mean a thing. I was a changed individual."

Her illness had brought that gift.

For Mrs. Reed—for many old people—life gets *better* amid the inevitable losses of old age, because, well, because they get wiser. Young adults often imagine that getting old is awful, and researchers have found that younger adults dramatically overestimate what they see as the serious problems of old age. For instance, only about one in five elderly people says that poor health and fear of crime are serious problems for them, and only about one in ten says that not feeling needed, not having enough friends, not having enough to keep busy, or loneliness is a serious problem. All in all, old people are a pretty happy bunch. Once a week, for instance, Mrs. Reed gets together for lunch with other old people at the North Brentwood Community Center. Today, fifteen people show up—about half of them men, half women. In an American culture that supposedly makes everyone crave eternal youth, not one says they'd like to be twenty-one again.

"My way of puttin' it," says one woman, "is that I'm glad I'm this far and not turned around and going back the other way. What's best about it is the journey. Waking up every morning and being able to put your feet on the floor. And being able to look back and think of all the good things that have happened to get this far." And consider the alternative, says one old man, only half joking: "You are going to get old or die young."

Usually, Anna Errico greets Mrs. Reed at the front door with a quip—something like, "Sorry, I'm not buying any today"—said in her pleasant, wavering, singsong voice. But today, Mrs. Errico is distraught: "Oh, I burned up my grandson's shirt. I am so upset." The smell of smoke is still strong in the house. Mrs. Errico, thin, delicate, and nearly blind at seventy-eight, has just extinguished a burning towel and rescued her grandson's University of North Carolina T-shirt, which was only slightly singed in the mishap. "I have an awful habit," Mrs. Errico confesses, explaining that although her son forbids her to go in the basement for fear she will fall, she navigated the steps to wash clothes today. When she went to iron the T-shirt it was still too wet, and so she flicked on the kitchen oven and draped a towel and the damp T-shirt from the top of the stove over the oven door. She then switched on what she thought was a rear burner to make soup. Accidentally, she turned on a front burner.

"Now how do I cover this up?" Mrs. Errico says of her excursion to the forbidden basement. She worries her son will say, "I'm gonna put you in a home if you don't listen to me and stop going downstairs." Then she adds, "He warned me about this a million times." She laughs gently, more relaxed now. "But I've been so successful with it. Once too many times."

"My father used to say, 'It's a good time to cuss,'" says Mrs. Reed, deadpan. "Now see, this is a good time to cuss."

Mrs. Errico laughs, a high-pitched, tight laugh that carries the hint of a sigh. "I'm a *damned* fool," she says, smiling and laughing freely now. Softly, she says, "I'm so glad you came."

When Mrs. Reed began visiting Mrs. Errico several years ago, the doctors had given her two months to live. Mrs. Reed looked at her and said, "Oh, no, you're getting well, my dear." She joked that it was lucky she wasn't around when they took Mrs. Errico to the hospital with pneumonia that last time, because Mrs. Reed would have doctored her instead from her "black bag"— Mrs. Reed's personal medicine bag that dates back five decades: coal oil for chigger bites, aromatic spirits of ammonia for fainting, oil of cloves for toothaches. Mrs. Reed says she'd have rubbed mutton tallow mixed and boiled with camphor and turpentine on Mrs. Errico's chest. She says her grandkids would be hoarse in bed and she'd tell them she was coming over with that concoction, and just the thought of it would have the grands up and feeling better. "Cure ya or kill ya!" she says. And the two old women laugh and laugh.

Truth is, Mrs. Reed believes Mrs. Errico, whose husband is dead, does try to do too much around the house, which she shares with her divorced son and her grandson. One day, she'll scrub the bathroom. The next, she'll stand on a step stool and wash the kitchen window. The next, she'll stand on a dining room chair and wash the crystal chandelier. She'll wait until her son leaves town and go downstairs to wash her bathroom rug. She'll exhaust herself scrubbing out the burned-on apple from the pie that overflowed in the oven. She'll bake rum cakes and delicate pizzelles flavored with anise, cook leg of lamb, pot roast, and lasagna for "the boys," as she calls her son and grandson. "There's so much to be done," Mrs. Errico will say. But Mrs. Reed doesn't discourage Mrs. Errico, because she knows that if she really does stop doing all the things she probably shouldn't be doing, she'll be worse off for it. For instance, Mrs. Errico had a house-helper provided by Maryland's social services department, but she didn't want her.

"With her around, I'm beginning to feel helpless," Mrs. Errico said just before she fired the woman. "When she's here, it's always, 'You should take a nap. You should do this, eat this, have one more piece.'" It made Mrs. Errico feel like a baby. "I don't want to feel like that." Mrs. Reed knows the feeling. After all, she also fired her own Medicare house-helper. Mrs. Errico knows people mean well when they try to help her. Her ex-daughter-in-law takes her grocery shopping every Saturday, for instance, and Mrs. Errico says it's a life-saver for her. But as they walk around the store, the woman will sometimes hold on to Mrs. Errico's coat as if she's guiding a child. "She really doesn't know what she's doing to me," Mrs. Errico says, adding that she never thought she'd have to stop driving, sewing, or reading the mystery novels she so loved. But then her eyes went. Says Mrs. Errico, "That's why I clean."

"Younger people don't understand that one of these days they're going to be the same," she says. "They don't believe it. They think they'll always be like they are now." Mrs. Errico knows because she remembers when her own elderly mother asked insistently that her daughter mark her belongings with the name of the child who was to receive each item after she died. No matter how many times her mother asked, Mrs. Errico didn't do it. It felt ghoulish to her, as if she were hovering over her mother's things, wishing her dead. But now Mrs. Errico has made the same request of her son and grandson, who keep putting it off, telling her, "You'll bury us all." Just as Mrs. Errico couldn't face the possibility of her own mother's death, she believes her offspring cannot face the possibility of her death, which she says she has faced many times. She sometimes feels so weak, as if she is going to pass out, and she will sit down and wonder calmly to herself if what she is feeling is death: "Well, is this it? Is my time now?"

"I'll tell you," Mrs. Errico says to Mrs. Reed, "if it wasn't for you . . ." and her voice trails off. Of old age, she says, "You have to be in it to appreciate it."

Mrs. Reed nods. "To understand what it's all about."

In the years she's been visiting, Mrs. Reed has watched Mrs. Errico recover from her pneumonia, but still look more and more frail. She wouldn't be surprised if her good friend lived another five or ten years, but she wouldn't be surprised if she died tomorrow. So many of her friends have died. While driving through the streets of North Brentwood, Mrs. Reed says, "Most of my friends are gone. All the people that once lived along here, the people that were my age, every one's dead." And, "That house there, those people are dead." And, "This house here, every one of them are gone, every one of them." Mrs. Reed says these things without emotion. She doesn't shake her head in disbelief, as a young person might, at the very idea of so many people missing, their homes now filled with strangers.

"I'm not afraid of death," she says. "If I gotta go—and I know I gotta go—it wouldn't bother me one bit. My life has been a beautiful life." To be able to say that, to believe it, is a real edge in old age. Mrs. Reed believes—and many experts agree—that people who led worthwhile, successful lives, people who got up and *did* things when they were young, are happier in their old age. No if-I-coulda-woulda-shoulda excuses for them. "I don't think I ever get depressed, to tell the truth," Mrs. Reed says. "I found the way to do things. If you find out it's cloudy today and you don't feel like cleaning the house, get out and do something else. Go shopping or bake, do something. Keep busy." Don't fuss with regrets.

About the only deep regret Mrs. Reed can recall in her life is that she wanted to be a schoolteacher, but gave up college to get married. "Like a stupid fool," she says, laughing. "But you know how it is when you're young and you're in love." If she had left Gibby in the early years, she probably would have gone back to her mother for help raising her son, and she would have finished college. But she didn't.

"It'll be three years," Mrs. Reed says, referring to the death of her husband. He died of kidney failure, and for the last two years of his life Mrs. Reed nursed him herself. She had a hospital bed put in the living room and she waited on him night and day. He was in terrible, awful pain at the end. The last day, she brought him a glass of water and helped him drink. He whispered, "Cool, cool water. No more." When she returned after taking the glass back to the kitchen, he was dead. She falls silent. "Three years," she says. More silence. "Good man." Silence again, until Mrs. Reed laughs out loud.

"He was born to be a grouch."

"He was nasty."

"He was like Scrooge."

"He got better, but he was still that old cranky man."

While she talks, Mrs. Reed keeps laughing fondly. "You try to look for the good things. My husband used to accuse me of that. He'd say, 'You can make more excuses for people than anybody I've ever seen in my life!' But you see, you try to not focus on the bad. I had to love him to stay with him that many years. They say love is—what?—one fool trying to seek the welfare of another." She laughs. "He was a good man." Mrs. Reed tells this story: As a young woman, she was a baseball fan. Well, not just a fan—an absolute nut. And for more than twenty-five years, Gibby got tickets to the World Series. "I didn't even know how Gibby got the tickets," she says, "but he got 'em."

So every year, the Reeds took two weeks of vacation and went to all the World Series games, no matter where they were played. The last year they went was 1966—the Baltimore Orioles versus the Los Angeles Dodgers, who were Mrs. Reed's team from their days in Brooklyn and her childhood in New Jersey. Hank Bauer was coaching the Orioles, and Frank and Brooks Robinson, Luis Aparicio, and Boog Powell were still playing for Baltimore. For Los Angeles it was Sandy Koufax, Don Drysdale, and Maury Wills. Mrs. Reed still has Gibby's hand-scratched scorecards from the games.

"The Dodgers didn't do a blessed thing!" she says, still miffed. But for one of the contests in Baltimore, the Reeds pulled their grandchildren out of school and took them to a game. A decade later, two months before her grandson died so unexpectedly, he told his grandmother, "It isn't every grandchild in the world who can say he has been to the World Series—and got a grandma and granddaddy to take him." Mrs. Reed says, "He was so proud that we carried him to the World Series."

Of Gibby, she says, "I would not want or wish him back to suffer like he did the last two years. But if he was back a well man, as well as he was three years before he passed . . ." Her voice fades. She asks rhetorically, "Are you gonna be sad? I don't know quite how to put it. You're not *glad* they're gone. You just have to say this is the way it is and learn to cope with it." Wishing or wanting Gibby back will not bring him back, and so Mrs. Reed figures she might as well embrace her new life without him. And she does: "I'm having a better life than I ever have, just as free as a bird! I'm not happy my husband's gone. I hope you understand. I loved my husband. He was a good man. He was a good father. He was a good provider. But he was a jealous man, and when you're living with a jealous man you got to think about every move you make. I'm free. I don't have to explain to anybody."

In Mrs. Reed's once-a-showpiece backyard, the white peonies that have continued to come and go without much attention for decades will be blooming soon, and when they do, Mrs. Reed will go out back, cut a bunch, and take them over to Gibby's grave. She has mastered the human art of being sad and happy, regretful and hopeful, kind and tough at once. She can look to the past and look to the future with equal joy. So she'll stand at Gibby's grave and talk to him, tell him that she misses him, that she's sorry he's gone. But she won't tell him that at age eighty-six she's also having the best time of her life. "I don't tell him that because he'd wake up from the dead!" Mrs. Reed says, laughing—*hee-hee*—cackling away. "He'd come back if I told him that! *Oooooh,* that jealous man! He would come right back, oh boy! He'd say, 'Doggone it, you're not gonna have it your way, *unh-unh!*'" And she laughs some more, before turning serious. "But I do say to him, 'Honey, you're here, but I'm doing fine. I'm doing all right. I'm comfortable. I love you and I did all I could for you. You're out of your suffering.' You know, silly stuff like that." Mrs. Reed pauses, smiles. "Tall, dark and handsome. That was Gibby."

June 28, 1992

Wesley Sadler.
Photo by Lucian Perkins.

Wesley's World

He is thirteen and he can see his life before him, running off on a hundred, no, a thousand, different and exciting roads. Like spokes in a wheel, the roads all begin with him at the hub. But they will never meet again, ever. And they will end far away and infinitely far apart in some dim and foggy time and place he cannot yet comprehend or imagine. Most of his life will be lived in that faraway place. He knows that. He really does. But right now, it seems that all his life is packed into each moment—each walk of the school hallway, each girl's smile, each snipe from a friend or a foe, each new rhythm he masters on his drums, each argument with his father, each crippling blow his man Cage lands on Raiden in Mortal Kombat II, each inverse variation he calculates. So much to learn . . .

Wesley tells himself: It is a matter of balance.

He is neither the tallest nor the shortest eighth-grade boy at Francis Scott Key Middle School in Springfield, Virginia. He's neither the strongest nor the weakest. He's popular but not *that* popular. He's a good student but not the best. His jump shot is nice, but other boys have nice jump shots too. His clothes are cool, but not the coolest. He spends enough quarters at the arcade to rank seventh in scoring on the Race Drivin' machine, but not nearly enough to rank first. Sometimes he has a girlfriend, sometimes he doesn't.

He tells himself: It is a matter of balance.

But how to strike that balance? It's every kid's dilemma. Wesley wants to be a man, to control his own life. But with that comes, as the grown-ups drone incessantly, *responsibility*. Most of the time, Wesley revels in the new freedom that comes with his age, marvels at all he's learning, breathes life in joyous gulps. But sometimes, nostalgic for childhood, he wants to run away from this boy-man world he occupies, a world that mystifies adults who have long forgotten its painful and promising subtleties, long forgotten that it is the best

185

and scariest of times. Wesley is clearly more responsible, mature, and thought-ful than many kids his age, but still, sometimes, he wants to run away—for an hour, a day, a week—just *not do* Mrs. Clo Brooks's sixty algebra problems. But if Wesley takes his eye off school for only a week, flunks one big test, he could book a C. "It's like if you just look away for one minute, then your grade has dropped." And grades, they decide the classes he'll take in high school, and high school decides the college he'll attend, and college decides the job he'll land, and his job decides his income, and his income decides how well he'll support his family, and . . . *oh, God!*

Sometimes he just has to shut down. Zone out. Hang out. Have fun. Drink Pepsi. Or he'd go nuts. Not long ago, Wesley read the book *Dogsong*. It's about a modern Eskimo boy who learns his people's lost ancient ways from a mys-tical old man who says that each Eskimo once had his own song, created his own song from his own life, a song that only he could sing, that only his head and heart could compose while he traveled a road that only he could travel. In his first year as a teenager, in the comfortable suburbs, Wesley Sadler is like that Eskimo boy. What song will he compose from his life? What song will be his alone? Wesley doesn't yet know.

But he tells himself: It is a matter of balance.

The vibraphone makes a resonant, mellow, distant sound, like a muffled bell ringing in the mist, and Wesley enjoys playing it. But at band practice this morning, it's hard to hear his rendition of Scott Joplin's "The Entertainer" over the ten other boys warming up on the marimba, xylophone, timpani, and bells to the tune of today's class assignment, J. S. Bach's gavotte from his French Suite No. 5. Think of a dozen wind chimes blowing in a good breeze—pleas-ant, but not exactly music. Through the easy jangle, two boys on the marimba next to Wesley hear "The Entertainer" and want to learn it. Wesley steps to the marimba, dinks it out, steps back, crosses his arms, poises his mallets like TV rabbit ears, bobs his head to their effort. They muff it. He dinks it out again, and this time they get it right. They smile and nod toward Wesley. Not a word is spoken.

"Now!" says Ms. Laura Deeds, a small woman who as school band director has learned to make her voice large, "we'll do a run-through. Ready? *One, two, three* . . ."

And something like a song arises . . .

Wesley loves music, loves band. Unlike some boys who goof off or slouch or yawn, he stands straight and attentive, his mouth open in a slight smile, his dimples charming and disarming, his hair buzz-cut on the wings and mowed to pinching length on top, his eyebrows dark and distinct, his skin clear, his nascent mustache a shadow, his left ear pierced, his outsize maroon Gap shirt hanging over the rump of his outsize, wide-legged, maroon Guess? jeans, his cuffs rolled up twice over his black-and-white Puma low-top sneakers. From the pages of *GQ* for kids.

And the band sort of plays on . . .

"Okay," says Ms. Deeds, cringing, "sticks down."

"Everybody collided!" hollers Wesley, laughing and conjuring the image of Bach's notes wandering the room in ragged 4/4 time, blindly bumping into one another like so many windup toy soldiers. His voice, like the voice of every boy in the room, sounds simultaneously listless and excited, while it warbles between manly and mousy.

"Are we making an aural picture?" asks Ms. Deeds.

It is a forced march to knowledge. The boys have mastered playing their eighth notes more softly, and today they work on their dynamics—recognizing how *very soft* is pianissimo, how *medium soft* is mezzopiano, and how *very loud* is fortissimo. They identify Bach's crescendos and listen for his dissonant notes that clash before arriving at a pleasing resolution. And they work on changing texture, how to go gracefully from many to fewer instruments playing. All in fifty-five minutes. So that before the year is done, each boy will play—after a fashion—at least ten percussion instruments.

"Tomorrow," says Ms. Deeds, "we get on the drums."

That's just first period. In Wesley's science class come concave and convex mirrors—concave mirrors are caved in; convex mirrors are pushed out. While images in convex mirrors are upright and smaller than the reflected objects, objects reflected in concave mirrors appear upright and larger, but only until the object's distance from the concave mirror reaches the focal point of a hypothetical circle created by the concave arc of the mirror, at which point the objects invert and become smaller. And turn in your lab papers.

In Wesley's algebra class comes a test on chapter 9, linear equations, which includes questions about: the slope of a line such as the vertical rise of an airplane shortly after takeoff (slope = rise/run = vertical change/horizontal change = difference between y-coordinates/difference between x-coordinates); an equation of a line (with slope 3/4 and passing through [-3,-2] the equation of the line is $y = 3/4$ multiplied by $x + 1/4$, or in standard form, $-3x + 4y = 1$); direct variation ($y = kx$, where k is a nonzero constant); and, finally, inverse variation ($xy = k$, where k is a nonzero constant).

"*Ohhhh*," whines Wesley, "not inverse, Mrs. Brooks."

Tomorrow begins chapter 10.

In English class comes a test on the diary of Anne Frank, plus reminders that the historical fiction stories the kids are writing are soon due and that the novel they are reading, *Roll of Thunder, Hear My Cry*, must be finished in two weeks. Then they review for Friday's vocabulary test.

"Dearth?" asks Wesley's vocab review partner, Tadz.

Wesley: "Dearth Vader."

Tadz: "Slumber?"

Wesley: "Party."

Tadz: "You gotta study. Like, man, you stunk up."

In civics class comes the writing of mock trial scenarios in which the kids play defendants, plaintiffs, and lawyers.

"What could it be on?" asks Wesley's partner, David.

"Arson," says Wesley.

"A pyromaniac!" says his other partner, Jeff, as the slapstick riff begins to roll.

David: "How 'bout a school set on fire? A boy named . . ."

Jeff: "Lyndon! He was upset about his name!"

Wesley: "Lyndon *Mary* Stewart!"

Jeff: "People teased him about his name!"

Wesley: "Do it! Do it!"

And then there's lunch and shop and gym.

And of course homework, usually an hour and a half.

Yes, sometimes Wesley just has to shut down.

He lies on his right side, curled up a bit, his head hanging over the front edge of the basement rec room couch, his homework done, the TV zapper held like a pistol in his left hand. *Zap:* Hillary Clinton's Whitewater press conference. Too boring. *Zap: The Brady Bunch. Zap: The Cosby Show. Zap: Batman. Zap: Lost in Space. Zap, Zap, Zap* . . . Back to *The Brady Bunch.* All too boring. *Zap:* TV off.

On some days, Wesley will go outside after school and shoot baskets, or he'll go over and play Doom on Tadz's computer. Or he might walk to the little strip mall near his house—a nice house with a big picture window and hostas, azaleas, two pink dogwoods, and a big magnolia in the front yard. No matter what, he'll talk on the phone in his room, because he does that every day for at least an hour. He'll talk to his friends Tony or Justin, but mostly he'll talk to Stephanie, Ingrid, Patty, and Viphalac, girls who are his friends. They are among the most popular girls at school, and Wesley has taken grief from guys about spending too much time with these girls rather than with his guy friends.

"You're just jealous," he tells them.

But today, Wesley gets up from the couch and rummages around for a 1980 video of his father and uncle and their friends playing in the reggae band One Love—named after Bob Marley's famous song. In the video, his father is twenty, only seven years older than Wesley is now. He plays the drums and wears his hair in long dreadlocks, while Wesley's mother dances in the audience. Wesley has watched this tape many times.

"They coulda been big," he says of the band.

His father is a financial counselor today, a man who wears nicely tailored suits and respectably short hair. His mother owns True Colours beauty salon in Washington. They usually get home about six, but with Wesley's mom opening a new shop, it's been later for the last few months. Wesley isn't alone, because his grandmother lives with them. But since he got his third-quarter grades—three A's, three B-pluses, and a C-plus in Mrs. Brooks's algebra class—he has been thinking about his mom and dad not being around as much. "I haven't been really focused," Wesley says of his schoolwork. "It takes a lotta work to keep your mind on it. The C-plus could be better, those B-pluses should be A's." But Wesley is of two minds about this. He mentions a boy who gets straight A's. "He's book-smart and that's all he is. And everybody makes fun of him." Wesley admits that he too makes fun of him. "He's just so strange." And, "He has a 104 average!" And, "No way, you gotta have a life!"

"If you're really that focused on it and you do your homework every single night, and you sit there after the test and study, anyone can do that. If you don't really have anything else to do but work." Wesley used to be in Gifted and Talented classes but got out, didn't want the three hours of homework every night. Wesley says most straight-A kids have no life outside school. "It's just kinda hard not to have that." It's also hard for Wesley to have his folks gone so much. His dad always helped him with his math, but more than anything his mom and dad kept a fire lit under him so that Wesley didn't have to rely only on his own motivation to keep his grades up. He says he's not trying to make excuses, but that he's found it tougher to stay "focused" with his parents so busy.

"I didn't really have that momentum from them anymore," he says. He realized with their absence that he'd always relied on his parents to give him "a kick in the butt" if his grades began to slip. "It was pretty much A's and B's in the first and second quarter and then everything just started, like, stacking up." And by third quarter, his algebra grade had really taken a nosedive. "If you don't understand something even a little bit and then you go to your next unit and you're still thinking about that past unit and you gotta think about this next unit, it's just a lot to be thinking about. Everything is like a big domino effect." From this, Wesley has taken a lesson that goes beyond grades and beyond his parent's temporary preoccupation with his mother's new business. "Each year, they're not helping you as much."

That realization is a little scary. Pretty soon, he'll be picking his college, his career, and his wife, then he'll be paying his own bills, making his own choices. He looks forward to that time, thinks about his eighteen-year-old cousin Mike, who is in college and always has enough money to buy nice Christmas presents and is never asked to leave the room when the grown-ups talk. But for all his craving for that independent time in the future, independence also frightens Wesley. And sometimes, when his folks are out late, he finds himself wondering: What if they don't come home? What if they're killed in a car accident? What would become of him? Where would he live? What would his life be like? Without his parents to kick his butt if he got too far out of line, would he behave? How much of him is still the child obeying the all-powerful parents? Would he let his grades drop way off? Steal a car for a joy ride? Do really stupid stuff?

"I don't like to think about it."

*   *   *

Wesley puts Bob Marley's reggae music on the stereo, goes to the cramped, unfinished, musty storage niche just off the rec room, a cavern filled with boxes of junk, half-used cans of paint, and old tennis rackets, and takes up a position behind his drums, a set his dad put together from his own old drums—a bass muted by a blanket stuffed in its innards, a snare muffled by a white T-shirt laid over its skin, high-hat, crash and splash cymbals, a mounted tom-tom, two floor tom-toms, a cowbell, chimes, and agogo bells. In this tiny room, when Wesley begins pounding, it's like an explosion.

For nearly a year now, he has played his drums every day, for an hour or two or even three. He set as his goal to play along to every one of his dad's more than two dozen Bob Marley albums, and he has done that. He seems never to get tired. "You just come down here and you put on music and you start playing," he says, one hand softly tapping out quarter notes, the other softly tapping out half notes, "and the time just passes away." And, "Gotta get good." Of his dad, he says, "He teaches me for when I get my band." And, "He says I practice more than he did at my age."

Wesley has what seems, for a thirteen-year-old boy, an unusual relationship with his father: He admires him. He doesn't broadcast this to his buddies, many of whom complain that their dads are stupid, that they're always wrong, that they're nerds. They say they hate their fathers. Wesley hears this constantly and discounts it, figures his friends don't really believe those awful things about their dads. "They feel differently in their hearts. They're just trying to look cool." He figures the chest-puffing comes with the age. But fearing his buddies might think *him* strange, he keeps his admiration for his dad quiet. But if his friends were to ask? "I would just say, 'My dad's not like that.'" And, "He knows things." And, "I just like him."

"If there's ever a problem, no matter what field it is, he knows a little bit about everything. If there was a plumbing problem, even though he's not a plumber, he still knows what to do. He knows a little about every single thing." Cars, computers, electronics, music, algebra, writing, girls, even handling bullies. Wesley says his dad knows how to break down a problem—"prioritize" it—and figure out what to do. He taught Wesley to check the weather before he starts his weekend yard work: If rain is predicted, cut the grass first. His dad knows how to buy a house, manage the construction at his mom's new beauty shop, negotiate the lease. Wesley is amazed. His dad, he says, is a wise man. And so Wesley tries to listen and learn from him. His dad studied engineering in college, and Wesley hopes to be an engineer someday. He pauses and laughs uncomfortably. "I'm just thinking about, like, he means a lot to me."

His dad's finest quality?

"There's no problem that's too big."

And, "He's just really balanced."

His dad, for instance, played in that reggae band and has a huge reggae recording collection. But he also has Duke Ellington, Frank Sinatra, McCoy Tyner, Herbie Hancock, Earth, Wind & Fire, Nancy Wilson, Jimi Hendrix, Stevie Wonder, En Vogue, and Boyz II Men. And besides reggae, he likes marching-band music, blues, jazz, rhythm and blues, rock and roll, and rap. His favorite drummer is the famous Tony Williams, who at age sixteen began touring the world with jazz great Miles Davis in the early sixties and helped create the melodic drum sound and fusion music—the blending of rock and jazz. Wesley can sit in the basement forever while his thirty-three-year-old father changes old records, plays individual cuts, and talks music.

"Now, you gotta listen for his dynamics," his father, also named Wesley, says of Tony Williams's drum playing. "He's like a conductor playing the drums. You got that rock flavor of the guitar and that funky bass. And then that jazzy keyboard coming in. He's a little guy with big sticks, and his technique is so good that drummers go and marvel at what he does naturally. His sticks fly off the drums, it's like—*flflflflflfl*—all over the drums."

"Double bass and everything," says young Wesley, excited.

"No, he isn't playing double bass," says his dad.

"I'm sure he *does*," says Wesley tentatively.

"He could, but he doesn't do that. He does it with one foot."

"But he plays *like* double bass."

"Yeah," his father says gently, letting Wesley's mistake pass and adroitly changing the subject. "Notice he's taking the drums into different colorations of sounds and they're holding the rhythm now and the drummer's going off playing the music. That's never been done before. *Na-na-naa, na-na-naa, na-na, na-na, na-na-naa, na-na-naa.* To musicians who study music, this is a masterpiece." He plays another album—*Miles Davis in Europe,* recorded in 1963 at the Antibes International Jazz Festival. On the recording, the band is introduced: "Miles Davis avec Tony Williams à la batterie." Wesley's dad repeats the words and then translates: "Miles Davis with Tony Williams on the drums."

"How do you know?" asks a skeptical Wesley.

"It's French."

"You took French?"

The son laughs and shakes his head. He is amazed. After a long time, the father must leave. Wesley goes to the cavern and gets on his drums. So much to learn . . .

"There's a lot of comparing between father and son," says Wesley. Yes, he admires his dad. But his dad also ticks him off. "He does some weird stuff."

At thirteen, Wesley misses no minor contradictions: A while ago, his dad told him to wash the car, although they were out of soap. When Wesley did, his father said, "This car's not clean." And Wesley said, "Dad, it's because we have no soap." His father said, "You keep on making excuses." Wesley got angry because he believed that if he had suggested washing the car without soap, his father would have said, "You can't wash a car without soap." And they would have gone to get soap.

At thirteen, Wesley misses no trivial hypocrisies: When Wesley cleans the house, his father makes him take a broom and sweep the dust out from along the walls before he vacuums. But Wesley has noticed that when his dad vacuums, he doesn't always sweep along the walls first.

At thirteen, Wesley misses no arbitrary rulings: When Wesley recently found in the fridge a bottle of juice that his dad had bought, he poured himself a glass. His dad said, no, that juice was for him, that Wesley would gulp it down in huge glasses. "I had a glass the same size. So then I see him, he has *another* glass—twice as much as I did, and I was, like, 'Dad, I didn't even have that much and look what you had.' And he goes, 'Stop complaining and stop counting food.' And I go, 'Oh, my God!' You know, you can't really do anything because he's your dad." And, "He says I'm always arguing." And, "Most times, I'll be right."

Father and son do a little dance. Wesley often gets in trouble for smarting off. Although he will deny it and say his father is pulling rank on him, deep down Wesley knows he's contesting his dad's authority. He knows, for instance, that he can say, "Don't get in my face," and probably get away with it, if he says it with a smile. And so he does. It feels good. His dad will say, "You'd better watch it," although he too, usually, will be smiling.

Wesley's mother is different. She notices when Wesley's depressed, when a girl has suddenly stopped calling. Once, when Wesley was in elementary school, he stole a piece of candy from the Giant supermarket and a friend told his mother. "That's normal," Wesley's mother, whose name is Michelle, told her son. "You're just going through what any kid does. But I want you to stop because you can get a bad habit." If that had been his dad, Wesley says, oh, man, he'd have gone ballistic: "'I can't *believe* you did that!' He'd be yelling. She's more understanding."

But despite the dance between father and son, despite Wesley's yearning and pushing to be a man, he also knows he's not yet ready to be his father's equal, that he's just playing with the idea, trying it on for size, as if maturity were a suit of clothes. Despite the dance, Wesley knows that if his folks didn't ride him about his chores—cleaning the house on Saturdays, taking out the garbage, cutting the grass—he might just let the jobs slide.

The road is bright blue, its shoulder orange, the grass iridescent green, the sky Day-Glo purple, the city skyline an eerie neon blur—Race Drivin' at the mall arcade. Wesley pops the quarters, selects the yellow speedster, turns the engine, revs it loudly, eases up to 40 for the gentle curve to the right, fires up to 90 in the straight, downshifts, takes the left curve at 60, rockets up to 80, 100, 120, flies through the air, feels the actual sensation of leaving the ground, lands with tires squealing, metal crunching—and explodes in a fiery ball.

"I love this game."

Nothing will take Wesley's mind off school and life and growing up as quickly as Race Drivin'—unless it's Mortal Kombat II, Street Fighter II, Terminator 2, Lethal Enforcers, or X-Men. These are not games, they are places a kid goes, other lands. To play well, every ounce of concentration must be focused *here,* on the screen, when the road angles suddenly to the right, when the legendary Chinese Ninja, Sub-Zero, fires his freeze ray, when the X-Men blow the robots into so many pieces of flopping, mechanical arms and legs and heads. A kid's gone, somewhere else. Einstein must have gotten lost like this in the pathways of physics. Just think if Wesley could focus this way on inverse variation or Anne Frank or the focal point of the imaginary circle created by the arc of a concave mirror. But then he'd be a geek.

He'd be like the kid who eats only Fruit Roll-Ups for lunch every day. Or the kid who cleans the label off his bottle every day before recycling it. He'd be like the kid who doesn't like girls. The kids who wear clothes without brand names, who wear tight jeans when baggy jeans are in. And he'd be harassed for it. Kids would chuckle when they walked past him and say, "Nice jeans."

"Kids would think of me like a smart kid, like nerdy and geeky and get all the good grades, answer all the questions, turn all the work in. It's cooler to be bad now. It's not really *cool* but it's not like anyone cares." Wesley had a brush with geekhood last fall and didn't like it. He was new in school and didn't know many kids yet, so he spent more of his time doing schoolwork. Impressed, his algebra teacher, Mrs. Brooks, took an obvious liking to him. "I just knew. She kept saying first quarter that it was a pleasure for me to be in her class and she was so happy she had me in her class. And I knew that if I kept on, then everybody would think I was a nerd." So for the sake of balance, Wesley had to pull back, not do quite as well, cut up a little bit more in class. He was rewarded with this note that Mrs. Brooks sent home to his parents: "Behavior is slipping." Says Wesley, "You still want to be good in class." But, "You still want to have your friends."

Imagine the school hallways as a political realm—with power struggles, constantly shifting alliances, real and feigned loyalties, ambitious people moving up and moving down, people with the power to defame or glorify others, people with no power at all, helpless people at the mercy of the strong. Sounds like life, doesn't it? Navigating this realm in school isn't only a diversion from academics. It is a life skill.

The rules according to Wesley:

It's okay to like kids who are geeks and even to talk to them, but always initiate the conversation yourself. "You don't want to be, like, he sees you, he says, 'Hi,' that kind of relationship." The popular kids would notice and think the geek was a *real* friend, so you have to draw the line. But the politics of it get complicated. For instance, there's a girl—a straight-A student—whom Wesley likes. But her friends are nerds. Now, he could talk to her, get to know her, and if she'd come over and hang out with him and his friends, leave her nerd friends behind, then he could get to know her better. But otherwise it's just too dangerous a move for a guy's reputation.

You don't have to wear expensive designer clothes all the time, just part of the time. The idea is to wear enough name-brand items—Polo, Guess?, Tommy Hilfiger, for right now, anyway—to prove that you *know* what's cool, to prove you care enough and are savvy enough to keep up with the trends, that you're not out of it, like parents who don't know the freshest styles and fads, who don't know that $135 sneakers, which were in a while back, are out now. When a kid wears "tight jeans," Wesley says, it's proof that he's out of it. The right styles and brand names are simply badges of membership, proof that a kid wants to belong and that he knows the rules of the game.

Don't talk about people behind their backs; don't take sides in silly disputes. Never get caught up in gossip about who said what about whom. Always de-escalate, don't escalate conflicts. Walk away from trouble. "Forget about it, drop it."

When kids ask you to keep a secret, keep a secret. Because most kids blab everything to everybody, you'll stand out as a friend who can be trusted—and thus have more friends.

"It's good to have popularity." Popularity means kids want to be your friend, talk to you, and talk about you. The worst thing for a kid, Wesley says, is "to not make your mark." That's why some kids would rather be troublemakers and class clowns than go unnoticed. At least "your name is coming up." The trouble is that the most popular kids often aren't the best students or the nicest people. But you want what they have and what they have the power to bestow—popularity. So even when it sometimes hurts to see a hotshot kid making fun of a nerd, it's wise not to say anything. "You just follow everybody else and jump on the bandwagon," says Wesley. "Because usually that person that's making fun of them is a popular person and you don't want to be telling him to stop. You want to be okay with him too." And, "You want to be *in*."

But not *too* far in, not *too* cool.

In enough, cool enough.

Not too far one way or the other.

"I'm where I want to be."

To see three boys out on the town, at Pizza Hut on a Saturday afternoon, is to see a display of pure self-absorption. It's as if outside the triangle of Wesley and his pals, Justin and Doug, no one else exists. Or if they do exist, it is only to provide the boys with more comedic material. Because the self-reflecting mirrors surrounding them are indeed concave—and the images reflected back to each and all are larger than life.

"Safety!" Justin hollers to the befuddlement of the Pizza Hut patrons around them. Wesley and Doug snicker, because "safety" is what a guy yells when he has loosed a gasser. If he doesn't yell "safety" before somebody else yells "doorknob," then everybody gets to punch his arm until he can find and touch a doorknob. People occupy the booths on either side of them. But, as is the teenage custom, the boys are relentlessly loud and relentlessly rude.

"Bend over," mumbles Doug.

Laughter.

"Bend over," mumbles Doug again.

Laughter.

The waiter arrives.

"This is Chris," says Justin, reading the young man's name tag. "He's a shift manager for Pizza Hut."

Wesley mumbles an obscenity about Chris under his breath.

Laughter.

"I'll take a Dr Pepper," says Doug.

"I'll take a Pepper, Doctor," says Wesley.

"An adult Pepsi, definitely adult," says Justin.

"What's on tap today?" asks Wesley.

"Nothin' for you," says Chris, smiling indulgently.

"Okay, nothin' for you too," says Wesley.

It's as if Wesley is two people: the young man who analyzes the schoolyard status hierarchy with the shrewdness of a sociologist, who respects his father and mother, who recognizes the transparent bravado of his friends, who wants eventually to become a musician, an engineer, and a father—and the snickering, laughing, mumbling boy in the Pizza Hut booth.

"Can we have some sauce?" Wesley hollers.

Laughter.

"I want some sauce, and I want it five minutes ago!"

Laughter.

"I wanta lick it," says Doug.

Laughter.

At one point, a Mazda Miata drives past, and the boys joke that they wouldn't want that little two-seater when they turn sixteen.

"We're gonna need a backseat pretty soon," says Wesley.

"What for?" deadpans Doug.

Laughter, laughter, laughter.

In quieter moments, away from the laughter, Wesley wrestles seriously with the matters of girls and sex. He knows "lots" of boys his age who claim to have had sexual intercourse. "It's like you're more of man if you've done it." Wesley thinks about sex a lot, but he hasn't yet had intercourse. He thinks also about AIDS, venereal diseases, and pregnancy. His mother tells him that kids his age aren't emotionally ready for sex. At the same time she constantly warns him that whenever he does begin, he should always use a condom. "Kids aren't really thinking about the downfall of it," Wesley says. "They're thinking it's going to feel good, be a man." But Wesley thinks of his mother's warnings often. He believes eighteen is the right age for first intercourse—a guy is out of high school, can get a job, make money to support a child if he must. "But who's going to really wait that long? Not even your best is going to wait that long." Wesley figures sixteen is a more realistic age.

Away from the laughter, Wesley wrestles seriously with the responsibility he believes he has to stay out of trouble, to do well in school, to break what he sees as the stereotype of the ignorant and violent young black male. That's why he doesn't like most rap music—he believes its lyrics are too often negative and destructive. "If you listen to that, then you're gonna start believing in that. Then who you gonna be?" Although race rarely comes up among Wesley and his friends—black, white, Asian, Hispanic—his dream is to attend Morehouse College, among the nation's most prestigious historically black colleges.

Away from the laughter, Wesley wrestles seriously with his belief in God. He has been raised to be deeply religious, attends Catholic church often, prays. But sometimes, he wonders: "Is He really there? Are we really praying to nothing? There are lots of Gods that people believe in, and how do I know that the one that my parents and everybody told me to believe in is the one? . . . You start to wonder is there really a God, and am I doing the right thing by praying to Him and what's the proof? . . . It's frightening what I'm thinking." Wesley even wonders if something is wrong with him for pondering this imponderable, if the very question is evil. "I don't even like to think about it."

But through it all, through the laughter and the music, science, algebra, English, and civics classes, hallway politics, parents, God, girls, sex, race, college, and careers, Wesley feels something else happening within him: He feels his childhood fears falling away, feels a new confidence surging. "The way I feel inside has changed," he says with a tone of awe. "The feeling that I had from before. I feel more sure about myself now than I did. Friends and girls and life. I just feel like I'm me." He ticks off his good traits—intelligent, strong-minded, mature for his age, independent, musical, athletic, easy to get along with.

"I know what I'm good at."

And, "I feel like I know who I am."

Perhaps these are the first lines of Wesley's song, the song only his head and his heart can compose.

Wesley has been studying more lately. On his Friday vocabulary test he got a 100. On his algebra test he got an 85, among the highest grades in the class. On his historical fiction short story he got a 98. On his Anne Frank test he got an 88. Wesley's English teacher, Ms. Peggy Dammeyer, says teaching Wesley is a joy. "Wesley is very capable," she says. "I'm excited for the day when he realizes how capable he is." Wesley blushes, says it feels good to have Ms.

Dammeyer say that about him. But he would not want his friends to know that Ms. Dammeyer had said that about him. Because Wesley is two people: He is a man. He is a boy. And, as he always tells himself, it is a matter of balance.

Back at the Pizza Hut, the food is dropped off.

"He's supposed to serve it!" complains Wesley.

"If I get burned—oh, I'm suin'!" says Doug.

"Where's our plates?" hollers Wesley.

Wesley burps, loudly.

Doug and Justin burp loudly too.

Laughter, laughter, laughter.

June 26, 1994

Deane Guy.
Photo by Chris Hartlove.

Of Dirt and Dignity

At this instant, Deane Guy is nowhere but where he is, squeezed into a small cubicle of space, behind a black steering wheel, behind a massive engine that is woofing and growling with each touch of toe to pedal, strapped so tightly to a seat molded for his torso that he is not so much sitting inside the car as he is contained within its works, a human addition to the physics of energy and motion that he is about to unleash. A race car is a systemic thing, not organic perhaps, but alive still, a network of pulsing actions and reactions, ten thousand possible combinations of individual pieces in all. A man strapped to its seat is wise to be humble, to always imagine himself as only a piece of the frame, no more significant than a suspension fifth-coil that cushions torque reaction where the tires meet the oval track, no less significant than a shock absorber that mediates the flow of weight as a car's inertia at 110 miles an hour in the straightaway is bent into an arc in the turn. Each, a sinew of the beast.

At this instant, Deane Guy is pristine in mind and emotion. He has no wandering thoughts or feelings. His blood pressure is elevated and his heart is running, but his mind is as clean and clear as a far blue sky. He knows of no moment in life that can compare. Around him are twenty-three other cars woofing and growling. Around them are two thousand people howling from the spindly grandstand of Maryland's Potomac Speedway. The night is hot and the wind is still. The sweet smell of alcohol exhaust is in the air, so pungent it burns the eyes. A cloud of amber dust that arose when the cars pranced into Pit Row hangs like a languid fog at the far end of the track, a high-banked, three-eighths-mile, red-clay track that before tonight's race glistens hard and dry beneath pale white lights. Atop a tall platform beside the front straightaway, a man in a red speedway shirt faces a low half-moon and prepares to launch the forty-lap race with an upward swipe and innumerable swirls of his green flag. The night, the heat, the dust, the pale white light, the swirling flag . . . Just now, is there anyplace else on earth?

No sound is quite like the roar of a race start. A jet engine is louder, but smoother, less jarring to the ears, a sophisticated *whirrrr!* A jackhammer is louder, but less subtle, a stupid *bam! bam! bam!* The sound of two dozen stock cars being punched at once is an instantaneously rolling, roiling, throaty, gigantic *ROARRRRRRRRRRRR*, each car bellowing in its own violent, guttural voice, noise climbing with so much body and volume that its force envelopes the senses, thunder and earthquake and squall, natural surround-sound, not sharp so that ear drums will puncture, but dull and deep so they will more likely vibrate to ashes.

Half a lap down . . . Deane Guy is runnin' third.

That quickly, he knows he's in trouble. Out of the front straightaway into turn one, he hit the brake for an instant and flicked the steering wheel quickly to the left so that the rear of his car would slide sideways to the right, toward the outside of the track, and come around almost ahead of its nose, leaving the car aimed straight across the second turn, aimed directly into the back straightaway. Just at the turn's apex, when Deane got back on the pedal, the flow of weight and energy through the car was supposed to straighten the front wheels automatically, the rear was supposed to halt its sideways slide, the tires were supposed to shift from their side-bite friction that keeps the car from spinning out, to their forward-bite friction that's meant to shoot it like a rocket into the straightaway.

But Deane's rear didn't stop sliding at the apex and instead got out of shape, went a few degrees farther around, like the hand of a clock going backward from 2 to 1, just far enough to force Deane to hold off the accelerator for an instant and turn the steering wheel to the right himself to stop the sideways chase. When he finally stepped on it again, the car's rear tires didn't bite the dirt instantaneously but spun helplessly for another instant. All of this took maybe an extra quarter-second. But when careering around a turn with a horde of 2,140-pound monster machines, a quarter-second is a long, long time.

Half a lap down, Deane knows . . .

He and the boys still ain't got her hooked up right.

Deane Guy is a hometown hero living in a time when most of our heroes are distant television visages, men and women whose skills and achievements are so grand that they are unimaginable and unattainable to those who live with their feet on the solid ground of everyday life. We may want to be like Mike, but we know that we never will. Deane Guy has made no commercials. He's not going to Disney World after tonight's race. He's a forty-one-year-old brick mason who quit school in the tenth grade. He's a little paunchy, with shoulders rounded from real work. He's got a relaxed, boyish manner, and when he smiles his cheeks swallow up his face. His distinctive laugh is a joyous, unapologetic *hahahahahaha* or *hehehehehehe*. He talks in that lyrical southern Maryland dialect that defies proper grammar, he's still married to his teenage sweetheart, and he lives only nine miles from the house in which he was born.

But at Potomac Speedway, a small world unto itself in a wooded glen in rural Budds Creek, Maryland, the young boys want to be like Deane. He has been Potomac's point champion of the year six times, more than anyone else in the speedway's twenty-one-year history. He's the only driver who has won the track's annual Gene Van Meter Memorial Race twice. He has also won the track sportsmanship award twice. In an era when so many people yearn for fast money and fast fame, Deane Guy won these honors in a way that, sad to say, seems almost quaint in America today. He began racing seventeen years ago, working evenings and weekends to pay for his hobby. His first year, racing a beat-up $200 Chevy Impala, he never finished better than seventh. But every evening, he and his friends worked on his car. And every year, Deane got better. His wasn't a dream, but a goal.

Every Friday night, he'd try to drive a bit better, try to have his car a bit improved, in the methodical way of the craftsman—backyard excellence built one adjustment, one detail, at a time. "It's just like anything," Deane says, as if it's all so obvious. "The more you practice, the more you take care, the more you do, the better you s'posed to be. My cars was better. And it come from workin' on the cars, where a lotta people didn't work on their cars. They just liked to run fast."

Every year, Deane invested a little more money in his cars. The red-and-white No. 44 race car he drives now is a $40,000 machine. In the winter off-season he and the boys, as he calls his pit crew, often go to racing classes in Pennsylvania. Crew chief Joey Pingleton harvests trees all day, cuts grass in the early evenings, and then works on Deane's car from about seven to eleven every weeknight. On the side, he reads books like *Auto Math Handbook* and *Dirt Track Chassis Technology*. Deane has never paid him a penny.

Joey and Deane—and Bobby Thompson, Ralph Noel, Wayne Guy, Pee Wee and Stevie Long, and a dozen others who work on Deane's car—are paid in a different coin, the coin of self-respect, something that's hard for working men to earn in a world increasingly populated by college-educated suburbanites. But Deane and the boys, aficionados of a sport the sophisticated consider a hillbilly pastime, offer a practical and moral primer for what everyone would claim to value—excellence for the sake of excellence. Because to be among the best, even at tiny Potomac Speedway, takes cooperation, dedication, hard work, and obsessive attention to the mind-boggling complexities of man, track, and machine.

It takes Deane Guy's philosophy of life.

Strapped inside his race car, Deane is still struggling with the unfortunate confluence of a clay track that's harder and drier than he has ever seen it, tires made of rubber compound hard enough for running on loose and damp dirt but too soft for this track tonight, and his car's suspension, which after months of tinkering is still letting the rear end chase up the hill and spin its tires.

After the first lap, Deane holds the steering wheel with his left hand in the straightaway, reaches down to his right, and twists a lever that adds brake power to the front wheels. That should help keep the car's nose down when he brakes into the turns, but it doesn't help much. Or if it does, the improvement is offset by his tires continuing to lose their gripping power. Or by the track continuing to dry and get even harder. No telling. No matter. Car 00 leads the pack with a 17.76-second lap time, while Deane clocks a disappointing 18.21. Running second is 44S. Then 01 passes Deane. Then 82. Now Deane's running fifth and barely holding off a charging car 75.

So he sets his strategy for the next thirty-five laps. He'll try to hold fifth by blocking out the faster 75, go into the turns well below top speed so he won't spin out and be sent to the rear of the pack, because he knows he'd never catch up again. He'll feather the gas pedal off the turns so he won't spin his tires, wear them down to nothing, and find himself in the track infield with a flat. His idea is to drive his tires to the edge of what they can take—no more, no less. Sometimes, he's halfway through the straightaway before the pedal's to the metal.

But behind him, cars are spinning out and crashing, tires are going flat. In Deane's words: "They done gone over the jagged edge." By lap twenty-eight, Deane still holds fifth, and only thirteen of the twenty-four original cars remain in the race. As Deane always says, laughing that distinctive *hahahaha-haha,* "You can't win if you're sittin' in the infield all torn up. Took me a while to learn that."

Two years to be exact. Deane was a twenty-four-year-old bricklayer who hadn't yet gone off to start his own masonry company when he came home one night in 1976 and told his wife, Linda, "I'm gonna buy me a race car." She answered, "No you're not." But Linda, who is just about as easygoing as Deane, relented when she saw the '64 red Impala, with its 283-cubic-inch engine and its windows broken out to let the air flow through unimpeded—No. 33X.

Deane: "I was tickled right to death."

He and Linda had gone to Potomac Speedway occasionally, but Deane had no racing experience—except for the racing he and the other country boys had done on the back roads. As a kid, Deane always had a hot car, usually a convertible. He bought his first when he was only fifteen—a blue '60 Impala. In rapid succession, he owned and wrecked three '64 Chevy Chevelle ragtops. Then he bought a showroom '69 Chevelle Super Sport, and it was one beautiful car—a green hardtop with a 396-cube, 375-horsepower V-8. Before Deane wrecked that beauty, the country boy was king of the road. Nobody could catch him after he squealed off the drag on the long, flat stretches of rural Route 234 or Route 242 at night, when he could see headlights coming from the other direction and had time to slow down and get out of the way.

It was a dangerous game, but that was life for Deane and his buddies. "You worked all week," he says, "for your insurance and your car payment." He's not proud that he'd usually been drinking when, going way too fast, he wrecked his cars, ran off those country roads and crashed into a tree or rolled over a few times. But he was always alone and he never hit another car. Miraculously, he was never hurt. Marriage and responsibilities finally ended the rampage—and put Deane behind the wheel of a little Ford Maverick, a three-speed on the column with a four-cylinder engine that expelled a sad, mournful whine when he toed the pedal.

But in his first race car, 33X, Deane again became that country boy who thought racing was speed without discipline. Pretty soon, Linda was sitting in Potomac's bleachers embarrassed at all the boos Deane was getting. He was the Darth Vader of the track, a bully. Sometimes, just for mean fun, he'd kiss the back bumper of a slower car and push it for an entire lap, before knocking it aside. "Outta control," Deane says. "I was just outta control." He also was losing big time, sitting in the infield, his car torn up only halfway home, watching men with slower machines win. Finally, a driver named Tex, a friend of a friend, told Deane to follow him, just do exactly what he did. Tex rammed nobody, kept his cool, let the hotheads bash it out and make their sorry ways to the infield. Then Tex won the race—and Deane took second.

Tex: "Did ya figure out what you're doin' wrong?"

Deane: "It kinda come to me."

The rest is speedway lore. In the next fifteen years, Deane Guy won at least one track championship in each race-car class, as he slowly worked his way up to the premier stocks, always the final and fastest race of the evening. He became known as a calm, judicious driver not only because he matured, but because he liked nothing—not even making love—better than winning. But when he moved up to the premier class three years ago, the winning stopped. Linda, who along with thirteen-year-old daughter Tonya and twenty-year-old daughter Deana had become Deane's biggest fan, began to worry to herself that he'd reached beyond his skills, that he would, like so many other drivers who dreamed of racing with the track's big boys, retire a loser. Deane, ever the craftsman, didn't know of her doubts and certainly didn't share them. He told his crew, "It's gonna take time."

The next year, last year, he was point champ again.

Linda, proudly: "He proved me wrong."

But that was last year. Over the winter, Deane had his 410-cube Chevy motor rebuilt by his engine man in Indiana, Earl Gaerte, into a 430-cube engine, which upped its horsepower. Even more important, it created more torque, which is the engine's twisting power that ultimately is transferred to the axles that turn the wheels. The added power has required suspension adjustments that still aren't right. "We're not havin' a *bad* year," says Deane, who's running third in points so far. "It just takes a lotta thought and a lotta effort. Sometimes it takes you a year to figure out what's the right tires. The fastest car don't always win. You gotta get everything workin' together."

And then came the new clay. For the first time in years, Potomac Speedway got its yearly six thousand tons of clay for the track from a different site. The clay turned out to be less powdery and laced with gravel. Although fifty thousand gallons of water are dumped on the track in the days before race night, this year the track has, by the final race, been dry and hard as bone. The track is hard enough that the cars bounce up and down on the rutted turns so fast and fierce that they look like pumping pistons themselves. In the early heat before tonight's forty-lapper, for instance, Deane's car hooked up fine when the track was still so tacky it stuck to Deane's shoes like chewing gum, and he won—earning third pole position to start the feature race. Joey'd put tires made of extra-soft rubber compound on the rear and the tires got good bite. The car was fast in the straightaways too, and back in the pits before the feature, Deane was downright effusive.

Deane: "Boy, she's fast!"

Joey: "How's it gettin' in?"

Deane: "It's gettin' in good—and gettin' off!"

Joey: "In the beginning you didn't look good."

Deane: "Right, until I got some heat in them tires. Then the car felt loose, gettin' faster and faster. *Good ta go!*"

Joey: "But it could go away. The track's gettin' harder."

Deane: "The next forty laps gonna tell the tale."

And they have. With thirty-five laps down, except for the lead cars that are running on much harder tires, the racers are skating around the turns like stones skipped on water. The earlier races have driven the track out—made it hard and dry—and mountains of dust are now billowing so thick that driving through them is like being in an airplane when it enters a cloud bank. But nobody's flying with instruments. By now, Deane's concentration is so intense that if every fan were to line up along the sidelines and wave at him to stop, he might not see them. As Deane says, "I don't drink and I don't take drugs, but out there I'm on my own." No phone jangling, no late-payers making excuses, no customers griping. No distraction.

And when Deane powers into a thick dust storm created when a car spins out on the fourth turn, he thinks calmly that, as with all of life, you never know what's on the other side. His best friend and fellow race-car driver, Gene Van Meter, leaned over to check the pressure in a tire one night at the track and fell over dead. Only weeks ago, Deane's brother-in-law was killed by a hit-and-run driver as he walked to work one morning. You never know what's on the other side. When Deane roars out of the cloud on the fourth turn, his mind is free and clear—completely, totally, unequivocally focused. But his optimism has hardened with the track.

Five laps to go . . . He's just tryin' to hang on.

*   *   *

All week, Joey Pingleton had pondered Deane's race car. While taking down trees for Van Meter Pulpwood, riding along on his big "Joey's Grass Service" mower, eating, or driving, even while he was nodding off, Joey was pondering that race car. At twenty-seven, he has been with Deane for a decade. He's the only crew chief the two-year-old No. 44 has ever known, and Joey and that car are on intimate terms. Racers have tried to lure him away, offered him real money for his time and expertise. Joey hired out a little but then gave it up, because it broke his concentration. How can a man nod off to sleep pondering the panhard bar setting of *two* race cars?

Sometimes, Deane and the other boys working on the car in Deane's garage will mill around quietly for more than an hour, listening to WFLS country twanging away, drinking up Deane's Diet Rites, checking every nut and bolt, removing the car's torn-up sheet metal and pop-riveting new skin to the frame, checking the oil and the brake fluid, replacing a broken motor mount and a leaky brake line, welding a cracked seam in the frame, greasing the ball joints and the steering rack, waxing the body. Even during the winter, the work goes on—with the entire car torn apart bolt by bolt, the red frame sandblasted and repainted, and every part checked and cleaned until it sparkles red, black, blue, silver, yellow, or gold, just like a child's prize model.

And the whole time, the boys will be jacking their jaws—about the time Bobby accidentally drilled four holes into a brand spanking new radiator, or the time Deane was running first in a race and some boy ran up and landed his car on top of Deane's hood, and Deane climbed out of his car and jumped up and down on the boy's roof, tore off pieces of the boy's car, howling wildly as he did. At that story, Deane will cock his red Deane Guy Masonry cap even lower over his left eye, laugh his famous *hahahahahaha* or *hehehehehehe*, and say with studied nonchalance, "I got outta control." But the whole time Deane and the boys are working and goofing, they will also keep an eye on Joey, who is a handsome, lean, pale man with a guileless, open face and a shy, wispy laugh. The whole time, Joey will be lying on a slide-board creeper on his back under the car looking up into its works. Just looking, trying to envision—imagine—how the power flows through the beast.

A stock car is such a pure device, an automobile reduced to essence, with nothing added for comfort, convenience, pleasure, or status. Underneath, Joey might be studying the panhard bar, which helps control roll—the way weight is distributed throughout the car's frame, springs, and wheels in the turns. The panhard bar runs horizontally behind the driver's compartment and has four possible high-to-low adjustments. Joey might study those adjustments and try to burn into his mind an image of just how the movement of force and energy would reconfigure if he were to make any of the changes.

Then he might try to imagine the effect of any change when coupled with a change in, say, a front shock absorber that pushes up and down with an equal

50-50 force as opposed to a 30-70 force. Or if either or both of those changes were combined with a lowered radius rod that runs from the left-wheel axle to the upper frame. Or combined with a shift in the front-to-rear weight distribution from, say, a 46-54 percent split to a 47.5-52.5 percent split. *Or . . . Or . . . Or . . .*

Deane: "It's more to it than it looks."

Joey: "You always have a problem. You're always changin' somethin'. Sometimes it works, sometimes it don't. Sometimes you change stuff and you go backwards."

Deane: "And if it goes backwards, I don't get upset. That's the only way you gonna find out."

This constant, methodical, determined search for doing better one day at a time is how Deane Guy has run his life. When he speaks of men he respects, the first description out of his mouth is always, "He's a hard worker." Deane was born poor, and he was more or less on his own by the time he was sixteen. "I failed first grade," he says, "and let me tell you, when you flunk sand piles it's rough." As a kid, he thought of himself as slow, and he wore a chip on his shoulder to cover up that belief. But he always was a worker. He learned the bricklayer's trade as a young teenager, and that's the job he took when he quit school. On the side, he tried his hand at waterman's work. One year, he tried sharecropping. "It cost me ninety-seven dollars to learn how to raise tobacco," he says, chuckling. For a decade, he and Linda lived from paycheck to paycheck, small ones at that. Then fourteen years ago he quit drinking and soon after went into business for himself.

As ever, he worked night and day and weekends, still does, usually up before the alarm goes off at ten minutes to five and never in bed before eleven. He and his seven-man crew work a good half a dozen jobs a week—a basement in Laurel Ridge, a patio floor and porch steps in Breton Bay, a foundation in Port Tobacco, a fireplace in Breton Beach, an office building foundation in Solomons. He goes checking up job-to-job, helping to lay bricks and sweep up the mess, taking the dump truck to pick up four or five tons of sand for tomorrow morning's job. Then he goes home to estimate bids in the early evening, before meeting the boys out at the garage about seven. Deane knows his masonry men will work whether or not he's with them. He will forgive a lot in a man, if he works from the heart.

Deane may have started with nothing, but if his life keeps up with "the same ol' same ol'," he figures he'll be worth near a million in a few years. Not in cash money, but in tangibles—the four nice work trucks with his name on the sides, the forklift and the masonry equipment, his own pickup, Linda's van, the house and land and big garage in the country, the few building lots he owns, the race car and the jet-black $25,000 trailer rig and Ford F-350 XLT Lariat he bought last winter for towing it.

To his work and his racing, Deane applied the way of the craftsman. There are no wunderkind craftsmen, no wunderkind bricklayers, carpenters, or mechanics. A craftsmen learns only as he goes, as he patiently does with his hands, his head, his tools, and his materials what the older and more experienced craftsmen have done before him. Deane learned to lay simple brick patterns, then he learned one bond style and then another. He learned how to fashion an ornate quoin corner in many styles, before he settled on the unadorned quoin corner that is his trademark. He learned the art and science of mixing mortar in different weather conditions as he met and mastered those conditions. A craftsman faces a new circumstance—grand or trivial—every day. If he does so for thirty years, he finally wakes up one day as one of the best.

In this way, time, experience, and determination—not natural genius—are life's teachers. The reason Deane insists that his work trucks and his race car be kept sharp and clean is because it means that he and his men are attending to even the smallest details, and details add up. A craftsman doesn't get to Step 10 until he has gotten to Step 9. And he doesn't ever, ever get there alone. Other people must draw up plans, excavate the site, pour the concrete, raise the frame, add the wiring, plumbing, and drywall. And it must all be done in orderly, detailed sequence, with each step building on the other. If a wall isn't plumb, then drywall can't be hung straight, then wall seams can't be made invisible and nails will twist and pop. By its nature, craft is teamwork.

"People don't appreciate a quoin corner anymore," Deane says. And more and more of the people he works for, mostly the suburban folks who have flooded Maryland's once-rural Charles and St. Mary's Counties, seem not to understand or respect men of the crafts. A customer making $40 an hour in an office job, for instance, will be outraged that Deane will pay a journeyman bricklayer $18.50 an hour and charge the customer $25 an hour for a job. "He thinks you're robbin' him!" Deane says. "But he makes more!" Yet, to Deane's way of thinking, that office worker who attributes more value and status to his job isn't creating a thing that will last. "I can pick that brick up and put it in that wall," he says, "and a hundred years from now it's still gonna be in that wall." Deane sees his racing victories in the same light. "We done what a lot of 'em can't say they done," he says. "That's something they cannot take away from you."

These days, the competition is getting tougher and tougher at Potomac Speedway, with Ray Kable, Roy Deese, a few others hooked up well and beating Deane regularly. But at Bert's Restaurant & 50's Drive-In, owner Bert Gagnon, a tall, hefty man who looks like a cross between John Wayne and Henny Youngman, still treats Deane, Linda, Tonya, and one of her girlfriends like royalty when they come in every Friday for eats before the race.

Racing is a family ritual for them. During the weekday evenings when the boys are working on the car, Linda and Tonya often drop by the garage, which is only thirty feet from the house. If daughter Deana weren't so pregnant, she and her husband would be going to the races tonight too. The races are always like old home week. Linda will wander around the pits all evening, often until midnight or 1:00 A.M., chatting it up with old friends and new—racers, crew, wives, kids, hangers-on, and helpers. Tonya and her girlfriend will read and listen to music in the air-conditioned dressing room at the front of the trailer rig, go out and sit in folding chairs to watch Deane and the boys work on the car, and then head off to the stands with Linda to cheer their favorite racers in the evening's different classes.

They always launch the night at Bert's Drive-In, where it seems that everybody knows Deane Guy. That's fitting, because Bert's is a memorial to a bygone car culture. Its walls are decorated with pictures of classic Fords and Chevys—and a picture of Deane Guy and his race car, as well as plaques that record his winning ways. In Bert's, Deane has a respect that indeed they can't ever take away from him. "I don't like sayin' I'm the best because I know I'm not the best," Deane says of his racing years at Potomac. Then he pauses with dramatic hesitation, winks, and adds, "*But,* I'm in the top five."

When Joey talks about why he works so hard for no money on Deane's car, he not only reveals the same pride, but even uses the same language as Deane. "We've done things that a lotta people can't say they've done," Joey says. "We've won championships more than anybody else around." And doing it from the heart makes it worth more. "It makes you feel like you accomplished more, not gettin' paid for it." Then he adds, "I hope people have respect for us."

That's why Joey is so determined to get 44 hooked up right. Last year, when Deane won the point championship, they also had trouble holding the turns and getting off, but the smaller 410 engine and the softer clay masked these failings, made them minor irritants. This year, they're spoiling the soup. Some drivers like a loose car, one that slides out of shape in the turns, but not Deane. He came up through the street stock car classes, where the cars drive *through* the turns, and he likes a tight machine that grips the track.

So a few weeks ago, Joey asked advice from Brian Johnston, a boy who used to hook up the car of Hagerstown Speedway racer Rodney Franklin, whose car frame and suspension are rigged a lot like Deane's. Brian suggested adding forty-five pounds of lead to the rear for more bite, lightening up the front right spring to accommodate the weight shift, moving the brake floater bar up one notch to transfer more weight and bite to the right rear tire, and changing to a lower gear in the rear end where the drive shaft meets the axles to kill some power from the big 430 engine that may be causing the rear wheels to spin. Joey made the changes.

But two weeks later, last Friday, Deane was still chasing the car around the track. Brian suggested radical adjustments—changing the entire suspension on the rear right from the stationary clamp-bracket the car has worn for two years to a flexible swing arm that will, theoretically, unload some of the weight from the rear right tire under acceleration and help drive the car through the turns tighter. But Joey, who keeps a written record of every single change he makes from week to week and a written record of Deane's description of the car's handling after every race, wasn't convinced. He told Deane, "I don't know whether that's the direction I wanta go." Three weeks ago, before he started with Brian's advice, the car was running better than the last two weeks. It wasn't *right,* but it *was* better. Now, that could've been the air temperature, the humidity, the way they graded the track before the race, the amount of water they poured on it that night. Could've been something they don't even know, but the car still *was* running better.

The Potomac Speedway forty-lapper is a big event, attracting hotshot racers from speedways in Hagerstown, Maryland, in Winchester, Virginia, and in Bedford, Pennsylvania, and Joey was afraid to take Brian's advice because he didn't want Deane going out there with an untested hookup that might leave him slipping and sliding around like some rookie. Embarrassing not only for Deane, but for Joey too. So after three days of pondering, he decided to scrap most of Brian's changes, go back to a tried-and-true hookup, and then start making changes—one at a time, week after week—like a scientist painstakingly altering experimental variables in individual succession. Like that scientist, if Joey changes too much at once he won't know what effect to attribute to what cause. Not to mention that even a few badly interacting changes can render a car literally undrivable.

Joey: "I'm goin' back to what we had three weeks ago."

Deane: "Do whatever you wanta do."

Joey: "I could take a torch and cut the frame in half and you wouldn't say too much."

Deane: "Nope."

Truth is, Deane never second-guesses Joey. Deane foots the $5,000 to $15,000 annual cost of racing and all the big capital outlays when they hit—a new engine can cost $25,000. A handful of sponsors—Bell Motor Co., Van Meter Pulpwood, W&W Racing Tires, Ray Long's Construction, Bert's—kick in about $5,000 a year total, but it's Joey's car to make good to go. Deane knows he's but a piece of the frame. Of his winning record, he says, "It come from the crew, it's not me. If it wasn't for my crew, I wouldn't be where I am at. It's just that simple. That boy out there, Joe, will work that car night and day. And you don't have many like that anymore. We're friends. You can't live in this world by yourself. You cannot do it yourself."

So in the days before tonight's forty-lapper, Joey went to work reversing the changes of the last few weeks. He went back to a higher gear in the rear end, removed the forty-five pounds of lead ballast from the back, put a stiffer spring back on the right front, and lowered the brake floater bar a notch.

Joey, in a voice that revealed his doubts: "I ain't sayin' it's gonna be exactly what we need."

Deane, with an easy shrug: "Joey's done his. Now it's my turn. If it works, it works. If it don't, it don't . . . *Mah turn!* . . . Go fast, turn left."

On the dusty infield now, with Deane still clinging to fifth place, his rear still walking across the track on the turns, Joey shakes his head. "We still ain't got her right," he says, scowling. "Gonna have to make some changes." The track has gone so parched by now that it's a huge spiderweb of tiny cracks and scarred with the long black rubber streaks of disintegrating tires. The clear plastic tear-offs all the drivers wear a dozen-deep on their helmet windows to collect the splattering dirt before they are discarded in sequence throughout the race now litter the track and as the remaining cars rocket by, the sheets swirl and fly and dive in the turbulence and flash under the lights like bursting white flames. The cars, so low and wide and aerodynamically wrapped, really do resemble jungle cats, with their giant rubber paws clutching the ground and their sheet metal bodies flexing like rippling muscles. Out of the first turn on the thirty-ninth lap, the nose of 75 brushes Deane's rear, throwing his car off its racing line for just an instant, enough time for the faster 75 to finally roar past him on the inside. Nothing Deane can do. He nurses his tires to the finish—sixth place.

Back in the pits later . . .

"There ain't none left," Deane says of his right rear tire, which to everyone's amazement has actually begun hissing air from a hole on its shredded face. Now that's driving your tires right to the edge, no more, no less, which makes Deane proud. He stands solemnly in a kind of matador's pose, exhausted, his hair and face and red racing suit soaking wet, his cap cocked low over his left eye, a Diet Rite held in his right hand before his waist, his jacket dangling from his left hand like a cape, its tip kissing the dirt, his shoulders cast back, his head cast down.

Deane: "Our left rear the same way, *goooone?*"

Joey: "Yeah."

Deane: "*Hahahahahaha . . .*"

Joey: "Ain't nothin' there."

Then, in the choking dust of the pit, beneath the pale white lights, amid a traffic jam of race cars, rigs, pickups, and men, women and kids winding down and heading home for the night, Deane and Joey and Bobby, Ralph, Wayne, Pee Wee, and Stevie lean against No. 44 and calmly relive the race, in its tangible detail and its intangible caprice. If they'd had harder tires, they'd for sure have run better. But if Deane hadn't swung out in a flash and missed a big crash in the warm-up laps, he'd never have made the feature race, never even have had the chance to run a sad sixth. There's more to it than it looks.

Tomorrow, the boys will start again. Deane will wash the car, that's his job. Everyone will begin poring over it, looking for cracks, leaks, twists. Then Joey's going to take Brian's advice, remove the clamp-bar suspension from the right rear, and replace it with a swing arm. Won't do much else, can't. Otherwise, next Friday night when they're standing and jawing in the same pit after the race, they won't know what effect to attribute to what cause. After next Friday's race, they will start again. Then again . . . And again . . .

One adjustment, one detail, at a time.

July 11, 1993

Jim Lachey.
Photo by Brian Smale.

A Violent Craftsman

The shudder in his ankle was almost imperceptible. Certainly, it would have gone unnoticed by Jim Lachey himself if the video he was studying in a darkened room two months ago had been rolling at real speed instead of slow motion. But watching it again and again in slow-mo, he could see the shudder begin, at the football's snap, as a slight twist on the ball of his left foot that then sent a vague ripple through the joint of his ankle that then caused his first backward step to leave his foot not perpendicular to the line of scrimmage, as it always should be, but at an angle to the line of scrimmage that was closer to forty-five degrees, his left toes seeming to point to ten o'clock rather than midnight, his shoulders corkscrewed slightly around to his left. Even if a Redskins coach had been carefully watching the Pro Bowl offensive left tackle from the sidelines, he couldn't have seen this flawed footwork. Tens of thousands of people in the stands at RFK Stadium and millions of folks watching on TV wouldn't have noticed it either. If they had, would ten in a million have known its dire meaning?

Well, *they* might not see it or understand it, but Jim Lachey did—as would even the saddest pass rusher in pro football if he were to see Lachey do it repeatedly. With maulers like Lawrence Taylor of the New York Giants or Clyde Simmons of the Philadelphia Eagles or Charles Haley of the Dallas Cowboys, that shudder would surely evoke muffled growls and crooked smiles: *Lachey's left foot's not nifty, he's out of form, off balance, and giving up his shoulders sideways in a two-way street that leaves a rushing lane on either side.* The nearly invisible flaw in Lachey's footwork would suddenly leave him open to the pounding inside club, the frightful dip 'n' rip, and the fleet-footed whirlybird spin. Word would travel fast, all right, just as it did decades ago when the New York Jets' ominous tackle Sherman Plunkett finally lost a step with age. Word hit the street, and the defensive assassins began firing past him like rifle

213

shots. A mauler's holiday.

Only one flawed step on one tape, yes. But Jim Lachey lives by an absolute rule: One screwup is a habit; two screwups are a *bad* habit. So for the next week, as he prepared to go off to summer training camp in Pennsylvania, Lachey mulled that step, the sad way it looked and the way it *should* have looked. He told himself again and again that his first step off the line of scrimmage in camp would, *must*, be perfect.

He imagined it repeatedly—visualized it, he says—in a kind of waking dream: Seeing himself in his three-point stance, sunk low at the knees, bent at the waist, head up, forward weight balanced on right knuckles, and left forearm resting on left knee, Lachey would dream of lifting his left foot off the ground, kicking it out from his body three inches and backward eight inches, where he'd plant that sucker like a giant oak, toes aimed like an arrow to midnight. And on the first snap at summer training camp, that's exactly what he did, in precise and perfect choreography. Because Jim Lachey has zero tolerance for error.

They call him Jimmy. He has been called that all his life, although it must have sounded discordant when a six-foot-six, 235-pound boy of sixteen was called Jimmy. Today, at thirty, after eight years in the pros, three Pro Bowl appearances, and a reputation as one of the finest offensive left tackles ever to play the game, he is still called Jimmy. Coaches, friends, mom and dad, wife all call him Jimmy because it fits. Sure, he's six feet six, packs 290 pounds. He's got a nineteen-inch neck, the circumference of a small man's thighs, and twenty-nine-inch thighs, the circumference of a small man's waist. Those thighs, the source of much of his football might, have the girth of a log yet to be quartered for the fireplace, the girth of a twenty-two-pound turkey in the Safeway freezer. But Jimmy is a quiet, polite, and gentle man, still boyish, still refreshingly earnest, less beastly than scholarly in his football ways.

That would be more odd if Jimmy Lachey played, say, linebacker and ripped and roared and gouged his way through mountainous hard-bodies on every snap. But Lachey has always played on the offensive line, the least glamorous and, after quarterback, most cerebral of football's positions. On the offensive line, a monster-man like Joe Jacoby, the Redskins' gnarled six-foot-seven veteran, can joke in a mockingly effete accent, "We consider ourselves more *civilized.*"

Football fans are often just that—fans who watch the football, as it travels from center to quarterback to rusher or receiver. They notice the offensive line only when it becomes a Maginot line and enemy troops swarm toward Paris. But in these fierce trenches some of the game's most critical confrontations are taking place. To study Jimmy Lachey is to marvel not only at football's grit and guts, but also at its craft, art, and magic. Lachey is the Compleat Offensive Left Tackle. He has always been physically gifted for the job but also yeomanlike in his dogged study of the position's intricacies. And he has always loved the sport, obsessively living and breathing and sensing it with an emotional depth that at times has made playing football an ethereal experience for him. To enter the world of Jim Lachey, to see the sport through his eyes, is to have a whole new game revealed.

Jimmy Lachey figures there are, on average, sixty offensive plays a game, each of which lasts, say, five seconds. That means about five minutes of *real* work each game, multiplied by sixteen regular-season games, which means eighty minutes of work a year. Divide that into Lachey's $1.35 million salary and *bingo*—$16,875 a minute! It sounds more outrageous than it is.

Jimmy Lachey's on-the-hoof value to the lucrative business of football began in tiny St. Henry, Ohio, due west of Columbus near the Indiana border. In high school, he was winning the hundred-yard dash *and* the shot-put competitions, as well as playing center on the state championship basketball team, as well as earning the title of All-American on the football team, as well as making the honor roll. The football seers came from UCLA, Notre Dame, Alabama, Ohio State, and on and on to salute and seduce him. He picked Ohio State, where he again became an All-American. In 1985, the San Diego Chargers drafted him in the first round, tossing in a then-remarkable $550,000 signing bonus. Why the fuss?

In a nutshell, it was a new football world. Teams were passing the ball more—and paying their quarterbacks unbelievable sums to do it. To encourage the passing game the fans loved and to protect the corporate investment in quarterbacks, old rules that forced offensive linemen to keep their hands and arms at their chests and then butt, brawl, and snout their invaders were scuttled in 1978 to let them hit, hammer, pound, hook, and grab in what became a below-the-neck boxing cum wrestling match. Jimmy Lachey, like some kind of football Robocop, seemed built by nature from the very pieces of mind and body that the new order demanded.

He was tall with a massive lower body. That combination is required today to get the necessary leverage to battle tall pass rushers. He had long arms. That's required because guys with little alligator arms can no longer do the job now that the goal of all offensive linemen is to keep attackers from even getting to their bodies. Instead, offensive linemen slug defensive invaders and ride them aside with their own momentum. And finally, he was smart. That's an absolute requirement with today's complicated offenses and constantly shifting defenses, which force all the men on the offensive line to make split-second individual "reads" on the line of scrimmage before and even after the snap and then to block in concert as if they'd had time to orchestrate it over coffee beforehand.

But Lachey had another gift, what's called *athleticism*, a description for a grab bag of physical traits that can't be achieved but must be God-given: fluidity of motion, grace, dexterity, reflexively quick hands and feet, the type of liquid balance—expressed in its pristine state in the flights of Michael Jordan—that allowed him to change direction in midstep, to absorb and then recoil like a spring after being hit with a bull rush, to quickly find his equilibrium when wrenched awkwardly out of form, to keep his upper body nearly erect while squatting so low that he looked like a bushman relaxing on his heels. Lachey was never "stiff"—a flaw that disqualifies any man, no matter how big or strong, from playing the offensive line, especially left tackle.

The Redskins' offensive-line coach, Jim Hanifan, a wry, rumpled master of colorful exclamation, growls, "I look at 'em like they're damned near ballerinas." Or he thinks of the differences among Clydesdales, thoroughbreds, and quarter horses. The Clydesdale is slow, steady, and powerful; the thoroughbred is sleek and fast in long distances. But the quarter horse, the short-sprinting horse, the one a rodeo cowboy rides when he ropes a steer, is a wonder of muscular equilibrium—just watch its feet make constant skitter-step corrections as the steer fights and pulls unpredictably, watch the large and small muscles in its body seem to flex independently of one another to keep its balance. No wasted movements. Naturally, a coach would like all his offensive linemen to have these ballerina/quarter horse qualities. But the man most gifted with them will always play left tackle.

Left tackles are the Mercedes-Benzes of offensive linemen. Most football players are right-handed, and the majority of offensive plays are therefore run to the right side of the offensive line. On the right, the offense often extends from the ball-hiking center to guard to tackle to tight end to wide receiver. Men roll on to the right like the Great Wall of China. But on the left, besides the wide receiver, the tackle is often the end of the line—the last fortification on an open frontier. It's called "playing on an island." So most teams put their best pass rushers on the vulnerable flank: Taylor, Simmons, Haley, as well as the Raiders' Greg Townsend, Buffalo's Bruce Smith, Minnesota's Chris Doleman, Detroit's Pat Swilling, Chicago's Richard Dent.

Perhaps the greatest left tackle ever to play the modern game, Anthony Munoz, now retired after thirteen years with Cincinnati, calls the challenge simply "the problem of open space." Playing left tackle is like guarding a man in open court in basketball: The man with the basketball has a wide territory to exploit while the defender has a wide territory to protect, which is why athletic speed, dexterity, and balance are at a premium. But in football, the price of failure isn't a single basket but a sack to the quarterback. And because most quarterbacks—including the Redskins' Mark Rypien—are right-handed and turn to their right to throw, a sack from the left is often a blind-side, confidence-busting, body-beating shot to the back. Which makes for a long eighty minutes.

Jimmy Lachey says, "My whole being is technique."

That sounds pretty ridiculous, or at least highfalutin, if you've ever watched, say, Kansas City sackmeister Derrick Thomas flash across the line of scrimmage, smash Lachey, and then scuffle with him for all of two seconds before Rypien passes and play halts. But it begins to look different once you've watched Lachey run through the simple "sandbag drill" with his offensive-line teammates. In the drill, a fifty-pound bag is held with both hands close to the chest and pumped in and out as rapidly as possible, while the feet slide sideways in rhythmic sequence.

The offensive linemen don't look like the rest of the Redskins. They are bulkier, meatier, more endomorphic than mesomorphic. They don't have those popping veins on their arms and calves, or the beautifully buffed and edged muscles of smaller men who have iron-pumped themselves into larger men. Unlike defensive end Charles Mann, they don't look as if they've been sculpted from stone into an artist's image of God's perfect Adam. No, these guys have arms and legs like country hams. Most have weighted stomachs and football pants that droop inelegantly beneath them. Jimmy Lachey has always stood out in this gang. He is a statuesque man. His body angles from shoulder to ground in an inverted pyramid, without stopping for a spherical detour from chest to thighs. Other linemen lumber when they walk, but Lachey has always had a springy step, a little stroll in his walk. In this crowd, he has always looked like a greyhound adopted by a family of bulldogs. In the sandbag drill, other men's sideways steps often seem disjointed, one at a time. You can almost hear the dance instructor: "*Step,* one, two, three. *Step . . .*" But Lachey's feet arc-and-land, arc-and-land in a seamless gliding motion. In foot-ball parlance, he can "dance on lightbulbs." And although the other men's biceps are every bit as thick as Lachey's, the bag in their hands pistons in and out more sluggishly, while in his hands it strikes and returns like a boxer's jab. As coach Hanifan always says, "Fast hands, fast feet to survive."

But not everything is God-given. When Lachey came out of college, he ran a 4.81-second forty-yard dash, which was lightning for a huge man then. Figure he has lost a step with age, and the fastest defensive ends today are now sprinting 4.7 or 4.8—and getting bigger and bigger, an average of maybe 275 pounds these days. Yet Lachey is probably better—more "skilled"—than he's ever been.

It's common to see the great running backs—Jim Brown, O. J. Simpson, Gale Sayers, Eric Dickerson, Marcus Allen—excel in their first seasons. In six or seven years, a running back's career can be over. Yet offensive linemen, like quarterbacks, often age on the bench like a good wine before they play. The Los Angeles Rams' great tackle Jackie Slater rode the bench for three years. Offensive linemen often play more than a decade, continuing to play even after they've slowed down and lost some of their athleticism, because the offensive line is home to some of football's truest craftsmen.

To hammer home the importance of craft, coach Hanifan has taken speed-sters like Ricky Sanders or Ricky Ervins—men who run a 4.4 to 4.5—and pass-rushed them against Lachey in drills. Big Jimmy would be pedaling backward and Sanders and Ervins would be rocketing forward, but Hanifan knew even they couldn't beat Lachey going inside or outside at the quarterback if Lachey's technique was picture-perfect, which is why Lachey became so obsessed with correcting that shudder-step. Nobody plays left tackle on natural ability alone. There's too much to learn. As Munoz says, "It's bring your lunch box and go to work."

To defend against the pass rush, a tackle must keep his body, from his toes through his hips and shoulders, in a squared-up alignment, with his feet set slightly wider than his shoulders. That way the defensive charger has more body to get around, and the tackle is best situated to follow him right or left, as well as best balanced to battle him with his hands. That first left-foot kick—out and back from the line of scrimmage—is the key, because it's an unnatural step, one that can be learned only through thousands of repetitions. Try it. Bend down in a three-point position and kick your left foot out and back. It wants to land toe outward and to take your knee, hips, and shoulders with it.

On a long pass play, where the quarterback will drop back seven steps before unloading, the tackle takes three, four, maybe five steps backward, mirroring those of his rusher, before making contact. These must be slide-steps—the technique used to defend in basketball, a game Lachey has played for years as footwork therapy during the off-season. One foot must always stay on the ground and the feet must never cross. The whole time the defensive man is roaring ahead he will be studying the tackle's technique, looking for his feet and hips and shoulders to be headed in different directions so he can shoot to one side or the other, magnify his opponent's disequilibrium, and then execute his next move depending on the advantage he can create.

Jimmy Lachey has always experienced these seconds in a kind of live slow motion, similar to the way many people experience car accidents. Sometimes, it can seem that a play is going to last forever. He can even remember thinking that this or that play must have lasted at least thirty seconds, although he knows that's impossible. In this time-compressed world a lot is always going down.

In a game, when Lachey lines up against a simple defensive alignment where he knows which man will be rushing him, he will examine him for cues. In sorry rushers it can be as obvious as a man lining up with his right hand on the ground if he's going right and his left hand on the ground if he's going left. But most cues are far more subtle. Lachey will look to see if one foot is set a few inches ahead or behind its normal position, because men often cheat a bit forward with the foot opposite the one they plan to move first. If Lachey sees a man's right foot forward, he figures he's probably going to take his first step inside with his left foot. If he sees the man's left foot forward, he figures he's going straight upfield with his right foot first. Lachey will look at his man's knuckles on the ground. If they are whiter than usual, it might mean that he's putting more of his weight forward and getting ready to bull rush—power rush—straight into Lachey. He'll also check his man's eyes, which will sometimes glance unconsciously toward his destination. All of this during the moments the quarterback is bellowing signals—and perhaps calling an audible that will completely change the play.

As the ball is hiked in a game, Lachey likes to jump the count an imperceptible tenth of a second. If the rusher is fast, Lachey will step almost straight back to keep as much distance between himself and the rusher as possible, because the later they collide the less time the rusher has to recover and go for quarterback Mark Rypien. If the rusher is slower, Lachey will step back and wider, which forces the rusher farther outside, stretches him out, and expands Rypien's pocket.

Lachey knows his man must declare his attack—go inside, outside, or straight ahead—by his third step. The clock is ticking, and even on a Rypien seven-step drop pass, if a rusher doesn't make his move by the third step he has just taken himself out of the play. It'll be over before he can get to Rypien. If it's a three-step or five-step drop, Lachey's job is made easier because Rypien will throw the ball quicker, meaning Lachey doesn't have to fend off his man very long. But as the rusher is taking his first three steps, it's cat-and-mouse: He's looking for Lachey to break form and give him an open lane, while Lachey is trying to stay squared up and wait for his man to declare.

Left tackle pass protection is a game of angles—"angles to intercept." No matter where the rusher goes, the tackle must always follow the Golden Rule of pass protection: He must keep his body between the rusher and the quarterback in what's called an "inside-out" position—meaning he must cheat slightly to the inside and downfield of the straight line between rusher and quarterback, because the rusher's shortest distance to target is the inside lane. A common rusher's move is the shake 'n' bake, in which he throws a series of rapid head and body fakes during his first three steps. Lachey knows that nine out of ten times, the shake 'n' baker will go inside. All those gyrations don't leave time to go outside. The danger with the shake 'n' bake for the inexperienced left tackle isn't in being faked out but in the tackle's not adjusting the timing of his backward movement to accommodate the slower speed of the rusher's forward motion. It's akin to a baseball batter awaiting a fastball and getting crossed up with a change of pace. A fraction of a second's backward drift can put the tackle suddenly out of his inside-out alignment between the rusher and the quarterback, creating a freeway for the inside rush.

When the left tackle and his rusher collide, a whole new battle of technique and experience unfolds. On impact, the tackle always wants his shoulder pads to be below his attacker's pads. This maximizes the physics of motion and leverage in his favor, because the lower he gets, the farther he can rise up with the lifting power in his lower body. He must not lean far forward at the waist, which would put him off balance, cast his face downward, and obstruct his vision, but bend his knees unnaturally low and squat on his haunches. In foot-ball-speak, it's called "anchorability," and it's a rare tall, big man who can sink as deep as Lachey. At the same time, his upper body should look as if a rod is holding it stiff from the base of his butt through his skull. From his waist, his torso should be angled only a few degrees forward. On pass protection, his neck should be craned back a bit, stargazing, as if exaggerating the importance of always keeping his head up and his line of vision clear.

A barbaric game of patty-cake then ensues: Lachey always wants "tight hands"—shoptalk for keeping his outstretched arms and hands close together so the rusher can't get his own arms and hands inside Lachey's, spread them, and get his body into Lachey's body, where a sumo wrestling match can take place, with the defensive sumo having the right to grab and jerk Lachey mercilessly. Instead, Lachey wants to punch his defensive man with his taped and gloved fists simultaneously in a curving arm motion that sweeps up and into the man's chest. "Strike, and strike up," in football argot.

The rusher will likely try to deflect Lachey's punch by batting his hands down, so Lachey often "flashes" his arms in and out quickly, hoping the rush-er will fall for the fake, try to bat Lachey's hands, miss, and then be carried off balance by his own forward arm motion. Lachey hopes his man will anticipate a flash on the next play and hold his arms back defensively so Lachey can then crush him with a punch or even a stab—a kind of roundhouse slug of his palm to the solar plexus that can slow a man down for several plays afterward.

When he does punch, Lachey sits down on his springy haunches with both feet planted, uncoils upward slightly, and imagines he's not striking the out-side of a man's chest but is instead reaching *through* his rib cage to grab and rip the man's spine. At times, Lachey can actually hear a man's forced wheeze of exhaled breath. In pro football there is a punch—and then there is a *punch!* Lachey has spent hours studying tapes of Rams tackle Jackie Slater, who has a punch so powerful it can temporarily immobilize a man. That kind of punch isn't God-given either, but rather learned in the way that a boxer learns to start a six-inch jab in his toes, channel it through his entire body, and strike with a force far beyond what he could seem to unleash. Lachey's punch—and per-haps a second punch too—is meant to freeze the rusher's motion for a fraction of an instant, destroy his timing, stand him up, buy that fraction of an instant for Rypien, and force the rusher to figuratively pause and regroup, take a breath, analyze what to do next.

The rusher's arsenal includes a straight bull rush that few men undertake against Lachey because of his strength, balance, and anchorability. He's far more likely to see and feel the inside club—a rusher's crushing left-hand blow to Lachey's right shoulder or, worse by far, to his ribs. It's meant to stun him, drive him to his left, to the outside of the passing pocket, so the rusher can then slip his right arm and shoulder outside Lachey's right arm and shoulder and leverage himself past Lachey to the inside lane. Or the rusher might unleash a dip 'n' rip to the outside, a move in which after contact he dips his left arm under Lachey's left armpit and tries to tear Lachey's arm up and out of its socket and then leverage himself around Lachey's body. Or he might go with a swim move—try to swim one of his arms over Lachey's head and opposite shoulder, hold down Lachey's arm, and leverage him aside. Or, in a speedster finesse move, he might suddenly stand up after contact and spin—whirlybird—backward left or right in an attempt to roll around Lachey as if he were dancing around a lamppost.

In these *mano-a-mano* matchups, each man is trying to find an inch's worth of advantage. "The longest inch," Lachey calls it. The great defensive pass rushers—Buffalo's Bruce Smith and the Redskins' Charles Mann, for instance—have an uncanny ability to see or sense when their opponent is off balance and instantaneously take advantage. Technique aside, that's when a tackle's athleticism, his speed and fluidity of motion, is all that stands between mauler and maulee. When Lachey was once knocked off balance by Smith, who then swam with his right arm over Lachey's right shoulder, it was only Lachey's piston-fast right hand getting to and pushing Smith's left hip to the outside at the last instant, adding enough force to Smith's outside momentum, that kept him from swimming past. Not pretty, but it worked. Indeed, no rusher has had much luck against Lachey so far. In his last sixty games, he gave up two sacks.

Truth is, pass protection—an offensive left tackle's raison d'être—has gotten easier and easier for Lachey, as his technique has matured and he has amassed a book on the league's rushers. He's also learned a few tricks—learned to alert the referees when a defensive rusher has illegally coated his jersey with silicone to make it as slippery as ice, learned to soak his own jersey with water to make it tighter and harder to grab. That's why, until a left tackle's knees or reflexes go far south, he can often outplay a younger, fitter man.

With age comes what coaches call football wisdom. Lachey, for instance, was once studying a tape of a superior defensive end whose name must remain a trade secret. He noticed that once, after the man lined up more squared up than usual at the line of scrimmage, he power rushed and then went with an inside spin. Lachey scoured films of the man for other times he went with the inside spin and discovered the same foot alignment again and again. So there Lachey was, down in his three-pointer in a game, when he saw the man square up. "Hey," he thought to himself, "this is why you study all this film." Lachey kicked back from his stance, careful to stay inside-out since he figured the man was going to spin inside. He kept his right arm cocked in a "strong arm" posture—and when the man tried the spin, Lachey used the man's forward momentum to ride him to the outside of the passing pocket and out of the play.

"That's when all the studying paid off."

Young offensive linemen must also learn self-control. They must play with what's described as "controlled aggression." They are like quarterbacks, who can never afford the luxury of losing their cool, complaining about a bad call, or getting angry at a botched play or a cheap hit. Quarterbacks have got to *think*, clearly and quickly, about the next play. That's also true for all the men of the offensive line, who function not as individuals but as an entity. They're not lone wolves, but animals who run only in a pack.

The Redskins' famous misdirection counter-trey running play is a good example of their symbiosis. When running the play to the right, the center, right guard, and right tackle block forward and to the left at the snap. Meanwhile, the left guard and tackle pull to their right and run along behind the line of scrimmage, sweeping in front of their backfield as it runs to the right. Lachey will often run with his hand on the lower back of the guard in front of him so that he can not only *see* which defender his guard blocks but *feel* the direction in which his guard is going to block an instant before he does, giving Lachey a split-second longer to concentrate on the next man in the way.

If one offensive lineman is angry at, say, a linebacker for a cheap shot on the play before and seeks revenge by going after him instead of his assigned block, the whole play will unravel. When it comes to zone blocking schemes, in which several offensive linemen will decide at the line of scrimmage which of several defenders they are to block depending upon how the defense has lined up, thinking and acting as one are equally crucial. Whether it's the demands of teamwork or because men who have often played on the unglamorous offensive line since high school don't get an inflated image of themselves, few show-offs or hotheads populate any offensive line.

Jimmy Lachey fits the profile. In his entire pro career, he has had only four or five penalties called against him, none for more than ten yards. He does exact revenge, but he'll patiently wait many plays, as he once did against the New England Patriots' Andre Tippett, chopping him from behind long after Tippett had speared his helmet into Lachey's ribs on an earlier play.

The challenge for every offensive lineman is to find a frame of mind that maximizes the edge emotional aggressiveness gives a man without ever letting that emotion get out of control, without ever losing his poise. Lachey, for instance, has had a reputation for more "trash talking" on the field than most offensive linemen. He'll tell a man he has just crushed, "You're gonna have to tighten your chin strap," or he'll tell him much worse. But Lachey doesn't talk trash in *reaction* to what other men say. He's really not even talking to *them* but to himself, psyching himself up. The idea is to play exactly at the outer edge of "controlled aggression" without ever crossing over.

His is an obsessive perfectionism—no rusher should sack or even pressure the quarterback, no "read" of a defensive scheme should be wrong, no block should be missed. Under the doctrine of zero tolerance for error, if Lachey got it right on fifty-nine plays and wrong on play sixty, he would think he'd played a bad game. That's true for the whole offensive line, where consistency is the creed. It's no good performing perfectly for half a game if the quarterback is then sacked and the ball lost. The motto: "Every play, every game."

Against the Cowboys in Dallas last year, Lachey couldn't hear the snap count amid the roar of the crowd and got off the ball a full second late. But when Charles Haley beat him and sacked Rypien, there could be no excuse. Lachey didn't even allow himself the luxury of feeling guilty. Noise or not, a man gets his job done. It isn't success but failure that Lachey tries to remember. He believes no man should take much joy in his accomplishments until he has retired. It might sap the hunger. Even in his dreams, Lachey is his own taskmaster. He doesn't dream of making great plays. No, he dreams of missing the bus, losing his pads, being late, of failure. No fan or coach or commentator could be harder on Jimmy Lachey than Jimmy Lachey.

Nobody watches more videotape than Lachey. He studies tapes of other great left tackles—Detroit's Lomas Brown, Atlanta's Mike Kenn, and, of course, Anthony Munoz. He studies so much film of Charles Haley that the man is like a science project for him. He takes tapes home and studies them in his rec room. Tapes of his opponents as well as of himself. He wants to study not only what he has done *wrong* in the past, but also what he has done *right*. In his mind he even wants to *feel* his muscles move on each imagined play. Watching hour after hour of tape has a kind of hypnotic effect that deepens Lachey's concentration before a game.

As a game approaches, he is off in a private zone, constantly visualizing his opponents' best moves and visualizing his responses. Like a lawyer who tries to anticipate every courtroom question, Lachey wants no surprises. In every aspect of his game, he wants to assertively control whatever he has the power to control: studying films, concentrating, working hard in the weight room and conditioning himself, staying off steak and eggs and junk. So much on the field cannot be controlled, Lachey seeks every tenth-percentage point of control off the field. Other guys can goof around, be loosey-goosey before a game. Not Lachey. He can't joke, can't laugh. He thinks like a soldier on the eve.

On game day, everything must be arranged in Lachey's locker just so. The Redskins' equipment manager, Jay Brunetti, must have Lachey's shoulder pads covered with his No. 79 jersey and hanging like a ghostly torso in his locker. He knows to give Lachey a new jock, socks, and T-shirt every week, although Lachey will reuse his gloves. Lachey tapes his own fingers, thumbs, and wrists, because he fears that if somebody else did it for him, a day might come when that person would be too busy or absent. Then someone else would have to tape his hands, thus defiling his concentration ritual.

When he dresses, Lachey puts everything on left to right: left knee brace, then right knee brace; left foot in his pants, then right foot in his pants; left sock, then right sock; left shoe, then right shoe. He then takes three aspirin to ward off the inevitable headache he'll get from butting heads. Finally, he goes again to Brunetti, who pulls Lachey's pads and jersey on over his head, shakes his hand, and says, "Good luck." Lachey never growls or bellows or pounds his fist. His is an offensive lineman's silent rage.

*   *   *

For all the technique, all the study, all the ritual, why one man can make it all come together on the field while another with equal gifts cannot is still unknowable. That, finally, is the reason Jimmy Lachey is so valuable. There are men who are drill dolls—guys who are often called upon by coaches to demonstrate technique and footwork in practice. But for whatever reasons, they can't make it happen when the troops are firing live ammo. In drills, a man knows what's coming. When drilling on pass protection, the rusher crashes into the offensive linemen as if he's certain it's a pass. The rusher needn't stay alert for the dozens of plays, variations on plays, and broken plays that might flash in a live show. And in drills the offensive linemen needn't stay alert for stunts, twists, and tricks—the endless, multiple-man, crisscrossing defensive rushing patterns meant to confuse the offensive linemen and make them miss an assigned block. No, the real thing can only happen on the field.

Imagine that the Redskins are planning a gut right running play over right tackle. Lachey lines up and reads a basic four-three defense, which means four defensive men are down on the line with three linebackers behind them. Lachey's defensive end has lined up wide, a body-and-a-half outside Lachey. Because the play is running to the right, Lachey plans to mostly ignore him and help his guard block the defensive tackle or block the outside linebacker in front of him. But during the count the linebacker moves way to the outside. Whatever the linebacker is planning is now moot, because the play's going away from him, which means Lachey now plans to block the defensive end and leave the defensive tackle to be blocked by the offensive guard.

But then, Rypien calls an audible and the gut is now coming directly over Lachey. Lachey and his tight end, lined up outside him on this play, now plan to block the defensive end together, and then Lachey plans to block the linebacker behind him. But then the linebacker moves to the inside, putting him right in the projected path of the ballcarrier. Instantly, Lachey knows he now can't give much help to his tight end, who is mismatched against a much larger defensive end. Lachey must first worry about the newly placed linebacker. But then the linebacker loosens up—moves to the far outside, taking himself nearly out of the play. Then the defensive end moves slightly to the inside. Lachey can now take over the defensive end from his mismatched tight end while the tight end blocks the linebacker lined up way outside.

Or imagine that the Redskins are running a draw play, a fake pass that becomes a run over Lachey, who with his guard and tight end must block the defensive tackle, defensive end, and a linebacker. The defensive men are lined up straight, meaning directly over the offensive men instead of being shaded into the gaps between them. Even though the rushers don't move during the count and complicate things more, the offensive linemen's blocking assignments are still not set in stone.

If the defensive men rush straight ahead, Lachey and company all block their own obvious men. But if the defensive tackle makes a hard move outside, Lachey takes him and the guard goes up and takes the linebacker while the tight end takes the defensive end. But if the linebacker pinches—slants hard to the inside—then Lachey takes him and the tight end takes the defensive end while the guard takes the defensive tackle. But if the linebacker goes outside and the defensive tackle over the guard plays it straight, then Lachey takes the defensive end. It's just that simple—and all in a few blinks of the eye.

It will never be a science . . .

No matter how many six-foot-six, 290-pound, smart, nifty-footed, fast-handed, hardworking, obsessive, live-ammo left tackles come out of the Ohio heartland, it will never be a science. Some men just love it more. They feel it more. For reasons unknowable, they enter an intuitive realm where thinking and doing are seamless, no longer opposites on a continuum but a closed circle. That is what Lachey will miss the most when he retires—the feeling, the literal high he gets playing the game. "Not being on the field is the worst," he says. Because on the field is the only place where the magic can happen.

Sometimes, when Jimmy Lachey is sprawled out beneath a crush of bodies, he will suddenly get a whiff of grass in his nostrils. For him, not only time but also sensation is compressed on the football field. On artificial turf, he believes, he can feel his cleats stick-and-go, stick-and-go with each step, that he can even hear them *suck* as he strides.

When Lachey and the Redskins are rolling, when they're ahead and churning and burning and Lachey is dominating his man, when a Clyde Simmons or a Bruce Smith takes a lick or two at the *right* side of the offensive line to avoid Lachey, when he's so tired he's playing on reflex and instinct, so tired he sometimes thinks he might see Jesus in the clouds, when the hits are juicy, like when he knocked out the Raiders' Jerry Robinson, hit him so hard that he had the odd feeling that he'd missed him, hit only air, that his shoulder hadn't even touched Robinson but had instead passed through him as if he were a ray of light. When Jimmy Lachey is playing in this sweet spot, it is delicious.

Sometimes, when the Redskins are way out front, he'll take a moment and look up and around him at the tens of thousands of people who have come to see him play, and he will feel not pride but humility, awe. The hours and the years of ambition and work and achievement seem to mingle with the smell of his pads and his sweat. In the crowded huddle, he breathes in that concoction like perfume. And sometimes, when he's battling a man at the line, he gets a blast that is so sour it's downright sweet, an instant so pure that thinking and sensing and doing have somehow become one.

That's not athleticism. Or technique. Or wisdom.

That's the magic.

September 5, 1993

Up and at 'Em

Mark Odum awakens at five minutes to five, lying on his right side on the left side of his bed. Backed up behind him is a motorized scooter, its swivel seat facing the bed. At five, the radio starts. Time to get up. With his left arm, Mark reaches down and flips the comforter and sheet off his body. He wears a nightshirt and his legs poke from it, bent forty-five degrees at the knees, his right ankle hooked around his left ankle and positioned to hitch a ride on his stronger left side.

Mark used to sleep naked, but his neck and shoulders often caught a chill and got stiff and sore during the night. So he switched to pajamas. But the pajamas would bind up and they were hard to loosen, especially on his right side, where he has been nearly paralyzed since the pool accident in 1974. The pajamas would bunch up and irritate his skin, which is the last thing a quadri-paretic person—a person with partial paralysis in all four limbs—wants, because it can lead to painful skin ulcers.

At age forty, Mark Odum lives by himself, independent of helpers. He has a steady girlfriend. He goes camping. Every day he drives his van around the Beltway from his home to his job. He's director of the National Rehabilitation Information Center. A regular guy. But each morning, Mark's life is a regimen of foresight, precision, and consciousness of matters that ABs—able-bodies—take for granted. For ABs, his routine would be like remembering to breathe.

Still lying on his right side, Mark places his left hand, the fingers of which can extend fully, flat on the bed in front of his body. He pushes and lifts him-self up. Mark's great fortune is that although his right side is largely crippled, the muscles in his right shoulder are strong. As he lifts his body, he plants his right elbow like a stake to prop himself up.

He now connects about a dozen discrete movements into one sweeping motion: He extends his left arm and reaches behind himself, pushes down on

226

his right elbow with his right shoulder to lift his body, throws his weight backward, pivots at his waist and hips, and slides his good left leg toward the edge of the bed, dragging his right leg with it. As he continues his roll, he hooks his right hand, the fingers of which have become locked into a claw, in the crook of his right knee, plants his left elbow on the bed, and pushes off; simultaneously, he grabs and pulls on the scooter with his left hand. His momentum carries his legs over the edge of the bed as what's left of his stomach and chest muscles pull up his torso and leave him sitting at bedside next to his scooter.

For ten minutes he catches his breath and stretches the muscles in his shoulders and neck, which are always stiff when he wakes up. Mark is now ready for his hardest maneuver of the morning—going from bed to scooter. It's tough because he must move to his left to get onto the scooter, meaning he must push off the bed with his weak right side and his nearly powerless right leg. He slides his butt as close to the seat of his scooter as he can without falling off the bed. He puts his left hand on the left armrest, which positions the scooter seat almost behind him. Using the muscles in his right shoulder again, he lifts himself on his right arm and pushes left toward the seat, pulls with his extended left arm, pushes on the floor with his left leg, and rotates and slides his butt to get a beachhead on the scooter's seat.

He scoots into position, unlocks the seat, and swivels it forward. He can lift his left leg the few inches onto the scooter's footrest, but his right leg is too weak to lift and his right arm is too weak to lift it. So Mark reaches down with his left arm, reaches beneath his left leg, and grabs his right ankle. He simultaneously pulls up and leans back, yanking his right leg onto the footrest. He turns his scooter around and backs into the tiny bathroom and up to the shower stall. He locks its wheels in place and crabs his feet around until he swivels the seat 180 degrees and faces the open stall. A three-inch-high metal frame on which the shower's glass doors slide is now between Mark and his shower chair.

He lifts his left foot just inside the shower. Ever mindful of skin lesions, he leans backward and allows the tendons in his legs to flex and lift and extend his helpless right foot as it slides slowly over the metal frame. He cannot feel minor external pain below his right knee, but Mark can tell from the gentleness of the scratching sound that he has done no damage.

He locks his scooter and seat in place and pulls the shower chair closer. He hooks his left foot behind his right ankle and extends his left leg in front of the shower chair, taking his right leg along. In a repeat of the bed-to-scooter maneuver, he lifts and rotates his body onto the shower chair, removes his nightshirt, and tosses it onto his scooter seat. He showers for twenty minutes to an hour and forty-five minutes, depending on how stiff he is. He can lift his hands high enough to wash his hair, although with his right hand he more scratches than massages his scalp. He can wash his back with a scrubber. The most difficult task is washing his toes and soles, and his left foot is particularly difficult: He must reach straight down with his good left hand, and his chest bumps into his knees.

To get out of the shower, Mark repeats his entry in reverse, except that the floor is now slick. He has twice landed on the floor at this juncture, sprawling naked with his legs still in the shower, his body wedged among the wall and the toilet and the scooter that has slid out from under him. This morning, after drying off and transferring to his scooter, he drives back into his bedroom and parks at a forty-five-degree angle to a chest-high set of drawers.

He has put out his clothes the night before. He slips on a T-shirt, which is easy. With his left hand he lifts his right ankle onto his left knee and slips his briefs over his right foot. With the same hand, he puts his right leg down, takes hold of the waistband of his briefs, works his left foot through, and pulls them up over his knees. The laundry returns Mark's shirts buttoned, except for his right cuff (his clawed right hand won't fit through). He pulls his shirt on over his head like a T-shirt and, with his left hand and teeth, buttons his right cuff.

Socks are next. Once again, he uses his left arm to pull his right leg onto his left knee. Then he plants his right forefinger into the mouth of his sock and with his left hand stretches it open and over his right toes. He pulls it up and over his calf with his left hand. To do this, he licks his fingers to create friction and smooths out any wrinkles, again to avoid damaging his skin. That is the easy sock. Because he can lift his left leg only a few inches straight up from the floor and his right hand is too weak to lift it onto his right knee, Mark takes his leather belt and drapes it like a lasso around his shin. Now, holding both ends of the belt in his left hand, he pulls up, leans way back, and hoists his left ankle onto his right knee.

He now uses his right hand to loop the mouth of his sock over his left toes, licking his hand repeatedly so he can maul the sock onto his foot. He hooks his left thumb into the sock's mouth, pulls it over his heel, and, with more licking of fingers, smooths the sock up over his calf.

To put on his pants, Mark again uses his left hand to lift his right ankle onto his left knee. With the same hand he snakes his pant leg over his right foot and works the cuff over his ankle. He lowers his right foot back on the floor, spreads his pants out in front of him, threads his belt through all but the last loop, and spears his left foot into the pant leg. He pulls the waistband up over his knees and bends so he can work the cuff past his left foot with his left hand. He then pulls his briefs and his pants up as high as they can go while he is sitting down.

The top drawer of his dresser is open six inches. In another sweeping motion, Mark pushes up on his armrests with the strength of both shoulders, lifting his body until the muscles in his left leg can take over. As he does this, he swings his right hand up and into the open drawer, hooks his wrist inside the top, and pulls until he is standing, his weight resting on his left leg, his knees held apart so his pants won't fall.

Balancing himself without his hands, he reaches down and pulls up his underwear with his left hand. He now pulls up his pants on the left side. With his right hand, he claws to catch the belt loop he has left unthreaded and, after several tries, gets it. He holds up his pants with his right hand while he tucks in most of his shirttail with his left. To tuck in the remainder, he swings his right arm behind him, between his shirttail and his pants, and lets gravity do the work.

Mark has one last touch: cowboy boots. They are difficult to get on, but Mark sees the boots as a statement about his freedom and his determination. His left boot goes on first because its inch-and-a-half heel gives him a little boost when it's time to lift his right foot off the floor. With many minutes of tugging, wrestling, thrashing, and stomping, his boots are on. After taking several more minutes to work his pant legs down over his boot tops, Mark leans back and lifts his left foot onto the footrest of his scooter. He reaches down with his left arm, reaches under his left leg, and grabs his right ankle. He pulls up and leans back, yanking his leg up and onto the footrest.

Breakfast is next.

November 6, 1994

The Client and the Caseworker

Shirley is the client.

Jackie is the caseworker.

They were united a year ago, on Tuesday afternoon, March 6, after the life of Shirley Rogers was routed Jackie Jordan's way via the usual, groaning channels of the poverty system. Shirley, fifty-five, was about to be evicted from her rented house in suburban Maryland's Prince George's County. Jackie, forty, was, and still is, what they call an intensive family services specialist. There aren't many like Jackie in the welfare system in America today. Most social workers are buried under scores of clients they see only in the office, nine to five. They don't have time to know their clients as people. Likewise, their clients don't have time to know them—or, more important, to trust them.

So Jackie is a rare breed. At any given moment, she'll have only half a dozen clients she might see two, three, four times a week, night or day. She'll go to their homes or their jobs, talk to their children, their spouses. She'll dog her clients, lobby for them with other social service agencies. For as long as six months, she'll try to win their trust, sort out the grab bag of woes in their lives, devise a strategy of attack, and then—charm, threaten, embarrass, or frighten them into *deciding* to change their lives.

In her first year on the job, Jackie Jordan has learned one lesson to share with those who insist that society uplift the poor and those who insist that society blame the poor: Changing the life of one lost and struggling person is quite possible and nearly impossible. At the same time. This is not a contradiction.

Shirley Rogers is proof of that.

Is she typical?

In this way: On Tuesday afternoon, March 6, last year, the life of Shirley Rogers was a mess. A year later, it's still a mess. But for different reasons. Progress, slight and slippery.

230

*   *   *

March 9, 1990. Shirley is too busy to see Jackie, at least that's what she has told her. Truth is, Shirley is sick of Meddling Millies like Jackie Jordan, the prissy pets from this or that welfare agency, with their prying questions, budgets, conditions, empty promises, and hints that they don't believe half of what Shirley tells them. Where's the beef? Where's the payoff for Shirley? No, Jackie, sorry, just can't make it, won't be home, gotta work today. Shirley—a short, large, somber-faced woman who, except at funerals and weddings, wears no-brand sweat suits every day, summer or winter—suddenly hits on the answer to her troubles: She'll be a bag lady. *Yes!* It's an answer from heaven, must be. She'll take Nick, her big, black, loping wolf dog, and join the Bag Brigade. No one will find her—not any of her seven grown kids, any of her fourteen grandkids. *And no more Meddling Millies!*

But Jackie is persistent. She'll be glad to come to Shirley's job and talk with her there, she says sweetly. Don't know, Shirley says, she's very busy cleaning, cooking, organizing for the disabled men who live in the Lt. Joseph P. Kennedy Institute's group home where she's the housekeeper. And it's way over past Rock Creek Park. No problem, says Jackie, in her warm and radiant manner, she'll find it.

Shirley is Jackie's first big case. She's been in her job only a few months. You might say she's a late bloomer, Jackie. After college twenty years ago, she tried to get a social worker's job but couldn't. Needed a master's degree. So she worked as a legal secretary, did some modeling. The secret be told, she'd still love to be an actress. She was an extra in *Broadcast News,* and she covets a part in a Spike Lee movie. But life has its own way of flowing, and over the years, Jackie married, divorced, remarried, and had a daughter, who is eleven. Through it all, Jackie clung to her early ambition, and after years of graduate school on the side, she finally earned her master's in counseling psychology and took a job at the Prince George's County Commission for Families. The commission isn't your average social service bureaucracy. Its job is to intervene aggressively to keep poor families together by attacking the social and psychological maladies that keep people down—but absent do-gooder naïveté. Because changing lives isn't easy.

Cold is really too nice a word for the way Shirley treats Jackie when she arrives at the little brick house in Northwest Washington where Shirley works. In her sweats, Shirley busies herself cleaning the bathrooms, getting dinner together, listening to classical music on the radio. *Rude* might be a better word for the way Shirley treats Jackie, who acts as if she doesn't notice. By now, Shirley has jumped through a series of social service agency hoops hoping to get help. But nobody has *done* anything, just talked—and made her feel like two cents worth of nothing.

Shirley's fall has been so swift that she almost can't believe it. For eleven years she'd been off welfare, working at the Kennedy Institute, earning about

$350 a week and loving every minute of it. Before taking the housekeeping job five years ago, she'd been an aide at the institute's main campus for disabled children in Washington. But Shirley was never *just* an aide, not Shirley. She taught ceramics classes at night, coached the floor hockey team to a city championship and on to a tournament game against the institute's arch rival, the Canadians. She set up a canteen at the institute's night school and used the profits to buy musical instruments from a local pawnshop—congas, bongos, guitars, a synthesizer, an organ, and a French horn. The Kennedy Kids orchestra had 'em dancing in the aisles. She wrote her own adaptation of *Swan Lake* for the children to perform. And always she was drawing and painting, creating scenery for the plays and holiday scenes around the building in what she called her "primitive style."

A year before Jackie's visit, Shirley might have pinched herself to be sure that her life wasn't a dream. For four years, she'd lived in a big rented house with her working son, who has sickle-cell anemia, his wife, and their three children; her working daughter, her daughter's four children and her long-time male companion, who also worked; and another grown daughter, Jonnie, paralyzed on one side and suffering from lupus and sickle-cell. It was a lot of personalities to balance, all right, but with several people working at low-paying jobs and the Social Security disability income that came to Jonnie, there was money for the $685-a-month rent, all the necessities, and a few frills. Just two Christmases before, Shirley had marveled at the monster pile of gifts beneath the tree. Why, even wolf dog Nick had his own Christmas tree with gifts under it. Life was going so well that Shirley took a vacation to Montreal, which she loved.

Then, crash . . . Shirley's working son and his family moved out to a place of their own. Another son got hurt, lost his job, and moved into the house without any income. Then Shirley's working daughter and her companion moved out, leaving a teenage daughter with Shirley. All Shirley had left were her wages and Jonnie's disability income. To buy food and other necessities for herself, Jonnie, her unemployed son, and her granddaughter, Shirley used her credit cards—and quickly ran up $3,500 in debts she couldn't repay. One night, she came home and was shocked to find police with guns drawn. They'd raided her house on a tip about alleged drug sales. No drugs were found and nobody was arrested, but Shirley felt as though her comfortable world was unraveling. To top it all off, three of her grandkids had landed in foster care, and Shirley was struggling with officials to win the right to care for them herself.

All in a year!

On the first day Jackie visits Shirley at work, Jackie is impressed. Although Shirley is, well, abrupt, she's smart and articulate, never finished high school but could pass for a woman with a college degree. She's also very proud, aloof, with a kind of defiant nobility. The toughness is a good sign. Jackie has learned that the best candidates for climbing up and out are people who take responsibility upon themselves rather than blame society, racism, or bad breaks for their predicament—even if society, racism, and bad breaks *are* to blame. The illusion of power can create the reality of power. Another good sign is that the home where Shirley works as the housekeeper is spotlessly clean and, as ever, decorated with Shirley's artwork—elaborate crazy-colored butterflies and sunbursts, or flat, perspectiveless paintings of Indian braves capturing wild stallions, also in psychedelic colors, or Christmas murals of camel-riding wise men dressed in Day-Glo orange, yellow, and blue robes and astride purple saddles.

"If you want to do something," Shirley finally tells Jackie, "then bring groceries." Shirley is down to cereal, milk, potatoes (potato pancakes, potato meat loaf, potato soup), and mulligan stew, a simmered mix of anything left on the shelves—say, Spam, rice, spaghetti, peas, carrots, macaroni, and ketchup. When Jackie leaves, Shirley figures it's the last she'll see of that debutante, with her beauty-shop hair, dangling earrings, and fancy clothes. But that evening, Jackie arrives with bags of groceries. Shirley is shocked: Somebody has finally delivered.

Jackie Jordan simply will not go away. She knew that the groceries would turn Shirley's head; she had planned on it. She knows that the more little things she can do to help, the more Shirley will trust her on the big things. Jackie visits Shirley at least twice a week, calls her on the phone even more often. She knows that she must position herself between Shirley and the social service workers and agencies that Shirley sees as the enemy—as cold, uncaring bureaucrats. There's more truth in Shirley's characterization of Jackie's colleagues than Jackie likes to admit. But even after only a few months on the job she understands what happens: Nearly every day, a client disappoints you—lies to you, promises to do something and doesn't. They oversleep for a sick child's doctor appointment that you've fought to set up. *They oversleep!* This is a very hard thing to take if you're a person who'd break down the door to get your own sick child to a doctor.

Cynicism sweeps over you as the only defense. And just as Shirley can no longer allow herself to get her hopes up over the promises of social workers, too many of whom have disappointed, social workers can no longer allow themselves to get their hopes up over the promises of clients. You just stop believing in the possibility of redemption. But Jackie's job is different, a luxury. As an antidote to the cynicism, she can actually see people's lives get better. She's actually *paid* to do what all social workers *ought* to be able to do: take the time to make a difference.

It will be weeks before Shirley smiles at Jackie, but when she finally does, Jackie will feel that they have now been joined. Jackie visits Shirley's landlady, who turns out to be no cartoon slumlord but a decent woman who has no desire to throw Shirley out, although she needs the rent money. She made an eviction request only because Shirley had to be threatened with eviction in order to qualify for emergency rental aid. She'd tried to help make Shirley's situation look even more desperate by adding the present month's rent to Shirley's past-due bill, but that only put the debt so high that Shirley couldn't qualify for rental help. Jackie gets it straightened out, gets the rent money. But it's finger-in-the-dike stuff. Shirley's finances are hemorrhaging.

March 23, 1990. First off, Shirley needs an affordable place to live. Commercial apartment buildings are out because her credit's shot. From Prince George's to Shirley's job in Northwest Washington is a two-and-a-half-hour one-way commute by bus, and finding a home closer to work would be smart. But Shirley has Jonnie in the Prince George's public medical system, and she's afraid to change to the District's. Jonnie is constantly in and out of the hospital, and Shirley figures there'd be some kind of screwup in the transfer and Jonnie'd end up without care in an emergency. She'd rather commute. So Jackie gets Shirley on the waiting list for several public housing projects in Prince George's, and goes with her to the Glenarden Apartments, a recently renovated project near Landover Mall, to fill out the applications. No regular apartments are available for months, but Glenarden has empty units for handicapped people, and Jonnie makes Shirley eligible. In only a few weeks, Glenarden officials have scheduled an inspection of Shirley's home to make sure she's a good housekeeper and a desirable tenant. Jackie isn't worried. Shirley is an immaculate housekeeper and an impressive woman.

Shirley doesn't know it yet, but Jackie has an ulterior motive for trying to get her into Glenarden. It's now that Jackie must play the uncomfortable role of God: She has decided that it's time for Shirley's children, who range from twenty-six to thirty-five years old, to stop returning to Mama when things get tough. Jackie feels the same way about another person in Shirley's life, someone with a drug problem who is very close to Shirley and whom Shirley often helps out with a place to stay. Glenarden will not allow any of Shirley's adult relatives or friends or grown children except Jonnie to share Shirley's new apartment. So if Jackie can get Shirley into Glenarden, she won't have to persuade Shirley to stop housing her children, because the problem will take care of itself. Back at the office, the staff psychologist has wondered aloud if Jackie isn't trying to break up Shirley's family when her job is to keep families together. But Jackie is adamant, not from some psychotheoretical reason, but from her gut.

In her many visits, Jackie has come to know the story of Shirley's early life, which on its face is a lot like Jackie's. Each girl lived with both parents at home—Jackie in the public housing projects of the South Bronx, Shirley in a rented house in Southwest Washington. Neither family was poor. Their fathers had good working-class jobs—Jackie's as a mailman and Shirley's as a construction worker. They lived in the same home and neighborhood all their childhood years, and both were bright, creative girls. But here the similarity ends, and the deeply personal reasons Jackie is today a successful professional and Shirley is nearly destitute start to emerge, reminding Jackie that giving money to poor people and getting them decent medical care and an affordable place to live isn't always enough.

Shirley's mother, who is dead, treated Shirley the way the wicked step-mother treated Cinderella—at least in Shirley's mind. She told her she was ugly and that she had a smile like the Joker from the *Batman* comic strip. She told her that her father had a girlfriend and that he was going to take Shirley's three younger sisters to live with his girlfriend, leaving Shirley behind with only her mother. Shirley loved to read at night, but her mother complained that she was wasting coal oil. Shirley'd sneak outside and read under the street lamp. Shirley loved classical music. Her mother listened to only gospel. Shirley was a tomboy and the only girl in the neighborhood's Dirty 32 Gang. Her mother dressed her in pinafores and had her hair curled like Shirley Temple's.

As a girl, Shirley fantasized that she'd been mistakenly given to her family at the hospital. From the movies, she picked the actress Beulah Bondi, who played Jimmy Stewart's mother in *It's a Wonderful Life,* as her grandmother, and she picked the actress and singer Ethel Waters as her mother. With John Wayne, they all lived on a homestead where everybody was always hugging Shirley and where fantasy mother Ethel Waters was always cooking something good in the kitchen.

Unlike Jackie, whose strong, loving mother inspired her, demanded excellence, demanded she go to college, Shirley had a mother who assaulted her little girl's psyche. Jackie, who went through some pretty rough times after college with her divorce, always believed she could conquer the world. Shirley always believed the world would conquer her. At age nine, Shirley became epileptic, a condition she later outgrew. But back then, neighborhood parents, fearful that the condition was contagious or that it was a mark of the devil, wouldn't let their children play with Shirley anymore. To this day, Shirley can still see the look of revulsion on her mother's face just before Shirley would lose consciousness during a seizure. It was as if her mother wanted the ground to open, swallow up her daughter, and make her disappear.

From Shirley's childhood, from her youthful history of allowing men to deceive her, leave her, return to her, and then do it all again, from her willingness to support her grown children, Jackie concludes—to use social worker buzz talk—that Shirley is locked in "co-dependency behavior": By allowing people she loves to take advantage of her, Shirley affirms their need for her, but at the same time allows and even encourages their selfish behavior. Jackie has decided these things, but she keeps them to herself while she waits for Shirley's move to Glenarden to be approved.

Then the other shoe drops: Glenarden rejects Shirley, claiming she has an "unpleasant attitude" and that her house is unkempt. Jackie, baffled, swings into action. Somebody—Shirley suspects one of her children who doesn't want to be left behind if Mama moves—had sabotaged Shirley's house, turned it upside down, just before the inspectors arrived. And Shirley—proud, well-spoken, and disdainful of social workers—also hadn't acted sufficiently grateful for the chance to move into Glenarden, at least that's what Jackie concludes. Shirley hadn't kowtowed or acted compliant at all. Instead, she had sat through her interview with a haughty, stone-faced expression. Shirley doesn't grovel for anybody, especially the Meddling Millies. Weeks go by and no public housing slot opens anywhere else, so Jackie goes back to Glenarden, hat in hand. She asks Shirley to cool out. She asks Glenarden officials to consider Shirley's fierce pride an asset, not a liability. She persuades them to inspect the group home where Shirley is the housekeeper, since it must pass strict cleanliness inspections. Jackie goes out on a limb: She vouches for Shirley personally. This time, Shirley is approved. If she wishes, she can move to Glenarden in August.

May 9, 1990. Two months after they meet, Jackie Jordan begins formal counseling sessions with Shirley. At first, Shirley doesn't want to hear about—what does Jackie call it?—"co-dependency." My God, somebody in your family's in trouble, what do you tell them, sleep on the street? Life's tough out there, honey! A family has to hang together, just like in the old John Wayne movies. Hang together or hang separately. Together, a family can make it. Alone, each person will crash and burn. That is Shirley's credo.

But Shirley, who is a thinker, mulls Jackie's comments over and over in her mind. She has come to trust Jackie, who is probably the best friend Shirley has had in years. She just isn't like all the others. She seems to actually *respect* Shirley. She's not condescending. And she has kept every promise. Jackie has given Shirley the gift of optimism. Folks outside "the system" just wouldn't believe what it's usually like.

Once Shirley had to send in a grandchild's birth certificate to a social service agency. She did, but heard nothing for weeks. When she called about it, she was told that the woman she mailed it to had a new job and that Shirley would have to send it to somebody else. Another time, when Shirley called an agency to set up an appointment, a recorded message told her that calls were only accepted after 2:30. But after 2:30 the lines were always busy. So Shirley took a day off work and went in. She was told that because she hadn't called ahead for an appointment nobody could see her. Jackie, ever since that day she dropped off those bags of groceries, has been different. So Shirley listens.

And, well, when Shirley thinks about it, she *has* let people walk on her, especially men—at least she did twenty, thirty years ago, before she gave up on men entirely. It's painful to admit. All her girlhood and even much of her young womanhood she spent trying, forever trying, to please her mother. What a waste! She never did. As her kids were growing up, Shirley was constantly racked with guilt about how she couldn't give them the nice things they wanted, about how she and her husband had divorced, leaving them without a father in the house. Come to think of it, "guilt" might well have been Shirley's middle name. She even feels guilty that two of her children were born with the genetic disorder sickle-cell anemia, as if her genes had volition.

When she really looks at herself honestly, Shirley realizes that even now, even as her children approach middle age, she still feels guilty about the ways she has failed them. She realizes that at least some of them seem to know this and throw it up at her, use it as a weapon. Jackie had asked, "When are you going to be strong enough to kick them out?" Shirley could never do that, but she now realizes that, first, she must think of her sick daughter Jonnie, of the three grandkids off in foster homes, and of the fourteen-year-old grand-daughter she's still raising—a granddaughter Shirley has just discovered is pregnant.

Glenarden it is!

August 6, 1990. Moving day is less than a week off, and Shirley isn't feeling very good about things. Her still unemployed son, a quiet and withdrawn man, seems hurt about being pushed out of the house. He disappears without a word. Meanwhile, Shirley is also deeply afraid for the person with a drug problem, who looks worse and worse, like a skeleton. Amid this gloom, Jackie Jordan makes her play. She suspects that the person with the drug problem sees the bottom of the awaiting pit without Shirley to fall back on. Jackie has purposely never talked to the person about drugs, but now she does. Indifference is the first response. But in three days, with Jackie's lightning help, the person is registered, admitted, and moved into a one-year residential drug treatment program. Shirley doesn't even know about any of this until after it happens, but she believes that Jackie has saved a life.

Two days later, Shirley, her pregnant granddaughter, and Jonnie move into Glenarden. They take Shirley's nice living room furniture, her several book-shelves full of books, her flourishing plants, and her two aquariums filled with fish. Jackie visits. It is a fresh start.

December 7, 1990. Jackie has been off Shirley's case for months now; it has been handed over to a social worker whose clients aren't considered to be in a crisis. But like old friends, they stay in touch. When Jackie visits just before Christmas, she discovers that Shirley has no money, no Christmas tree, and no presents for her children or grandchildren. Jonnie has been in the hospital so many days this year that Shirley has overdrawn her vacation time without realizing it. She had planned to use her last paycheck before Christmas for gifts, but now there will be no check. And Shirley, who has high blood pressure and osteoarthritis, has been feeling down lately.

For months she has struggled to get her three grandkids out of foster homes and into hers. She took a class to become a foster parent but won only tempo-

rary foster parent status and must be recertified in a few months. She has gotten one of the three grandkids—the precocious child who loves to read, just
like Shirley did. But the two other grandchildren are still in foster care. They
were moved to another home recently, and Shirley didn't even hear about it
until she ran into the former foster father at Landover Mall. He said, Shirley,
get them back, they're miserable.

Shirley can't understand the holdup. The foster care woman keeps telling
Shirley that she can't afford the other two grandkids, that her health is bad,
and that she doesn't have a car, so how would she get them to the hospital in
an emergency? Shirley tells her, "The same way I got my kids to the hospital—
by taxi or ambulance." Shirley isn't told this, but part of the holdup is her own
kids. Three of her seven grown children are working and getting on all right,
but the foster care people have told Jackie they're reluctant to give Shirley the
two other grandchildren she's seeking because of the serious problems several of Shirley's own children have had. They want Shirley's life running
smoothly *before* she gets the grandkids. To Shirley, this is hooey. She figures it's
got to be better for her grandkids to be with her than with strangers. Family is
family! Indeed, if Shirley could win foster parent status, she could take her foster parent income, combine it with early retirement from her job, and stay
home and raise the grandkids full time.

In pursuit of the grandkids, Shirley has found a day-care woman in
Glenarden. Shirley's got the public voucher payments for the day care
approved, but she has to figure out a way to get home by six o'clock to pick
up the kids. She has been experimenting with new hours at work, trying to get
in early so she can leave early. It's trouble, though, because if she takes the first
bus at 6:00 A.M. from the liquor store near her home and then transfers to four
other buses before arriving at work, she still can't get there much before 8:30—
and that's if all the buses run on time. That would mean she could leave work
at 3:30 in the afternoon, but the bus commute back would still often run her
past six o'clock. Shirley could take the subway, but that would be an extra
$4.60 a day, which would put her budget in the red and probably make the
foster care folks say she can't afford to feed and clothe the grandkids so she
can't have them.

In the meantime, Shirley's now fifteen-year-old granddaughter has had her
baby, who goes to the home of one of Shirley's daughters during the day.
Jackie had gotten the granddaughter into a home study program and then
back in school, but recently the granddaughter has stopped going to school
again. But right now, that helps Shirley, because when Jonnie is home from the
hospital somebody has to be there to take care of her. Shirley has been on several waiting lists for months now to get Jonnie into some kind of day-care program. No luck so far.

She tells Jackie that Jonnie could die before she gets off the damned waiting
list. And Jonnie does seem to be getting worse, with some apparent heart damage now, seizures, and shooting pains up the back of her neck. One of Shirley's

sons, the one with a wife and three children and who also suffers from sickle-cell, has been sick lately. Shirley worries that the day will come when he'll not be able to work, and she might have to help his family. Another son, the one who moved out of the house without a word last August, hasn't been in touch with Shirley for months, and she doesn't know where he is. Still another son, who is dyslexic, is in prison on a drug charge and will be eligible for parole soon, and Shirley feels bad that, living in Glenarden, she'll not be able to offer him a place to live while he's getting back on his feet.

They can call it "co-dependency behavior" if they like, but, for God's sake, Shirley just can't turn her back on her family. Truth is, she often thinks she'd love to be free of them all. To move into Glenarden she had to get rid of her wolf dog Nick! She almost couldn't do it, thought about putting his doghouse back in the woods and hiding him there, visiting him every day. But she heard that gangs of drug dealers work the woods, and she was afraid they'd hurt him. If she had thought everybody could get along fine without her, she'd have taken Nick and disappeared, gone back to writing—did you know, she wrote an unpublished novel a decade ago? Used the name Theus V. Mitchell. Titled it *The Night Lovers.* She'd start ceramics again, coach floor hockey, paint. But how can she? After all, what would you think of her if she abandoned her family?

After her Christmas visit, Jackie puts out the word that Shirley needs help, and several agencies come through with Christmas gifts for the grandkids. Then, while Shirley is walking across the parking lot one night, she notices a little artificial Christmas tree in the trash and takes it home. She sprays it with disinfectant and decorates it. She takes a few dollars she's been hoarding, and at the Dollar Store she buys three teddy bears, three Raggedy Ann dolls, crayons, a coloring book, and a thousand-piece puzzle. Her family has a little Christmas after all.

December 25, 1990. Jackie takes the good things in her life less for granted these days, especially at Christmas. Her job is to change people's lives, but her job also has changed her life, which seems more fragile to her now. She thinks more about how each day could be the last good day of her life, how it can all change overnight. She still plans for the future, like any good Middle American, but she's less certain about it all.

Since Shirley's case, Jackie has had half a dozen new clients whose lives are a mess—families with drug and booze problems, incorrigible children, homelessness, pregnant teens, handicapped kids. Lack of money is a woe they all share. Jackie has decided that having money makes people's troubles no less awful but a lot more manageable. And not only for what money can buy. Jackie has come to believe that the less experience her clients have had with money—with "the good life"—the less hopeful is their prognosis. Everyone says they want a steady job, a nice place to live, a stable and loving family. But for those who have never experienced these things, the ambitions are more like dreams than goals. People can describe the good life, but it is something akin to the way Jackie might describe what she'd do with a million dollars from the lottery. The talk is fantastic.

Jackie thinks of the time she was listening to a man play classical piano during an event at the mall. Standing there, she overheard a beautifully mannered little girl tell her mother, "Oh, listen, Mommy, he's playing Bach, and it's my favorite piece." The little girl wasn't being snotty. Bach was simply the world she knew, and that knowledge—and all the other kinds of knowledge that go with it—will matter in that girl's life, because she will not be able to imagine herself any other way. Her idea of herself will create the person she will be. *Things,* Jackie has come to believe, are not all that money buys.

You don't get clients like Shirley Rogers every day—people for whom you can have hope and from whom you can draw hope. And if Shirley is judged a success in Jackie's career, just think of the failures—the alcoholic mother she tried and tried to get into treatment but who relapsed and is now on the run from the child welfare people who want to take her child away, or the family of seven children and an out-of-work husband and wife living in a house without running water who listened and listened to Jackie, agreed with everything, but who never got off the dime and changed their lives. A good eight of ten clients get better, Jackie figures, but already she knows she can't do this forever. Or she too might become one of the clock-punchers Shirley so despises.

February 1, 1991. Perhaps you expected a happy ending? Sorry, this is a Cinderella story without a prince. Shirley is grateful for all the help she got from Jackie—especially for the apartment. At least she and the grandkids won't land on the street. And at least the person in drug rehab is alive. But Shirley's troubles are only diminished, not finished. Because she is a victim of the unpredictability of living on the edge in a family of people who live on the edge.

Her two grandkids are still in foster care. Her son who had disappeared when she moved to Glenarden has turned up living in a shelter, and Shirley would like to help him. Her teenage granddaughter still needs to be gotten back into school. Of course, the credit card folks are still dogging her; she pays ten or twenty dollars when she can. But worst of all, Jonnie has been in the hospital off and on for weeks, which means Shirley has had to find time to visit her every day. She has missed too much work again. Jonnie also wants a rented TV in her hospital room, which costs Shirley twenty-four dollars a week that she doesn't have. But she can't say no to Jonnie. And as if Jonnie's illness weren't enough, just a few days ago, Shirley's son landed in the hospital with a sickle-cell crisis. He's home, but very weak. Will it ever stop? Shirley wonders.

This morning Shirley is at work, has just gotten off the phone with Jackie, when the hospital calls: Jonnie is dead. From a heart attack. Shirley is numb. Her first emotion is guilt. She had gone right past the hospital on the bus this morning, and been tugged to stop and look in on Jonnie, but she hadn't, figuring she'd go by tonight. If she'd stopped, been with Jonnie when the attack came, she could have called for help. She knows CPR. She might have saved her. A voice in her head had told her to stop. Why hadn't she listened? Why hadn't she listened?

The first person Shirley calls is Jackie.

February 15, 1991. A week after the funeral, which Jackie attended, Shirley gets a letter telling her that Jonnie finally has been placed in day care. Shirley calls the bastards: "She doesn't need you anymore. She's dead." When Shirley tells Jackie that she has done this, Jackie simply nods.

What is there to say?

May 26, 1991

ACKNOWLEDGMENTS

All thanks to the *Washington Post,* the rarest of institutions, the rarest of newspapers. Each day, it's a gift to its readers and to the profession of journalism. The stories in this collection I owe to my editors and colleagues there. *Post* Executive Editor Leonard Downie and Managing Editor Robert Kaiser created the environment where my work was appreciated, encouraged, and rewarded. The steady and demanding hand of former *Post Magazine* Editor Bob Thompson made each story better, as did the brilliantly persnickety editing of John Cotter.

Thanks also to the *Post*'s Linton Weeks, Bill O'Brien, Liza Mundy, Tom Frail, Deborah Stewart, Steve Coll, Deborah Fleming, Karen Tanaka, Lauren Hicks, Kelly Doe, Sandy Schneider, Rich Ploch, Carol Melamed, Mary Ann Werner, and Jane Genster. Thanks to Bill Dickinson and Suzanne Whelton of the *Post* Writer's Group. Thanks to my book editors Beverly Jarrett and Jane Lago. Thanks to my agent Amanda Urban. Thanks to my friends and colleagues Pete Earley, Mike Sager, David Finkel, Steve Weinberg, Steve Petranek, Jay Lovinger, Madeleine Blais, Edmund Lambeth, Joyce Hoffmann, Paul Hendrickson, Yvonne Lamb, Peter Carlson, and Peter Perl. Thanks to my wife, Keran, and my children, Matthew and Kyle, for tolerating strange hours and strange obsessions.

And thanks to the people who let me write about them.

Photo by Molly Roberts

For more than a decade, Walt Harrington was an award-winning writer at the *Washington Post Magazine*. He is currently Professor of Journalism at the University of Illinois at Urbana–Champaign and the author of *Crossings: A White Man's Journey into Black America* and *American Profiles: Somebodies and Nobodies Who Matter* (University of Missouri Press).